A Mother's Grace

Rosie GOODWIN
A Mother's Grace

ZAFFRE

First published in Great Britain in 2018 by
ZAFFRE PUBLISHING
80–81 Wimpole St, London W1G 9RE
www.zaffrebooks.co.uk

A CIP catalogue record for this book is
available from the British Library.

ISBN: 978-1-785-76239-0

also available as an ebook

1 3 5 7 9 10 8 6 4 2

Typeset by Palimpsest Book Production Limited, Falkirk, Stirlingshire

Printed and bound in Great Britain by Clays Ltd, Elcograf S.p.A.

Zaffre Publishing is an imprint of Bonnier Zaffre,
a Bonnier Publishing company
www.bonnierzaffre.co.uk
www.bonnierpublishing.co.uk

This book is for the very special new member of our family,
Poppy Victoria, my beautiful little granddaughter.
Welcome to the world sweetheart xxx

Tuesday's child is full of grace

Prologue

'You'll do,' Gertie remarked cryptically as she tied the ribbons of her niece's bonnet beneath her chin, but despite her kind words her eyes were concerned. 'But you *do* know you don't *have* to do this, don't you? There will always be a home for you with me.'

Madeline, her niece, smiled. 'I know that, Aunt Gertie, and I appreciate the offer but I *want* to marry Jacob,' she assured her as she surveyed herself in the long cheval mirror in her bedroom. Yet despite her brave words her stomach was churning. It was only a few weeks since her beloved father, the vicar of the parish where she had lived all her life, had died. She was still mourning him and yet here she was about to get married. Everything had happened so quickly that she had barely had time to take everything in. But I *will* be happy with Jacob she told herself to quell the little ripple of unease in the pit of her stomach. She hadn't realised until after her father's death just how poor they were, in fact, she barely had a penny to her name. But then she shouldn't have been surprised. Her father had been such a kind man, he would have given a beggar the bread from his own mouth.

She hadn't known which way to turn when he died, for she wasn't trained for any kind of work and had no idea what was to become of her, but then Jacob Kettle, who had attended her

1

father's services for many years, had come forward like a knight on a white charger in the fairy stories she had been so fond of in her childhood. He had expressed sincere feelings for her and had told her that he would be honoured if she would become his wife. Admittedly, Jacob was many years older than herself and she didn't love him but she was sure that this would come with time and he *was* very handsome. She was aware that many of the spinsters in the parish had had their eyes set on him for some long while but he had never responded to any of their advances as far as she was aware and she had been flattered. He was rich too and she knew that she would never have to worry about money again. Surely, she had pondered, Jacob was the answer to all her prayers. And so, in her innocence she had agreed and had quite come to terms with it until Aunt Gertie had appeared.

Aunt Gertie was her father's younger sister and Madeline had spent many happy summers with her on her smallholding in Wales when she was a child so she had been distressed when very soon it became apparent that Gertie and Jacob had not taken to each other. But they will when they get to know each other, she told herself hopefully as she turned her eyes back to the mirror. Jacob had given her money to buy the new gown and bonnet she was wearing despite her protests and it was by far the finest quality gown she had ever owned, although, as Aunt Gertie had pointed out, it was very conservative. Jacob had expressed a wish that she would not buy anything too flamboyant. She had quite agreed, it would have been disrespectful when she was still in mourning for her father and so she had chosen a fine wool dress in a soft green colour edged with black braid. The colour matched her eyes and set off her flaming auburn hair to perfection.

'I *still* think you could have chosen something just a little more stylish,' Aunt Gertie huffed as she lifted a small posy of cream rosebuds and handed them to her. Jacob had had them delivered to her that morning and Madeline thought what a kind gesture it was.

'This is just right,' Madeline insisted as she leaned forward to peck her aunt's cheek. 'Now come along. I don't want Jacob to think I've jilted him at the altar.'

She paused in the doorway to look back at her bedroom one last time and she had to swallow hard to stop the lump in her throat and blink back tears. All her clothes had been transferred to Jacob's home the day before and this was the last time she would ever see this small room where she had known such content-ment. With a little sigh, she followed her aunt down the stairs and went out to the carriage that Jacob had sent for her. It looked very grand, although Aunt Gertie was clearly unimpressed.

'Huh! I still can't believe that you're not even going to have a proper wedding breakfast,' she remarked as she clambered in behind her and settled against the leather swabs.

Madeline squeezed her hand. 'I've explained that Jacob and I didn't think it would be fitting so soon after father . . .' Her voice faltered, but then pulling herself together with a great effort she went on, 'At least I shall have you there to give me away and that's all I want. And I'm sure the meal we shall have back at Jacob's will be splendid. He tells me his cook is very good.'

'Well, I just hope it's something hot,' Gertie grumbled, wrapping her arms about her waist. 'The wind's enough to cut you in two today. I wouldn't be surprised if it didn't snow – it's certainly cold enough. I just hope it holds off till I get back to Wales on the train.'

They lapsed into silence until soon after the carriage pulled up outside St Peter's Church where the vicar who would be taking over her father's parish was waiting for them. It felt strange to think that later that day he would also be moving into the vicarage that had always been her home, but she tried as best she could to push the gloomy thoughts away for now. At the door she took her aunt's arm and they glided down the aisle towards Jacob. He had a broad smile on his face and looked so handsome that her

3

concerns momentarily faded away. I'll be a good wife to him, she promised herself.

The service was over in the blink of an eye and before she knew it they were back outside. It was not the wedding that Madeline had dreamed of as a little girl. There was no one waiting to shower them with rose petals and rice but she was trembling with a mixture of nervousness and excitement all the same. She was now Mrs Kettle, the wife of a well-respected judge.

'I trust you will have time to return to my home for a meal before you have to catch your train?' Jacob addressed Gertie but there was no warmth in his voice.

She was equally as icily polite as he when she answered, 'That would be very pleasant. Thank you.'

And so the newlyweds climbed into the carriage while Gertie followed in a second one with Frederick Marshall, one of the judge's colleagues who had stood as best man for him.

When they arrived at the judge's home, Gertie was forced to admit it was very impressive. Three storeys high and surrounded by low iron railings, she judged that the downstairs alone must be as big as the whole of her cottage put together. Not that she would have swapped it. Gertie had never set much store by material possessions.

The judge ushered them all through a thick oak door into a long hallway and then into a dining room where a large table was set with fine china and crystal glasses for a meal. There was a large fire burning in the grate and Gertie headed for it instantly to warm her cold hands as the judge sent a maid away to fetch them all a tray of tea.

The meal followed shortly after and although it was plain, Gertie was forced to admit that it was wholesome and filling. They were served with leek and potato soup followed by roast beef with all the trimmings and finally a jam roly-poly pudding and custard.

At the end of the meal, Jacob stood and, after the maid had

4

filled their glasses with wine, he proposed a toast, 'To my lovely new wife!'

It was short and sweet but Madeline was touched none the less. Soon after Gertie glanced at the clock and said reluctantly, 'I'm afraid I should be heading for the station now if I'm to catch my train.'

'I shall have the carriage sent round for you immediately,' Jacob responded and when he bustled away Gertie took Madeline's hands in her own. She still couldn't take to her niece's new husband. There was just something about him that she didn't like. Perhaps it was the way his smile never seemed to quite reach his eyes?

'Now, you know where I am if you need me.' Gertie, never one to show much affection, found that she was choked, especially when Madeline's eyes filled with tears.

'I know . . . but I shall be fine . . . really.'

They exchanged a brief hug and shortly after Gertie took her leave along with Frederick, who was returning to work.

Once alone with her new husband, Madeline felt suddenly shy and her heart sank when he informed her, 'Do excuse me but I too need to go to my office for a few hours. But I'm sure you will find something to do. Perhaps you could help the maid to put your clothes away? I shall be back for dinner this evening.'

Disappointment coursed through her. She had imagined that they would spend the day together but then she knew what a busy man Jacob was and as they had got married on a week day he was bound to have things to do.

'Of course, Jacob.' She forced a smile although she was feeling totally out of her depth. 'You go along, I shall be fine.'

Once he had gone she went upstairs to look for their bedroom. She had only visited the house once before and still didn't know her way around. However, she found it without difficulty and once she entered she found the maid busily emptying the small trunk that held her clothes.

'Good afternoon, ma'am.' The maid bobbed her knee and Madeline blushed. She'd never had a maid before and this girl looked barely older than she was.

'Oh please, call me Madeline,' she answered but the girl looked horrified at the very suggestion.

'No, ma'am. I don't think the judge would like that. He's told us all to address you as ma'am, but my name is Fanny.'

They worked quietly together and within no time everything was put away apart from the fine lawn nightdress trimmed with lace at the collar and cuffs, which Jacob had also bought for her. Madeline blushed furiously as she saw it laid across the bed and thought of the night ahead. She had never so much as kissed a man let alone lain with one and she wasn't at all sure what to expect, although she had a rough idea after all the parishioners she had visited with her father. Fanny pottered away leaving Madeline alone with her thoughts. There was a small fire burning in the little grate but the room was still quite chilly and she paced up and down as she waited for Jacob to come home.

He was home for his evening meal as promised and once it was over, he suggested, 'Why don't you go up and prepare for bed. It's been a long day and you must be tired.'

Madeline had hoped that they might sit together and chat for a while but all the same she nodded obediently.

'Very well . . . I'll see you shortly.' Hot colour again flooded into her cheeks as she scuttled from the room.

Fanny was in the hallway as she made her way to the staircase and she grinned at her as she passed causing Madeline to blush yet again. Her new husband must be very keen to consummate their marriage if he was sending her up to bed so early, she thought as she climbed the staircase as sedately as she could. In their room she found that Fanny had filled the jug on the washstand with hot water for her and shrugging out of her wedding outfit as quickly as she could, she hung it neatly away and washed herself thoroughly

6

from head to foot. She then took the pins from her hair and brushed it until it gleamed and leaped into bed, pulling the covers up to her chin. She lay watching the door with a mixture of nervousness and anticipation. Slowly, the clock on the little shelf above the fireplace ticked away the minutes, then the hours and the house became still. By then Madeline was struggling to keep her eyes open. Perhaps Jacob was not going to come to her this evening after all?

She had almost given up seeing him when the door suddenly barged open and he appeared. Without a word, he crossed to a chair and began to undress. Madeline looked away, deeply embarrassed. She had never seen a man completely naked before but she supposed she would have to get used to it now that she was a married woman. Minutes later, she felt the covers lift and Jacob slid in beside her. She turned her face to him, a shy smile on her face expecting him to kiss her and whisper sweet words but to her horror he tossed the bedclothes back and roughly dragged her nightdress above her waist making her cringe with embarrassment. Then without further ado he straddled her and thrust himself into her making her cry out with pain and distress.

'J-Jacob . . . you're *hurting* me,' she gasped but he took no notice. He was bucking now and Madeline felt as if she were being rent in two. His thrusts became more and more frantic as she lay there feeling dirty and humiliated but then suddenly he stiffened and she felt something hot and sticky between her legs. Jacob seemed to collapse on top of her but then he rose from the bed and dragged his trousers back on. 'B . . . but where are you going?' She was openly crying now.

'To my own room, of course,' he informed her, then without so much as another word he left.

Once he had gone she curled herself into a tight ball and sobbed uncontrollably. She felt defiled and soiled. She crawled from the bed and washed herself with the now cold water but she still felt dirty. Will I ever feel clean again? she wondered in despair. There had been no tenderness or love in their coming together and she wondered if Aunt Gertie had been right. It seemed there was truth in the old saying, 'Marry in haste repent at leisure!' But it was too late now, the deed was done. She was a married woman for better or worse and, somehow, she was going to have to try and make the best of it.

Slinking back to the bed she pulled the blankets over her head and cried herself to sleep.

Chapter One

Nuneaton 1892

'Our furniture and personal possessions will be delivered over the next few days. Make sure that someone is in at all times to receive them. We shall take up residence a week from today. I will sleep in my late uncle's room and you will prepare another room for my wife. I also expect the rooms above the stables to be cleared out and made habitable for my groom and two stables made ready for the horses. My meals will be served on time and I do not believe in waste so I expect you to be thrifty with the housekeeping money. Is that quite clear?' The stern-faced man stared down at the cook-cum-housekeeper who was standing to one side of the front door with the young general maid. She bobbed her knee. Her head was spinning, for he had not stopped barking orders at her since the second he arrived.

'Perfectly, sir.' How would they possibly have everything ready in time? The stable block and the rooms above it had stood empty for years and she dreaded to think what a state they would be in. As for being thrifty, she had always prided herself on keeping a good table without being extravagant. Her old master had certainly never had cause for complaint. And how strange that he and his young wife were to sleep apart.

The man's dark eyebrows beetled into a frown as he eyed her

disdainfully. 'You will address me as Judge Kettle at all times, woman.'

'Yes, si— judge,' she answered trying hard to keep the resentment from her voice. He was an imposing figure – she estimated that he must be well over six feet tall. His enormous frame almost filled the doorway and he had hard, pale blue eyes and steel-grey hair. His nose was large and hooked and she found herself thinking that it would have looked more in place on a boxer.

He glanced over his shoulder then at his young, heavily pregnant wife and barked, 'So what are you waiting for, woman!' She scuttled past him towards the carriage waiting outside, her eyes downcast.

Nodding towards the servants he rammed his hat on and followed her without another word.

'Phew! I'm glad he's gone, that's all I can say, though I dread to think what our lives are goin' to be like when he moves in.' She shook her head sadly as she stared at the mess in the dining room. 'It's hard to believe that him an' our lovely old master were related, ain't it? The old master were a gentle soul but the same can't be said for his nephew. Apparently, he didn't have a lot to do wi' him when he was young. He was an unwanted child an' were packed off to boarding school almost before he were in long trousers.'

Mabel, the maid, nodded in agreement as she blinked back tears. Their master's death had come as a great shock to both of them and she was still struggling to come to terms with the fact that he was gone. He had been so kind and had it not been for him she and her family would have been destitute, for he had given her a job when her father had been injured in a pit fall.

Now she too glanced towards the dining room, which was littered with empty glasses, cups, saucers and plates of discarded food. The last of the mourners from the funeral had left over an hour ago but Judge Kettle had remained, going through paperwork at his late uncle's desk. He had also left them a seemingly endless list of things he wanted doing before he returned and she was wondering how they were ever going to manage it all in a week.

'I reckon you're right, Batty,' she answered, using the affectionate nickname their late master had given her. 'It's just our hard luck that the dear soul left nearly everything he owned to the judge. It would have been so different if only he and the late mistress had been able to have children of their own. While the men were at the funeral the women were like a pack o' vultures pickin' over who should have what. One of 'em even took the ormolu clock off the mantelpiece. Another went through the china cabinet an' took one of the late mistress's favourite figurines sayin' it had been promised to her years ago. Funerals allus seem to bring out the worst in folks, don' they?' She sighed. 'Anyroad, I dare say we'd best get on wi' the clearin' up. It ain't goin' to do itself.'

Mrs Batley nodded. 'Did you hear how he spoke to his poor wife? She seemed terrified of him. God knows what the poor lass saw in him in the first place. He must be old enough to be her father.'

'Ah well, I heard a bit o' gossip about that an' all,' Mabel confided. 'It seems she met him at church in Leeds where he lived followin' the death of his first wife. She was recently orphaned an' her father had left debts, so the relatives reckon she must have married him for a bit o' security. I bet she's regrettin' it now, though,' she added as she began to pile the dirty pots onto a tray. 'She seems like the sort as wouldn't say boo to a goose!'

'I dare say she is. An' I bet he'll make a few changes to the old master's law business an' all.'

The late Mr Kettle had owned a thriving law practice in the town centre but that too was now the property of Judge Kettle and she foresaw major changes ahead, which she had an idea the late Mr Kettle's colleagues would be none too pleased about, not that they could do anything about it.

It was almost two hours later when Mrs Batley sank into the cosy chair at the side of the inglenook fireplace in the kitchen and eased her swollen feet out of her shoes. Both she and Mabel had already been working for two whole days, cooking and baking for the funeral feast, and they had been up since five that morning laying it out. At Judge Kettle's insistence, only males had attended the funeral service while the female relatives waited for them to return to the large residence in Swan Lane. It was a grand house and Mrs Batley had worked there happily for so long that she almost regarded it as her own. She was a plump, homely soul with silver-grey hair, which she wore in a tight little bun at the nape of her neck, and lively, bright blue eyes.

As Mabel poured them a well-earned cup of tea, she smiled with satisfaction as she looked around. The brass pans suspended along the thick oak beam above the fire gleamed and the flag-stoned floor was so clean that Mabel often teased they could have eaten off it. The large table that took up the centre of the room had been scrubbed until it was almost white – the old master had joined her and Mabel to eat his evening meal there many a time, insisting that it wasn't worth them setting the dining room table just for one. Somehow, she couldn't imagine their new master doing that. She had an idea that he was going to be a stickler for protocol, although his young wife had seemed pleasant enough on the rare occasions she had dared to open her mouth.

Mabel pressed a steaming cup into her hand and she smiled gratefully and pointed to the chair at the other side of the fireplace. 'Sit yourself down for a while, pet. You look fit to drop an' what we ain't managed to do tonight will keep till morning now.'

The young maid willingly did as she was told, holding her feet out to the flickering flames. Then after taking a noisy slurp of her tea she said thoughtfully, 'Well, I suppose it ain't *all* bad. There'll be a new baby in the house soon, which is somethin' to look forward to at least.'

Mrs Batley's head bobbed in agreement as she thought of the nursery the late mistress had prepared all those years ago. Sadly, it had remained empty but now at least it would be used.

'Aye, yer right there, lass. This great house was made to ring to the sounds o' children's laughter. Perhaps when he has a little 'un to love the judge will soften a little.'

Mabel snorted. 'Happen it'd take more than a baby to soften *him*.'

Mrs Batley smiled affectionately at the girl. Mabel was as thin as a beanpole, in spite of all the good food the kindly cook insisted she should eat, and her dull, mousy hair was as straight as a die. But her eyes were a lovely pale grey that sparkled when she smiled. She also had a kind nature and a heart as big as a bucket and Mrs Batley had grown fond of her. They sat together in a companionable silence for a while until Mabel stifled a yawn and said, 'I reckon I might turn in now, Batty, if yer don't mind. I can hardly keep me eyes open. Do yer want me to lock up afore I go to bed?'

'No, pet, you go on up. I'll see to it.' Mrs Batley smiled as Mabel trudged wearily across the flagstones then, bending, she scooped a large ginger cat onto her lap and stroked him affectionately. She had taken in Ginger some years ago when he had come begging for scraps at the kitchen door.

'Are you missin' yer master too?' she whispered as the cat arched his back with pleasure. He meowed in response and she sighed as she absent-mindedly stroked him. So very much was about to change.

A week later, on the evening before their new master and mistress were due to arrive, they sat together in the kitchen enjoying a cup of warm milk. The week had been long and busy with new furniture being delivered, and more cleaning and tidying than she could ever remember doing, but finally Mrs Batley was satisfied that the house was spotless and just as the judge had ordered it to be.

It was a bitterly cold night and outside the wind was howling as rain lashed at the windows.

'It were on a night just such as this some years ago that the old master came into the kitchen to me to wish me goodnight,' Mrs Batley said reminiscently. 'He allus stuck his head round the door to say goodnight afore he went to bed but on this night I were feelin' right poorly. I'd had a terrible cough an' cold that I couldn't seem to shift an' on this particular night he noticed that I'd not bothered to wash the dinner pots an' the fire was burnin' low.' Her eyes welled with tears as the memories flooded back. 'Bless him. He came in and rolled his sleeves up and did the pots himself before makin' the fire up, then he fetched me a blanket and made me tea sayin' I was to stay down here in the warm fer the night. I can't see the new master doin' that, can you?'

Mabel looked troubled when Mrs Batley smiled at her. 'Don't get frettin', pet. Perhaps it won't be as bad as we're expectin'.'

'Perhaps not,' Mabel agreed, although secretly she didn't quite believe it.

Chapter Two

It was mid-afternoon on a frosty November day when a fine carriage drawn by two matching black stallions drew up outside the house in Swan Lane.

'This is it, then,' Mrs Batley muttered as she peeped round the snow-white lace curtain that hung at the hall window. 'Straighten your mob cap and smooth your apron, Mabel,' she said as she hurried to open the door. Judge Kettle climbed down from the carriage and strode towards her, leaving the coachman to help his wife alight.

Some gentleman he is, Mrs Batley thought, but she fixed a smile to her face and bobbed her knee. 'Good afternoon, judge. Welcome to your new home.'

He completely ignored her, sweeping past and unbuttoning his coat, which he almost threw at Mabel along with his hat.

'Did all our possessions arrive?' he asked shortly.

'Yes, judge. And they've all been put away in the correct places, although they can always be rearranged if anythin's not to yer likin'.' Mrs Batley was still doing her best to get off to a good start with him but felt as if she was failing dismally.

He nodded. 'And have you a meal ready? My wife and I have had a long journey and we're tired and hungry.'

'There's a lovely piece of pork roastin' this very minute. I can have the meal on the table in half an hour,' she assured him. 'But first, perhaps you and your wife would like to freshen up? I'll get Mabel to bring you some hot water and a tray of tea up to your rooms right away.'

Mrs Kettle entered the hall then and Mabel rushed to help her off with her cloak and bonnet as the judge went on an inspection of the house. He paused halfway down the hall to run his hand across the top of the console table on which stood a vase of holly, clearly looking for dust. Mrs Batley bristled.

'I think you'll find everything is in order,' she told him in a clipped voice, and he continued on his way without even glancing in her direction.

'Eeh, Mrs Kettle, yer look worn out,' Mabel said kindly once she had hung the woman's outdoor clothes on the tall coat stand. 'Would yer like to go to your room fer a rest or I could bring yer a tray o' tea into the drawin' room?'

'A cup of tea sounds lovely, and I'll have it down here if it's no trouble,' the woman said gratefully.

Mabel hurried away to prepare it while Mrs Batley led her towards the drawing room.

'I think you'll find all your things in place,' she told her as she guided her to the fireside chair. 'But if there's anythin' as yer want changin' me an' Mabel can swap it about in a jiffy.'

'No, everywhere looks wonderful, Mrs Batley. Thank you.'

As the woman sank onto the chair, Mrs Batley smiled. At least the new mistress seemed a nice enough soul, which was one blessing.

She found Mabel in the kitchen preparing two trays and remarked, 'We'd best take a drink over to the groom an' all. No doubt the chap will be glad o' one when he's settled the horses.'

Mabel nodded in agreement and once they had delivered the trays to the new master and mistress, she prepared another one.

'You take it across,' Mrs Batley urged. 'I want to get this dinner dished up. While yer over there show him his rooms an' ask if he has everythin' he needs, then bring him back here to eat wi' us. It's too cold to take his meals over there.'

Minutes later fifteen-year-old Mabel was gingerly picking her way across the treacherously slippery cobblestones towards the stables. She noticed that the carriage had already been put away in the small coach house so she headed for the stables where she guessed he'd be. She found him brushing down one of the horses who had a thick blanket slung across his back and his nose buried in a nose bag and said shyly, 'Hello, I'm Mabel. I've brought you a warm drink.'

He turned and gave her a smile that made the colour flame into her cheeks. He had blonde hair and deep blue eyes and looked to be not much older than her. It was only when he moved towards her that she noticed that he was very bandy-legged and had quite a severe limp.

What a shame, he'd be really handsome if it wasn't for that, she found herself thinking and then blushed an even deeper shade of red.

'Thank you. Er . . . I'm Harry. Harry Grimes, miss.'

'You don't have to call me miss.' Mabel giggled, making her plain face look almost pretty. 'I'm just a maid here.' She handed him the mug. 'Would you like me to show you your rooms? They're up that ladder there.' She gestured towards the far wall beyond the small tack room. 'I've done the best I can with them and put extra blankets on the bed for you, although I'm afraid it may be rather cold up there.'

'I'm sure they'll be very comfortable, thanks.' He shuffled from foot to foot self-consciously but when Mabel set off towards the ladder he followed her up. It was a large room divided by a heavy curtain. Against one wall was a brass bed piled high with blankets and there was a small table and chair beneath a window where Mabel had hung bright floral curtains in an attempt to make it look a bit homelier. There was also a rather dilapidated wardrobe

17

and a mismatched chest of drawers, which Mabel had polished until they gleamed. Beyond the curtain was a washstand on which stood a large jug and bowl but other than that it was empty. It was, as Mabel had warned, bitterly cold up there, and their breath hung on the air in front of them. Even so, Harry seemed pleased with what he saw.

'You've made it really cosy for me,' he observed and she grinned.

'Well, perhaps it won't be so bad. I dare say you'll be busy throughout the day and in the evenin' yer can spend yer time in the kitchen where it's warm wi' me an' Mrs Batley till it's time fer bed. Mrs Batley is the cook-cum-housekeeper . . . Oh, an' she said to tell yer that you'll be eatin' in there wi' us, an' all,' she ended lamely as she ran out of things to say. Then turning about, she rushed off down the ladder so fast that she almost fell.

Perhaps there would be advantages to having a new master after all.

Chapter Three

'Phew, well that's the first day over wi',' Mrs Batley remarked late that evening. 'You did remember to make the fires up in their bedrooms an' put the hot bricks in their beds didn't yer?'

Mabel nodded. 'I did an' I helped Mrs Kettle wi' her undressin' as well. She was struggling with the buttons on the back of her dress.' She shook her head. 'She seems such a nice lady. I don't understand why the judge is so harsh with her.'

'I know. And have yer seen the way he talks down to her.' Mrs Batley snorted as she poured herself a tiny glass of gin. It was her nightly treat before bedtime. 'But that red hair an' those green eyes of hers are glorious, ain't they? Admittedly she's only a little slip of a thing an' not particularly pretty but those features make yer look at her.'

Mabel nodded in agreement. 'They certainly do. She was so tired that I talked her into letting me brush her hair for her an' when she released it from the pins it spilled right down her back in a riot o' curls.' She sighed enviously as she fingered a lock of her own mousy hair that had escaped from her mob cap. Then her face brightened as she thought of Harry. 'Harry's nice too, ain't he?'

Mrs Batley gave a wry smile. If she wasn't very much mistaken young Mabel was smitten.

'Yes, he is nice,' she agreed. 'Although he didn't have much to say fer himself when he joined us, did he?'

'He's probably just shy. I'm sure he'll come out of his shell when he gets to know us,' Mabel answered, then she frowned. 'I wonder what the master wants to see us about tomorrow? Yer don't think we've done summat wrong already do yer?'

'Course we haven't. He asked to see the household ledger I keep; I dare say he's just goin' to discuss the monthly outgoin's.'

Mrs Batley had always been a stickler for keeping the ledger up to date so she had no qualms whatsoever about showing it to Judge Kettle. She downed the rest of her drink and stifled a yawn, then after wishing Mabel goodnight she pottered away to her room.

Sometime later, after laying the fires ready to light the next morning, Mabel drew her curtains and smiled when she saw a candle glowing in Harry's room across the courtyard.

Mrs Batley and Mabel were in the kitchen the following morning preparing lunch when Judge Kettle appeared in the doorway. Mabel stopped her merry humming and glanced at him nervously. His large frame cast a shadow across the floor and his eyes were as cold as a fish's.

'A word if you please, cook.'

Mrs Batley hurriedly threw a damp towel across the dough she had been kneading and laid it on the hearth to rise before following him to his office.

At a glance, she saw that he had the housekeeping ledger open on the desk in front of him and she smiled as she wiped her floury hands on her apron. His first words wiped the smile from her face.

'I have been going over the household accounts and feel that there are cuts to be made.' Sitting in the worn leather chair, he steepled his fingers and peered at her over the top of them, making her feel like a naughty schoolgirl called up in front of the headmaster.

Mrs Batley bristled with indignation. 'What do you mean? I'm very thrifty wi' the housekeepin' money an' every single penny I spend is accounted for in there!'

He sniffed and stabbed his finger towards the coal bill. 'We could save here for a start. I notice that there are fires lit in the bedrooms as well as the drawing room and the day room each day. An unnecessary extravagance, I believe. In future, a small fire in the day room will suffice unless we are entertaining. My wife can spend her time in there. It's a smaller room and won't cost so much to heat. And the fires in the bedrooms need not be lit until shortly before we retire.'

As Mrs Batley's lips tightened, he went on, 'And the food bill. I'm sure you could save on that. Tea and sugar are extravagances, I think we could halve the weekly bill.'

Mrs Batley was beginning to bubble with rage. The late Mr Kettle had never questioned her like this. On the contrary, he had always praised her for keeping such a good table and had trusted her implicitly.

'The butcher's bill,' he went on. 'We can manage perfectly well on cheaper cuts. A good cook should be capable of making tasty meals out of scrag ends and we can certainly cut down on the breakfast menu. There was an awful lot returned to the kitchen this morning, I noticed.' She had served him thick, crispy rashers of back bacon, juicy sausages and sizzling kidneys, which had been slow cooked in butter, as well as devilled eggs, toast and a pot of home-made marmalade.

Mrs Batley contained her anger with an effort. The food that wasn't eaten by the master had always fed herself and Mabel, then Mabel usually delivered what was left to her mother who was always glad of anything. They were feeding Harry too now and she wondered what they were supposed to dine on if she was only allowed to cook enough for the master and mistress. Not that, going by this morning, Mrs Kettle ate much, bless her. Mrs Batley

21

supposed it was because she was having a baby. But did this arrogant man think that servants could exist on fresh air?

He went on to suggest other places where she might make savings before adding, 'And Mr Grimes. From now on, when he is not attending to my horses or chauffeuring me about, he will attend to the gardens and do any jobs that need doing about the house. I am sure we will find enough to keep him fully occupied and that will do away with the need to employ tradesmen. Idle hands make work for the devil is the saying and I don't believe in squandering hard-earned money.' He slammed the ledger shut and handed it to Mrs Batley. 'That will be all for now. Go about your business.'

'Just one thing, judge.' Mrs Batley forced herself to stay calm. 'I can't help but notice that your wife is very close to her time . . . for givin' birth, I mean, an' I was wonderin' if yer'd like me to speak to the doctor an' the midwife for her to have 'em on standby?'

'Thank you, Mrs Batley. The midwife perhaps, but I see no need to waste money on a doctor's fee unless it is absolutely necessary. My wife is young and healthy so I foresee no complications.'

'But what if there are? Your wife is very dainty.'

He waved his hand dismissively. 'We'll cross that bridge if and when we come to it. And now, if you wouldn't mind, I would like to get the rest of my uncle's affairs in order before I go into town to look at my new business. I shall only require a light lunch before I go out and then dinner will be served promptly each evening at six p.m.'

'Yes, judge.' Gripping the ledger so tightly that her knuckles turned white, Mrs Batley turned and almost flounced from the room. She hadn't expected the judge to be as kind a master as the late Mr Kettle but it appeared that he was going to be even harder to work for than she had feared.

When she got back to the kitchen she relayed to Mabel what the judge had said. Mabel chewed her lip nervously.

22

'You don't think he'll dismiss me, do yer, Batty? With him tryin' to cut down on household costs, I mean. He might decide that I'm not needed.'

'Huh! I'd soon tell him if he tried,' Mrs Batley responded heatedly but the conversation was stopped from going any further when Harry Grimes popped his head round the kitchen door, letting in a blast of icy air.

'Sorry to disturb you but you did say to come in at eleven o'clock for a tea break.'

Mabel flushed prettily as Mrs Batley glanced at the kitchen clock and started. 'Goodness, I hadn't realised it were that time already. Come on in, lad, an' you, Mabel, get the trays ready fer the master an' mistress. We don't want to give him anythin' else to moan about.'

Fifteen minutes later, when the trays had been delivered, the three of them sat down to snatch a cup of tea for themselves.

'This is one o' the things he told me we've to cut down on,' Mrs Batley grumbled as she spooned sugar into three cups.

'Well, I don't mind doing without sugar,' Mabel piped up.

Mrs Batley shook her head. 'You'll do no such thing, me girl. We work hard an' the way I see it we's entitled to a cuppa when we feel like it.' She glanced at Harry and asked tentatively, 'Is the judge always this difficult?'

He flushed to the roots of his hair. 'I, er . . . yes, I suppose he is.'

'So why did you leave Leeds an' your family to come here wi' him then?' Mrs Batley was curious.

'I don't have a family,' Harry confessed. 'Me ma died some years ago an' I never knew me dad. I was the eldest an' the young ones were all taken into the workhouse. They would have taken me too but I managed to avoid it and after that I lived on the streets any way I could. I got rickets then, which is why me legs are as they are an' things got harder.'

Mrs Batley clucked her tongue sympathetically. In the squalid courts around Abbey Street where Mabel had been raised, rickets was rife, caused by poor diet, and now she understood why Harry's legs were so deformed.

Harry went on, 'The master found me in a shop doorway one day an' offered me a job working in his stables. That was about two years ago, and I've been with him ever since.'

Mrs Batley would have liked to think that the judge had done this out of the kindness of his heart but already she guessed that he would have probably worked poor Harry almost into the ground. His next words confirmed it.

'He can be a bit harsh . . . very harsh, really, an' he's whipped me on more than one occasion if I haven't done something exactly as he told me to but at least I ain't on the streets anymore. Anythin' is better than havin' to go back to that. And the mistress is kind . . . when he ain't about, that is.'

'Is she afraid of him then?' Mabel asked, appalled.

He shrugged. 'I'm not sure to be honest. I've never known him to raise his hand to her, but I don't think he lets her ever forget that he rescued her when her father left her penniless, poor thing. I know she has an aunt who offered to take her in at the time, she lives somewhere in Wales, but I think the mistress was too proud to take her up on her offer.'

He clammed up then, no doubt worried that he'd already said too much and Mabel and Mrs Batley wisely didn't push him for any more information.

❦

After his light lunch, the judge left for the town in his smart carriage and Mabel and Mrs Batley breathed a sigh of relief.

'Phew, he ain't even been here fer a whole day yet an' already I'm glad to see the back o' him,' Mrs Batley remarked, then she

24

started when she glanced up to see the young mistress standing in the kitchen doorway.

'Oh, I'm *so* sorry, missus,' she muttered, red-faced, but Mrs Kettle merely smiled.

'I was wondering, would one of you have time to show me where the nursery is located? I don't wish to disturb your work.'

'I'll take you up there,' Mrs Batley offered. 'You carry on preparin' them vegetables for dinner would yer, pet?'

Mabel nodded and Mrs Batley led her new mistress towards the staircase. 'The nursery is right up on the top floor,' she wheezed as she puffed her way up the stairs, her plump face red with exertion. 'It's never been used, more's the pity, so it'll need a good airin'. In fact, it might possibly need redecoratin' after all these years.'

At last she flung open a door and the mistress stepped past her into the room. Mrs Batley hurried forward and began to whisk the dustsheets off the furniture. She secretly hated this floor, for it always brought back sad memories of her former mistress who had chosen every stick of furniture up there with such loving care for the children that had never come along.

'Oh, that's quite beautiful,' Mrs Kettle exclaimed as a wooden swinging crib was revealed.

'The moths have got into the little blankets,' Mrs Batley said regretfully as she stroked them and they crumbled to dust. 'But the crib is still in fine condition by the looks of it. Just as soon as we have any spare time me an' Mabel will come up here an' give the whole place a good scrub fer you. There's a small bedroom next door for a nanny an' the other door leads to what was to be the schoolroom.'

'How sad that it was never needed,' Mrs Kettle said softly, her voice heavy with tears as she thought of the heartache Jacob's aunt must have suffered. Her hand then fell protectively to her swollen stomach. Hopefully this little one would breathe life into the empty rooms.

'I could come up and help you, Mrs Batley,' she offered, but the older woman shook her head vigorously.

'You'll do no such thing so close to your time . . . beggin' your pardon, ma'am. No offence intended.'

Mrs Kettle smiled and her whole face was transformed. 'None taken.'

Mrs Batley cleared her throat then before asking, 'Do yer mind me enquirin' when the baby's due, ma'am? Only I were sayin' to yer husband earlier that we should be preparin' the midwife to be on standby.'

'Early in the New Year.' The woman smiled. 'But I won't be needing a nanny. I shall be looking after the baby myself and would prefer to have it in my room with me for the first few months.'

Mrs Batley made no comment although she still found it strange that a married couple should wish to sleep apart after the birth of their baby. She had supposed that the judge had taken his own room so that his wife could rest but it appeared that this wasn't the case, not that it was any of her business, she reminded herself silently.

'Perhaps I could get young Harry up here to give the place a coat of limewash for when the baby does move upstairs?' she suggested tactfully, and Mrs Kettle nodded in agreement.

'It would certainly brighten the place up,' she agreed. 'Meantime, a little closer to my time, perhaps we could have the crib carried down into my bedroom?'

'That would be no trouble at all. Me an' Mabel could do that. Have you got together any baby things yet? Blankets and night-dresses and such?'

'Oh yes. I've made most of them myself. My mother taught me to sew, she was a very fine needlewoman.' Mrs Kettle's face clouded. 'I wish that she and my father were still alive to meet their first grandchild but my mother died when I was twelve. Father was

26

never quite the same after that but we were very close. He was such a kind, gentle man.'

Mrs Batley squeezed her arm sympathetically, feeling the young woman's pain.

'My father was a vicar,' Mrs Kettle said and Mrs Batley's eyebrows rose in surprise. She'd had no idea.

'He had his own parish in Leeds. We lived in a lovely old vicarage attached to the church but I'm afraid he was rather too generous to people in need for his own good, which is why I found myself almost penniless when he passed away. And by the way, my first name is Madeline. It was my grandmother's name and I'm quite happy for you to address me as such.'

'Why, that's a lovely name but I fear the judge wouldn't think it seemly,' Mrs Batley pointed out.

The young woman seemed to think on her words for a moment then slowly nodded. 'Perhaps you're right. Jacob is quite strict about such things. But maybe sometimes when we're alone we need not be quite so formal?'

'We'll see.' Mrs Batley patted her hand. 'But now I really ought to be getting back to work. I don't want to end up in the master's bad books on his first full day here.'

'Oh, of course. How thoughtless of me. I'll come down with you.'

Mrs Batley smiled to herself. The young mistress was a lovely person and soon there would be a baby in the house.

Chapter Four

A week later, Mrs Batley was once again summoned to the master's office to present the household accounts.

'Hmm . . .' He ran his finger down the page of the week's expenses. 'I see you have managed to save a few pence on the coal bill by following my orders, although the food bill doesn't look to be much improved.' When he stared up at her she felt as if his cold eyes were boring right through her.

Mrs Batley straightened her back, ashamed to find that her hands were trembling slightly. 'I've changed the menus so that for three days a week we have fish instead of meat and that's saved a bit,' she objected defensively. 'But it's hard to cut down on certain other things. Vegetables tend to be expensive at this time of year, and so is tea, even though Mabel goes to market and looks for the best prices she can.'

His eyebrows drew together as he continued to examine the accounts. It was clear that he intended to see that every single penny was accounted for.

At last he opened a drawer and carefully counted out a sum of money. 'That is the housekeeping allowance for next week,' he told her and she saw at a glance that it was vastly reduced. Right, she thought angrily. She'd certainly make cuts, starting with his wine bill, and see if he was still so keen to keep her short of funds this time next week. His wife would never be so mean, she was sure of it. Only that day she had commented that Mrs Kettle's clothes looked dangerously tight on her and suggested that she should approach her husband to ask him for some new ones, but the young woman had shaken her head and flown into a panic.

'Oh no, there'll be no need for that,' Madeline had gabbled. 'I'm sure I can let the ones I have out just a little more, then I can take them all in again once the baby is born.'

Mrs Batley had stared at the tight, plain bombazine gown her mistress was wearing and sighed. Madeline Kettle would never be classed as a beauty, admittedly, but with her striking hair and lovely eyes, Mrs Batley was sure she could be very attractive were she able to dress in more fashionable clothes. The judge, on the other hand, was always immaculately dressed in fine waistcoats and smart suits.

Now she simply took the money, dropped it into the pocket of her apron and strode from the room. He wanted cuts? Well, she would make sure he got them.

That evening, as Mabel was about to go up to light the fires in the master and mistress's bedrooms, Mrs Batley told her, 'Don't light the fire in the judge's room, pet. He wants us to cut down on household expenses.'

The judge had gone out in his carriage over an hour before, and goodness knew what time he would roll in. Already they had discovered that he went out in the evenings a great deal, often not returning till long after they were in bed. A couple of times Mrs Batley had tentatively questioned Harry about where the master went but each time Harry had closed up like a clam.

'But, Mrs Batley, it will be freezing up there!' Mabel looked concerned but Mrs Batley merely grinned and went back to her knitting. She'd bought some wool from a shop in town and was making a little matinee coat for the new arrival.

29

'Let me worry about that if he complains,' she answered complacently. 'You just go and see as the mistress's room is nice and warm for her.'

The next morning when Mabel placed the serving dishes on the sideboard at breakfast, the judge stared down at the measly few rashers of bacon and two eggs and asked, 'Where are the sausages?'

'I've no idea, judge. Mrs Batley just asked me to bring it through.' Mabel gulped nervously as the colour rose in his cheeks.

'Send her in to me *immediately*,' he roared and Mabel scuttled away so quickly she almost tripped over her skirts.

'Batty, the master wants to see yer this instant,' Mabel gasped as she burst into the kitchen. 'An' I should warn yer, he ain't in the best o' moods.'

Mrs Batley wiped her hands on a length of huckaback and headed towards the door. She'd been expecting this and was ready for him. Deep down she had come to fear him almost as much as Mabel did but she would have died rather than admit it to anyone.

She found Mrs Kettle seated at the dining room table with her head bowed while her husband stood with his hands clasped behind his back rocking backwards and forwards on his heels.

'Yes, judge, yer wished to see me?'

'What is the meaning of this?' he spluttered. 'How is a man supposed to do an honest day's work on such a meagre meal?' He had now taken up his role as a judge in the law courts in Coventry where he went each day on the steam train from Trent Valley railway station.

'But, sir, I was just doin' what you told me an' cuttin' back,' Mrs Batley replied innocently. Despite her calm countenance, her heart was thumping painfully. She was sure, just for a moment, that she saw a shadow of a grin flit across his wife's face.

30

'*Cutting back!* Go to the kitchen and get me a proper meal, woman,' he ordered through clenched teeth.

Mrs Batley calmly shook her head. 'I'm afraid I can't do that. I cut sausages off the shoppin' list, see?'

He seemed to swell to twice his size but then, controlling himself with an effort, he told her, 'I don't have time to wait about for you to cook anything else anyway or I shall be late for my train but see that you do better in the morning! And by the way, my room was freezing when I went up to bed last night. The maid clearly forgot to light the fire.'

'I told her not to,' she told him boldly. 'After all, yer did reduce the housekeepin' money an' I have to make cuts somewhere. I thought yer'd approve.' And she strutted away with a sweet smile on her face.

Entering the kitchen, she blew out a breath and said shakily, 'I'll show the bugger, you just see if I don't! I wouldn't dream o' walkin' into his court an' tellin' him how to do his job an' I'll be blowed if I'll let him come in here tellin' *me* how to do mine!' She felt as if she and Judge Kettle were engaged in a battle of wills.

Mabel was sitting at the kitchen table with Harry enjoying a cup of tea and they grinned at each other as Mrs Batley went to pour one for herself.

'I reckon the master don't know what he's taken on wi' our Mrs Batley,' she whispered. 'She can be as stubborn as a mule when she has a mind to be.'

Harry nodded but made no comment. He himself had no complaints whatsoever since coming to live in Swan Lane. Mabel had even begun to put warm bricks into his bed each night and he had never eaten so well. Already the waistbands on his trousers felt a little tighter and although his room above the stable was cold, it was his and he loved the peace and quiet of it.

'I'd best be off,' he said, glancing at the clock. 'I have to get

31

the carriage out and the horses harnessed in time to get the judge to the railway station otherwise he'll have me guts for garters.'

Mrs Batley tutted. Why the judge couldn't get himself to the station she had no idea. It was only around the corner, less than a ten-minute walk away. Harry swallowed the rest of his drink in a gulp and seconds later he was gone, leaving Mabel to stare after him with a dreamy look in her eyes.

'I reckon someone not a million miles away has got a soft spot fer a certain young man,' she teased.

Mabel flushed and rose to carry the dirty pots to the sink. 'I don't know what yer talkin' about,' she snapped a little too quickly.

Mrs Batley let the subject drop, for now at least.

The judge arrived home as usual at five thirty that evening. He appeared to be in a particularly ill humour as his wife went to meet him in the hall.

'Have you had a good day, dear?' she questioned with a perfunctory peck on the cheek as she helped him off with his hat and coat. It was raining cats and dogs outside, freezing rain with a promise of snow in it.

'Not particularly.' He glanced down at her swollen stomach with a look of repugnance. What men found attractive in pregnant women he would never understand.

'Never mind, come through to the day room. There's a bright fire in there and you can get warm. Mrs Batley has the dinner almost ready.'

He did as he was asked and once inside he crossed to the small table where the whisky was kept and poured himself a generous tot. He scowled at the almost-empty decanter.

Soon they were summoned to the dining room and when Mabel placed a pie in the centre of the table, he frowned. 'What do you call this? It's working men's fare. Where is the joint of meat? Send Batley to me *at once*!'

Mabel scuttled away as fast as her legs would take her.

'He wants you in the dining room right now,' she informed the cook the second she set foot in the kitchen and the older woman nodded.

'What the *hell* do you do you call *this*, woman?' growled the judge when she entered the room. Disgusted, he stabbed a finger towards the offending pie as she stared innocently back at him.

'Why, it's a steak an' kidney pie. Is it not to your likin'?'

'I expect a *proper* meal when I've been working all day,' he thundered. 'Especially after the measly meal you served me at breakfast.'

'I-I'm sure it will be delicious, Jacob,' Madeline ventured timidly, hoping to calm him, but her words only seemed to incense him further.

'Speak when you are spoken to, woman!' He cast her a withering look and she seemed to shrink in her seat.

'*Well?*' He turned his attention back to Mrs Batley who returned his stare calmly.

'I can only make the reduced housekeeping money stretch so far,' she pointed out. 'An' you *did* tell me to cut down on the butcher's bill, if I remember correctly. I cut the wine order in half as well, you'll be pleased to know. After all there's two extra mouths to feed now to what there were when the old master were alive an' I was managin' on the same money as he always gave me. But now . . .' She spread her hands and shrugged as his face turned puce.

'We will discuss this later,' he told her abruptly. He sliced into the pie and placed a generous portion on his plate. 'Oh, and by the way, I shall be having a dinner party here next Thursday for my colleagues from the law courts. There will be eight of us dining that evening and I shall expect something special served.'

'Huh! Not on the housekeepin' you give me there won't be,' she said bluntly and turning about she left the room, closing the door softly behind her.

When she recounted what had been said to Mabel, the girl was appalled. 'Eeh, yer never did,' she gasped.

Mrs Batley nodded. 'I did, true as I'm standin' here.' She puffed her chest out. 'There's only one way to treat bullies an' that's to give as good as yer get an' that man in there is a bully, all right! Why, even his own little wife is afraid o' him, bless her. But he'll not get the better o' me, you just mark my words. If he wants a warm house an' good food on the table then he'll have to pay fer it.'

Harry joined them then and unlike Judge Kettle's, his eyes lit up at the sight of the steak and kidney pie Mrs Batley placed on the table with a dish of vegetables.

He smiled at Mabel and took a seat. 'Oh, that smells lovely,' he said appreciatively.

Mrs Batley's face brightened. It was nice to cook for someone who appreciated it and she piled the young man's plate high, much to his delight.

When they'd eaten, Mabel served the judge and his wife with apple pie and thick creamy custard – at least he didn't moan about that – then hurried back to the kitchen to have hers. No one could cook an apple pie like Mrs Batley, as far as Mabel was concerned.

When the meal was over, the judge went to his room to get ready to go out as he did most evenings, while his wife retired to the day room to read for a while before going to bed.

'Where the hell does he find to go to?' Mrs Batley mused as she put her feet up at the side of the fire while Mabel tackled the dirty dishes.

Harry just stared into the dancing flames and pretended he hadn't heard her so she wisely didn't push the point.

When Mrs Batley went to present the weekly accounts to the judge later that week, he hastily read through them and pushed a pile of coins across the desk to her.

'You will find some extra there,' he told her as if he were bestowing her with some great gift. 'Please make sure that my dinner guests are presented with a good meal. My wife will discuss the menus with you.'

'Right y'are, judge.' She pocketed the money and left the room with a smile on her face. Happen he wouldn't be such a skinflint in future.

Mrs Batley went to discuss the menu with Madeline later that day, and the poor young woman flew into a flap.

'But I haven't a *clue* what to suggest,' she told the older woman truthfully. 'My father and I dined very simply and I have no idea what Jacob would like.'

'It's all right, pet,' Mrs Batley soothed. 'The old master had a few posh dinner parties himself from time to time so I'm happy to make suggestions. What about a nice melon for starters, something fresh for the palate? Then we could have beef with a red wine sauce – my sauces are quite tasty I'm told – followed by a fresh cream trifle an' a selection o' cheese an' biscuits?'

Madeline clapped her hands with relief. 'Oh yes. That all sounds wonderful . . . but won't it make rather a lot of work for you?'

'Don't you get frettin' about that, lass. I enjoy cookin' an' I've got Mabel to help me.'

Madeline looked relieved. 'Thank you, you are so kind.'

Mrs Batley gave her a crafty wink. 'If the master should ask I'll tell him you came up with the menu, eh? That'll put you in his good books.'

Madeline giggled, totally transforming her usual serious features and Mrs Batley was saddened. She was such a nice young lass and deserved to be married to a man that appreciated her.

The dinner party was a huge success, although Mrs Batley suspected that Madeline didn't enjoy it. The judge had invited two lawyers, another judge and their wives. The other women looked like multi-coloured butterflies in their silks and satins, and Madeline felt dull and dowdy by comparison.

'As you can see, my wife is in a somewhat delicate condition,' the judge apologised as he introduced them to her in the hallway while Mabel took their cloaks and bonnets. 'So please excuse her for not looking her best.'

Poor Madeline seemed to shrivel as she pulled her shawl about her and blushed, and the evening got no better for her as they sat down to the meal. One of the women present had known Jacob's first wife and without even thinking how it might make Madeline feel she commented, 'I do *so* miss, Julia, Jacob. We were such good friends and she was *such* a beautiful person. How sad that she should die giving birth to your child. Still' – she glanced towards Madeline – 'at least you are about to become a father now. How clever of you it was to marry a younger woman. I'm sure she will not have to endure losing one child after another as Julia did.'

The conversation moved on to other things but for Madeline the night was ruined. Had Jacob married her simply because he hoped she could bear him a child? She thought it more than likely. After their disastrous wedding night, Jacob had only come to her rarely, and when he did the act was over in seconds. He had seemed relieved when she'd told him she was with child and had not attempted to touch her since, for which she was grateful.

But now was not the time for such thoughts, so she fixed a false smile to her lips and tried desperately to get through the rest of the evening.

Chapter Five

'The food last night was wonderful, Mrs Batley,' Madeline told her the next morning when she ventured into the kitchen after Jacob had gone to work.

Mrs Batley glanced up from trimming the pastry on a mince pie she was preparing for their pudding that evening. The girl looked pale.

'Why don't yer come an' take the weight off yer feet an' share a hot drink wi' me an' Mabel,' she invited. 'We usually have one round about this time.'

Mabel immediately pushed the kettle onto the hob and pulled out a chair for the mistress who sank onto it gratefully. She felt so ungainly now and seemed to waddle rather than walk.

Mrs Batley dusted the flour from her hands and popped the pie into the oven before joining her young mistress. Madeline often slipped into the kitchen to have a word and the older woman sensed that she was lonely and bored. Still, she thought optimistically, all that will change once she has a baby to look after.

'So how are you feeling?' she asked as she laid three cups out and measured sugar into them.

'Huge! Like a beached whale!' The mistress grinned as she looked around the kitchen appreciatively before saying, 'You keep this room so nice; the whole house in fact. And young Harry is doing a lovely job of decorating the nursery.'

'It's nice of you to say so, and yes he is,' Mrs Batley replied. 'He seems to be a nice lad although he's very quiet. He doesn't give much away about his past, if you know what I mean.'

Madeline nodded. 'I do know; I've found the same. He'd been working for my husband for about a year when we first got married but apart from the fact that I know Jacob rescued him from the streets, he's not said anything else.' She sighed and glancing towards the window said sadly, 'I do tend to get bored lately. I was always busy when my father was alive, helping him with something or another.'

'Perhaps a bit o' fresh air might perk you up?' Mabel suggested. 'It's market day today and I have to go and get a few things for Mrs Batley. It's not far to walk but if you fancy comin' you'll need to wrap up warm. It's enough to freeze the hairs off a brass monkey out there.'

'Hmm, I'm not so sure that's a good idea.' Mrs Batley looked out of the window. It was so cold that the frost hadn't thawed at all. 'Everywhere's goin' to be very slippery,' she pointed out. 'An' we don't want yer goin' yer length so close to yer time.'

'I hadn't thought o' that,' Mabel answered gloomily but Madeline seemed quite excited at the prospect.

'I could hold on to your arm and take my time,' she said. 'And I'd love to see a little of the town. I haven't been anywhere apart from to church since we moved here.'

'I've got to drop a few bits in to me mam an' I'm afraid it's not very posh where she lives. Not at all the sort o' place you must be used to,' Mabel added worriedly.

'Oh, that wouldn't trouble me at all,' Madeline assured her. 'Believe me, I visited some very squalid slums with my father when I lived in Leeds . . . Not that I'm suggesting your parents' home will be like that,' she added hastily.

She noticed Mrs Batley adding half a loaf to a large wicker basket and the woman explained, 'I've done a fresh batch o' bread this mornin' an' the old master always encouraged me to send anythin' as we couldn't eat – leftovers an' whatever – to Mabel's mam. She's allus glad of it, bless her, wi' so many mouths to feed an' her husband crippled an' it's better than throwin' it away. I hope that's all right wi' you?'

Madeline smiled and nodded. 'Of course it is.' Then, glancing at Mabel, she pleaded, 'Please may I come? It would be so nice to get out of the house for a while.'

Always obliging, Mabel nodded. 'Of course, but as I said be sure to put yer warmest coat on an' I'll see you back here in ten minutes.'

Ten minutes later, Mabel lifted the heavy basket and the two young women set off down Swan Lane.

As they passed St Mary's Abbey Church, which Madeline had recently started to attend, Mabel said, 'Did you know that the church used to be a priory with monks livin' in one side of it an' nuns in the other?'

Madeline was amazed. 'No, I had no idea,' she admitted as she gripped tight to Mabel's free arm. As they'd feared, the paths were treacherously slippery, and she didn't want to fall. When they came to the end of the lane they turned left.

'This is Queen's Road, the main road through the town. We'll come to the shops an' the market stalls soon.'

Madeline couldn't stop smiling. It was lovely to be out in the fresh air even if it was bitterly cold. She had put on her thickest coat and warmest dress and although it was fairly plain, she still looked very smart compared to Mabel who was forced to brave the winter weather with nothing more than a woollen shawl about her shoulders. As they approached the shops, Madeline looked about with interest. There was a baker's shop with loaves of crusty bread and cakes displayed in the window and a butcher with braces of pheasants and pigs' heads dangling from large hooks. Madeline quickly looked away from that. Next was a hardware shop displaying metal buckets and ceramic bowls, sweeping brushes and seemingly everything anyone could need for a kitchen. Next to that was a dress shop and further on a haberdasher and a milliner with a smart bonnet trimmed with peacock feathers displayed in the window.

'Ain't that just the most *beautiful* bonnet you ever saw? One day I shall have a bonnet like that.' Mabel sighed as she paused to stare at it longingly and when Madeline agreed that it was indeed very fetching she reluctantly moved on.

Soon they were assailed by a myriad of sounds and smells as they arrived at the stalls that had been erected in rows all down either side of the street. One stall was piled high with what appeared to be second-hand clothing and this was one of the busiest stalls of all as women with pinched faces rummaged eagerly through them.

'That's the rag stall. Me mam gets all the kids' clothes from there,' Mabel informed Madeline. 'You can get some rare old bargains. She sells second-hand boots an' all an' sometimes yer can drop on a pair that have hardly been worn. I got these from there fer tuppence.' She stuck out her foot proudly to show a sturdy black lace-up boot. They were very cumbersome and quite ugly and Madeline felt they would have been far more suited to a man, but Mabel was clearly very happy with them so she smiled and nodded.

'I'm just goin' to pop into here,' Mabel told her, pointing to a shop that was displaying brightly coloured hanks of wool in the window. 'Batty asked me to pick her up a roll o' black wool fer darnin' her stockings.'

While she was gone, Madeline pounced on a red item that she had spotted amongst the tumble of clothes on the rag stall. It turned out to be a muffler, thick and warm with hardly any signs of wear so she paid for it hastily and when Mabel reappeared she handed it to her with a smile.

'This is for you, I thought you looked rather cold.'

Mabel's mouth gaped with pleasure and surprise at the kind gesture and in seconds she had wound it about her neck.

'Ooh, it's just lovely.' She giggled as she admired her reflection in a shop window. 'An' me neck an' shoulders are as warm as toast now. Thanks, missus, it's one o' the nicest gifts I've ever been given.'

With one hand still stroking her present, they moved on and soon came to the cattle market where pens that held a variety of loudly protesting animals – pigs, cows, horses, and chickens in cages and nearby farmers were loudly bartering their worth.

'We'll drop these off to me mam then we'll get the things Mrs Batley asked for,' Mabel told her as she headed off up Abbey Street. Soon they came to a long, narrow alley and as they moved along it, a sickening smell met them.

'That's the shared privy an' the pig pen,' Mabel said apologetically. 'All year round the people from the court feed the pig on scraps, then just before Christmas the pig is slaughtered an' they all get to share it fer Christmas dinner. Then in the New Year they buy another piglet from the cattle market an' it all starts over again.'

Secretly, Madeline was sure that she couldn't have eaten an animal that she had nurtured all year but then she supposed that needs must. She found herself in a dismal courtyard with four tiny cottages, two on either side of it.

'This is where me family lives,' Mabel told her, heading towards the furthest door. 'They were originally built fer the ribbon weavers that used to live an' work here. The attic used to house their looms but people use 'em as an extra bedroom now.'

Seconds later, she stepped into a small room and beckoned Madeline to follow her. It seemed to be full of children of various ages ranging from a baby crawling about the flagstones to a girl who looked to be slightly younger than Mabel.

'Hello, Mam.' Mabel looked towards a woman busily sewing beside the room's one small window.

At the sight of Mabel, the woman's face lit up and she clumsily rose from her chair. Madeline saw at a glance that, like herself, she was in an advanced state of pregnancy and wondered how they would possibly manage to fit another body into this tiny house. Her eyes were drawn to a man who was lying on a wooden settle at the side of the fireplace with a thin blanket wrapped about his legs. His face was drawn and wracked with pain and she guessed that this must be Mabel's father.

Mabel's mother looked at Madeline curiously and Mabel hastily introduced her. 'Mam, Dad, this is Mrs Kettle, me new employer. She just bought me this lovely scarf, look. She came out wi' me to get a breath o' fresh air.'

'Well, that was very kind o' you. How do you do, ma'am.' Mabel's mother dipped her knee as her hand self-consciously rose to brush a stray wisp of hair behind her ear. Then looking back at Mabel, she scolded gently, 'Yer should have warned us yer were bringin' a visitor, our Mabel, the place is barely fit to be seen.' She pulled a hard-backed chair out from the wall. 'Won't yer sit down, ma'am. I'll just put the kettle on. I dare say as yer could do wi' a hot drink to warm yer up.'

'Oh, please don't go to any trouble on my account,' Madeline objected, but the woman was already bustling about preparing the kettle then the teapot as the children fell silent and stared at the visitor's fine clothes in awe.

Madeline smiled at the man then and said, 'Good day, sir. And how are you keeping? Mabel told me of your unfortunate accident.'

'Oh, I shouldn't complain, ma'am.' He smiled politely as he tried to heave himself up on the settle. He was obviously very weak and Mabel rushed over to help him, propping him up on some flat, out-of-shape pillows. 'At least I'm still here to tell the tale, which is more than can be said for some o' me mates. It's

42

me lass I worry about.' His eyes settled on his wife who was flitting about like a butterfly. 'It's her who has to do the lion's share o' the work now. Sewin' till all hours every day by the light of a candle an' when she ain't doin' that she's takin' in other folks washin' an' ironin'.' He sighed heavily and Madeline's heart went out to him. 'Sometimes I think it might have been better if I hadn't come up either, at least she'd have had a small widow's pension then,' he confided in a hushed voice.

His wife, however, had heard him and she wagged a stern finger at him. 'Ain't I told yer before not to say such things,' she rapped. 'We might not be rich but we're managin' well enough, ain't we? It ain't often we go to bed hungry, partly due to our Mabel, that is.' She flashed a smile in the girl's direction. 'An' I'm managin' to pay the rent an' all, well, most weeks anyroad, wi' what our Mabel brings me. What else could we wish for if we still have each other?'

Mabel's father hung his head sheepishly and, wishing to lighten the atmosphere, Mabel said brightly, 'Right, let's see what Mrs Batley has sent yer today then.' The second she lifted the basket on to the rickety table, the children crowded around her like bees around a honeypot, their eyes wide with hunger and anticipation.

'Hmm, now here's half a loaf left over from yesterday. There should be enough fer yer to have a slice each. An' here's some leftover slices o' steak an' kidney pie. That's one o' yer favourites, Dad. Oh, an' there's some apple pie here an' all, an' a pot o' drippin' from the pork she cooked last night. Yer could have that on the bread, it'll be right tasty wi' a bit o' salt on it.'

The children licked their lips at the thought of the feast ahead, but before they could touch anything, Mabel's mother whipped the whole lot away into the pantry.

'Yer can all keep yer eyes off, yer greedy little buggers.' She glanced at Madeline. 'Sorry, ma'am. Yer'll all have yer fair share at the proper time.'

43

The children sloped away, and Mabel chuckled as she reached into her pocket. 'Here, there should be one each fer yer to keep yer goin' till dinner time. Mind yer don't get chokin' on 'em!'

She tossed a brown paper bag to the nearest boy and when he glanced inside he whooped with delight.

'It's gobstoppers,' he declared and instantly the children all held their hands out.

'Eeh, our Mabel, yer shouldn't be doin' that,' her mother told her gently. 'Yer hand over most o' yer wages to me as it is wi'out you wastin' the little yer keep on this lot.'

Mabel shrugged as she poured a drop of milk into three cups and soon they were all sipping the unsweetened tea.

Eventually, Mabel told Madeline regretfully, 'We ought to be goin' to get the shoppin' done an' gettin' back to Mrs Batley now. She'll haul me over the coals if I ain't there in time to help wi' the dinner.'

'Of course.' Madeline smiled at Mabel's parents. 'And thank you for your hospitality, it's been a pleasure to meet you.'

'You too, ma'am. Wi'out these bits you allow us to have I don't know how we'd manage.'

Madeline felt humbled as she shook her head. In future, she intended to make sure the family had a lot more than just leftovers.

Chapter Six

Madeline was tired but happy when she and Mabel arrived back at the house. However, the smile faded from her face when the judge himself opened the door with a face like thunder and demanded, 'Just where the hell do you think you've been, woman?'

Before she could open her mouth to answer, he grabbed her none too gently by the arm and hauled her off to his study as Mabel looked on in distress before scuttling away like a frightened rabbit towards the servants' entrance at the back of the house.

Madeline frowned, her heart thudding painfully as she was dragged along the corridor. What was Jacob doing home at this time of day? And what could she have done to upset him so? Surely it wasn't a crime to leave the house for a breath of fresh air?

Once the study door was shut behind them, he let her go. 'Well?' he growled, his face red with fury.

'I decided to walk into town with Mabel to get a little exercise,' she answered calmly, her hands joined tightly at her waist above the mound of her stomach, trying not to show how frightened she was.

'Walk into town? In *your* condition! Whatever will people think? And with a common maid too!'

Hoping to change the subject she asked, 'But why are you home so early, dear?'

'Snow is forecast and I didn't want to be trapped in Coventry if the trains stopped running, so I decided to bring some work home with me. But let's get back to what we were talking about. I wouldn't even have known you were leaving the house if I hadn't seen you disappearing down some godforsaken alley in Abbey Street.'

He was speaking as if she had committed some unforgivable crime but ever the peacemaker, Madeline tried to remain calm as she answered in a small voice, 'We called in to see Mabel's parents, she had something she wanted to drop off to them. They live in the courts off Abbey Street.'

'And you *dared* to expose my unborn child to the disease that is rife there?' Jacob looked as if he was about to explode. 'Are you aware that those courts are running with vermin? And whatever possessed you to venture out onto the slippery pavements in the first place *anyway*? You might have fallen and brought the birth of the baby on early!'

'But I didn't, I was most careful,' Madeline replied levelly, although there were tears in her eyes. 'And poor Mabel's parents' home was very clean and tidy considering how many of them live there.'

Jacob ran a hand distractedly through his hair as he fought to control his temper. 'You are *not* . . . I repeat *NOT* to go there ever again; do you hear me? In fact, I think it would be best now if you were to confine yourself to the house until after the child has been safely delivered!'

Madeline gasped with dismay. 'But what about attending church? You know how I love to go at least three times a week and what will people think if I suddenly don't put in an appearance?'

'People will accept that you are putting the welfare of our child first, as you should.'

Madeline opened her mouth to protest but he put up his hand, totally unmoved by her obvious distress. 'There will be no arguments. I have said all I am prepared to say on the subject so just make sure you abide by my wishes. One more thing . . . I noticed that the maid was carrying a rather heavy basket up the alley. What was in it?'

Madeline thought quickly. Jacob was so mean she was sure he would not agree to leftovers going to Mabel's family anymore were he to find out.

'It was shopping that Mrs Batley had asked her to get,' she lied and didn't even feel guilty.

He stared at her suspiciously. 'Very well. As it happens, I have been meaning to speak to Mrs Batley about Mabel. Send her in to me immediately.'

'What about Mabel?' Madeline dared to ask.

His stare was colder than the frost outside. 'It is nothing to concern yourself about. Now, please go and do as I ask.' He turned his back on her and began to shuffle some papers on his desk, so with a sigh she left the room, so upset that she forgot to close the door behind her.

'I know you're busy, Mrs Batley,' Madeline said apologetically in a wobbly voice when she entered the kitchen. 'But my husband wishes to see you in his study.'

'Does he now?' Mrs Batley frowned. 'I wonder what he wants me to cut back on now?' And moaning beneath her breath she headed for the study.

'You wanted to see me,' she said bluntly as she approached the desk.

He turned to face her. 'I've been giving the matter some thought and I believe that we could dispense with Mabel's services. After all, there is only my wife and myself to look after.'

'*And* young Harry an' a new baby any time soon,' Mrs Batley snapped as her eyes flashed fire. She shook her head, refusing to let him intimidate her. 'No, Mabel stays. There's no way I could see to everything.'

He stared her out for a moment, silently cursing his late uncle who had clearly been very fond of her. So fond, in fact, that he had had a codicil put in his will to the effect that Mrs Batley's job should be safe for as long as she wanted it. He had also left her fifty pounds for when, or if, she retired, so he was stuck with the old besom!

'Then what about if we reduce her hours?'

She wagged her head again. 'No. As I've said, I need the help. I'm too old to be runnin' about the place like a blue-arsed fly!'

He visibly flinched at her common outburst and pointed a shaking finger at the door. 'Very well, we will leave things as they are for now. But should I find Mabel trying to lead my wife astray again I shall reassess the situation.'

'Lead her astray? What, just by letting her walk into town wi' her? Hmm, I didn't realise the poor lass was a prisoner!'

Totally unaccustomed to anyone standing up to him, Jacob Kettle blustered, 'I . . . I am only thinking of my unborn child's welfare!'

'Of *course* you are!' Mrs Batley's voice was heavy with sarcasm. 'So why don't you just lock her in her room an' have done wi' it?' And on that note, she turned and left him staring after her.

Jacob's hands clenched into fists. First his wife had dared to argue with him and now the housekeeper! He had just seen another side to Madeline that he did not at all care for. She had seemed so pliable when he had decided she would be the one to bear him children, and following their marriage the conception had come about far more quickly than he had dared to hope. He had never really enjoyed the physical side of marriage. He was hoping for a son, although it wouldn't really matter if it was a girl. Once he was a father his colleagues would have a new respect for him. The majority of them had families and when he had been married to his first wife he had hated the sympathetic glances they bestowed on him each time she lost a child. And then there was that *damned*

Mrs Batley. Why his late uncle had thought so much of her he would never understand.

Glancing towards the window he saw the first flakes of snow fluttering down and his mood worsened. He just prayed that it would not come down thick enough to leave him housebound with all these women!

In the day room, Madeline's mood was not much better as she too stared at the snow from the window. Jacob had seemed like an answer to a prayer following the death of her father, but now he was becoming more and more controlling and she was beginning to feel like a prisoner. Just then the child inside her moved and her hand flew to her swollen stomach as a smile hovered at the corners of her mouth.

'Not long now, my little one,' she crooned. She could hardly wait to hold the child in her arms for she knew already that it would be the most important person in the world to her. And it wasn't really so bad that Jacob had forbidden her to go to church for the time being. She had her Bible to read and she could still pray. Feeling happier she sank down onto the sofa. She hadn't realised until now just how much the unaccustomed exercise had tired her. Within seconds she was fast asleep with her arms folded protectively across her unborn child.

Thankfully the snow stopped falling after a couple of hours and so the judge was able to go to work as normal the next morning.

Mrs Batley was baking cakes when the kitchen door leading from the hallway creaked open and Madeline asked, 'May I come in?'

Mrs Batley chuckled. 'Why shouldn't you, lass. It is your house.'

Madeline glanced about before asking, 'Where's Mabel?'

'Oh, she's upstairs cleanin' the bedrooms. Why, did yer want her?'

The young woman shook her head. 'No, actually it was you I wanted to see. You see, I was wondering if from now on when you bake you could do a little extra for Mabel's family.'

Mrs Batley raised an eyebrow and Madeline hurried on. 'Perhaps just an extra loaf and an extra cake here and there if you could manage it. I'm sure they would be grateful for it. They're such a lovely family and I so enjoyed meeting them.'

'They are nice an' I'm sure they would be grateful for a bit extra an' all. But I ain't so sure the master would be so keen on the idea.'

'He doesn't have to know, does he?' There was a mischievous twinkle in her eye and Mrs Batley chuckled again.

'Right you are then. I'll start right now an' Mabel can drop some bits round to 'em tonight when all the jobs are finished, if yer quite sure?'

Chapter Seven

As Christmas approached, a routine developed in the Kettle household. Monday to Friday each week the judge went off to the law courts in Coventry or visited his lawyer's office in the town, then after dinner on Friday night he would disappear, sometimes for the whole weekend, which suited the women of the household just fine.

Harry always took him wherever it was he went in the carriage and returned with the master, but when questioned he never let on where they'd been.

'I can't see why he should be so secretive,' Mrs Batley grumbled as the three women sat together by the fire in the kitchen one Saturday night early in December. 'It ain't as if the master is particularly kind to him. He speaks to him like he's dirt half the time.'

Madeline was forced to agree and could say nothing in her husband's defence. He spoke to her the same way most of the time now, although he had never as yet raised his hand to her. Her dreams of making him a good wife were fast fading and she was more convinced than ever that he viewed her as merely a vessel to carry his children. He certainly never went out of his way to spend any time with her and he never showed her any affection. She secretly hoped that one child would be enough for him, for the thought of having to share a bed with him again made her break out in a cold sweat. But still, he had helped her out of a terrible financial mess, and he had given her a fine house to live in, so she supposed she should be grateful for that at least.

The following week when Mrs Batley tendered the weekly accounts to the master, she ventured to ask, 'I was wonderin' if I might be allowed to spend a little o' the housekeepin' on a small Christmas tree for the drawin' room? The old master always used to come home with one round about now an' I know the mistress would like one.'

He had seemed to be a little more relaxed for the last few days, possibly because the birth of his child was drawing nearer, but now he frowned. 'Why ever would I want to waste hard-earned money on fripperies?' he said with a sneer. 'I consider such things to be quite unnecessary!'

Mrs Batley shrugged and gave a sly little grin. 'I suppose it all depends how yer look at it. Yer did tell me last night that you'd be havin' a dinner party fer some o' yer colleagues the week afore Christmas an' I just thought they might think it a bit strange if they arrived to find the house wasn't decorated festively. Still, I dare say they've all got big posh places an' they can afford to be a bit extravagant.'

The judge's brain ticked over. He supposed, much as he hated to admit it, that she was right, and he didn't want to appear mean to his colleagues. Appearances for a man in his position were all-important.

'Very well,' he agreed somewhat grudgingly. 'I shall give you a little extra to make the house look festive. But there's no need to go mad. I want it looking tasteful, is that clear?'

'Crystal clear, judge!' She contained her mirth as he counted out her housekeeping money and added an extra half a crown.

She nodded and dropped the money into her apron pocket then went back to the kitchen with a spring in her step.

'You an' Harry can go into the market tomorrow an' pick a tree up,' she informed Mabel gleefully. 'I reckon I just shamed the tight-fisted old devil into lettin' us have one. I ain't under no illusions, though, it weren't for his wife or us he agreed to it!'

'Well done, Batty!' Mabel beamed. The job of decorating the Christmas tree fell to her each year and it was one she thoroughly enjoyed.

The mood in the house improved even more the next morning when Madeline went into the kitchen to tell them, 'My husband has just informed me that he won't be here for Christmas, Mrs Batley. Apparently, he has some unfinished business back in Leeds to attend to so he will be leaving the day before Christmas Eve and he won't be back until the twenty-seventh.'

Mrs Batley kept her eyes fixed firmly on the pastry she was trimming so that Madeline wouldn't see how happy the news had made her. In truth, the young mistress didn't actually look too heartbroken about it herself. Perhaps she'd be able to wangle it for Mabel to spend a bit of time with her family on Christmas Day now? If there was only Madeline and Harry to cook for she could easily manage by herself, but she would address that with the mistress nearer to the time.

'Right you are,' she answered. 'I've been meaning to talk to you about the Christmas dinner. Our old master always liked goose but if there's something else you'd prefer—'

'Oh no,' Madeline said hastily. 'Just do whatever you normally do, please. I'm sure it will be delicious. As you know, I'm struggling to eat big meals now anyway. I don't think there's any room left in here and I feel as if I'm about to pop.' She grinned as she stroked her stomach.

'Not long now.' Mrs Batley smiled. Then a thought suddenly occurred to her. 'But you're so close to your time. What if you have the baby while your husband is away? Shouldn't he perhaps delay going until you've safely given birth?'

'Not at all,' Madeline said hastily, trying not to show how pleased she was at the news that he was to be away. 'I'm quite happy for him to go. If anything should happen I know I'll be in safe hands with you and Mabel.'

The two women exchanged a smile then Madeline waddled away to read her Bible. She was missing going to church enormously, especially now it was nearly Christmas. As she thought back to the Christmases she had spent visiting the poor with her father, a lump formed in her throat. He had been such a kind man. She could clearly remember him taking the boots off his own feet one Christmas Eve and giving them to a youth who was huddled in a shop doorway with nothing more than rags on his back to keep him warm. Another Christmas he had delivered their whole Christmas dinner to a starving family, much to the chagrin of their long-suffering cook, and they themselves had dined on bread and dripping. She hadn't minded, in fact she had been proud of his kind heart and often she wished that Jacob could be just a little bit more like him.

I must remember to give him his present before he leaves, she thought as she settled in a chair in the day room. She doubted he would have bought her anything but she didn't care. Perhaps they would be able to have a fire in the dining room on Christmas Day and she would invite the staff to join her at the table. That would be so much nicer than eating alone or having to endure Jacob's company. Happily, she lifted her Bible and soon she was intent on her reading.

Later that afternoon, Harry delivered the Christmas tree and Madeline watched him set it in a sturdy bucket of earth in the drawing room before Mabel set about decorating it.

'*Wonderful!*' Madeline clapped her hands when it was done, her eyes as bright as a child's as she and Mabel stood side by side to admire it.

'The little glass baubles belonged to the old mistress,' Mabel informed her with a sad smile. 'Batty told me that the old master bought 'em for her in London shortly after they were married an' she treasured 'em. They are pretty, though, ain't they? I always feel a bit nervous when I'm doin' the tree in case I break one.'

'They are beautiful,' Madeline agreed as Jacob strode into the room.

'Look at the tree, dear. Doesn't it look pretty?' Madeline smiled at him but he merely gave it a cursory glance.

'I find all these festive trimmings rather vulgar.' As he eyed her coldly, the smile slid from her face. 'And as the daughter of a vicar I would have thought you would too. Surely Christmas is supposed to be about celebrating the birth of Christ?'

'Well . . . yes . . . Yes, of course it is but . . .' Her voice trailed away as he turned and left abruptly. Flushing with embarrassment, she glanced at Mabel apologetically. 'He's probably just had a bad day in court. But never mind. I think you've done a fine job of it. Thank you, Mabel.' Then she lifted her skirts and waddled from the room as quickly as she could, clearly upset.

The days rushed past and the day before Christmas Eve, Madeline dutifully pecked her husband's whiskery cheek as he was about to depart. 'Merry Christmas, Jacob. I hope you manage to conclude all your business successfully.' She actually thought it was rather odd that anyone would be working over Christmas but was too astute to say so.

'Hmm.' He rammed his hat onto his head and left without

another word, throwing his bag into the waiting carriage and clambering in after it as Madeline stood on the step waving.

'Drive on, Grimes.'

Harry set the horses into a gentle trot and, shivering, Madeline hurried back inside. It had started to snow again and already the roads were white all over. I hope this doesn't stop the trains from running, she thought as she followed the delicious smells issuing from the kitchen, and instantly felt guilty.

'Mm, mince pies,' she said as she saw them cooling on a rack.

Mrs Batley smiled and placed one on a plate for her. 'Here, try one. There's plenty more in the oven.'

'Delicious,' Madeline told her seconds later as she sprayed crumbs across the table.

Mrs Batley chuckled. The young mistress appeared almost light-hearted and she had an idea it was because the master would be gone for a few days.

She drew in a breath; now seemed as good a time as any to ask. 'I was thinkin' . . .' she began tentatively, 'if perhaps we could let Mabel have Christmas Day off to spend wi' her family? She does so miss 'em at this time o' year an' I can manage to cook fer me you an' Harry wi' me eyes closed.'

'Why, of course she must. What a brilliant idea.' Madeline nodded. 'And I was thinking that we might all dine together on Christmas Day.'

When Mrs Batley looked uncertain, she rushed on, 'Oh, *please* say yes. I shall feel quite lost if I have to have Christmas dinner all on my own.'

'In that case, it sounds wonderful; we'll do just that.' Mrs Batley went back to mixing the sage and onion stuffing she was making to stuff the goose, humming merrily.

Chapter Eight

Harry, Madeline and Mrs Batley had a most enjoyable Christmas Day, although both of the women were thinking of Christmases past. Mrs Batley was remembering old Master Kettle; Madeline was thinking of the ones she had spent with her father; and who knew what Harry was thinking of. His past was still, in the main, a secret although he seemed to enjoy himself. Sadly, Madeline could only pick at the lovely meal Mrs Batley had prepared but Harry did it full justice and even had second helpings of everything, much to the cook's delight.

Mabel had gone off early on Christmas morning with a spring in her step and a basket heaving with treats for her family. Mrs Batley had bought and cooked a fowl for them out of her own money. She had also sent vegetables, mince pies and a Christmas pudding, so hopefully they would all enjoy their Christmas too. She had been tickled to see how sad Harry had been to see her go and had high hopes that eventually the two would admit their obvious attraction. The trouble was they were both shy with the opposite sex but she hoped this might disappear as they got to know each other a little better.

After dinner, they opened the small gifts they had bought for each other. For Harry, there were two white handkerchiefs, which Mrs Batley had embroidered with his initials in the corner, and there was a warm hand-knitted sweater from Madeline. He was touchingly thrilled with them. For Mrs Batley, there were some lavender bath salts and matching soap from Madeline and a pretty scarf from Harry, which she insisted she would keep for best. Harry had also bought Madeline some lovely burgundy gloves to go with the scarf Mrs Batley had given her and she was so touched that she insisted they were the nicest she had ever owned, causing him to flush with pleasure.

After insisting on helping Mrs Batley and Harry with clearing and washing their plates, Madeline then retired for a couple of hours for a rest. She grew very tired now and could hardly wait for the birth to be over. As she was lying down her back began to ache and she commented on it when she went back downstairs in time for tea.

'I think I must have laid funny,' she grumbled as she rubbed the base of her back.

Mrs Batley eyed her suspiciously.

Madeline's backache was worse the next morning and the kindly older woman kept a close eye on her. They were all sitting together in the warm kitchen enjoying a cup of hot milk before retiring when Madeline suddenly started and spilled some of her drink down the bodice of her dress.

'Ouch!' Her free hand clutched at her stomach and the colour drained from her face.

'What is it, pet?' Mrs Batley was beside her in a second and after a moment Madeline smiled self-consciously.

'I'm so sorry. I didn't mean to startle you but I just had this sharp pain and it caught me unawares.'

'Hmm, well you just sit there now an' let's see if it comes again, eh?'

She was watching her mistress like a hawk and suddenly the younger woman asked, 'You don't think this might be the start of the baby coming, do you?' She had longed to meet her child and yet now she was suddenly afraid.

Mrs Batley patted her hand and chuckled. 'I think it may well be. Harry, we might need you to go for Mrs Robins soon so get wrapped up warm.'

As Harry gulped, Mrs Batley grinned. If she wasn't very much mistaken they would be meeting the new arrival very soon but there was no time to ponder, there were things to do.

'Harry, you go up to the mistress's room and make the fire up then come down here and get as much water on to heat as you can. I'm going to go up and make sure the crib is ready and get the towels out.' She patted Madeline's hand reassuringly. The poor girl had paled to the colour of lint and was clearly afraid of what might lie ahead. 'Meanwhile, you sit there and keep warm and time how far apart the pains are if you have any more. It might be a false alarm but better safe than sorry, eh? It's a bitter night an' wi' the snow settlin' it might take Mrs Robins some time to get here, so I ain't takin' no chances.'

Twenty minutes later she was back. 'The pains are coming about every fifteen minutes now,' Madeline told her.

'Right then, we'll wait till they're a bit closer together afore we send fer Mrs Robins. I believe first babies like to take their time in comin'. Is there anythin' yer want, lass?'

Madeline shook her head. She looked absolutely terrified. 'Jacob won't be very pleased if I have the baby while he's away,' she remarked.

'Huh! Then he shouldn't have left yer so close to yer time, should he? Now, let's get you upstairs and changed into your nightgown, eh? You'll be more comfortable up there.'

Madeline willingly followed her, stopping halfway up the stairs as another pain took her breath away. 'That must have been ten minutes after the last one, they're coming closer together now,' she gasped in a panic.

Mrs Batley helped her to her room and once she was settled on the bed, she fled down the stairs as fast as her feet would take her to tell Harry, 'You'd best go for Mrs Robins, I think, lad. I don't want this baby comin' afore she gets here. Yer know where she lives, don't yer?' Over the last couple of weeks she had told him of it often enough.

Harry nodded, almost tripping over his feet in his haste to get to his coat. 'Aye, I know all right. She's in Fife Street, ain't she?'

'That's it, now off yer go an' be as quick as yer can.'

The last sentence was unnecessary as Harry had disappeared through the door before she had chance to finish it.

He arrived back with Mrs Robins almost an hour later and their coats were both white with snow, which began to melt and steam in the heat of the kitchen.

'Eeh, fancy startin' on Boxin' Day, I were just sittin' by the fire enjoyin' a nice glass o' stout wi' me hubby,' the elderly woman grumbled as Mrs Batley hurried to help her off with her coat. 'Still, babies have a habit o' comin' when they're good an' ready. Now where's the mum-to-be? I'll go an' have a look at her then a nice hot cup o' tea wouldn't go amiss.'

Harry hurried over to the sink to fill the kettle while Mrs Robins followed Mrs Batley upstairs.

Madeline was sitting in bed clutching the eiderdown to her chin when they walked into her room. The woman smiled at her. 'Hello, pet. I'm Mrs Robins. Now, how about yer lie down an' let me take a look at yer.'

Madeline did as she was told and when the examination was over the midwife told her, 'Everythin' is comin' along nicely but I reckon you'll be a good few hours yet. Is there anythin' yer want?'

'M-my Bible please.' Madeline pointed to the book on the dressing table and once she had it, she gripped it to her chest and began to pray quietly as the two women went back down to the kitchen to enjoy the tea Harry had brewed for them.

'I'd like you to stay here, if yer don't mind,' Mrs Robins told

60

him. 'Just in case we need the doctor. Yer never know wi' first babies an' her upstairs is only a wee scrap of a thing. Not that I'm envisagin' any problems, mind,' she added hastily as Harry's eyes popped. She chuckled as she shook her head, setting her double chins wobbling. Mrs Robins was a small woman, almost as far round as she was high with greying hair and twinkling blue eyes. Over the years, she had delivered dozens of babies in the town and she was known for liking a tipple and having a very good sense of humour. 'You men are all the same,' she said teasingly. 'You're keen to be there at the makin' o' the babe but not so keen to watch it come into the world. I tell yer, if men had to have the babies the population would die away. Ain't that right, Enid?'

Harry blinked with surprise. The midwife finished her drink in a long gulp, then wiping the back of her hand across her mouth, she heaved herself out of the chair, saying, 'Right then, let's go back up an' have a look how the little lass is progressin'. Can I take it you'll stay to help if need be, Enid?'

'Of course,' Mrs Batley said with a confidence she didn't feel. She had never attended a birth before but she supposed there was a first time for everything and with her husband being away, Madeline deserved to have a familiar face beside her.

The two women pottered away as Harry settled himself in the fireside chair and prepared for the longest night of his life so far. He wished he could look at the newspaper that was lying on the settle but no one had ever taught him to read and he was too ashamed to ask anyone to teach him.

The night dragged on as the snow continued to fall softly and at last, countless cups of tea later, as dawn was just streaking the sky, Mrs Robins told Madeline, 'Nearly there now, lass. Now yer must listen an' do exactly as I tell yer. When the next pain comes push as hard as yer know how, there's a good girl.'

Madeline barely knew where she was by this stage and lay

61

exhausted against the pillows praying for death. Surely nothing could be worse than this terrible agony? Her hair was plastered to her head with sweat and she felt as weak as a kitten; even so she gathered what little strength she had left and, gripping tight to Mrs Batley's hand, she did as she was told groaning and whimpering with the effort. Her bottom lip was raw and bleeding from the many times she had bitten down on it to stop herself from screaming and Mrs Batley was full of admiration for her. Most women would have been screaming blue murder but Madeline had been very brave.

'*That's it* . . . I can see the head now,' the midwife crowed as the pain died away. 'Now on the next one let's have the same again. Push as if yer life depends on it!'

Mrs Batley watched her young mistress's face closely as she lifted her head and pushed again and suddenly a tiny body seemed to almost explode from her body to lie in a bloody heap between her legs.

Mrs Robins lifted the child and slapped its rounded little backside soundly and suddenly the room echoed with the sounds of an indignant newborn cry.

'Well done. You've got yourself a little daughter an' a right bonny little lass she is an' all,' she cried triumphantly as she hastily wrapped the babe in the towel that Mrs Batley held ready for her and passed the child to her.

'Eeh, she's beautiful.' Mrs Batley was overcome with emotion as she stared down at the precious bundle in her arms, tears pouring unashamedly down her cheeks. 'An' she's got your red hair an' all, pet. An' blue eyes, I reckon, though I'm sure I can see a hint o' green in 'em.' She was suddenly painfully aware of what she had missed by never becoming a mother herself. It hadn't been for the lack of trying. She and her late husband had dreamed of having a houseful of babies when they were first wed but it had never happened for them.

'All new baby's eyes are blue, they'll most likely change,' Mrs Robins informed her as she hung over the new mother with a frown on her face. Madeline was barely conscious and there was a terrifyingly blue tinge about her lips as her eyes began to roll back in her head. She was also bleeding profusely. Grabbing a towel, the midwife attempted to stem the flow as she suddenly hissed urgently, 'Take the child away an' bathe it an' get Harry to run fer the doctor quick as he knows how! There's somethin' badly amiss here.'

Mrs Batley had to force herself to stay calm as she hurried away as fast as she could. Oh, dear God don't let anything happen to the poor lass now, she silently prayed as she negotiated the stairs.

Harry was off like a whippet when she told him that the doctor was needed and once he had gone she busied herself with bathing the child. Sometime later, clad in one of the tiny nightgowns her mother had painstakingly stitched for her, and swaddled in the shawl Mrs Batley had knitted, she looked like a little angel.

'Tuesday's child is full of grace,' Mrs Batley whispered as she cradled the baby to her. And then she prayed that God might spare her mother long enough to see the little mite grow up. God help the poor little thing if she was left to the mercy of her father, who certainly didn't appear capable of loving anyone. 'But you'll always have me,' she crooned tenderly as she rocked the precious child to and fro, and from that moment on her heart was lost.

Chapter Nine

'Here yer go then, pass her to me,' the young woman said as she walked into the kitchen and shook the snow from the shawl she'd had wrapped about her shoulders. It seemed poor protection for such harsh weather.

Madeline's child was now three days old and thanks to this young woman, she was being well fed. Mrs Robins had delivered Cathy Barnes's baby only the week before and she had kindly offered to step in as a wet nurse until Madeline was well enough to feed the child herself. Thankfully, Madeline had survived the birth, just, but she was still very ill and weak and Mabel and Mrs Batley had their hands full, what with looking after her and the baby – not that they minded. Harry had been a brilliant help; between feeds he would sit for hours cradling the baby, leaving the women free to get on with other things.

Now he passed the child to Cathy and as she took a seat at the side of the fire and unfastened her drab dress, he blushed and hastily averted his eyes.

'Eeh, I feel as if I'm pingin' back an' forth atween here an' home on a bit of elastic.' Cathy giggled as the child fastened her rosebud mouth to her nipple and began to suck greedily. There was certainly nothing wrong with her appetite and, thankfully, Cathy had plenty of milk for both this baby and her own son.

'I'll get yer a nice hot drink, pet,' Mrs Batley offered as she hurried across the flagstones to fill the kettle. 'That's the least we can do for yer. Goodness knows what would have happened if you hadn't stepped in to help. And don't worry, when the judge comes home, an' I say *when*, I'll make sure as yer properly paid fer your trouble. He should have been back the day the lass was born but we ain't seen hide nor hair of him. He don't even know he has a daughter yet.'

Cathy smiled as she rocked the baby gently. 'Well, I must admit the money will fair come in handy but it's been a pleasure seein' to this little 'un. In truth, I don't think I've ever met such a placid baby, me own included. He howls the house down half the time.'

A rap came on the front door then and Mabel hurried to answer it to find the judge standing outside.

'Well, don't stand there with your mouth gawping open like a goldfish, girl,' he barked in a fine ill-humour. 'Stand aside and let me in, can't you. I do live here!'

Mabel hastily stood aside as he stormed past her. Then, after glancing about, he roared, 'And where is my wife?'

'She's upstairs in bed.'

'Oh, and why is that? Surely she should be up and about at this time of the day.'

His head snapped around as Mrs Batley's voice sounded behind him. 'As it happens, she gave birth to yer baby the day after Boxin' Day, the day you were due to come home.' Mrs Batley's voice was laced with sarcasm and she had his full attention now. 'Unfortunately, there were complications an' she almost died. In fact, the doctor is due at any minute. He's visited every day since.'

'And the baby . . . did that survive?'

She nodded. 'It certainly did. There's a wet nurse feedin' it in the kitchen right now.'

'But I expressly said that there was no need for a wet nurse.'

''Twere either that or let the little soul starve. The mistress were certainly in no fit state to feed it.' Her eyes flashed with contempt and he had the good grace to flush.

'I see . . . then in that case I suppose it was necessary,' he answered grudgingly. 'And was it a boy?'

Mrs Batley shook her head. 'No, you have a fine healthy little lass, the double of her mother.' She thought she saw a flash of disappointment in his eyes for just a second.

'I see.' Without another word, he strode towards the kitchen. Entering, he found the babe still glued to Cathy's breast and flushed, just as Harry had done, and hastily turned away.

'I shall be about another ten minutes,' Cathy informed him and with a nod he left.

In the hallway, he found Mabel showing the doctor upstairs and he followed him and began to pace the landing while the doctor went in to see his wife.

'Well, how is she?' he demanded the second the man left the room.

The doctor eyed him disapprovingly, noting his rather dishevelled state. Jacob looked as if he hadn't shaved for days and his clothes were crumpled.

'Slightly improved. But I'm afraid it's going to be a very long time before she's properly well again and even then, she's going to have to take things easy. She lost an awful lot of blood and I also discovered your wife has a heart condition which had gone undetected. It was probably the strain of having the child that highlighted it.' The doctor paused then and chose his words carefully before going on. 'I should inform you that another pregnancy could prove fatal for her. Do you understand what I'm saying?'

Jacob nodded slowly. He understood perfectly; he would never father a son now.

'Very well then, I shall take my leave but I shall be back tomorrow to check on your wife's progress. Should you need me before then, you know where I am.'

He dipped his head and was gone down the stairs before Jacob could say another word. He stood for a time digesting what the doctor had told him, then, after taking a deep breath, he straightened his back and opened the door to his wife's room. She was lying in bed with her head turned towards the window and he was shocked to see how ill she looked. She seemed to have shrunk to half her size and there were great black shadows beneath her eyes.

She turned her head slowly and managed a weak smile. 'Jacob . . . we were concerned about you when you didn't come home on the day you said you would.'

He walked stiffly to the side of the bed. 'I apologise for that. I was unavoidably detained and had no way of getting word to you.'

'Never mind, you're home now. Do you know that I had the baby?'

'Yes . . . a girl, I understand.'

She nodded, sensing his disappointment. 'A very beautiful little girl, as it happens and she's healthy too. I just wish I could spend more time with her.' He could hear the frustration in her voice. 'Have you seen her yet?'

He shook his head. 'No, not yet. She is being fed at the moment.'

Madeline felt as if she was speaking to a stranger rather than her husband. 'We should think of a name for her,' she said then. 'She was born on Tuesday so I thought perhaps Grace?'

To her surprise, he shrugged his approval. 'I dare say that's as good a name as any,' he replied unenthusiastically. 'And we shall have Victoria for her middle name in honour of our queen.'

'Grace Victoria . . . yes, I think it's perfect,' she agreed.

'Good.' He began to back towards the door.

He closed the bedroom door quietly behind him and once out on the landing again he shook his head. *A girl!* And no chance of a boy now either! Still, at least he had a child, that was something.

Slowly he made his way back down to the kitchen just in time to see Cathy leaving. 'I'll be back in three hours,' she promised Mrs Batley as she wrapped her shawl about her shoulders and vanished into the swirling snow.

Mrs Batley was holding the child and she moved towards him while Mabel swept the floor. 'She's sleepy now cos her belly is full,' she told him. 'But she's got a good pair o' lungs on her, I warn yer, although I have to be fair an' say she's as good as the day is long an' only cries when she's hungry.'

He nodded, staring down at the contented little bundle. Mrs Batley held the baby out to him, and he automatically opened his arms and took her. It was then, as he gazed down at the fluffy red down on her head and her wide blue-green eyes that were sleepily staring trustingly up at him, that the most amazing thing happened. His whole face softened and when the baby curled her tiny hand around one of his fingers, he sank abruptly onto the nearest chair. Jacob Kettle had yearned for a son, and now here he was holding a daughter and the only child he was ever likely to have. But suddenly it didn't matter. This tiny being was his flesh and blood, a part of him and, for the first time in his life, he fell in love.

'She . . . she's quite exquisite,' he breathed in awe and, despite everything, Mrs Batley almost liked him.

'She is that.' She smiled as she watched the father staring in wonder at his newborn baby.

'We have decided to call her Grace Victoria,' he informed the housekeeper then, and she nodded her approval.

'That's a lovely name an' very fittin' seein' as she were born on a Tuesday.'

He glanced up at her. 'This . . . this wet nurse you have employed in my absence . . . Is she clean? I don't want her passing on any germs to my daughter.'

'Cathy is poor but clean as a whistle,' Mrs Batley responded sharply. She had thought his softening was too good to last. 'An' we were very lucky that Mrs Robins were able to ask for her help.

She will want payin' fer all the trouble she's goin' to o' course. The poor lass is rushin' backwards an' forwards atween her own home an' here like a yo-yo an' it ain't so long since she gave birth to her own son. She must be fair exhausted an' goodness knows what we'll do if her milk dries up.'

Jacob looked alarmed. 'Then we must ensure that that doesn't happen. She will move in here until she is no longer needed.'

Mrs Batley sniffed. 'I doubt she'd do that, judge. She has her own baby to see to an' all an' she ain't goin' to be inclined to neglect him, is she?'

He frowned for a moment. 'Then her child will have to come here too. You may prepare the nursery and they can all stay in there. Get a fire going up there and make sure that the room is warm for Grace. We don't want her catching a chill!'

'I suppose I can put it to her when she comes to do the next feed,' Mrs Batley ventured doubtfully.

'She'll come when I've spoken to her.' There was a determined look on the man's face. 'I shall make her an offer she can't refuse, so please inform me the moment she arrives.'

He stood and gently passed the now sleeping baby back to Mrs Batley. 'I shall go and bathe and change. Have Mabel bring hot water up to my room. And then I want the nursery prepared.'

Mrs Batley shrugged. 'As you wish.' She and Mabel watched him stride from the room then Mabel let out a long breath.

'Well, who'd have believed it, eh? He does have a heart after all.' She chuckled.

'You could be right but now you'd best get that hot water upstairs else he'll be soon shoutin' the roof off again.'

Mabel nodded and hurried away as Mrs Batley stared down at the sleeping infant nestling in her arms.

'So, little Grace,' she cooed. 'It seems you've won yer papa over good an' proper. Let's hope it stays that way, eh? Now we'll change yer binder an' take yer upstairs fer a little visit with yer mam. Yer know how she loves to see yer. I just pray for her sake that she'll be well enough to spend a bit more time with yer soon.'

By teatime that evening, Cathy and her son were installed in the nursery with baby Grace tucked snugly in her crib in front of a roaring fire. Jacob Kettle had offered her a sum of money that had made her eyes pop to ensure that his daughter would be properly fed. Even so, she had made a few stipulations of her own.

'In between feeds o' both babies I want to pop home an' see me husband sometimes.'

Gritting his teeth, he had nodded.

'An' I also want him to be able to come here fer a good meal each day when he's finished his shift at the pit. I can hardly cook for him if I ain't there, can I?'

At this point, Cathy wondered if she had pushed him too far as his hands clenched into fists, but after a moment he had nodded again. 'Is there anything else?'

Ignoring the sarcasm in his voice she shook her head. 'No, that'll be all.'

With his lips set in a firm line, he nodded and strode from the room without another word.

Chapter Ten

June 1897

'Oh, Papa, here she comes, look!' Standing at her father's side in the City of Westminster, Grace clapped her hands with delight as the queen's carriage rattled towards them. The crowds were celebrating Queen Victoria's Diamond Jubilee, and Jacob Kettle had brought his young daughter to London specially to see the queen waving to the crowds from the carriage window as she was driven to St Paul's Cathedral for a thanksgiving service in her honour. The crowd were wildly enthusiastic, just as they should be, Jacob considered. The queen's reign had seen more changes than in any other era in world history. Since she had ascended the throne, the world had seen the advent of motor cars, the telegram, the telephone, steam trains and steam ships and the coming of electricity. Once the carriage had passed, Grace hopped from foot to foot and asked, 'What shall we do now, Papa?'

'I thought I might take you for a ride on a boat on the River Thames and show you the Tower of London.' Jacob smiled at his daughter indulgently. Grace was the light of his life and in his eyes, she could do no wrong, and she rarely did. She was a placid, good-natured child with a ready smile and a kind word for everyone. Even on the way to see the procession she had stopped abruptly when she saw a blind beggar sitting on the pavement

71

and had pleaded with her father to put some money in his bowl. Jacob would normally have passed the man by without giving him a second glance, but seeing the sympathetic tears in his daughter's eyes he had grudgingly planted some coins in her hand and she had placed them in his begging bowl.

'These are for you, so as you can buy yourself some dinner,' she had whispered and the man had smiled and touched his cap.

'God bless yer, child.'

Grace had tripped happily on her way then, holding her father's hand tightly with a smile on her face. It was a glorious sunny day and she looked sweet in her new blue dress. She just missed being termed as pretty: her nose was a little too small and her chin a little too pronounced and in the summer her pale skin was prone to erupt with freckles, but her glorious deep green eyes, striking red hair and gentle nature more than made up for that and she was adored by all who knew her – her father especially.

There appeared to be three loves in Jacob Kettle's life, as Mrs Batley had commented. First was Grace, who could wrap him around her little finger, secondly came his horses, and lastly his latest toy, a brand-new Daimler Shooting Brake fresh from the factory in Coventry where it had been manufactured. Jacob had noticed that motor cars were much more common in London whereas back in his home town they were still quite a rarity.

But today was for his daughter, and now they set off in a high state of excitement for a ride on the pleasure boats.

Back at home, Mabel was taking the mistress her morning tea. Madeline had never fully recovered from Grace's birth and was now a semi-invalid, although she did still make an effort to attend church at least three times a week. Other than that, she rarely left the house and when she did overtax herself her lips would turn a frightening shade of blue and she'd become breathless, which would send Mrs Batley and Mabel into a panic. They had come to love the young mistress over the years and both thought that young Grace was very like her in nature. They were both kindly and undemanding, which was more than could be said for the master. Sadly, he hadn't mellowed at all towards them.

As Mabel entered the drawing room she found Madeline sitting in a chair enjoying the garden from the open window. Harry was working out there and she smiled as Mabel entered.

'I wonder if Grace got to see the queen's procession?' She sighed wistfully as Mabel laid the tray down on a small table. 'I should so have loved to have gone with her but I fear I would have spoiled it if I hadn't been able to keep up.' Madeline loved her little girl dearly and the love was returned. Grace adored attending the church with her mother and never tired of listening to the Bible stories she would read to her.

'I bet she's havin' the time of her life,' Mabel assured her. The house was so quiet without her. 'An' never fear, her nanny is there to make sure she comes to no harm, not that the master would let it.'

Jacob had employed a nanny to care for the child soon after her wet nurse was no longer needed and Grace now lived up on the nursery floor with her, much to Madeline's disappointment. She got so frustrated because she wasn't able to take proper care of her only child herself but sadly there was nothing she could do about it.

Mabel paused to stare out of the window and her heart skipped a beat as she caught sight of Harry expertly scything the grass. Over the last few years he had turned from a skinny lad into a strapping, handsome young man thanks to Mrs Batley's cooking. His legs were still somewhat bandy, admittedly, but Mabel never noticed that and had realised long ago that she loved him. Not that it had done her any good. Although Harry always treated her kindly and was free with his smiles, he had shown no inclination to take their relationship any further as yet and Mabel got frustrated sometimes. Surely he must know how she felt about him? She tried to show it in a hundred little different ways. But still, she thought optimistically, he was sure to get the message sooner or later. Could he ever feel the same about her?

'It's such a beautiful day, it makes you want to be out there in the sunshine, doesn't it?'

Madeline's voice brought Mabel's attention back into the room and she grinned. 'Well I can soon get Harry to take a chair out into the garden fer you. A bit o' sunshine would do yer the power o' good. You could perhaps sit and read out there awhile till Mrs Batley's got yer lunch ready.'

Madeline's green eyes lit up. 'Do you know what, I think I'll do that. I get so tired of being stuck indoors all the time. Oh, and by the way, did you enquire about the Sunday school at Chilver's Coton?'

'I did actually. I spoke to Mrs Lockett, the vicar's wife who runs it, an' she said she'd be happy fer Grace to start goin' just as soon as she likes. I could always walk her there an' back an' I'm sure she'd love it. She gets lonely never mixin' wi' other children her age.'

'I know she does.' Madeline sighed. 'Jacob and I are at loggerheads at the moment about what to do about her education. He wants to hire a private tutor to come in and teach her each day but Grace wants to start at the local school so that she can make some friends. What do you think would be best for her, Mabel?'

'Personally, I reckon she'd be happier at the school in Abbey Green, not that it's really my place to comment.'

'I agree with you.' Madeline took the tea that Mabel held out to her and sipped daintily from the china cup. 'I think I'll get Grace to speak to her father herself about it when they get home. She can always get round him whereas anything I suggest just seems to fall on deaf ears.'

Mabel chuckled. 'I reckon yer right there. But now you finish yer tea an' I'll go an' get Harry to lift one o' the kitchen chairs out into the garden for you. Oh, an' I'll slip upstairs an' get your sun parasol an' all. We don't want you gettin' sunburn.'

A short time later, when Madeline was settled comfortably under her parasol, Mabel returned to the kitchen to help Mrs Batley prepare the lunch. They were going to just have cold cuts of meat left over from the day before and salad today along with some freshly baked bread and pickles. The heat and the fact that they were all missing Grace seemed to have robbed them all of their appetite.

'I shall be glad when Grace is back.' Mrs Batley sniffed. 'The place don't seem the same without her, does it?'

Mabel nodded in agreement as she began to chop a lettuce into the salad bowl. 'I miss her too, but the master will take good care of her.'

'Hmm! If yer were to ask me, he's takin' *too* good care o' her! He seems to resent any time she spends with the mistress.'

'I know what you mean. It's the poor mistress I feel sorry for. When he's home she don't get a chance to spend any time at all wi' Grace an' she does love her so. I reckon Nanny gets cross wi' him too, he's always disruptin' the little girl's routine!'

'I dare say I'm bein' a bit hard on him an' we should make allowances,' Mrs Batley said. 'He probably wants to make the most of her cos he knows he ain't goin' to get any more children.'

'I'm tired now, Papa.' Grace yawned and rubbed at her eyes as they wandered along the Mall after admiring Buckingham Palace.

Jacob Kettle swung her up into his arms. 'I'm sorry, sweetheart.' He kissed her forehead. 'I've kept you out far later than I should have. I'll get you back to the hotel now; Nanny will be waiting to put you into bed no doubt.'

Holding Grace with one arm, he went to the edge of the kerb and hailed a hackney cab.

After hastily giving the driver the address of their hotel in Marylebone, he gently lifted Grace inside and within minutes she was sound asleep on his lap with her thumb jammed into her mouth.

Nanny was indeed waiting in the foyer and she looked none too pleased as she hurried to take the sleeping child from him.

'Really, judge, this is far too late for Grace to be out,' she scolded.

He looked shamefaced. 'I know, Nanny, and I apologise. We were having such a good time I didn't realise how late it was.'

'Hmm!' The woman glared at him. 'I shall have to leave her bath until morning now and it's far too late to take her into the dining room.'

'Oh, don't worry about that. I shall have something sent up to your room for her.'

She inclined her head and hauled Grace off to the lift, mumbling beneath her breath. Just like Mrs Batley, Nanny was not afraid to stand up to her employer although she disliked the man intensely.

As he headed off to the bar for a much-needed drink, Jacob let out a low whistle of relief. Truthfully, he would much rather have brought Grace to London by himself but as his wife had pointed out, it wouldn't be seemly for him to have to see to her bathing and her personal toilet now she was a little older. Grudgingly he had been forced to admit that she was right. Hopefully he wouldn't have to see the dratted woman again till the morning and then he would whip Grace away on another sightseeing trip. They only had another two days of their holiday left and he was determined that Grace should see as much of London as she could before they headed for home.

76

'The mistress has been sat by that front winder all afternoon,' Mabel commented to Mrs Batley as she carried Madeline's afternoon tea tray into the kitchen. 'An' she ain't touched this nice cake yer sent her in.'

Mrs Batley shrugged. 'She rarely does no matter what I try to tempt her wi'. In fact, she hardly eats enough to keep a bird alive. It's no wonder she's never got no energy. Still, happen she'll perk up again when Grace gets home.'

Just then they heard the horse's hooves on the gravel drive.

'This sounds like them.' Mrs Batley grinned. She was another one that little Grace could wrap around her little finger and she had missed her sorely. Sure enough, seconds later they heard the sound of the judge's key in the lock and Grace exploded into the hallway in a smart new coat and bonnet that her father had bought her from Selfridges in London.

'Grace, my love.' Madeline had come to stand in the hallway and when the child caught sight of her mother she flew into her arms, her dark red curls dancing on her slim shoulders.

'Oh, Mamma, I've *missed* you . . . but we had a wonderful time.' The little girl's striking green eyes were shining as she gabbled on. 'Papa took me to see the Palace, an' Westminster Abbey an' the Tower of London an' *all sorts* of wonderful places.'

'Did he now?' Madeline bent to kiss her. 'Then you must come into the drawing room. I want to hear all about it.'

Both Mabel and Mrs Batley noticed that the judge and his wife barely glanced at each other but they were used to that now. Sometimes the couple seemed to go for days without a word passing between them.

Nanny followed Mrs Batley and Mabel into the kitchen, saying, 'Phew, I could really murder a cup of tea. That train journey seemed to go on for ever. And a slice of your delicious cake wouldn't go amiss either, Enid.'

Like Mrs Batley, Betty Donovan was a widow, hence her need

to earn a living. Both of them were childless too but there any similarity ended. Mrs Batley was a short, rounded little woman whereas the nanny was tall and thin as a whistle. She was also very firm but fair and it tickled the staff that the master seemed to be afraid of her.

'So how did the trip go?' Mrs Batley asked when the nanny had a hot cup of tea and a slice of cake in front of her.

Nanny sipped at the tea delicately. She was a great one for etiquette and was trying to drill some into Grace. 'It went pleasantly enough but as usual, Grace's father spoiled her shamelessly and kept her out until all hours!' She shook her head in exasperation. 'I'm telling you, that man still looks upon her as a baby. I gave him a right telling-off one night when he brought her back to the hotel way past her bedtime!'

Mrs Batley chuckled as she pictured the scene.

'It's time some decision was reached about Grace's schooling. I am a nanny not a tutor and that child has a brain like a sponge. She can already read passages from the Bible. As it happens, I'm intending to speak to the judge about it again. Grace would like to attend the local school and personally I think it would do her the world of good.'

'I think it would an' all,' Mabel piped up. 'It ain't natural the way the master tries to keep her shut in all the time. The poor mistress don't even get a look-in with the child when he's about an' she rarely goes out of the house except to go to church with the mistress.'

Nanny sniffed. 'You're right. In fact, I'll go and have a talk with him just as soon as I've finished my tea.'

She swallowed her tea and wiped the cake crumbs from her fingers with a napkin, then with her shoulders squared as if she was about to do battle, she set off to speak to the judge.

Chapter Eleven

July, 1902

'I thought we could travel there in my car, staying at hotels along the way. Cornwall is a beautiful place, I'm sure you'll enjoy it.' The judge smiled at his ten-year-old daughter as she stood listening solemnly on the opposite side of his desk.

And then she surprised him when she answered, 'Actually, I would rather spend the school holidays here with Mother, if you don't mind, Father. She isn't at all well.'

Forcing himself to keep the smile fixed on his face, he took a deep breath before pointing out, 'But your mother has the staff here to look after her, Grace. She would not wish you to miss your holiday.'

'Even so, I wouldn't enjoy myself if I were to leave her.'

He could feel his anger rising. Lately, Grace had not seemed so happy to spend time with him and it hurt. She was by far the most important person in his life and he was jealous of any time she spent with anyone but himself.

Glancing down at the papers on his desk, he said dismissively, 'I suggest you go away and think about it, my dear. I have gone to a great deal of trouble to make myself available to take you away and I've no doubt that many children would jump at the chance of a holiday. Oh, and please tell Nanny that I wish to speak to her.'

'Very well, Father.' Glad to escape, Grace scurried from the room, breathing a sigh of relief as she closed the study door behind her.

Mabel, who just happened to be passing, saw her reaction and suggested, 'Why don't yer come along to the kitchen, pet? Batty's just made a nice jug o' lemonade.'

Mabel felt sorry for the child. Admittedly, she had been allowed to attend school for some years now, so at least she was mixing with children her own age – although the judge hadn't been at all happy about it. He felt that it wasn't right for his daughter to mix with children from working-class families but the only other alternative had been to send her away to a boarding school, which Madeline had been adamantly against. In truth, he hadn't liked the idea either, so in the end he had reluctantly relented. But he never allowed her to bring any of her friends home, or even to visit them in their homes. The fact that she mixed with children who were not as well dressed as she was didn't seem to trouble Grace in the least. If anything, her gentle nature and kindly ways drew her towards such children and whenever she could she would sneak tasty treats from the kitchen to take to school for them.

Her special friend was Olivia, or Libby as she was affectionately known. Her father ran a small hardware store in Edward Street and she was a Catholic. Everything that Libby told Grace about the Catholic faith fascinated her. She loved the rosary beads that Libby had been given on her first communion and listening to Libby talk about the lengthy church services. On a few occasions when her father had been away from home, Madeline had allowed her to attend the Catholic church with her and now Grace almost wished for him to go away so that she could go again.

'I just have to tell Nanny that Father wants to see her,' Grace told Mabel.

She flew up the stairs, her red curls bouncing, and with a smile, Mabel went on her way.

Grace found Nanny putting away her freshly ironed washing

and the woman glanced up and smiled at her. 'So, where's the fire then? You seem in a rush?'

Grace took a deep breath before saying, 'Father wants to see you in his study. And I should warn you, he isn't in the best of moods.'

'Oh?' Nanny raised her eyebrow. 'And why would that be?'

Grace squirmed uncomfortably as she lowered her eyes and fiddled with a fold in her skirt. 'I think it might be because I just told him that I don't wish to go away on holiday with him this year.'

'I see, and why is that?'

'Well . . .' Grace paused. 'I don't really want to leave Mother with her being so poorly. She wasn't even well enough to attend church with us last week, was she?'

The nanny's face creased in a sympathetic smile. 'She's just going through a bad spell,' she comforted. 'She'll come through it, she always does, so you shouldn't worry about that.'

Grace sighed and threw herself into the chair at the side of the empty fireplace. Through the open window, she could hear the sound of the birds singing and suddenly she envied them. They were free to fly where they wished, whereas she was trapped. Lately she had begun to feel that she was being pulled two ways. Her mother needed her and yet her father begrudged every second she didn't spend with him. She wanted to please them both, but it was impossible.

'Anyway, I'd best go and see what his lordship wants.' Nanny straightened her skirt and winked at the child as she breezed from the room and slowly Grace rose to make her way to the kitchen.

'Ah, Nanny Donovan, do come in, take a seat.'

The woman eyed Jacob Kettle suspiciously as she sat down

opposite him. He was leaning on the leather top of his desk eyeing her over his joined hands and she felt a little wriggle of unease in her stomach.

'I've been meaning to speak to you for some time.' Jacob gave her a sickly smile that didn't quite reach his eyes. 'Grace is getting rather too old to need the services of a nanny now.' Seeing the alarm flash in the woman's eyes, he hurried on. 'I'm giving you notice . . . Shall we say a month? And I will of course provide you with a reference.'

'You're *dismissing* me?' Nanny's eyes grew large as the colour drained from her cheeks.

'It's simply that your services are no longer required and I'm sure a month will give you plenty of time to find another post.' In actual fact, he could hardly wait to see the back of the dratted woman. She was always interfering when he wanted to spend time with his daughter and had even banned him from visiting the nursery saying that Grace needed to be kept in a routine.

She rose stiffly and inclined her head, then without another word she stalked from the room, her back rigidly straight. However, once the door had closed behind her, her shoulders sagged and she had to stuff her clenched fist into her mouth to stop herself from crying aloud. She had a bad feeling about this. Oh yes, she did! Jacob Kettle's devotion to his daughter had been touching to see when she was a little girl but to her mind it was becoming unfair on the girl. When he was home he barely allowed the child out of his sight and he had even taken to escorting her to Sunday school and back. Even so, deep down she supposed that he *did* have a point. Grace was too old for a nanny, but how she would miss her. The child was such a good little soul and she had come to love her over the years. Still, all good things must come to an end, she told herself and after mopping her eyes with a large white handkerchief, she squared her shoulders and went to break the news to Grace.

82

She was still in the kitchen with Mabel and Mrs Batley, sitting at the table with Ginger curled up on her lap and a large glass of lemonade in front of her.

'What? You're going to *leave*?' Grace looked horrified as tears flooded into her eyes. She stood up abruptly causing Ginger to fall in an undignified heap on the flagstones. He flexed his claws and hissed before stalking away as Grace flew into Nanny's arms.

'But you *can't* leave, I *need* you,' she sobbed.

'No, pet, you don't – not really anymore.' Nanny kissed the child's hair as Grace clung to her. 'Your father is right. You're at school all day apart from the holidays and when you come home you'll still have Mabel and Batty.'

'B-but what will *you* do? Where will you go?'

'Well, you know my first thought was that I would look for another post but it's just occurred to me that this might be the ideal time to retire.' Nanny grinned. 'I'm not getting any younger and my sister, who was widowed some two years back, has been pestering me for some time to go and live with her in London.'

'Will I ever see you again?' Grace asked tremulously.

'Why, *of course* you will.' Nanny forced herself to sound jovial. 'Perhaps your father would allow you to come and visit?' She secretly thought that there was very little chance of that happening. 'And we can always write to each other, can't we? London's not so very far away now that we can hop on a train.'

'I suppose not.' Grace wiped her freckled nose on the back of her sleeve in a most unladylike manner but just this once Nanny chose to ignore it.

'We're goin' to miss yer.' Mrs Batley's voice was heavy with tears. 'But as yer rightly told Grace, we can still keep in touch. In fact, I might just pluck up the courage to come an' see yer meself one o' these days. If I can force meself to get on one o' them there noisy trains that is!'

Nanny thought that was highly unlikely. It was a known fact

83

that Mrs Batley rarely ventured as far as the marketplace and then only when Mabel couldn't go.

'I don't think I'll like sleeping up on the nursery floor all by myself,' Grace remarked sadly.

'That's nothin' to worry about,' Mabel reassured her. 'I'll have a word wi' your Ma an' ask her if I can get one o' the bedrooms close to hers ready for you. I reckon yer old enough to come down from the nursery floor now.'

Grace perked up a little. She liked the thought of having a grown-up bedroom. 'I'd better go and find Harry and tell him about Nanny leaving,' she said, and slowly she made her way out into the sunshine.

'Oh no! But you're like one of the family now, Nanny.' Madeline was dismayed when Nanny Donovan relayed her news to her.

The woman smiled and patted her mistress's hand where it lay on the arm of her chair by the open window. It was the closest she could get to being outside, for she had been too unwell to leave her room for the last week or two, and today there was a distinct blue tinge about her lips.

'I'm sure you will manage very well without me.' The kindly nanny followed the mistress's eyes to where Grace was skipping towards Harry in the garden. He was busy pruning the roses but they saw him glance up and smile at her as she raced towards him.

'Of course, this will make it rather difficult as regards Grace holidaying with her father,' Nanny said hesitantly. 'He was hoping to take her to the seaside for two weeks next month. I shall have left by then but I'm not sure that he will be able to see to all her needs without a woman present.'

Madeline frowned. 'To be honest, I don't think Grace is that keen to go. She's getting a little old for holidaying alone with her father.' She sighed. 'Things would be so different if I were able to go with them . . . I feel that I'm letting Grace down all the time. I haven't even been able to accompany her to church the last few times.'

'Nonsense,' Nanny consoled her. 'Grace understands that it isn't your fault and she loves to come in here and read her Bible with you.'

They went on to speak of Nanny's plans for the future and Madeline was pleased that the woman was going to enjoy her retirement with someone she was close to.

'I wish you the very best of luck,' she told her sincerely. 'And I thank you for all the love and care you have lavished on Grace over the years.'

'I can truthfully say it's been my pleasure,' the older woman responded with a warm smile. 'She's turned into a lovely, caring child. Mrs Lockett, who runs the Sunday school, is quite taken with her. I have a feeling she'll go into a caring profession when she grows up.'

'Oh, I doubt that.' Madeline looked momentarily angry. 'Her father keeps such a tight rein on her I'm fearful that he'll never let Grace marry and leave home. In Jacob's eyes, no one will ever be good enough for her and financially she has no need to take a job.'

'Well, I think most men feel like that about their daughters, but no need to start fretting about it just yet,' Nanny advised, before excusing herself and leaving Madeline alone with her thoughts.

Each evening, as he considered his duty, Jacob visited his wife's room, and when he arrived following Nanny's visit he found her ready and waiting for him.

'I understand you have given Nanny notice,' she greeted him coldly.

Slightly taken aback at her abrupt attitude, he nodded. 'Yes, I feel that now Grace is ten she no longer needs her.' He stood with his hands clasped behind his back.

Madeline inclined her head. 'That is your decision, although I would have appreciated you speaking to me about it before you dismissed the woman. I am Grace's mother after all, even if I am incapacitated.' He opened his mouth to defend himself but she rushed on. 'And of course, this will change many things. For a start, it would not be right for you and Grace to go holidaying without a chaperone in future. And also, I don't want her shut away on the nursery floor on her own, so I have instructed Mabel to prepare a room close to mine.'

Jacob's eyes grew hard, but he could think of nothing to say. He wasn't used to his wife being so assertive and now he was wondering what he'd started.

'I see no reason why Grace should be moved to another bedroom—' he began.

Madeline held her hand up to silence him and surprisingly it did. 'I have decided that Grace can spend her summer holiday with Aunt Gertie,' she went on. 'She has been expressing a wish to see Grace again for some long time and I think it would be nice for Grace to visit her.'

Gertie was Madeline's only living relative and she was aware that Jacob wasn't fond of the woman. They hadn't got on at all well when they first met, nor on the few occasions she had come to visit them, which Madeline suspected was why Gertie had not been for the last couple of years. Their only contact had been by post. She was very fond of Grace and never missed sending her a birthday card.

'But she lives in Wales,' he objected. 'How is Grace supposed to get there? It's much too far for her to travel on her own.'

86

Madeline nodded in agreement. 'Yes, it is. I've already thought of that. There would be nothing unseemly about you holidaying there with her.'

When he shook his head, she nodded. 'I thought that's what you would say and so I've decided that Harry shall travel with her. He's a sensible young man. They can go on the train and once he has seen her safely settled he can come back and then go and fetch her when it's time for her to come home.'

Jacob's lips set in a grim line. 'Then if this is what you want, I suggest you ask Grace how she feels about it.' Given his earlier conversation with her, he was confident that Grace would refuse to go and he managed a smile. 'I shall get Mabel to fetch her and we'll put the idea to her right now.'

Minutes later the girl trooped into the room looking worriedly from one parent to another and wondering what she had done wrong.

Madeline quickly asked her how she would feel about going to visit Great-Aunt Gertie and just for a moment, as Jacob had hoped, the child frowned.

'But I don't like to leave you while you are ill, Mother,' she said in a small voice.

Madeline smiled and when she opened her arms Grace flew into them and nestled against her chest, making Jacob scowl with jealousy.

'Don't be silly, pet. I have Mabel and Batty here to look after me and your Aunt Gertie would so love to see you. So, what do you think to the idea? It's quite beautiful where she lives, right by the sea, and I'm sure you'd enjoy yourself.'

'Well . . .' Grace glanced apologetically at her father. 'If you're quite sure that you will be all right then I'd love to go.'

Madeline smiled with satisfaction. 'Then I shall write to Aunt Gertie straightaway and make the arrangements.'

Once Jacob had left the room in disgust, and Grace had gone

to see Nanny, Madeline sagged back in her seat and pressed her hand to her rapidly beating heart. It had been so long since she had had the confidence to stand up to Jacob but now that Nanny was leaving she realised she would have to do it more often. The thought was daunting, for Jacob was a bully, but somehow she was determined to find the confidence. Grace deserved it.

Chapter Twelve

'Now, you be a good girl and do as Aunt Gertie tells you,' Madeline said as she tied the ribbons of Grace's pretty new bonnet beneath her chin. 'And make sure you stay close to Harry on the journey . . . Oh, and don't go wandering off onto the beach on your own once you're there. And—'

'Mother, I shall behave, I *promise*,' Grace interrupted tearfully. It was early in the morning of the day she was to leave for her holiday and the parting was proving to be far more painful than she had thought it would be. But then, Grace consoled herself, it's only for four weeks! The time would surely fly by and she *was* looking forward to seeing Aunt Gertie again.

'We, er, ought to be off,' Harry said after glancing at the dainty ormolu clock that stood on the mantelpiece. 'The train won't wait fer us, little 'un.'

'You're quite right, Harry,' Madeline answered guiltily. She gave Grace one last peck on the cheek before pushing her gently towards the door, forcing a brave smile to her face. 'Off you go then and have a wonderful time and I shall want to hear all about your adventures when you get back. Give Aunt Gertie my love. Goodbye for now, sweetheart.'

They arrived on the train platform with barely minutes to spare and Grace hopped from foot to foot as Harry checked their tickets for at least the tenth time since they had left the house. He was clearly far more nervous than she was, and as the train chugged into the station, belching steam and smoke, he visibly paled.

'Crikey, it's some beast, ain't it?'

Grace laughed and caught his hand. 'You'll love it,' she promised.

Soon they were seated in the carriage with the basket of food Mrs Batley had packed for them to eat on the way, and their luggage stored safely in the baggage van at the back of the train. There was the slam of doors and a whistle and slowly the train chugged back into life, picking up speed as it left the station.

⚜

It was early evening when the train shuddered to a halt. Grace was tired by then and longing for the journey to be over.

'We're here, Harry,' Grace shouted joyously as she stared out of the window. They had pulled into a small station and the sign on the wall stated that they were in PWLLHELI.

Hastily they gathered their belongings and tumbled onto the platform where Harry instructed a porter to fetch Grace's case from the baggage van. As they were waiting for him, a tall man in a smart jacket approached to ask in a curious accent, 'Would you be Miss Grace Kettle, *bach*?'

Grace nodded solemnly and stared at him, wondering what bach meant. Over the next few days she would discover that both bach and *cariad* were a form of endearment.

'Ah good. Your Aunt Gertrude sent me to fetch you, cariad. I have the horse and trap outside. And you, young man, I believe are heading back the way you've come on the next train?'

Harry nodded.

'Well, the mistress said to tell you that you'd best come back with us for the night as there's no trains till the morning. You won't want to sleep on the platform now, will you, boyo?'

'Not really,' Harry agreed as he flashed the man a grateful smile. He would be quite happy to stay, as it happened. He had never seen the sea and had hoped he'd get a glimpse of it before he had to head home.

Once the porter had delivered all their luggage the man led them outside, introducing himself to Grace on the way. 'I'm Aled Llewelyn. I work for your aunt, cariad. A sort of Jack of all trades, you might say I am. I do the garden an' any odd jobs as need doing and I run her about in the trap when there's a need to. My wife, Cerys, keeps house for her and does the cooking. You'll meet her when we get back.'

They emerged on to cobbled streets that were lined with stone cottages and Aled stopped at the side of a fine bay horse that was lazily munching at a nosebag.

'There, me fine lad.' Aled removed the nosebag and stroked the horse's silky mane before throwing Grace's case into the back of the trap. 'Up we go then, me fine little *merch fach*.'

Grace frowned, not understanding what he meant. He seemed to sense that she was confused and chuckled. '*Merch fach* is Welsh for little girl,' he explained as he lifted her onto the bench seat. Soon Grace found herself sandwiched between Harry and Aled and they set off. Eventually the town gave way to twisty lanes with stone cottages dotted either side of them and then, as they crested a particularly steep hill, the sea suddenly came into sight and Grace clapped her hands with delight.

'Look, Harry . . . there's the sea!' Even the air felt different here, Grace thought, and when she licked her lips she could taste the salt from the sea on them.

Open-mouthed, Harry stared at the vast expanse of water. It seemed to stretch away for ever and he was sure that he would never again see a sight quite so beautiful. Frothy waves were lapping onto a sandy beach and in the distance the sun was just beginning to sink, its reflection making the water look as if it had been sprinkled with diamonds.

'It's a fine sight, is it not, boyo?' Aled said proudly and Harry could only nod in wonder.

They continued on their way in silence, admiring the scenery, until they spied another small village nestling at the bottom of a valley. 'That is Sarn Bach,' Aled informed them. 'Your aunt lives on the other side of it close to the coast. Not far to go now and my Cerys will have a tasty meal waiting for you, no doubt.'

Grace's stomach rumbled. It seemed a long while since she had eaten on the train and she was very hungry and tired.

As the horse trotted through the village, Grace realised that she had very little memory of it. It consisted mainly of huddles of stone fishermen's cottages and in some of the tiny front gardens the fishermen's wives were sitting in the late afternoon sun repairing fishing nets and they waved to them as they passed. Some way into the village they passed a quaint old church surrounded by a graveyard. The salt air had long ago eroded the names on the older tombstones and they leaned drunkenly while the more recent ones stood erect. They passed a blacksmith and a village shop displaying everything from groceries to buckets and brooms, and further on along the main street was a butcher, a baker and a number of other small shops. Eventually, they came to a small harbour where boats of all shapes and sizes bobbed on the water. Ruddy-faced fishermen were unloading their catches into huge wicker baskets and Grace found herself feeling sorry for the wriggling silver fish that would no doubt be on someone's dinner plate the following day. It didn't stop her being excited, though. Everything was so new!

Leaving the harbour behind, they passed pastures full of sheep and cows, after which the woodland about them grew more profuse. They continued along the coast road for some way before turning up a narrow tree-lined lane.

'Here we are then.' Aled winked at them as he shook the reins to hurry the horse along. 'This is Beehive Cottage.'

As her aunt's residence came into view, Grace thought it quite strange for it to be termed as a cottage, for it was a large, two-storey house in the shape of a beehive with a charming thatched roof and a myriad of tiny leaded windows that twinkled in the late sun. Hollyhocks, delphiniums, a profusion of roses every colour of the rainbow, and all manner of wild flowers grew around it, and it reminded Grace of the picture on the lid of a box of chocolates her father had once bought her. The house nestled close to the side of a hill and behind it was a steep incline covered in woodland.

'Phew!' Harry whistled admiringly. 'This is some place!'

'Glad you approve.' Aled sounded proud as he drew the horse to a halt at the front door. 'These gardens take some keeping up, I don't mind telling you, but the mistress likes her flowers and she potters out here herself whenever she has the time.'

Aled hopped down and lifted Grace from her seat as if she weighed no more than a feather. He was a giant of a man in height and breadth with wiry grey hair and twinkling grey eyes that always seemed to be smiling.

He hooked Grace's case from the back of the trap and led them to the stout, studded oak door. Before they reached it, the door was flung open by a homely looking, plump little woman with a broad smile.

'Ah, so you're back, Aled, and this must be little Grace. Welcome cariad.' She enveloped Grace in a bear hug that left her breathless, before smiling a welcome at Harry. 'It's right welcome you are,' she gushed. 'Now come along in and say hello to your aunt, cariad. She's so looking forward to seeing you, then I'll whisk you away to the kitchen where I have a meal keeping warm. You must be hungry after your long journey.'

Grace glanced at Harry and smiled. It had indeed been a long journey but she couldn't have wished for a better welcome and suddenly she had the feeling that she was going to very much enjoy this holiday.

Chapter Thirteen

As they entered the house four dogs of different shapes and sizes rushed to greet them, their tails wagging furiously.

'You might not remember but your aunt is a great one for taking in injured wildlife and strays.' Cerys Llewelyn shook her head. 'To be sure, right at this moment we have a baby hedgehog that she found with a broken leg and a piglet in the kitchen that she's bottle-feeding.' She chuckled fondly. Before she could say any more another door in the hallway opened and Aunt Gertie appeared with a wide smile on her face.

Harry blinked in amazement. She was quite short and was clad in men's breeches and an old shirt that reached almost to her knees. Her hair, which must once have been as vibrant as Grace's but was now peppered with grey, was pulled into an untidy knot on the top of her head. Here, he thought, is a woman who was definitely not a follower of fashion.

'Hello, my dear.' Aunt Gertie hurried forward to give Grace a peck on the cheek. She then held her at arm's length and exclaimed, 'My goodness, you're the spitting image of your mother when she was your age.'

She ushered them towards the kitchen, saying, 'You'll have to excuse the animals. The kitchen tends to act as our hospital for waifs and strays. Cerys is always scolding me about it but I know she doesn't mind them being there really.' She gave the woman an affectionate smile as she led them into a huge, sunny room at the back of the house. The walls were curved, even the fireplace was curved, and although everywhere was clean it looked lived in. Not like at home where Father insists that everywhere was just so all the time, Grace thought regretfully. A book lay open on the scrubbed table, the kettle was singing merrily on the hob and there were cats of all colours and sizes curled up on almost every available seat. The back door was open and through it Grace could hear the birds singing in the trees as they roosted down for the night.

'Now then, let's get you two young people fed.' Mrs Llewelyn was bustling about fetching cutlery and making tea as Aunt Gertie checked on the tiny piglet that was curled up fast asleep in a box at the side of the empty fireplace. 'Sit yourselves down, now. We've already eaten so it's just you two to see to tonight.'

Grace was so excited that she could scarcely contain herself. She had always longed for a pet but her father had forbidden it and now all at once she was surrounded by animals.

Mrs Llewelyn shooed two cats off the chairs at the table and within minutes she had placed plates full of pork chops and roast potatoes in front of them, along with a dish piled high with a variety of vegetables and a jug full of thick, juicy gravy.

Grace's stomach rumbled in anticipation and she and Harry ate everything on their plates in record time.

'That was lovely, thank you,' they said together and Mrs Llewelyn laughed as she swooped on the empty plates. 'It's nice to see young people with good appetites,' she said approvingly. 'But I hope you've left room for some of my apple pie. It's your aunt's favourite and I've made some nice creamy custard to go with it.'

Grace and Harry nodded enthusiastically as Aunt Gertie settled in the fireside chair to give the piglet a bottle of milk. Grace watched her from the corner of her eye as she ate her pudding and by the time she was done she was already more than a little in love with the tiny creature.

'Might I be allowed to try that one day?' she asked timidly.

Aunt Gertie nodded. 'I don't see why not. There's nothing to it really. Once you've guided the teat into its mouth it does the rest itself.'

The meal was rounded off with cups of steaming sweet tea. Harry declared that he was so full he was sure he was going to burst. Surprisingly, neither he nor Grace were tired now and he dared to ask, 'Is it far to the beach from here?'

Cerys Llewelyn raised an eyebrow, 'Not so very far. Why do you ask?'

Harry blushed to the roots of his hair. 'Oh . . . I just wondered, that's all. I've never seen the sea before, you see?'

'Ah, and you would like to see it properly before you go back?' The woman smiled at him.

'Well . . . yes, I would rather.'

'Then you must go now before it gets dark. The tide will be coming in and it's a sight to behold.' She pointed towards the open door. 'Go left across the lawn then follow the path through the woods. It will take you down to a cove but don't linger too long. You don't want the tide to cut you off.'

'May I go too, Aunt Gertie?' Grace asked hopefully.

The woman glanced up. She had finished feeding the piglet and was checking on the wounded hedgehog now.

'I don't see why not, so long as you don't go wandering off.'

They hurried out into the fading light and shot off in the direction they'd been told. They found the path with no trouble and plunged into the wood beneath a thick canopy of trees. It was gloomy in there but they were in such high spirits they barely noticed. The path wound steeply downhill and the further they went the louder the sound of the sea became.

'Your aunt . . . she's not what I expected,' Harry said tactfully.

Grace giggled. 'No, she's quite strange for a lady, isn't she? Father says she's eccentric and he doesn't like her at all, but I do. She

97

wears weird clothes and she makes me laugh. But Mother says she wasn't always that way. Aunt Gertie was my grandfather's sister and when she was young she fell in love with and married a very wealthy young man. Mother says they doted on each other and were really happy, but not long after they got married her husband fell from his horse and broke his neck and Aunt Gertie was never the same after that. They had a huge townhouse in a smart part of London and she sold it and moved here, where she's been ever since. I think all she really cares about now is her animals. It's sad, isn't it?'

Harry nodded in agreement. Eventually, through a gap in the trees ahead of them, they caught a glimpse of the sea. The leaves underfoot gave way to sand and as they emerged from the trees they both stopped and stared in awe at the view in front of them. Far away on the horizon a great red sun was sinking into the sea, washing the waves in scarlet and crimson, and closer to, white-capped waves slapped gently onto the shore. On either side of the cove, the hills rose around them and they felt as if they might be the only two people left alive. Seagulls dipped and dived gracefully into the water as they fished for their supper and Harry suddenly wondered if he had died and gone to heaven.

'Eeh . . .' His voice was full of wonder as he stared down at the shells scattered like treasure across the beach. 'I never imagined it would be like this.'

Grace giggled as she bent to undo her shoes, then she grabbed his hand and yanked him towards the water. 'Come on. We can't go back without having a paddle.'

He laughed as he too kicked off his shoes. As the water lapped over their toes, they began to splash each other. Harry was usually so serious and quiet that Grace was surprised to see him like this, so clearly enjoying himself. After a time they wandered along collecting shells and stuffing the special ones into their pockets for mementos. Harry spotted a large building high on top of the hill and he pointed to it.

'I wonder what that place is. It's huge, look.'

Grace shrugged. 'I have no idea but no doubt Aunt Gertie will tell us when we get back. It looks like some sort of church to me.'

They came to a rock pool and Harry watched, fascinated, as a crab moved sideways beneath the water. When they glanced back towards where they had kicked their shoes off, they saw the tide had almost reached them.

'Aunt Gertie did say it came in quickly, didn't she? We'd better hurry up else our shoes will be washed away.'

They skittered back up the beach and after retrieving their footwear they went to sit in the shelter of the trees to brush the sand from their feet and put their shoes on again. Grace was so happy she wished this day would never end.

'I could sit here all night and watch the sea,' Harry admitted. 'But we'd best make our way back. It's getting dark now and we don't want to get lost in the woods.'

It was much darker in the shelter of the trees now and Grace was a little nervous as she glanced to either side of her. They had gone some way when a dog fox suddenly barked and she reached out and clutched Harry's hand.

'What was that?'

'Oh, just some animal or other,' he said reassuringly. 'Don't worry, it'll probably be more scared of you than you are of him. But let's get a move on, eh? Time is running on.' In truth, he was almost as afraid as she was. Harry had grown up in towns and cities and had never known country life, although after today, he knew that he'd like to.

At last they saw the lights shining from the kitchen window of Beehive Cottage and hurried towards it. Harry's legs were paining him now and he would be glad to rest but he knew that he would remember the short time he had spent on the beach for the rest of his life; it had been magical.

Mrs Llewelyn had mugs of hot milky cocoa and a plateful of

home-made biscuits ready for them and despite the fact they'd already had an enormous meal, both Harry and Grace tucked into them.

'Now then, boyo. I'm afraid it will have to be a very early start for you tomorrow if you're to catch the train back to the Midlands.' As she spoke Mrs Llewelyn piled yet more biscuits onto the plate in front of them. 'So, when you're done here I'll show you where you're to sleep and you'd best say your goodbyes to Grace this evening. There will be no point in getting her up in the morning to see you off.'

Harry nodded, wishing that he didn't have to go back.

Aunt Gertie had joined them to give the piglet yet another bottle and Grace asked curiously, 'How often do you have to feed it?'

'At least every two hours till it gets a little bigger and stronger.'

'Hmm, an' she feeds it all through the night as well!' Mrs Llewelyn shook her head. 'She's slept in the chair by the fire ever since it came. I keep telling her it's too much for her, but will she listen?'

'I'm fit as a fiddle,' Aunt Gertie protested. 'Stop fussing, woman. I'll tell you when it's time to put me out to grass. I'm only in my early fifties, only a couple years older than you! I might be getting on but I'm not in me dotage yet!'

Grace and Harry exchanged an amused glance as Mrs Llewelyn ushered them towards the door.

'Goodnight, Aunt,' Grace said.

'Goodnight, Mrs, er . . . and thanks fer puttin' me up,' Harry added.

Gertrude smiled at him. 'No problem at all. When you get back tell Madeline that I'll let her know when Grace is coming back so that you can come and fetch her home. Perhaps you could come early and sneak a couple of days' holiday for yourself at the same time?'

Harry's face lit up at the thought, as he followed Mrs Llewelyn and Grace upstairs.

'This will be your room, boyo.' Mrs Llewelyn flung a door open and Harry glanced around. It was too dark to see much from the open window but he could hear the waves crashing on the shore beyond the woods.

'Goodbye, Harry, and thanks for bringing me. Give my love to everyone at home, won't you?' Grace felt tears prick at the back of her eyes.

'O' course I will. Bye fer now, Miss Grace.'

Leaving Harry to settle in, Mrs Llewelyn moved on to another room a little further along the landing.

By the light of the oil lamp, Grace could see it was a very pretty room, although the wallpaper, which was covered in tiny pink rosebuds, was a little faded.

'This was your mother's room when she was a girl and she used to come to stay,' Mrs Llewelyn informed her.

'Really?' Grace smiled. Then she remembered something. 'Mrs Llewelyn, what is that large building perched high on the edge of the cliff that you can see from the cove?'

'Oh, that'll be the convent.'

'Really? Do nuns still live there?' Grace was intrigued.

Mrs Llewelyn was in the process of turning the bed back. 'They most certainly do. They open their chapel to the villagers for Sunday morning worship if ever you wish to go.'

'Oh, I'd love to,' Grace declared as Mrs Llewelyn passed her a nightdress.

Grace snuggled down in the bed with the breeze from the open window gently blowing the curtains. She could hear the waves on the beach and somewhere an owl was hooting. Grace smiled into the darkness. She felt safe here. There was no chance of her father coming into her room and perching on the side of the bed. It was funny, she thought, how not so long ago she had actually enjoyed all the attention he showered on her, but now his attention was beginning to feel a little suffocating. He even resented the time

101

she spent at Sunday school. The only saving grace was that he still went off on his weekend jaunts to wherever it was he went. She and her mother had stopped asking him where it might be some long time ago, for he always evaded answering them and, truthfully, neither of them much cared. The house was always so much lighter without his presence. And now she had at least a whole month here with Auntie Gertie to do as she pleased. It was a shame Harry couldn't have stayed with her, though. On their walk that evening he had said more than she had ever heard him say in her life. It was as if he was a different person. Perhaps it was the fresh air, she mused. She decided she would get up early to see him off and yawned as she wondered what she might do the next day.

Chapter Fourteen

The next morning Grace woke to another beautiful day and the sound of the birds singing in the trees outside. Something was rustling in the thatch above her and she lay disorientated for a second until she remembered where she was. Then, with a big grin, she hopped out of bed and dressed without even taking the trouble to wash. She had no idea what time it was but with a bit of luck she would catch Harry before he left.

She thumped down the stairs in a most unladylike manner – after all, her father wasn't there to scold her – and burst into the kitchen to find Mrs Llewelyn standing at the stove stirring something in a large pan. Aunt Gertie was in her usual seat feeding the piglet and a young girl who looked to be about her own age was sitting at the kitchen table eating a large bowl of porridge.

She gave Grace a shy smile before lowering her eyes and turning her attention to the food in front of her.

'Ah, here you are, pet.' Aunt Gertie grinned as she laid the piglet back in his box and carried the empty bottle to the sink. 'I was beginning to think we'd need a crowbar to get you out of bed.'

'Why? Is it very late? Have I missed Harry leaving?'

'It's almost ten o'clock,' Aunt Gertie informed her. 'And Harry left ages ago. I should think he's been on the train for at least a couple of hours now.'

'Oh!' Grace glanced towards the girl sitting at the table again, trying hard not to show her disappointment.

'This is my granddaughter, Myfanwy,' Mrs Llewelyn told her with a proud smile in the girl's direction. 'She lives in Pwllheli with her parents but she spends a fair amount of time here with me and her *taid*.' When Grace looked slightly confused she explained. 'Taid would probably be grandfather to you and I am her *nain*. Show some manners and say hello now, our Myfanwy.'

'Hello,' Myfanwy said quietly and as Grace nodded to her she felt quite envious. Myfanwy was easily the prettiest girl she had ever seen. Her hair was as black as coal and hung down her back in a silken sheet and her eyes were the colour of bluebells. She had a heart-shaped face, a rosebud mouth and dimples in her cheeks when she smiled. Even though she was sitting down, Grace judged that she would be much taller than she was. Suddenly she felt very plain and dumpy.

'You and our Myfanwy are the same age all but for a couple of months,' Mrs Llewelyn went on as she spooned porridge into another dish. 'I thought you might be able to entertain each other while you're here. But now come and get some of this down you.'

'I'd be fat as anything if it was left up to my nain,' Myfanwy whispered as Grace sat at the table with her and Grace noticed that she had the same accent as her grandparents. But at least the ice was broken now and the girl seemed friendly enough.

'Myfanwy knows her way about,' Mrs Llewelyn informed Grace as she spooned a large dollop of honey collected from the beehives that Aunt Gertie kept at the bottom of her garden into her bowl. 'So she'll be able to show you about so's you don't go getting lost.'

Grace nodded. She had never really been allowed to spend time with anyone close to her own age, apart from Libby when she was at school and she liked the idea of possibly making a real friend.

'I'll show you all around Beehive Cottage first, there's lots of animals for you to meet,' Myfanwy volunteered.

Grace nodded eagerly and as soon as they'd finished their porridge, they left via the back door.

'Be back for some lunch now,' Mrs Llewelyn's voice floated after them and Myfanwy gave a cheeky grin.

Grace was quite shocked to see just how big it was at the back of the cottage. There was an orchard where the branches on the trees dipped beneath the weight of apples and pears, a pigsty where an enormous sow snuffled in the dirt as ten chubby piglets chased after her, and there were chickens, ducks and a rather feisty goose who chased them territorially.

'That's Esmeralda,' Myfanwy informed Grace. 'She thinks she's a dog and tries to see everyone off.' The tour continued and at one point they saw Aunt Gertie marching purposely towards the woods with a rifle slung beneath her arm. Today she was dressed in men's corduroy breeches and yet another flannel shirt that flapped about as she walked. Her feet were encased in heavy black boots and her hair was scraped back with a ribbon at the base of her neck. From a distance it would have been very easy to take her for a man.

'Where do you suppose Aunt Gertie is going?' Grace asked musingly.

Myfanwy chuckled. 'Off to shoot some rabbits in the woods no doubt.' She tossed her long black hair across her shoulder. 'We're overrun with them here, so she doesn't mind shooting them because they can be eaten. My nain makes a wonderful rabbit stew, so she does. But she'll never kill an animal just for the sake of it. I think Gertie likes animals more than people.'

'Does she ever . . . you know . . . dress normally?'

Myfanwy shook her head. 'Well, I've never seen her in a skirt, if that's what you mean. My taid usually gets all the provisions from Pwllheli but even when she's away from the cottage, she still dresses as you see her now. Lots of people hereabouts think she's strange but she isn't. She just doesn't care much for conven . . .

convenshi . . . Well, she don't care what folks think, that's what me mam says anyway.'

'Hmm.' They were wandering in the direction of the beach now and Grace asked, 'And what does your father do? For a job, I mean.'

'Me dad is a fisherman,' Myfanwy told her proudly. 'He owns his own boat and has a crew that work for him. It's a good living in the summer but me mam worries something terrible when he's out at sea in the winter. Storms can blow up from nowhere and me mam has spent many a long night up on the cliffs watching for a sign of his boat returning home. We respect the sea around here, see? It can be brutal, so it can, and has claimed many fishermen's lives. That's why me mam and dad always go to chapel to say a prayer afore he sails.'

'And do you have any brothers or sisters?' Grace asked then.

'Just the one brother, Dylan, he's two years older than me. There were two more, both girls, but they died of scarlet fever just after I was born. Me mam said I was very lucky that I didn't get it too.' She glanced at Grace in her pretty clothes and asked curiously, 'What does your dad do?'

'He's a judge.'

'*A judge!* What, in a court of law?'

Grace nodded as she kicked at a stone. It was something that her father considered extremely unladylike and she would never have done it in his presence but she was just discovering that she could get away with things here.

'Yes, and I don't think he's very popular around where we live,' Grace confided. 'I overheard Mrs Batley and Mabel, our staff, talking one day and they said that he's known as "the hanging judge" because he's so stern and he gives criminals who are brought before him very heavy sentences.'

Myfanwy's pretty blue eyes stretched wide. 'And is he strict with you?'

106

'Not really . . .' Grace paused as she chose her words carefully. 'But he likes me to do what he says and he doesn't like me to have friends. When he's at home I have to spend my time with him.'

'I see.' Myfanwy didn't think that Grace's father sounded very nice at all. 'And what is your mam like?'

Grace's face broke into a smile. 'Oh, she is lovely. But she's an invalid and can't get about too easily. Aunt Gertie is really her aunt and my great-aunt. She was my grandfather's younger sister and Mother says they were very close until my grandfather died. I never knew him because he died before I was born.'

'That's sad,' Myfanwy commented, then as they glimpsed the sea through the trees she giggled. 'Last one to reach the waves is a rotten egg.' And she was off running with her glorious black hair flying behind her.

For the first time in her life, Grace was discovering what it was to be allowed to be a child. No one grumbled at her if she scuffed her shoes or got grass stains on her dress, and no one told her to mind her manners or speak only when spoken to.

One evening, Aunt Gertie said, 'I reckon I'm going to sort out some old clothes for you to wear while you're here. That father of yours would have a fit if he could see the state of you.' She stared at the hem of Grace's skirt, which was wet from paddling in the sea and covered in sand. Her hair resembled a bird's nest from the many brambles that had snagged it as she and Myfanwy raced through the woods, and her skin, red and angry for the first few days of the holiday, was now almost as brown as Myfanwy's, on top of which, freckles had exploded across her nose and golden highlights had appeared in her flame-red hair.

'Sorry, Aunt Gertie,' Grace murmured. She was feeling comfortably sleepy following a delicious fish meal and a day spent racing about with Myfanwy. She and Myfanwy were already inseparable and Grace loved every single minute they spent together.

Her aunt laughed. 'You don't have to say sorry to me, pet. As far as I'm concerned, they should have sent you with more suitable clothing, not all these fancy London togs! But then, what do I know about children never having ever had any of my own? Your mother will tell you that I was always considered to be the black sheep of the family. I never did bow down to convention and fashion; give me comfort any day.' She paused for a moment, before adding, 'Oh, and you might be happy to hear that Cerys has asked her daughter if Myfanwy can stay here for the rest of your holiday,' Aunt Gertie informed her.

'Oh, I *do* hope she's allowed to,' Grace said excitedly. 'She's going to take me to see the convent on the top of the cliffs tomorrow.'

Gertie raised her eyebrow. She had noticed Grace reading her Bible, and praying on a few occasions, which might explain her fascination with the convent. Then again, Madeline had always been very religious, and her brother had been a vicar, so she shouldn't be that surprised. Since the untimely death of her beloved husband, she herself no longer practised any religion. After all, if there was a God, how could He have allowed such a terrible thing to happen? Even so, she had no objection to those who believed.

Grace looked at her aunt, who was cleaning her gun by the empty fireplace, and was suddenly overwhelmed with love for her; she might be a little eccentric, but beneath her cool veneer, there beat a heart of gold. Unable to stop herself, she got up, threw her arms around her aunt's neck and kissed her soundly on the cheek.

'You're *so* kind,' she told her sincerely. 'If it weren't for missing Mother I'd be happy to stay here with you for always.'

'And what about missing your father?'

Grace flushed and lowered her eyes. 'Well . . . I suppose him too . . .' But somehow her words didn't ring true.

✤

Long after Grace had gone to bed, Gertie sat staring into space, remembering the time Grace's grandfather had passed away, leaving Madeline penniless. He had always been a generous soul, bless him. But his generosity had almost certainly been his daughter's downfall, and then Jacob Kettle. Gertie scowled. She had never approved of him. For a start, as she had tried to point out to Madeline, he was far too old. And, after making a few discreet enquiries, she'd discovered that his reputation left a lot to be desired as well and he had made many enemies. But, unfortunately, being young and naive, Madeline's head had been turned by the attentions of an older man and nothing Gertie had said had discouraged her from marrying him.

Gertie shook her head and wondered how Madeline felt about him now. She had been shocked to see her niece the last time she had visited her, for she was merely a shadow of her old self. But then at least one good thing had come from the marriage, Grace. She smiled as she listened to the child humming merrily as she got ready for bed upstairs. She was such a good little soul. Too good, Gertie thought. At Grace's age, she herself had had a rebellious streak but Grace was so polite and well mannered that Gertie feared she hadn't been allowed to do the things that children should do. Still, she thought, as a smile split her face, at least she's coming out of her shell now, thanks to Myfanwy. I shall have to have Grace here more often, if that father of hers will allow it. Then she set about finding a more suitable outfit for the child to wear the next day.

Chapter Fifteen

'Wait for me,' Grace panted as she laboured up the steep hillside behind Myfanwy. She was clad in one of her aunt's old shirts, with the sleeves rolled up to the elbow, and an old pair of trousers that were at least four sizes too big – her aunt had crudely chopped some length from the legs, and they were tied round her waist with a piece of string. To say they were inelegant would have been putting it mildly but Grace had to admit they didn't hamper her running about and climbing nearly so much as her full skirts had. Even so she was lagging far behind Myfanwy who was as sure-footed as a mountain goat. Her feet were bare but she didn't seem to notice the stones and twigs she raced across and as far as Grace could see she hadn't even broken into a sweat. She moved as swiftly as she could trying to keep Myfanwy in sight and at last her friend paused and leaned with her back against the trunk of a tree to wait for her.

'You townies are so unfit,' Myfanwy teased as Grace eventually drew abreast.

Grace glared at her as she struggled to get her breath back. 'Am not,' she said petulantly when she was able to. 'It's just that I'm not used to climbing.'

Myfanwy giggled. 'Well, we're almost at the top now, look.' Myfanwy nodded ahead to where Grace could see a gap in the trees. 'Once we're out of the woods we'll be on the outskirts of the convent.'

The girls moved on more slowly and soon emerged into brilliant sunshine. Just as Myfanwy had said, the convent was sprawled before them and Grace stared at it admiringly. It was a huge place with tall, arched stone windows, which sparkled in the sunshine. From within she could faintly hear the sounds of singing.

'It's probably the nuns at their morning service in the chapel,' Myfanwy said.

Grace paused to admire the view. It was another lovely sunny day and far out at sea she could see the fishing boats bobbing on the waves. The sea looked as if it had been sprinkled with diamond dust and the water was violet blue.

'It's *so* beautiful here,' she breathed. 'I shall miss all this when I go home.' Had it not been for the fact that she was missing her mother she knew that she wouldn't have wanted to return home at all, especially now she had met Myfanwy.

'Oh, it's far too soon to be thinking about that just yet.' Myfanwy pulled some leaves and twigs from her hair. 'We've got over three weeks of your holiday left yet and I've still got so many places I want to show you, though why you wanted to come here, I don't understand.'

'Are you not particularly religious then?'

Myfanwy shrugged. 'I go to chapel from time to time with my mam an' dad when they make me but with Dad being away at sea so much it's not very often.'

'I go to church whenever I can,' Grace informed her new friend proudly. 'And I'd go even more often if I was able to. There's something about the inside of the church that I love, especially a Catholic church. It's always so peaceful in there and I feel so close to God.'

Myfanwy raised an eyebrow but didn't comment as they began to skirt the gardens surrounding the convent. Most of it had been left to grow wild and flowers grew here and there amongst the tufts of lush green grass. Then, as they moved on, they saw some women, most of them very young, clad in white habits, tending a very well-maintained vegetable garden.

'They're the postilan . . . postu . . .'

'Postulants,' Grace corrected her. 'They're sort of trainee nuns who haven't taken their final vows yet.'

'Huh! Don't I already know that?' Myfanwy said scathingly. 'One of our neighbour's daughters, Angharad, joined the order just last year. We rarely see her now. But how do you know about them?'

'A girl I know at school is a Catholic,' Grace informed her. 'And on odd occasions I've visited her church with her. Most times I go to church with my mother, when she's well enough that is, and when she isn't we read the stories in the Bible together. But isn't Angharad allowed to come home and see her family and friends then?'

'Oh yes, occasionally.' Myfanwy suddenly pointed. 'There she is over there, look. I wonder if she'll spot us.'

Grace followed Myfanwy's pointing finger to a serene-looking young woman who was hoeing between a row of radishes. The girl was tall and slim and the fringe beneath her bandeau, which held her white veil in place, was white blonde.

'She had a sweetheart before she decided that this was her calling,' Myfanwy whispered. 'And when she told him that she was going to join the convent he was heartbroken and left the village.'

'She's very pretty and her hair is such a lovely colour.'

Myfanwy nodded. 'Yes, it is, although when she is ready to take her final vows it will all be hacked off and she'll go into a black habit.'

This didn't seem to faze Grace at all but she had no chance to comment because just then the girl looked up and gave a friendly wave before starting towards them.

'Is she allowed to talk to you?' Grace asked. 'I thought nuns lived by a vow of silence.'

'Only once they've taken their final vows and even then, it's only at certain times of the day.'

'Myfanwy, how lovely to see you. And who is this then? I don't think we've met.' Angharad was standing in front of them and close up she was even prettier than Grace had thought.

'This is Grace, she's staying with Gertie Adams in Beehive Cottage. Gertie is her aunt.'

Grace was quite in awe of the girl and gave her a shy smile.

'It's so nice to meet you, Grace. Will we be seeing you at any of our Sunday services?'

'I-I hope so . . .' Grace stuttered. 'But I would have to come alone. I don't think Aunt Gertie is much for that sort of thing.'

Angharad laughed. 'The chapel is open to the villagers at ten o'clock every Sunday morning. Do come if you can.' She glanced over her shoulder then and said reluctantly, 'Well, I really should get back to work now but it's been lovely meeting you, Grace. Goodbye for now, both.'

As she turned, the breeze caught her white habit and veil and Grace sighed. She looked like an angel and Grace envied her. 'How wonderful it must be to devote your whole life to God,' she muttered.

Myfanwy looked horrified at the very thought. 'Hmm, I tell you now it wouldn't do for me.' She sniffed. 'All those rules and regulations they have to live by! And me mam said that they actually *marry* Christ.'

Grace had a dreamy look in her eye but then Myfanwy took to her heels, eager to show her a cormorant's nest with babies in that she'd found on the cliff face a little past the convent, and Grace had no choice but to race after her.

※

'Right, now lie down flat on your belly and wriggle right to the edge of the cliff and then you can peep over,' Myfanwy ordered bossily when they had gone some way further on.

Grace eyed the cliff edge apprehensively. It looked an awful

113

long way down to the waves that were crashing on the rocks far below, but even so she didn't want to appear to be a coward, so she gingerly did as she was told. And then as her eyes lit on the nest with the tiny chicks tweeting away inside it, her face broke into a wide smile.

'Their mother must be out looking for food for them,' Myfanwy whispered and sure enough, seconds later a large cormorant with a large worm in its beak flew towards the nest and started to circle in the air, eyeing the intruders suspiciously.

'We'd best go,' Myfanwy hissed, wriggling away from the edge of the cliff. 'We don't want her to abandon her babies.'

Grace followed her and soon they were flying along hand in hand as the sun shone down on them.

They arrived back at Beehive Cottage by mid-afternoon. Grace was starving and more than a little tired, although Myfanwy still seemed to be bursting with energy.

'Hmm, and what time do you call *this*?' Mrs Llewelyn stood with her hands on her hips trying to look cross but there was a twinkle in her eye. 'Your dinner was ready hours ago! It's a good job I kept it warm for you, isn't it, now?'

Grace hung her head while Myfanwy grinned. She knew her grandmother would forgive her almost anything.

'Sorry, we lost track of time,' Myfanwy told her as Grace hurried away to wash her hands. Cerys Llewelyn smiled indulgently.

'I really don't know where that granddaughter of mine gets all her energy,' Mrs Llewelyn said minutes later as she placed a plateful of steak-and-kidney pie in front of Grace. Myfanwy had been sent off, muttering beneath her breath, to wash her hands.

Grace smiled and began to tell her what they'd been up to that morning and the woman laughed. 'Well one thing's for sure, cariad.

You won't get bored for the rest of your holiday with our Myfanwy to keep you company. She could talk the hind legs off a donkey, so she could.'

Grace nodded before asking tentatively, 'The postulant we saw working in the gardens up at the convent said that I would be welcome to go to the service in their chapel on Sunday morning. Do you think my aunt will allow me to go?'

Mrs Llewelyn laughed. 'I can't see why not, just so long as you don't expect her or Myfanwy to go with you.'

Smiling with satisfaction, Grace tucked into her meal. Staying here was just getting better and better!

That night there were a lot of giggles as Grace and Myfanwy slept top to toe in Grace's single bed. Aunt Gertie had said that Myfanwy was welcome to sleep in the other spare room but both girls were adamant they wanted to stay together.

'What do you want to do when you grow up? Grace asked.

Myfanwy laughed. 'I hadn't really thought about it but I dare say I'll marry a fisherman. Most girls from around here do. Either that or I'll go to London and go on the stage! We had some actors here once who did a play in the village hall. What about you?'

'Hmm, I think I'd quite like to be a Sunday school teacher, or something like that,' Grace mused as she thought of Mrs Lockett.

'Just hark at the pair of them,' Aunt Gertie said as their laughter floated down the stairs. 'I shouldn't be surprised if they keep us awake all night!'

'I don't think there'll be much chance of that happening.' Cerys looked up from the sock she was darning, yet another unladylike item of clothing belonging to Gertie. 'They've been on the go non-stop all day. They'll go out like a light in a minute, you just mark my words!'

Sure enough, minutes later there was a sudden hush and when Aunt Gertie peeped into Grace's room sometime later both girls were sleeping like tops. She smiled as she gently closed the door. It was nice to have children about the house. Many years ago when she had been first married she and her husband had dreamed of having many children. With a rueful little sigh, she moved on to her room with the oil lamp balanced carefully in her hand. Electric had not yet arrived at Beehive Cottage but then Gertie was happy with things as they were. As far as she was concerned, she had all she needed and she didn't care if things stayed the same for ever.

The next two weeks passed in a blur for Grace. She and Myfanwy roamed the hills collecting wild flowers that they presented to Aunt Gertie at the end of each day and which were promptly transferred into jam jars that adorned the kitchen window sill. They sploshed in the silver streams that gurgled down the hillsides, visited the tiny harbour to watch the fishing boats and told each other all their hopes and dreams. One day, Myfanwy took Grace to meet her parents in Pwllheli. They lived in a tiny cottage close to the harbour and Grace was enchanted with it.

'It's like something out of a fairy-story book,' she whispered as Myfanwy's mother sat them at the table and served them with glasses of frothy milk and fresh-baked griddle scones. She looked just like a younger version of Mrs Llewelyn. Myfanwy's brother, Dylan, a lanky, skinny lad with a mop of coal-black hair and blue eyes exactly the colour of Myfanwy's, was sitting on the outside step repairing a fishing net and he gave Grace a friendly wink as she entered the cottage.

'Dylan wants to go to sea with me dad when he's a little older,' Myfanwy confided and Grace nodded. There were herbs and wild flowers strung from the rafters and the tiny leaded windows gleamed in the sunshine. Outside, the garden was full of little piles of shells that Myfanwy had collected over the years, and fishing nets and lobster pots; Grace couldn't help but think how different their lives were.

Each Sunday, Grace attended the service in the convent's chapel and they were the highlight of her holiday. She loved to watch the nuns gliding across the floor in their long black habits and the postulants in their white ones, looking so innocent and pure. And the singing . . . Oh, the singing! Each Sunday Grace sang her little heart out as a sense of peace stole over her. The chapel was quite breathtaking with stained-glass windows that reflected the sun's rays and Grace couldn't remember a time when she had enjoyed herself more and wished that it might never end.

Then one afternoon, towards the end of the third week, they arrived back at Beehive Cottage late one afternoon, tired but happy, to see a horse and trap standing outside the door of the cottage.

'I wonder who that could be?' Myfanwy raised an eyebrow. 'I don't reckon your aunt usually has many visitors.'

Grace playfully poked her in the ribs. 'There's only way to find out. Come on – I'll race you.'

Giggling, they set off at a run side by side and seconds later they exploded into the kitchen.

When Grace saw the stiff-backed figure sitting at the kitchen table, the smile instantly slid from her face and she skidded to a halt.

'Hello, Father,' she muttered.

Chapter Sixteen

Jacob Kettle raised his eyebrows as he stared at his daughter before saying sternly, '*Whatever* are you wearing, Grace? You look like a gypsy child!'

Gertie, who was sitting opposite him looking none too pleased and sipping lemonade, sniffed. 'I found out some more suitable clothes for her to play in,' she informed him stiffly. 'She could hardly go out and do the things children like to do in the fancy ones you sent with her.'

Grace glanced down at the grass stains on the knees of her ill-fitting breeches and wet shoes and socks and gulped. Her red hair was tangled and tied with string at the nape of her neck and her hands and face were grubby.

The dislike between the two adults was so tangible that both she and Myfanwy felt that they could almost reach out and touch it.

'The things children *do*?'

'Yes. Like paddling in the streams and climbing trees!'

'Climbing *trees*?' Jacob looked horrified. 'Grace has been brought up to be a young lady.'

'It's quite possible to be a young lady and still enjoy yourself,' Aunt Gertie replied tersely. 'But hadn't you better tell her why you have come?'

'Oh, yes . . . yes of course.' Turning his attention back to his daughter, Jacob flashed a false smile. 'I've come to take you home,' he informed her and now it was Grace's turn to look horrified as tears sprang to her eyes.

'B-but why? I still have over another week of my holiday here left.'

'Ah, but the thing is your mother isn't too grand and I thought if I brought you home it might make her feel a little better.'

Seeing the child's distress, Aunt Gertie patted her arm comfortingly, 'Never mind, pet,' she whispered. 'You are very welcome to come back when you have your next school holiday.' She then glared openly at Jacob before asking Mrs Llewelyn, 'Would you mind helping Grace back into her own clothes please, Cerys, and doing her packing for her?'

'Of course.' Taking Grace's hand, the kindly woman led her from the room.

'I hope this isn't going to take too long.' Jacob took a solid gold Hunter watch from his waistcoat pocket and glanced at it. 'I hired a trap from the village to get me here and get us back to the station but the next train leaves in just under two hours.'

Gertie shrugged. She was far from pleased at the child's holiday being cut short but was wise enough to know there was little she could do about it. Jacob was her father after all. She hurried away to fetch Myfanwy a cold drink, aware that the child was feeling as miserable as Grace was.

They sat in an uncomfortable silence until Cerys and Grace reappeared some half an hour later with Grace looking tidy and demure once more in a pretty blue muslin dress and little black buttoned boots. Her face and hands had been scrubbed and her hair had been brushed and was now tied back with a blue ribbon, but she looked utterly dejected.

'That's better,' her father said approvingly as Cerys dropped her heavy case onto the floor at the side of the table and openly glared at him. 'So if you have everything shall we be off?'

Grace followed him outside without a word and as he heaved her case into the trap she turned to Myfanwy and held her hand out politely, once more the young lady. 'Thank you so much for showing me around, I've really enjoyed it.'

A tear slid down Myfanwy's cheek and she angrily swiped it away with the back of her arm.

'You just come back again soon . . . and remember we're best friends now,' she muttered thickly.

'For always,' Grace whispered back solemnly and she knew that it was true. She would never forget the special time they had spent together and hoped that there would be many more of them, for young as she was she knew that a precious bond would tie them together for ever. But then Jacob swung Grace up onto the seat of the small trap and she didn't even have time to say a proper goodbye to her aunt.

Grace glanced at Myfanwy helplessly. She didn't know how she could bear going back to her father's strict regime.

'Right then, you just see you get this girl home safely,' Aunt Gertie rapped out as Jacob climbed into the driving seat and took up the reins. She had never found it easy to show her affections openly but Grace was aware that there were tears lurking in her eyes too.

'Goodbye, Aunt Gertie, and thank you so much for having me.'

'Be off with you then. You'll not want to miss your train,' Gertie answered as she took a man's handkerchief from her pocket and noisily blew her nose, then without another word she turned and strode back into the cottage.

Jacob flicked the reins and the horse set off as Grace turned in her seat to wave to Myfanwy and Mrs Llewelyn who were still standing there. She waved until they were lost to sight as the horse began to labour up the steep hill out of the valley. In the dappled shade of the woodlands she glimpsed wood anemones and ramsons, or wild garlic as Mrs Llewelyn referred to them, growing in wild profusion. Myfanwy had told her that in the spring the floor of the woods was a massive carpet of bluebells and she regretted that she wouldn't be there to see it. Dog roses and honeysuckle clambered up the hedges and they passed bushes heavy with shiny blackberries. Grace smiled as she remembered the day they had gone to pick some for Mrs Llewelyn who wanted to make a blackberry and apple pie. They had eaten just as many as they had taken home and on that evening poor Myfanwy had been violently sick. They passed clusters of foxgloves, oxlip and cow parsley and Grace was proud that she knew the name of them all now. Jacob, however, seemed oblivious to everything apart from getting to the station on time, so she sat silently at his side hanging on to the narrow seat for all she was worth. At the top of the hill she turned and there was Beehive Cottage nestled in the valley far below her. There was no sign of Myfanwy or Mrs Llewelyn now so she merely tried to lock away her last sight of it in her memory before they rounded a corner and it was gone.

When they eventually clip-clopped into Pwllheli, her father lifted her down from the seat and returned the horse and trap to the farrier's where he had hired it from before rushing her off to the train station. He was panting by the time they reached it.

'You've ten minutes to spare,' the stationmaster informed them and Grace felt a little ripple of disappointment. She had half hoped that they would miss the train so that they could go back to Aunt Gertie's for another night.

She and her father sat on a bench to wait and once seated he took her hand, which made her feel uncomfortable and surprisingly resentful. Why couldn't he have just left me alone to enjoy the rest of my holiday? she thought. And then instantly felt guilty. If her mother really *was* ill, then she supposed she should go home.

'What is wrong with Mother?' she asked, turning her head to look at him.

'Oh, I think it's probably just missing you has brought her

down.' He ran his finger around the inside of his shirt collar. It was a habit Grace had noticed he adopted when he was annoyed or uncomfortable about something. 'But I'm sure she will perk up again once you are back. I've missed you too,' he added, but she didn't respond and his lips set in a prim line as he asked, 'Haven't you missed me?'

Grace flushed. She couldn't lie. 'I, er . . . I've been so busy going out and about that I haven't really had time to think about it,' she admitted in a small voice.

They heard the rumble of the train in the distance and thankfully the conversation was stopped from going any further as he lifted her case, gripped her hand and stood to wait for it.

The journey passed uneventfully. Grace sat as far away from her father on the carriage seat as she could, feeling disgruntled. She was tired from her adventures with Myfanwy that day and so they hadn't gone too far when she fell asleep. The next thing she knew her father was shaking her awake.

'Come on, sleepyhead, we're home.'

It was very late and when they emerged from the station they found that the streets were deserted.

'Never mind it's not too far to walk,' her father said as he again gripped her hand. After asking the porter if he would keep Grace's case there till the morning, they set off. The house was in darkness when they arrived home. Mabel and Mrs Batley had obviously retired to bed and Grace knew that her mother would have been asleep for hours.

'Never mind, I'll help you get ready for bed,' her father told her as they crept up the stairs so as not to disturb anyone.

Grace looked dismayed. 'But I'm old enough to get myself ready now, Father,' she objected. Lately she had begun to feel uncomfortable when he walked into her room without knocking, especially if she was in the process of getting undressed.

'Nonsense, you're still just a little girl,' he insisted as he nudged her bedroom door open and placed her overnight bag on the floor. 'Now, come along, you can wash in the morning, let's get your nightdress on.'

With her cheeks burning she stood still as her father fiddled with the buttons on the back of her dress.

'There, that's got it!' He lifted it over her head and she self-consciously folded her hands across her undeveloped breasts as she stood in her petticoats and undergarments.

'M-Mother says it isn't seemly to allow a gentleman to see you in your underclothes,' she protested but he merely laughed.

'It doesn't count if the gentleman in question is your father.'

Grace was mortified as he continued to undress her as if she was a baby until eventually she stood before him naked.

Grace was glad that the only light in the room was that of the moon shining through the window. She flushed as she felt his eyes on her but after hastily unpacking her nightdress he tossed it to her and she gratefully wriggled into it. She then yanked back the covers of the bed and hopped in, pulling them up to her chin as he leaned over her.

'Goodnight, my angel.' His eyes were gleaming in the moonlight and before she knew what was happening he had leaned across and kissed her forehead. He strode from the room and she breathed a sigh of relief as she snuggled down into the blankets.

❧

The next morning Mabel woke her with a tray of tea, toast, a boiled egg and a wide smile.

'Your father just told us you were back so I've made you yer favourite.' She smiled and Grace was pleased to see her although she was still smarting because her holiday had been cut short. 'And your mam will be delighted.'

Grace pulled herself up in the bed. 'Father said Mother was

ill.' she said and Mabel frowned as she drew back the curtains allowing the sunshine to pour into the room.

'Did he? She's no worse than usual.'

'Oh!' Grace sliced the top off her egg and proceeded to dip her toast in it.

'She's not too pleased about the guests your dad's had stayin', though,' Mabel went on as she hoisted Grace's case onto a chair and started to unpack it. Harry had fetched it from the station for her early that morning.

'Over a week they were here an' right unsavoury characters they were an' all, if you were to ask me. Still, they've gone at last an' now that you're home happen things will return to some sort o' normality. Your dad were skulkin' about like a lost soul without you, I don't mind tellin' yer. Now, you stay there an' finish your breakfast an' I'll go an' fetch some hot water so you can have a nice wash afore you go to see your mam.' And with that Mabel pottered away leaving Grace to wonder who the guests might have been.

'Darling, how I've missed you.' Madeline held her arms out to her daughter the second she stepped into the room and Grace flew into them. 'Have you had a wonderful time?'

'Oh yes.' Grace nodded enthusiastically. 'I made a best friend. Her name is Myfanwy and we had *so* much fun together. And Aunt Gertie was so kind to me. But how are you? Father said that I had to come early because you were ill.'

Madeline frowned as she stroked Grace's thick auburn curls. They were already escaping the ribbon she had tied them back with.

'I'm no worse than normal,' Madeline assured her. 'And I'm very annoyed with your father for making you cut your holiday short. But never mind about that for now. Tell me all you've been doing.'

So, after perching on the edge of her mother's bed, Grace did just that and as she spoke her mother noticed how animated her face became.

'But the best times were my visits to the chapel on the clifftop,' she ended breathlessly. 'The nuns live there but they're not a closed order – they're working nuns. Some of them are nurses. Others work in offices in local towns and the postulants work in the vegetable gardens growing fruit and vegetables that they sell at market. All the money they earn goes towards keeping the convent going and they were all *so* nice. I felt as if I could have stayed with them for ever.' Looking slightly guilty then she hurried on, 'Although I missed you, of course. But there was just something so . . .' She tried to think of the right words to explain. 'Peaceful, I suppose. One of the nuns let me have a look inside the convent and that was wonderful as well.'

Madeline smiled indulgently. 'Well, perhaps next summer you can go back again,' she said. 'I'm sure Aunt Gertie loved having you.'

Grace giggled then as she confided, 'I don't think Father was very pleased when he arrived to fetch me. Aunt Gertie had given me some old clothes to play in and he looked horrified when he saw me in her old trousers and boots.'

The image she conjured up made Madeline smile too. Jacob was a great one for convention, especially when it came to Grace. They talked for a while longer, mainly about Myfanwy who Grace was missing already, until Madeline grew tired. Grace left her to rest and skipped down the stairs to scrounge a jam tart off Mrs Batley, her mind racing ahead to the following year when hopefully she would return to Sarn Bach and her very best friend, Myfanwy.

Chapter Seventeen

Grace had only been home for a few days when she woke one morning with a raging sore throat. The inside of her mouth felt sore too, even her tongue hurt, and after she had dragged herself out of bed and dressed, she made her way down to the kitchen feeling rather sorry for herself.

'Why, pet, yer look a bit flushed. Are yer feeling all right?' Mrs Batley sat her down at the table and felt her forehead then clucked in dismay. 'You've got a temperature. Let's have you back to bed straightaway. Mabel can bring yer breakfast up on a tray.'

'I don't want to go back to bed and I don't want any breakfast,' Grace croaked as Mrs Batley fussed around her.

'Well, whether yer want to or not that's where yer goin',' Mrs Batley said firmly. 'An' if you ain't no better in the mornin' I shall get your father to ask the doctor to call in an' take a look at you. Now come along, there's a good girl, let's be havin' you.'

Once she was back in bed, feeling very miserable and sorry for herself, Mabel tucked the blankets up beneath her chin and asked, 'Now, how about I go an' make you a soft-boiled egg an' some bread an' butter fingers, eh? They'll be easy to digest an' happen you'll feel a bit better with summat inside you.'

Grace shook her head. She really did feel quite strange. 'I'm not hungry really . . . Perhaps just a cup of tea?'

Mabel nodded and scurried away, but when she returned some

minutes later Grace was fast asleep so she placed the tray down and tiptoed from the room.

Grace woke mid-afternoon and groaned as she opened her eyes. Her mouth and throat felt even worse but she felt too ill to go downstairs. When Mabel checked on her a short time later, she was alarmed to find that Grace's temperature was even higher.

'Open your mouth,' she ordered and when Grace did, Mabel was horrified. The girl's tongue was swollen and covered in blisters and angry red bumps were appearing on her arms. 'I'm goin' to have a word with yer mam,' she muttered. 'I reckon we need to get the doctor in to you now.'

Twenty minutes later, Harry was dispatched to fetch the doctor. Madeline had gone to sit by Grace's bed, watching as her daughter drifted in and out of sleep. 'Do you think it might be measles or chickenpox, perhaps?' she whispered to Mrs Batley, who'd popped in to check on Grace.

Mrs Batley shook her head. 'Far as I know chickenpox looks like tiny blisters on the skin. These are like little red lumps an' I've never seen anythin' like them blisters in her mouth. Poor lamb, no wonder she can't manage to eat or drink anythin'.'

Madeline chewed worriedly on her lip and prayed fervently that the doctor would come soon. Thankfully, Harry managed to catch him just as he was about to start his afternoon surgery and the kindly man came straightaway.

'Right, little lady, let's have a look at you, shall we.' He smiled at Grace, whose eyes were feverishly bright, as he removed his stethoscope from his bag. He conducted a thorough examination and when he was done his face was grave.

He patted her hand then motioned for Madeline to follow him outside onto the landing.

'Well? What's wrong with her?' Madeline looked frighteningly pale. 'Is it the measles?'

He shook his head. 'I only wish it was but I'm afraid it's much more serious than that. I think Grace has scarlet fever.'

Madeline's hand flew to her mouth as panic set in. 'But isn't that a killer?' Her voice came out as little more than a croak.

Dr Busby hesitated before answering. 'It can be,' he admitted. 'But hopefully we have caught it in time.'

'So, what do we need to do? Will we need to get a nurse in or—'

He held his hand up. 'Unfortunately, scarlet fever is highly contagious. She will have to be admitted into an isolation hospital.'

'B-but we can look after her here,' Madeline protested tearfully.

Dr Busby shook his head. 'No, she must go into isolation. Meanwhile everyone who has had contact with her must wash their hands thoroughly and do not allow anyone else into the house. Once she has gone you must burn her clothes and thoroughly scour her room.'

Both Mabel and Mrs Batley were wringing their hands, but the doctor hadn't finished. 'There have been no reports of any outbreaks in Nuneaton, as far as I know,' he said thoughtfully. 'Has she visited anywhere else?'

'Yes,' Madeline hastily told him of her holiday in Wales.

'Then you must get in touch with them and tell them to be vigilant. It could be that someone there was incubating it and has passed it on. Do you have a telephone? I need to phone the hospital. I think the nearest isolation one to us is in Coleshill. It's run by nuns.'

As Madeline thought back to the conversation she'd had with Grace the evening before about the nuns in Wales, tears sprang to her eyes. Grace had been so impressed with them. Now she would be spending more time than she would have liked with them. It seemed ironic.

'It's in the hall,' she informed the doctor in a shaky voice. 'And when you've finished making your calls I shall have to ring my

128

husband. He'll be at the courts in Coventry but I'm sure he will want to come home.' As the doctor strode towards the door she asked then, 'Shall we pack a bag for her to take with her?'

'No, that won't be necessary,' he said grimly. 'They will burn whatever she is wearing when she's admitted and then she'll wear a hospital gown for the duration of her stay.'

He rushed off, taking the stairs two at a time, leaving Madeline staring helplessly at her daughter.

It was almost two hours later when the ambulance arrived and when she was told that she wasn't permitted to travel to the hospital with her daughter, Madeline openly wept. 'But she's only ten years old, she'll be frightened on her own,' she implored the driver, a tall, skinny man with a beaked nose and enormous bushy eyebrows. Both he and his assistant were clad in a white uniform that covered them from head to foot.

'Sorry, missus. No one's allowed into the ambulance or the hospital apart from the doctor,' he said, as he and the assistant lifted Grace onto a stretcher.

Madeline went even paler if that was possible. 'What do you mean? When *am* I allowed to visit then?'

He shrugged. 'Not until you come to fetch her home an' that could be months away. But you can ring to see how she is each week.' He gave her a sympathetic smile, then he and his colleague began to manoeuvre Grace out of the room. Grace didn't even stir and Madeline was suddenly terrified that she had lost her beloved child already.

'Try to be brave, my dear,' the doctor told her kindly. 'And be sure to do as I asked and contact the people she has been staying with.'

Madeline nodded numbly. Mrs Batley had helped her down the stairs and now she stood and watched as the men gently lifted her daughter into the back of the waiting ambulance. The doctor climbed in beside her and the doors were firmly closed then it was off and suddenly Madeline spurted forward with tears streaming down her cheeks.

'I didn't kiss her goodbye,' she sobbed as Mrs Batley caught her arm and dragged her to a standstill. 'And I didn't tell her how much I love her!'

'You had no need to, pet,' she soothed in a wobbly voice. 'Grace knows how much she is loved. Now come inside.'

They had just turned when a figure racing along the pavement brought them to a halt.

'Madeline!'

She turned back to see Jacob, who was red in the face and breathless from his dash from the train station. He had left the judge's chambers following her phone call and caught the first train to Nuneaton.

'How is she? *Where* is she?'

Madeline pointed back the way he had just come. 'You're too late. She was in the ambulance you just passed.'

He grit his teeth in frustration. '*Damn you*, woman! Why didn't you make them wait until I got home?'

Mrs Batley rounded on him defensively. 'Don't you understand? Your little girl is very ill . . . she could *die*! Ain't that reason enough for 'em to want to get her to the hospital as soon as they could?'

He gulped. 'Yes . . . I suppose so. But now I must go to her. Tell Harry to get the car out immediately.'

Mrs Batley shook her head. 'You'd be wastin' your time. No one's allowed to see her now till she's better.' *If* she gets better, she silently thought.

'Huh! She's my daughter, let them *try* to stop me seeing her,' he sneered.

'Suit yerself!' she muttered. Then she turned and led Madeline, who was sobbing uncontrollably and leaning heavily on her arm, back into the house.

130

Mrs Batley was all too aware that the judge would be haring off on a fool's errand if he tried to get into the hospital, but what did she care? All her concerns were for her poor mistress at that moment. And, of course, there was also an enormous amount of cleaning to do now. When she glanced behind her before going back through the front door there was no sign of him. He'd no doubt rushed around to the back of the house to get the car. Well, let him go, she thought, and closed the front door firmly behind her.

Sometime later, Jacob Kettle drew the car to a halt outside the huge iron gates of the isolation hospital in Coleshill. They were set into a ten-foot-high wall that completely surrounded the building, ensuring no one got in without permission.

He got out of his car and shouted, 'Hello there.'

A small lodge stood to one side on the inside of the gates and a man appeared.

'Yes, sir, can I help you?'

Jacob glared at him impatiently. 'Yes you can, my man, by getting theses gates open immediately.'

He had drawn himself up to his full height and made quite a daunting figure, but the man seemed unimpressed.

'Sorry, sir. I can't do that,' he answered calmly.

'What do you mean *you can't do that*?' Jacob's face was so red with rage that he looked in danger of bursting a blood vessel. 'My daughter has just been admitted here and I demand to see her! *Do you hear me*? I am Judge Kettle so open the gates *right now*!'

The man sniffed. 'Makes no difference to me if you're the king, squire,' he replied. 'My strict instructions are to let no one in apart from doctors and nurses. Even I ain't allowed near the hospital. A lot of the patients have contagious diseases, see? Sorry. I'd advise you to ring up and speak to the sister in charge. Good day to you, sir.'

Jacob was hopping from foot to foot in his frustration and rushing forward, he shook the gates. 'How *dare* you disobey me!' he roared. 'Your head will roll for this.'

The man shrugged and disappeared back into the lodge.

Back at home, Mabel stood at the sink quietly crying as she thought of Grace, and Harry, who had just come back into the room, bit his lip. Mrs Batley was no doubt upstairs trying to calm the mistress so he and Mabel were alone for once.

'Don't cry, lass,' he soothed as he went and awkwardly put his arm across her shoulders. Never having known what it was like to be loved he wasn't sure quite sure how to handle this. But he knew that it hurt him inside to see Mabel upset.

'Oh, Harry, the *poor* little mite.' She turned abruptly and buried her head in his chest and feelings he had never known before surged through him. Instinctively his arms went about her and he wanted to take away her pain. He wanted to kiss away her tears and look after her for ever, but of course he knew that this was never going to happen. Mabel was lovely, the most beautiful girl he had ever met, both inside and out, so what chance was there for him? He had nothing to offer her and worse yet, his legs were crippled with rickets. Why would a girl like her ever look at him when she could surely have any chap she set her cap at? And so he merely stood and comforted her as she cried, and kept all the feelings he had for her hidden away.

Chapter Eighteen

'But you've been telling me that for the last month, sister, *surely* you could be a little more specific. When *can* I visit my daughter?' Jacob Kettle was struggling to remain polite but losing his patience by the second.

'I'm sorry, sir, but I repeat, Grace is as well as can be expected at this stage of the illness and is holding her own. That is the best we can hope for. Now I must bid you good day, sir.'

The phone went dead and Jacob slammed it back onto the cradle and groaned with frustration. It was now late in September but despite his threats and entreaties he had still not been allowed to visit Grace. It seemed that his status as a judge meant nothing to the nursing sisters and they treated him exactly the same as the other patients' parents.

'How is she?' Madeline's voice interrupted his thoughts and he turned on her. As usual, she was flanked by Mabel and Mrs Batley, who hovered around her as if *she* was the one who was ill, and it irritated him even further.

'How the *hell* should I know? All those idiot nuns will tell me is that she is holding her own and is as well as can be expected! *Holding her own indeed!* What's that supposed to mean? For two pins, I'd go and demand to take her out of there! There has to be another hospital that would treat her where I was allowed to visit.'

'There isn't, I've already made enquiries,' his wife informed him dully.

The separation from Grace was hurting her just as much as it was hurting him, but Jacob was oblivious to that. Oblivious to everything except the fact that he could not visit his child. Strangely enough, Madeline could sympathise with him on that count. She of all people knew just how much he adored their daughter and although she felt his adoration sometimes went beyond the normal, she could feel his pain. She had shared a wonderful relationship with her own father but she could never remember him treating her as Jacob treated Grace. It wasn't as if he was the only one concerned for her, after all. She herself lay awake night after night worrying. Was Grace conscious and thinking that they had abandoned her? Was she in pain with no one there to hold her hand? Was she getting better or was she worse? Round and round the questions went until sometimes Madeline thought she would go mad. Each time the phone rang her heart sank. What if it was the hospital calling with bad news?

Just then, some mail plopped through the letterbox and with a strangled grunt Jacob went to lift it from the mat before disappearing into his study.

'Come on, pet.' Mrs Batley gently took Madeline's arm. 'They do say no news is good news. Let's get you into the day room, there's a nice fire in there and I'll bring you some coffee. And perhaps a bit of that jam sponge sandwich I made yesterday? You like that, don't you.' Since Grace had gone, Madeline had lost even more weight and looked almost skeletal, despite her and Mabel's best efforts to get her to eat more.

Madeline forced herself to smile at Mrs Batley. She was trying so hard to please her, forever cooking treats to try and tempt her, but somehow everything tasted like sawdust and stuck in her throat.

Once in the day room Madeline stared sightlessly out of the

window that overlooked the garden. Over the last couple of weeks, the weather had changed dramatically. There was a nip in the air and the nights were fast drawing in. Leaves had begun to drift down like confetti and only the late-flowering roses lent any colour to the garden. After a while she sighed and moved to the small escritoire in the corner. She would write to Aunt Gertie again, that would pass a little time. Time seemed to be something she had far too much of lately and it hung heavily on her like a shroud. She and Aunt Gertie had been corresponding regularly and keeping in touch via the phone. Lifting her pen, Madeline dipped it into the inkwell and tried to concentrate.

At that very moment, in a small ward in the hospital in Coleshill, Grace had just opened her eyes. They felt gritty and her head hurt as a young nun rushed to her side.

'Ah, you're awake.' The nun smiled as she swiped a damp cloth across Grace's feverish forehead. 'How about a little drink?' She lifted Grace's head and carefully trickled some water between her dry, cracked lips, but within seconds Grace had vomited it up again and dropped back against the pillow, exhausted. Her whole body was covered in angry red lumps and she felt as if she was on fire.

'How is she?' An older nun appeared and the young one shook her head. 'Not good, I'm afraid, sister. The fever is still raging. I don't know how much longer her body can cope with this temperature. I'm doing all I can but it doesn't seem to be doing any good.'

The senior nun gently squeezed the young woman's shoulder. 'She is in God's hands now, my child,' she whispered and then glided away.

The next time Grace woke she found that she was encased in

a strange white light. 'Mamma, Myfanwy,' she croaked deliriously, and as if by magic Myfanwy was suddenly there, her huge blue eyes serene and calm.

The girl took her hand and gently kissed the hot fingers. 'Come along now,' she ordered in her usual bossy way. 'I am your best friend and I order you to get better . . . for me.'

'I . . . I'll try,' Grace breathed and with her friend's hand gripped in her own she drifted off to sleep again.

When she woke it was daylight and she blinked as the weak autumn sun streaming through the windows hurt her eyes.

The young nun who had cared for her so tenderly was the first face that swam into her vision and she asked, 'Where am I?'

'You're in the hospital. You've been very poorly indeed. But your fever has broken. For a while there you seemed to hover between life and death, but our dear Lord clearly has plans for you to stay on this earth. You'll start to get better now.'

Grace tried to nod but it hurt to move her head or try to speak. Instead she lay quietly and felt a warm glow as she thought of Myfanwy's visit. Her dear friend had come all that way to see her when she was ill. She was disappointed that she hadn't been allowed to stay longer but she remembered how strict the nuns were about visitors. Myfanwy had done well to get past them if only for a short time. Eventually she raised her hand and felt her shorn head. She vaguely remembered the nuns giving her the pudding basin cut shortly after she had arrived. They said that it was necessary, for long hair sapped a person's strength. Grace wasn't overly concerned about it. No doubt it would grow back. This time when she fell asleep, it was a healing sleep and she determined to put all her efforts into getting well again. The sooner she was better the sooner she would go home again and see her mother. Strangely she gave no thought to her father.

Christmas that year without Grace was a sad affair. So sad that Madeline decided she didn't even want to go to the trouble of putting up a Christmas tree. Jacob was spending Christmas in Liverpool again and Mabel would be spending Christmas with her family, so it would be just her, Mrs Batley and Harry. The news from the hospital was optimistic, however, so they all hung on to that knowledge in the hope that Grace might be back home with them soon.

'Where do you suppose the master goes off to?' Mabel mused as she and Harry sat enjoying a mug of cocoa late on Christmas Eve. Mrs Batley had gone to bed and it was just the two of them.

Harry bowed his head and Mabel sensed he knew more than he was letting on. 'Come on, if you know, let me in on the secret,' she urged. 'It'll go no further an' it ain't as if I care about him. He's a vile man!'

'He ain't all bad, actually,' Harry said in the master's defence.

'But how can you say that? He treats us all like dirt!'

'Aye, happen he does,' he admitted. 'But when we lived in Leeds I overheard some chaps that knew him talkin' once. They'd just got off a train an' they paid me to carry their bags to a hotel an' when I heard the master's name me ears pricked up. Apparently one of 'em was a friend of his first wife.' He paused then, as if he was unsure if he should go on.

'And?' Mabel urged.

Harry frowned. 'Well, he was carted off to a boarding school at an early age by all accounts, and he rarely went home. It seems his mother had him late in life an' he was an inconvenience. The school was a harsh place from what I could gather. The children were beaten by the masters there. Both his parents died within months of each other while he was still at school. When our master came out he used the money his parents had left him and worked his fingers to the bone to put himself through law school. An' then he met his first wife. Seems her father never thought the master were good enough for her but she married him anyway

137

an' he were keen to start a family.' He shook his head. 'I reckon it were cos he'd never had no family of his own before that cared about him, an' that's probably why he's so possessive of Grace. His first wife lost one baby after another, I heard, an' he started to go to these clubs in Liverpool.'

'What clubs?' Mabel was intrigued now.

Harry looked uncomfortable, wishing he'd never started this in the first place. 'I ain't sure,' he hedged. 'But I won't forget that as surly as he is he saved me from the gutter.' He longed to tell her the rest but in a strange way he felt he owed some loyalty to the man. It was one of the reasons he couldn't disclose his feelings to Mabel and she wouldn't want him anyway, he was sure.

Mabel felt there was more to it than what he was telling her, but she didn't push him. 'Hmm, well, what you've told me is sad,' she admitted. 'But I still don't like him! He's a mean old bugger!'

Harry didn't know how to answer that so he turned his attention back to his cocoa.

⚜

Grace spent a lot of her time in prayer. Since recovering a little she had enjoyed joining the nuns in their services in the chapel attached to the hospital and now she was even well enough to write to her mother, Myfanwy and Aunt Gertie. She had no idea that the letters were never posted for fear of them being contagious. The young girl who had spent some weeks in the next bed to Grace with the same illness had sadly not survived and so now Grace counted herself extremely lucky. She wondered if God had spared her for a reason. She had no idea what it might be as yet but was certain she would find out in the fullness of time.

On Christmas Day the isolation hospital took on a completely different atmosphere. The nuns had placed bowls of holly here and there and helped those of the children that were well enough to

138

make paper chains, which they strung across the ceiling. In the morning after breakfast they gave each of the children a small gift. For the boys, there were liquorice sticks and gobstoppers, for the girls there were small oranges – a rare treat – and pretty ribbons to tie in their hair. They then conducted their Christmas morning service in the ward and as Grace listened to their sweet voices, she was entranced. Many of the children were still too poorly to have much of an appetite but even so they were each served with slices of succulent goose and roast potatoes followed by Christmas pudding and warm mince pies. In the afternoon, the sisters read stories to them and served them with rich Christmas cake, and although Grace missed her mother and the staff back at home, she enjoyed every minute of it and was almost sad when the day was over.

Soon after Christmas the snow arrived, thick and deep, making everything beyond the hospital window look brand new. Grace felt totally at home and safe with the nuns now and enjoyed learning all she could about the Catholic faith. In February, a thaw set in and the rains came and suddenly they were into March and the world started to come alive again. Primroses peeped from beneath the hedgerows, tender green leaves began to unfurl on the trees and the air was filled with birdsong.

One day when the sun was shining tentatively the older nun, Sister Agatha, who was in charge of the others, came to see her.

'Sit beside me, child,' she invited, patting the bed. 'I have good news for you. We feel that you are clear of the fever now and so we are going to allow you to go home. I shall be ringing your father this afternoon to arrange for him to come and fetch you.'

'Really?' Grace felt a mixture of emotions. Of course, she was happy at the thought of seeing her mother again and yet she also felt sad to be leaving the nuns. She had come to look upon them almost as family and she knew already that she would miss Sister Agatha. The elderly nun had never shown her anything but kindness and after seeing the way she selflessly nursed the sick, Grace was full of admiration for her. Sister Agatha had even given her a set of rosary beads, which Grace would always treasure, and had taught her a great deal about the Catholic faith. Grace found it fascinating. So much so that she intended to ask her mother for permission to attend more of the services in Our Lady of the Angels Catholic Church in Riversley Road when she got home.

'When do you think I might be able to go?' she asked. It seemed such a long time since she had seen her family and the people she really cared about.

'I see no reason why you shouldn't go home this Sunday, providing your father is able to fetch you of course,' the kindly nun told her.

On Sunday afternoon, Jacob Kettle once more pulled up at the hospital ready to do battle to be admitted if need be, but this time, the gatekeeper opened the gates immediately and even tipped his cap to him.

'Afternoon, sir.'

Jacob glared at him before roaring down the drive. Once he was admitted a nun took the new clothes he had brought for Grace to go home in and he paced up and down impatiently as he waited for her.

At last he heard footsteps approaching on the highly polished tiled floor and looking up he saw Grace walking towards him gripping the hand of an elderly nun.

He forced a smile and tried not to look shocked, for he scarcely recognised his own child. She was taller but her new clothes hung from her skinny frame and she was deathly pale with huge dark circles beneath her eyes. But it was her hair that shocked him the most. Where once it had hung almost to her waist in thick, gleaming waves, it was now chopped to just below her chin, although it was still the same rich, vibrant auburn colour he had been so proud of.

'Grace . . .' He was so choked with emotion that for a moment he was rooted to the spot then he hurried forward and clasped her so firmly that she gasped.

'Please be gentle with her, sir,' the nun scolded. 'And try to remember that she has a way to go until she is fully recovered. She is still very weak and she will need to rest often.'

'Oh . . . yes . . . yes, of course, sister. I apologise.'

She smiled then as she turned to Grace and gave her a gentle hug. 'Go with God, my child, and may He watch over you.'

'Thank you, sister.' Suddenly Grace wasn't so sure that she wanted to leave. Here in the hospital she had felt safe and serene but now she would have to go out into the world again and it was a daunting thought. But still, at least I will get to see Mother, she told herself sternly and forced her legs to propel her towards the door. She had thought that Sister Agatha would come outside to wave her off but the nun turned and walked away. Her job with Grace was done, now there were others that needed her attention.

Once she was seated in the car, her father tucked a warm travelling rug about her legs and seconds later they were off. Grace snuggled down into the seat and said very little on the way home. After the close confines of the hospital everywhere suddenly felt so big and she knew it was going to take some getting used to.

Grace dozed on the journey home and when they arrived, despite her protests, her father lifted her from the car and carried her inside. Her mother, Mabel, Mrs Batley and Harry were all in the hallway waiting for her and at sight of their dear faces Grace burst into tears. She hadn't realised until that moment just how much she had missed them all.

'But what have they done to your beautiful hair, pet,' Mrs Batley cried as she stroked her shorn curls.

'I had to have it all cut off because they said it would sap my strength,' Grace informed her solemnly. 'But it's growing back again already. It's past my chin now. When they first cut it, it was just below my ears.'

Secretly they were as shocked at their first sight of her as her father had been. Mrs Batley decided there and then that it was up to her to cook some tempting treats so the child would put a bit of meat back on her bones again. There was no time like the present so she asked, 'What do yer fancy for dinner, lass? I'll cook whatever yer like.'

'Actually, Sister Agatha informed me that she must eat little and often,' Jacob told her as he placed his arm about Grace's frail shoulders. 'Nourishing things like chicken soup and fish. And she must also get plenty of rest so I wonder if she shouldn't go upstairs for a little lie-down.'

'Oh, but Father, I slept on the way home and I'm not tired yet,' Grace objected. 'I'd like to go into the drawing room and speak to Mother for a while, if you don't mind. I can lie on the sofa if I get tired and Mother can read to me.'

'Very well,' he replied grudgingly. He had hoped to spend some time with her himself but he didn't want to upset her on her first day home. He watched then as she took Madeline's hand and walked away before turning on his heel and retiring to his study with his lips pursed in a thin line.

Over the next few days, Grace slept a lot. Mrs Batley plied her with home-made egg custards and chicken soup and anything she could think of to tempt her to eat and Mabel fussed over her like a mother hen. Grace was happy to be home and gradually a little colour crept back into her cheeks and she began to gain a little weight.

'I shall be very fat at this rate,' Grace told her mother one afternoon as they sat either side of the roaring fire in the drawing room. 'I'm beginning to feel a little stronger already. In fact, I think I might write to Myfanwy this afternoon. She must have been very worried about me and I was so pleased when she came to see me at the hospital.'

Mrs Batley had just entered the room bearing a tray laden with jam tarts and a pot of tea and she almost dropped it as she glanced at Madeline in alarm. The look was not lost on Grace and she asked innocently, 'Is something wrong?'

'Just when did Myfanwy come to see you, darling?' her mother asked gently.

Grace screwed up her eyes and tried to think. 'I'm not sure but I think I had been in the hospital for about four weeks, so it must have been round about the end of September. None of the nuns ever mentioned her visit so I didn't either in case Myfanwy had managed to sneak in. I knew we shouldn't have visitors. But I do remember I was very poorly and she came very late one night. Why do you ask?'

Madeline gulped.

Grace noted she had gone quite pale and then in a very small voice her mother told her, 'It couldn't have been Myfanwy, sweet-heart. You see, she got scarlet fever too and sadly she died round about the time you say she came to see you. So I'm afraid she can't have come to visit you. I was waiting until you were a little stronger to tell you. I'm so very sorry. Aunt Gertie and Mr and Mrs Llewelyn are all heartbroken.'

Grace looked stunned. 'But she *can't* be dead!' Her head wagged from side to side in disbelief. 'She *was* with me. She told me she was my best friend and she ordered me to get better . . . for her.' And then suddenly, as she realised that what her mother was saying must be true, she began to sob – great tearing sobs that shook her whole body.

Chapter Nineteen

It was on a cold and frosty morning in November that Grace walked into the kitchen unexpectedly to find Harry and Mabel with their heads bent over a book, which Mabel hurriedly slammed shut.

'Oh . . . we were, er . . .' Mabel began, but Harry interrupted her.

'It's all right,' he told her. 'I don't mind Miss Grace knowing.' Then turning to Grace, shamefaced, he explained. 'The thing is, Mabel discovered some time ago that I couldn't read or write . . . so the long an' the short of it is, she's been teachin' me in any spare minutes we have.'

'And very well he's doin' too,' Mabel butted in proudly. 'He can read almost as good as me now an' he only struggles on the hard words.'

'But you should have told me, Harry. I would have helped you too,' Grace assured him.

He shook his head. 'Thanks for the offer, miss. But I don't reckon your dad would take very kindly to that.'

'Mm, I suppose you're right,' Grace admitted. Her father didn't like her mingling with the servants more than she had to, although Grace looked upon them as part of her family. 'But I could help you in the day when Father is at work and Mabel is busy. I do tend to get very bored. I shall be glad when I can go back to school.'

She did actually look much better now, although the news of Myfanwy's death had set her back terribly for weeks. Nothing anyone said could convince her that Myfanwy hadn't visited her at the hospital and she would carry that belief close to her heart for the rest of her life. It was only after she had spoken to Aunt Gertie on the phone that she was forced to accept that her friend was really gone and she had grieved for her.

Now Harry answered doubtfully, 'Well . . . I suppose if I have nothin' to do an' you're not busy we could.'

Mabel nodded her approval. She knew how bored Grace got and thought helping Harry might give her something useful to do.

Grace took a seat at the table while Mabel made a pot of coffee. Looking from Mabel to Harry, she noticed how much more relaxed they seemed in each other's company these days. She had often heard Mrs Batley tell her mother that Mabel had a soft spot for Harry and she wondered if now a romance might be developing. She hoped so because she loved them both dearly and wanted them to be happy. Still, there's plenty of time yet, Grace thought as she went to join her mother for morning coffee in the day room. Father O'Rourke from Our Lady of the Angels was visiting, and Grace was looking forward to seeing him.

Over the last couple of weeks, she had been visiting the Catholic church with her mother's permission. After almost losing her, Madeline was quite happy for Grace to do anything that made her happy, within reason. Harry would drive her there and back, for everyone felt that she wasn't fully recovered yet, but she didn't mind that. Within the walls of the church she had found the same peace as she had in the chapel in Sarn Bach and in the hospital, and Father O'Rourke, the priest, had taken a great shine to her.

'There is something about her,' Father O'Rourke told Madeline as they waited in the day room for Grace to join them. 'Something indefinable that seems to shine from within her. She is full of grace and joy. But how do you feel about your daughter embracing a

145

different faith? I believe you and your husband are Church of England?'

Madeline nodded as she strained tea into a dainty cup and saucer. 'We are,' she agreed. 'But truthfully I believe at the end of the day that we all worship one God so if Grace gets happiness from attending a Catholic church I have no objections.'

'And your husband?'

Madeline looked slightly embarrassed. How could she tell him that she believed her husband only attended church at all because he felt he should? As a judge, it was expected of him but she didn't think he was particularly religious. In fact, the services seemed to bore him.

'Whatever makes Grace happy makes him happy,' she replied cautiously and the priest seemed content with that explanation.

Later that day, Mabel was dusting in Jacob's study, humming softly to herself. There were a number of papers on his desk and she lifted them gingerly to dust beneath them. As she did so a piece of paper fluttered to the floor and she silently cursed. The judge had always told her that she was not to disturb anything in there but the desk had looked so dusty that she hadn't been able to resist giving it a quick wipe. She bent to lift the paper and put it back in its place, but as she did she couldn't help seeing what was written on it in a large scrawl. *I'M WATCHING YOU.*

Mabel dropped the paper as if it had bitten her and gasped in shock. Then, deciding that the study was tidy enough for today she scuttled away to the kitchen where Mrs Batley was kneading some dough for a new batch of bread.

'You'll never guess what I've just seen in the judge's office,' she whispered after glancing around to ensure that they were alone.

When Mrs Batley raised an inquisitive eyebrow, Mabel hastily told her.

'Well, he's a judge, ain't he? He sentences people to prison so he's bound to have enemies.'

'Mm, I suppose yer right.' Mabel shivered. 'But it still gave me the creeps.'

'It could have been anybody,' Mrs Batley pointed out. 'Perhaps someone who's just come out o' prison, or maybe a relative o' someone he's put away? I dare say he's used to it.'

Despite her reassuring words, from then on Mabel found herself watching the judge's post more closely. As far as she was concerned, there was no doubt that someone wished him harm.

By the time Christmas came around again, Grace and Mabel between them had Harry reading almost as well as they could and now they were teaching him basic maths. Grace was as bright as a button and Mabel was the first to admit that Grace knew far more than she did.

'I went to school when I could if me mam didn't need me,' she admitted. 'So, although I know the basics I can't hold a candle to Miss Grace even though she's just a child.'

'Not such a child anymore,' Mrs Batley replied regretfully. 'Since bein' so ill an' losin' that little friend of hers, Miffan – Myfen . . . Oh, whatever her name was, Grace seems to have grown up all of a sudden. I think she's far too old for her years but then I think part o' that is down to her father. It ain't natural how he still don't like her mixin' with folks her own age. But she'll rebel, you just mark my words. She'll probably run off wi' a chimney sweep or the first chap to show her a bit of attention soon as she reaches sixteen.'

'Oh, I think Grace would have more sense than to do that.'

When Mrs Batley glanced at her she saw that she was blushing and asked, 'An' is there anythin' *you* want to tell me?'

'No . . . well . . . yes.' Mabel got all flustered. 'Harry's asked me to go to the music hall with him this Friday evenin' . . . that's if you don't need me for anythin', that is,' she added hastily.

'*Hallelujah!* It's only taken him eleven years to get around to it.'

Mabel blushed an even deeper shade of red as Mrs Batley threw a damp cloth over the yeast and put it on the hearth to rise.

'We're just going as friends,' Mabel retorted and Mrs Batley chuckled.

'Well, it's a start, I suppose, an' yer know what they say, everythin' has to start somewhere.' Then with a wry grin she got on with her chores.

Late that night, Grace heard her bedroom door creak open. She peeped over the top of the blanket and saw her father approach her bed. She quickly closed her eyes and pretended to be asleep hoping he would go away. These night visits were becoming a regular occurrence and they made her feel uncomfortable. Not that her father had ever hurt her; he would just stand there and look at her for a time and then he would kiss her forehead before leaving the room. But only a few nights ago, he had actually kissed her on the lips and Grace hadn't liked it.

'You are my perfect angel,' he had crooned and Grace had shuddered. 'You will stay with me always and be a comfort to me in my old age when your mother has gone.'

Grace didn't much like the thought of that. She didn't know what she wanted to do when she grew up as yet but she did know that she wouldn't want to live with her father for always. She hadn't told him that, of course, but she had tentatively asked her mother if she was old enough to have a key for her bedroom door now.

'Why ever would you want to lock your door, darling?' Madeline had looked surprised. 'What if you were ill? If your door was locked no one could come in to help you. No, let's wait until you are a little older, shall we?'

Grace had nodded. It looked like for now she would just have to put up with her father's night visits. Now she lay very still and tried to regulate her breathing. She could smell the peculiar mixture of him: Macassar oil, cigar smoke and whisky all rolled into one. After a moment, he leaned forward and stroked a lock of her hair from her face then thankfully he tiptoed from the room. Grace let out a sigh of relief.

The following morning Grace was woken by the muffled sound of raised voices coming from her father's study. She pulled herself up onto one elbow and frowned, wondering what time it was. Dropping her legs over the side of her bed, she yanked her dressing gown on and padded downstairs. Mabel was in the hallway wringing her apron between her hands.

'I don't know who it is, Miss Grace,' she said in a hushed voice. 'I heard a knock on the door an' when I opened it this bloke barged in demandin' to see yer dad.'

'Oh well.' Grace yawned. 'I'm sure Father will sort him out. Is there a cup of tea going? There's not much point going back to bed now.'

Mabel smiled. 'Come through to the kitchen. We'll soon get you sorted.'

As Grace had still not fully regained her appetite, both Mabel and Mrs Batley were always only too pleased to oblige when she wanted anything to eat or drink.

Mrs Batley was sitting at the table enjoying a tea break. The smell of bacon hung on the air as she had already served the master his breakfast and he had been just about to leave for work when his visitor had arrived.

'So, what's goin' on out there then?' She cocked her head towards the door and Mabel shrugged.

'Haven't got a clue but the chap that barged in looked a right nasty piece o' work. Soon as the master saw him he grabbed him by the elbow and dragged him off into his study. They're still there now an' it sounds like they're havin' a right old ding-dong!' Then remembering Grace was just behind her she said hurriedly, 'Sit yerself down, pet, an' I'll fetch you a cup.'

She had barely finished pouring the tea when the master appeared in the kitchen doorway, his face red with rage. He raised an eyebrow when he saw Grace sitting there but then told Mabel curtly, 'Prepare the spare bedroom. We have a guest who will be staying. When it's ready show him up there.'

'A guest? For how long?' Mrs Batley asked. After hearing the raised voices, she was shocked to discover that the visitor would be staying.

'Just for a few days,' Jacob answered, clearly none too pleased with the idea. Then directing his attention to Grace, he asked, 'And what are you doing in here in a state of undress? I suggest you go upstairs and make yourself presentable as soon as possible.'

It was so unusual for her father to be annoyed with her that Grace looked shocked before muttering, 'I'm hardly in a state of undress, Father, I have my dressing robe on.'

He gentled his tone. 'Even so, while we have our guest staying I would ask that you present yourself respectably.'

'Yes, Father.'

Jacob turned on his heel and marched from the room just as Harry appeared to take him to the station.

'What's wrong wi' him today?' he asked. 'Get out the wrong side o' the bed, did he?'

'You tell me,' Mrs Batley grumbled. 'It appears we have a guest stayin' so I shall have to send Mabel out for some more shoppin' today.'

With a shrug, Harry left and after draining her cup, Grace rose from the table. 'I'd better go and get dressed.'

'Yes, pet, might be as well,' Mrs Batley agreed.

Harry and her father had just left when Grace entered the hallway to find a man there puffing away on a cigar. He eyed her appreciatively up and down and Grace squirmed uncomfortably.

'Well, hello there, little lady, and ain't you a pretty little girl, eh?' The man stuck his hand out but Grace chose to ignore it. 'The name's Charlie Biggs,' he went on, nonplussed. 'I knew Jacob had a daughter but he never mentioned what a little beaut you are.'

Mabel bustled towards her then and seeing how uncomfortable Grace looked she took her hand protectively, saying, 'Come on, pet. I'll see yer to yer room.' She eyed the visitor disdainfully. 'An' I suggest you take a seat in the drawin' room, sir, while I get yer room ready.'

He flashed her a charming smile. 'O' course, me dear. I don't mind takin' the weight off me feet for a while.' He headed off, leaving a trail of ash in his wake and Mabel tutted with annoyance.

'Let's just hope *he* won't be stayin' fer long,' she commented as she ushered Grace ahead of her up the stairs. 'He looks like trouble to me.'

Grace nodded in agreement, wondering what her mother was going to make of their new house guest.

It was later that evening when Grace found out. They were seated at the dining-room table and after dabbing her lips with her napkin, Madeline asked tentatively, 'How long is your guest likely to be staying, Jacob?' The person in question had wolfed his meal down then headed off for the nearest pub.

151

Jacob had the good grace to look slightly uncomfortable. 'Not for long. I have a little business to conclude with him and then hopefully he'll be on his way.' He hadn't at all liked the way Charlie had stared at Grace throughout the meal and could she have known it he was just as keen as Madeline to see the back of him.

'Good. I really don't like the thought of that type of person being under the same roof as my daughter!' She rose from the table without another word and left.

Charlie was still there three days later when Aunt Gertie phoned Madeline to check on Grace's progress and when Madeline told her about their unwelcome house guest she came up with a solution to get Grace out of his way.

'Why don't you let her come to me to finish her convalescence?' she suggested. 'The sea air would do her the power of good and if this man is half as horrible as you say he is, I dare say Grace will be pleased to get away from him. I'm shocked that Jacob would even entertain his sort knowing what a snob he is!'

Madeline paused. She supposed Aunt Gertie was right although she hated the thought of losing Grace again, even if it was only for a little while. But then only that morning she had discovered Charlie Biggs holding a tiny bit of mistletoe he had found left over from Christmas trying to kiss Grace in the hall, and it had made her feel nauseous. She had advanced on him with a strength she hadn't known she still had and snapped, 'How *dare* you, sir! Please keep your hands to yourself!'

'I were only havin' a bit o' fun,' Charlie had said sullenly as she hauled Grace away to the drawing room. She was absolutely fuming. He was an obnoxious little man, almost as round as he was high with a penchant for gaudy suits and waistcoats. His hair, which was thinning and badly in need of a cut, was always plastered flat to his head with Macassar oil and his crooked teeth were yellow and decaying. Jacob appeared to dislike him almost as much as she did so she could only assume he was still there because Charlie had something on him. Perhaps getting Grace away, at least until he was gone, would be a good thing.

'I'll ask her how she feels about the idea,' she promised her aunt.

When her mother asked her if she'd like to go to Wales, Grace had mixed feelings. Half of her longed to go back to Sarn Bach, she had been so happy there, but the other half of her was still mourning Myfanwy and she knew it could never be the same without her. But then she detested Charlie Biggs. He was always trying to touch her – just like her father did – when they were alone and she'd taken to staying in her room throughout the day just to keep out of his way.

'I'll go,' she said.

Now all Madeline had to do was inform Jacob and make the necessary arrangements. When Madeline told him, Jacob was none too pleased at the thought of Grace going, but until Charlie Biggs left, he felt he didn't have much choice so he had reluctantly agreed.

Chapter Twenty

On a bitterly cold morning late in January, Harry and Grace set off for the train station with Grace muffled up to the eyeballs in warm clothes. Madeline was tearful as she waved them off from the door but Grace was tickled to see the way Mabel had pecked Harry on the cheek before they left and the way Harry flushed and grinned.

'Take good care of her, Harry,' Madeline shouted.

Harry nodded. 'O' course I will, Mrs Kettle. Yer need have no worries on that score.'

Soon they were on the train and Grace was shocked at how tired she was already. However, she managed to stay awake until they had changed trains in Birmingham and then within minutes of being settled in their carriage she fell fast asleep and didn't wake again until they drew into the station at Pwllheli.

'I didn't like to disturb you,' Harry told her as he helped her down onto the platform. 'But you must be starving hungry now.'

'I'm all right,' Grace answered as she knuckled the sleep from her eyes and peered up and down for a sign of Mr Llewelyn. And there he was, striding towards them with a smile on his face. She thought he looked older and despite his smile his eyes were sad, but then she supposed he too was probably still grieving for Myfanwy.

'Why, cariad, it's so good to see you,' he greeted her, although secretly he was thinking how frail she looked. 'Now come along. The trap is outside and it's keen I am to get you home and out of the cold. I can smell snow in the air.'

This time as the horse jogged along Grace recognised places she had visited with Myfanwy the summer before last and the memories were bittersweet as tears pricked at the back of her eyes.

It was getting dark but luckily Aled Llewelyn knew these roads like the back of his hand and at last he drew the horse to a halt outside Beehive Cottage and swung Grace down from the trap. Grace could smell the salt in the air and hear the waves thundering onto the beach in the distance and she was suddenly glad she'd come.

'You two get away in now while I go and get the horse settled in his stable,' Mr Llewelyn told them kindly. 'I believe my Cerys has a nice dish of stew and dumplings all ready and waiting for you.'

Harry smiled at him gratefully, then taking Grace's hand in one of his, he lifted her case with the other and propelled her towards the cottage door. There was a bitterly cold wind blowing and Grace's teeth were chattering so she was grateful when the door suddenly opened and Mrs Llewelyn and Aunt Gertie appeared and hurried her inside.

'Why, your poor little nose is glowing red,' Mrs Llewelyn declared as she pushed her gently towards the roaring fire in the kitchen. Aunt Gertie meanwhile stood by watching. She had never been a great one for being openly affectionate but her smile said it all.

She was clad in her usual outlandish clothes: an old shirt and ill-fitting trousers with her hair tied back simply in a ribbon. 'I'll take your case up to your room,' she told Grace. 'Cerys lit a fire in there for you so it should be nice and warm.'

Grace nodded as she held her hands out to the fire. It was strange, she thought, that she could almost sense Myfanwy's presence.

At that moment, back in Nuneaton, Jacob was facing his house guest across his desk. 'You're telling me that you need yet *more* money, Biggs? But I only gave you five pounds a couple of days ago. And may I ask exactly how much longer you are planning on staying?'

'Hmm, now that all depends.' Charlie made a great show of examining his fingernails. 'See, the thing is, until I've got enough in me pocket to find some decent digs in London, I'm stuck here, ain't I? I mean . . . yer wouldn't want to see me out on the streets, now, would yer? I don't think you'd like me to message yer little wife either, especially if it were like the one I sent you. I reckon it'd scare her.'

Jacob's nostrils flared. 'You do know this is blackmail, don't you?' he spat as he stared at Charlie with loathing.

Charlie chuckled. 'Now, don't be like that, me old son. You an' me should stick together. We're cut from the same cloth, see? Shall I say . . . we both share the same little . . . fetishes? It would never do if it were to come out what a respectable pillar o' the community did in his spare time, would it? An' just think what it would do to your wife an' daughter. She's a tasty little piece, that Grace!'

Jacob's heart lurched. 'How much?' he ground out from between clenched teeth.

'Let me see now.' Charlie tapped his lip as if he was in deep thought, enjoying the power he had over the man. 'I reckon a hundred quid would keep me goin' fer quite some time.'

'A *hundred*?' Jacob was visibly shocked. 'But I don't keep that sort of money in the house.'

'Then how about you give me another fiver for tonight an' get the rest out o' the bank tomorrer? I'll be gone out o' your hair quick as a flash then.'

Jacob gulped before withdrawing his wallet from his pocket and extracting five one-pound notes. He held them out wordlessly and Charlie snatched them and stuffed them into his own pocket.

Jacob just wanted to see the back of this despicable character. He'd been on tenterhooks ever since he'd arrived.

'And if I give you this hundred pounds, will that be an end to it?'

Charlie sniffed. 'I should think so . . . for now. But the pub's callin' me, so I'll be off. Ta-ra, see you later an' don't forget to tell Mabel to make the fire in me room up fer when I get back. I'm getting' quite fond o' me home comforts, though I'd like 'em even more if I had a nice tasty little piece like your daughter tucked in at the side o' me! We likes 'em young, don't we, Jacob!' He swung from the room whistling merrily as Jacob stared up at the ceiling. Things were going from bad to worse and he felt there was only one option left open to him now.

The front door had no sooner closed than Jacob peeped out into the hallway. It was deserted so, grabbing his coat, he stealthily left the house and began to follow his unwelcome guest.

Much, much later that evening, Jacob watched as Biggs staggered out of the Fleur de Lys pub. He was swaying dangerously and singing loudly. Jacob cursed from his hiding place behind a tree. Why couldn't the bloody fool be quiet! The last thing he wanted was for the bloke to draw attention to himself. He set off after him, keeping a safe distance, his teeth chattering with cold and his hands and feet so chilled that he could hardly feel them. Biggs swayed beneath the Coton Arches then veered off across the field leading to Riversley Park. Jacob smiled into the darkness. This was going to be easier than he'd hoped. Biggs stopped once to relieve himself up a tree trunk, but Jacob kept a cautious distance. He needed to be sure that there was no one about. Eventually, Biggs emerged into the park and took the path alongside the River Anker where the weeping willow trees trailed their leafless branches into the sluggish waters. Jacob bided his time until the moon sailed behind the clouds, then slipping on his gloves, he crept up behind the man and tapped him on the shoulder.

'What the . . .' Biggs almost jumped out of his skin as he turned, startled to see who it was. Jacob brought his arm back and Biggs, seeing the cold flash of metal, moved quickly to one side and raised his fist. But drink had made him unsteady and he stumbled to his knees, holding his hands up to try to defend himself. His flailing fist caught Jacob on the knee and he grunted with pain. But then Jacob was on him again and swinging his arm forward with all his might he managed to thrust the knife into the man's heart. Instantly blood began to bubble from Bigg's lips and he made a desperate, strangled noise in his throat. There was a moment's recognition in his eyes as he looked up at his attacker before they began to close and, as if in slow motion, he toppled forward making a strange gurgling noise.

Jacob stood there, his heart thumping wildly until the noise ceased then cautiously he turned Biggs over with the toe of his shoe. The man's eyes were staring sightlessly up at the sky and for a moment Jacob thought that he was going to be sick. However, he pulled himself together with an enormous effort, and heaving and grunting, Jacob pushed and rolled the dead weight to the edge of the riverbank, then putting his foot in Biggs's back he gave a final heave. The man's body hit the water with a satisfying splash and as the water closed over him silence fell, save for the beating of the judge's heart.

Suddenly he realised his mistake. He should have found some rocks to weigh the body down, but it was too late to do anything about it now. If anyone should see him arriving back at the house dripping wet the game would be up; he would just have to take his chance. Jacob glanced around nervously. Satisfied that he was quite alone, he took to his heels, before forcing himself to stop and take his gloves off. With shaking fingers, he hastily filled them with stones and tossed them into the river, throwing the knife in after them. Suddenly, the full horror of what he had done hit him and he sagged against a tree, exhausted. But he couldn't stay; he needed to get home immediately. It was imperative that the staff should think he had been there all night. Forcing one foot in front of another he set off with his head bent. Despite the bitterness of the night, a cold sweat had broken out on his forehead.

He was pleased to find the house in darkness save for one oil light burning on the console table in the hallway. He crept up to his room where he lit a candle, gasping as he saw the blood on the cuff of his shirt. He threw it off, screwed it into a tight ball and stuffed it into the leather bag he used for work. He would have to dispose of it away from the house. Then he washed himself thoroughly and fell into bed. It was only as he lay there, shivering uncontrollably, that another problem presented itself and he sat up abruptly. Biggs's clothes! They were all still in his room. Slipping his arms into the sleeves of his robe, he tiptoed across the landing to Biggs's room where he lit a candle, yanked the man's bag from the bottom of the wardrobe and rammed everything he could find into it. But now he was faced with yet another problem. What was he to do with the bag? He wanted the staff to think that Biggs had simply upped and gone, but it was too late to dispose of his possessions tonight. Finding no alternative, he thrust the bag as far beneath the bed as it would go. He would have to get rid of it at the first opportunity, which wouldn't be easy with the staff always pottering about.

Then, like a thief in the night, he crept back to his room.

'Mr Biggs didn't come home last night,' Mabel informed Jacob the following morning as he was breakfasting in the dining room.

'He didn't?' He kept his eyes fixed on his plate.

'No, sir. I just went up to ask him what time he wanted breakfast an' his bed hadn't been slept in.'

Jacob shrugged. 'I shouldn't worry about it. He's a grown man so quite entitled to stay out if he so wishes. Or perhaps he decided to go back to his own home.'

Mabel's head wagged. 'I don't think he's done that, sir. I spotted his bag all packed an' shoved under his bed. Surely he would have taken it an' told you if he was intendin' on goin'?'

Jacob silently groaned but managed to maintain his composure. 'I'm sure he'll come back for it when he's good and ready, Mabel. But now would you tell Harry I'm ready to leave. I have to be in court early this morning.'

She bobbed her knee and hurried away, leaving Jacob grinding his teeth in frustration. Glancing at the clock he hurried into the hall where Harry was waiting for him.

'All set then?'

'Yes, sir.'

Jacob nodded and followed the younger man from the house just as he did every other normal working day.

The next day, under a large headline, the local evening newspaper reported that the unidentified body of a man had been found floating in the River Anker. The article stated that he had been stabbed, gave a brief description of him and what he had been wearing, and requested that anyone who might know who the man was to come forward to the police.

'Eeh, yer don't think it could be Charlie Biggs, do yer?' Mabel said as she sat reading the paper at the kitchen table.

'It certainly sounds like it could be.' Mrs Batley paused. She was stirring a pan of gravy on the range for their evening meal. 'An' the description o' the clothes he were wearin' fits an' all.

160

Seems too much of a coincidence to me. The judge has just got home, perhaps we should ask him what he thinks.'

Mabel took the newspaper and tapped at the judge's study door. 'Yes?'

Mabel thought he sounded irritated, but then that was no surprise. The judge never went out of his way to be polite to the staff.

'Sir, I thought perhaps yer ought to see . . .' Mabel's voice trailed away as she saw that he already had a copy of the newspaper on his desk.

'I was goin' to show yer the headlines in this evenin's paper but I see you've already got it,' she flustered. 'The chap on the front page . . . the one that's been murdered an' dumped in the river . . . me an' Mrs Batley were wonderin' if perhaps it could be yer friend, Mr Biggs.'

He curled his lip. 'Really, Mabel, you have a very vivid imagination,' he said sarcastically. 'The man they found could have been anybody. He was probably some vagrant that was sleeping in the bandstand.'

'But his description an' what he was wearin' matches—'

Jacob held his hand up to stay her flow of words. '*Please*, I really don't wish to hear any more of this nonsense. I've had a very long day so if you will excuse me I would like to finish my drink in peace before you serve dinner.'

Chastened, Mabel flushed and nodded. 'Yes, sir.' She flew from the room so quickly, she almost tripped on her skirts.

When she entered the kitchen, she found Harry had just returned from Wales and she smiled at him shyly. They still went out together occasionally, although as yet Harry hadn't officially asked her to be his girl, which was very frustrating, but then Mabel lived in hope that one of these days that might change.

'What did he make of it?' Mrs Batley asked as she attacked the potatoes with a masher. The judge loved his mashed spuds.

161

'*Huh!*' Mabel tossed the paper onto the table in disgust. 'I might as well have saved me breath,' she grumbled. 'He'd clearly already read it and he won't even entertain the thought that it might be Charlie Biggs.'

'Ah well, happen the police will get to the bottom of it. But now get into the dinin' room and lay that table fer one, would yer. The mistress is eatin' in her room this evenin'. She don't feel well enough to come down.'

Later, as Mabel was putting away the clean pots, someone rapped on the front door.

'Go an' see who that is,' Mrs Batley told her. 'I'll finish puttin' these away.'

Opening the door, Mabel found two policemen standing on the doorstep and her heart did a little flip.

'We'd like to speak to Judge Jacob Kettle please, miss,' the older of the two informed her.

'Of course, won't you step inside.' They entered, bringing a blast of icy air with them, and politely removed their helmets as Mabel darted off to tell the judge, who asked her to show them into his study.

'How may I help you?' he asked the policemen as they stood in front of his desk.

'You are probably aware that a body has been found floating in the river, sir?'

The judge nodded, his face grave.

'We have reason to believe that it may be a gentleman who was staying with you. He went by the name of Charlie Biggs.'

The judge looked concerned. 'Yes, I do have a guest of that name staying here, although he didn't come home last night . . .' He gripped the back of his chair, looking shocked. 'Goodness me, you don't really think the body is Charlie's, do you?'

'It's possible. We were wondering if you would come with us to the morgue to identify it. And if it is the said Charlie Biggs

162

we'd like to know why he was staying here and where he is from.'

'I can answer that quite easily.' Jacob's heart was hammering although he was outwardly quite calm. 'I have no idea where Charlie comes from exactly, except I know he lived in the East End of London somewhere. I met him occasionally in a gentleman's club I sometimes frequent in London. Then, out of the blue, he turned up here a while back. He was clearly down on his luck so I took pity on him and said he could stay here for a time while he got back on his feet. Rather foolish of me, you might say, gentlemen. After all, he could have been a rogue, but that's me, I'm afraid. I've always been a soft touch for someone who is down on their luck. But now if you like I'll come with you to look at the body. Unpleasant a task as it is, we may as well get it over with.' Jacob was fairly confident that they would never trace Charlie Biggs, for that wasn't his real name.

When he left with a police officer either side of him a few minutes later, Mabel's fertile imagination went into overdrive.

'Eeh, yer don't think the master's been arrested, do yer?' she squeaked, much to Mrs Batley and Harry's amusement.

'I shouldn't think so fer a minute but we'll just have to wait an' see, won't we?' Mrs Batley answered with a grin. What a turn-up for the books that'd be, she thought, then she went back to what she'd been doing.

163

Chapter Twenty-One

The snow started to fall in Sarn Bach three nights after Grace arrived and when she rose the next morning she was sure that she had never seen anything so pretty. In the town where she lived the snow was turned to dirty slush in no time by the many feet that trod the pavements, but here everything looked clean and fresh, as if nature had taken an enormous brush and painted the landscape pure white while they all slept. However, once she was dressed and had made her way down to the kitchen, she found that Aunt Gertie wasn't quite so enamoured of the weather.

'It doesn't take much for us to get snowed in here sitting at the bottom of the valley as we are,' she grumbled. 'Still, at least we have plenty of food in for ourselves and the animals for a few weeks at least.' Her aunt prided herself on their self-sufficiency.

Grace yawned as she took a seat at the table. She had not been sleeping particularly well since her arrival. There were so many memories of Myfanwy everywhere she looked and it made her sad. No one had really mentioned her much as yet and Grace thought perhaps they were afraid of upsetting her, although she had caught Mrs Llewelyn crying softly into her handkerchief a couple of times. She must be missing her too.

After much coaxing, she ate most of the breakfast that Mrs Llewelyn cooked for her and when she had finished her meal, Aunt Gertie asked, 'So what are you planning on doing today,

Grace.' She was in the process of pulling her boots on over a pair of thick woollen socks.

'I, er . . . I *was* thinking of visiting the churchyard. I'd like to say a proper goodbye to . . .' When her voice trailed away her aunt smiled sympathetically.

'What a nice idea. The fresh air will do you good so long as you wrap up warmly. And you could perhaps take some scissors and cut some holly to place on the grave on the way. Myfanwy would have liked that. She always collected holly for the vases at Christmas time for us.'

'But, Gertie . . . the weather. Grace still isn't properly well yet,' Mrs Llewelyn objected as she glanced worriedly towards the window.

Gertie waved her hand dismissively. 'Poppycock! Good fresh air never hurt anyone. A brisk walk will do her far more good than being shut away in here. It's only about two miles or so to the church. No distance at all for a girl like her. Stop mollycoddling her, Cerys,' she said as she went off to see her beloved animals.

Cerys Llewelyn sighed ruefully. 'That told me, didn't it? If you're sure you're up to it I suppose you'd better start getting wrapped up. The old boots you wore the last time you were here are in the cupboard under the stairs if they still fit you. And I've a nice thick woollen hat and scarf you can borrow.'

Ten minutes later, Grace found herself bundled up to the nines, as Cerys put it.

'Right now, you can't go wrong really, just follow the lane at the top of the drive into the village and you'll see the church ahead of you. But if you start to get tired just mind you turn around and come right back.' She adjusted the scarf tied about the girl's neck then with a gentle tap on her backside she sent her on her way.

Grace was panting for breath by the time she reached the top of the hill. Already the snow had found its way over the top of her boots and her feet were wet and frozen, but she was enjoying herself. It was nice to be out in the open air with no one breathing down her neck and fussing over her. From here the sea looked as calm as a millpond and after enjoying the scene for a while, she trudged on. Half a mile or so further on, she came to a bend in the lane and glancing down into the next valley she saw the village below her. It looked like a scene on a Christmas card and knowing that it was downhill from here on she set off again, pausing beside a holly bush laden with bright red berries from which she cut a good-sized bunch. The snow was coming down thick and fast now and her hands and feet were so cold that she couldn't feel them, but she could see the church spire ahead and knowing that she was close spurred her on.

At last she arrived at the lychgate where she stopped to catch her breath and enjoy the quiet of the place. The streets were deserted and there was not a sound to be heard, even the birds weren't singing and Grace had the eerie feeling that she was the only person left on earth. Mrs Llewelyn had told her where Myfanwy's grave was so she skirted the church and marched around to the back of it. She stopped and peered amongst the tombstones, many of them leaning precariously after the many years they had stood there. She spotted Myfanwy's final resting place over by the wall: a simple wooden cross sheltered by a yew tree. Quietly she made her way towards it and stood staring down at the mound of earth covered in snow.

'Hello, my dearest friend,' she whispered as icy tears slid down her cheeks. 'I brought you some holly. Aunt Gertie said it was one of your favourites.' Bending, she reverently placed her offering before the cross and laid her mittened hand on the ground. 'I just want you to know that you will *always* be my best friend and I shall never forget you even though we only got to spend a short time together.' She wondered, as she remembered Myfanwy's visit to her in the hospital, why it was that she had survived and yet her friend had not. Her mother had tried to persuade her that the visit had been nothing more than a dream, but Grace was not convinced.

After gently kissing the cross she turned and left her friend sleeping her eternal sleep to begin the journey back to Beehive Cottage. At the corner of the church she turned to look back and just for a second she was sure that she saw Myfanwy peeping from behind the yew tree with a wide smile on her face. Grace blinked and looked again but there was nothing and she supposed she must have imagined it. With a sad smile, she left the churchyard.

'Why just look at you, you're frozen through,' Mrs Llewelyn scolded when Grace eventually tumbled into the warm kitchen. Within seconds she found herself standing in a puddle of water as Cerys frantically yanked her outer things off her. 'Now go and sit down by the fire while I get you a hot drink,' the woman ordered. 'Otherwise I can see you being ill again and we don't want that, now, do we?'

Grace held her cold hands and feet out towards the roaring fire and as the feeling returned to them, they began to throb painfully. Although she was exhausted, Grace was glad she had gone. She felt better now that she had said a proper goodbye and hoped that from now on she would think of Myfanwy and smile instead of crying all the time.

Shortly after, Aunt Gertie came in and threw a dead chicken onto the table, telling Cerys, 'You may as well get that plucked and in the oven for dinner. It had stopped laying so it's no good to me now.'

Grace shuddered. Aunt Gertie could be heartless, or so Grace thought, when it came to her livestock. 'There's a big difference between livestock and pets,' her aunt had informed her when she'd questioned how she could bring herself to wring a chicken's neck or slaughter a pig she had nurtured for a whole year. 'I feed my livestock well and give them the best life they can have while they're here but I never lose sight of the fact that they are here for a reason. They are our food source.'

Grace understood what her aunt was saying, but she had avoided having too much to do with the livestock. It was too painful knowing what fate was eventually going to befall them!

It snowed steadily for the next few days and just as Aunt Gertie had predicted the lane to the cottage was soon covered in drifts.

'We'll not be getting out of here till the thaw sets in,' she warned Grace. 'So I should prepare yourself for a long stay if I was you. I shall have to tell your mother what's happened. She thought you were only staying for a couple of weeks. I'll ring her this afternoon, that's if the phone lines haven't gone down!'

Grace was quite happy with that, although she missed her mother dreadfully. But at least here she didn't have the oily Charlie Biggs trying to corner her at every opportunity, or her father pawing over her all the time.

The trip to the churchyard had tired Grace more than she had realised and for the rest of the week she was happy to stay in by the fire reading and writing letters to her mother, not that they were able to get out to post them. But when Sunday dawned she asked tentatively at breakfast, 'Will I be allowed to attend the service up at the convent this morning?'

They all looked up from their meals as one and glanced towards the window where the snow was still steadily falling.

'It would be a bit of a hike in these conditions, cariad.' It was Aled who voiced his opinion.

'But I could climb up there through the woods. The snow won't be so deep in there,' Grace answered hopefully. 'And once I come out of the woods I'm almost there. I'm sure I can remember the way. Oh, *please* may I go?'

'I suppose I could always take you,' Aled answered.

She flashed him a grateful smile that lit up her pale face. Her hair had grown back again now and was once more a riot of curls, still a deep rich red that only seemed to emphasise the pallor of her skin. 'Would you? Would you *really*? Oh, *thank you*. I'm sure I can find my own way back if I can only get there and I do so miss going to church. I've been taking instructions at Our Lady of the Angels Catholic Church back home.'

'Really?' Aunt Gertie raised an eyebrow. 'And what do your mother and father make of that?'

'Mother doesn't mind at all and Father hasn't really said much,' Grace told her, skipping away from the table to get ready.

As she had hoped, apart from it being a very steep climb, the paths through the woods were relatively snow-free and she and Aled made good time, although they were both out of breath by the time they reached the cliff top.

'Phew, I just realised I'm not as fit as I used to be,' Aled panted with a grin as he clutched the stitch in his side. 'Still, at least it's all downhill on the way back.' The convent stood before them and Grace's eyes lit up at the sight of it. She had happy memories of the time she had spent there on her last visit.

'Thank you for bringing me,' she told him. 'But you needn't wait for me, really. I shall be back in time for lunch.'

And so, with a wave Aled set off back the way he had come as Grace hurried towards the chapel. The postulants were there already, although she noted none of the villagers had ventured there that day. Angharad, the young woman who had spoken to Grace when she came with Myfanwy, recognised her instantly and smiled at her as the nuns filed in. Then the young priest who would be leading the service arrived and took his place at the altar and the air was filled with song as the nuns began their mass. This priest was much younger than the one Grace remembered. He was tall with silver-blonde hair and violet-blue eyes that seemed to be smiling all the time. Grace briefly thought how handsome he was but then she was swept along with the service and she forgot everything else.

When the service was over, the nuns left the chapel first and Angharad came to have a word with her.

'It's nice to see you again,' she welcomed her. 'And I'm so sorry about what happened to Myfanwy. We said a mass for her and the other five young children from the village who died. I hear you were very ill too?'

'Yes, I was.' Grace nodded solemnly. 'I almost died. But the strange thing is . . . one night when I was in a fever in the hospital I could have sworn that Myfanwy came to see me. It would have been round about the time that she passed away.'

'Perhaps she did come,' the young woman said kindly. 'After all, strange things happen between heaven and earth.'

Grace smiled radiantly. Angharad was the first person who had not pooh-poohed her when she'd spoken of it.

The young priest joined them then and held his hand out to Grace, saying, 'Good morning. Are you from the village?'

Grace quickly explained where she was staying with her aunt and he smiled. 'It seems you may be here for longer than you intended with the snow. I do hope we see you again.'

'Oh, you will,' Grace assured him as he walked away with his black cassock swaying about his long legs.

'That's Father Luke,' Angharad informed her. 'He'll be taking the place of Father Michael when he fully retires in the summer. But now I really must get on. Goodbye, Grace.'

The young woman rushed after the other postulants with her white veil making her almost invisible in the snow, and alone in the chapel Grace let the peace of the place wash over her. It was then that it came to her. One day I shall be a nun, she vowed, then buttoning her coat she headed for the woods. She didn't want to be late for lunch.

Chapter Twenty-Two

December 1908

'Happy birthday, darling. I can't believe my baby is sixteen and all grown up now.' Madeline squeezed Grace's arm as her daughter tucked the blankets on her bed more tightly about her. Although she smiled at her daughter, Madeline's heart was heavy. Grace should be out and about enjoying herself but instead, after leaving school at fourteen, she had become her mother's full-time carer, only leaving the house to shop when it was absolutely necessary and to attend church.

Madeline lifted her arm and pointed to a small box on her dressing table. 'There's something on there I want you to have,' she said weakly and frowning Grace went to fetch it.

'Open it,' Madeline insisted and when Grace did she gasped.

'But I can't accept this,' she whispered as she stared down at the shining hoop of emeralds and diamonds. 'This was your mother's engagement ring and I know how much you treasure it.'

Madeline smiled sadly. 'I'm hardly likely to wear it again, am I?'

'Don't say that.' Grace felt tears at the back of her eyes. Over the last year she had watched her mother fading away before her very eyes. 'You will wear it again when you're better.'

'Oh, my beautiful girl.' Madeline took her hand and stroked it gently. 'I think we both know that isn't going to happen now.'

Grace made to turn away. She didn't want to hear this but Madeline gripped her hand. '*Please* listen,' she implored. 'I don't have long left now, darling, and I'm worried about what will become of you when I'm gone.' As she said this, the sound of her husband's rowdy visitors, drinking and laughing in the drawing room below, drifted up to them and Madeline shook her head. It was an all too regular occurrence now and she didn't like the type of men her husband was associating with at all.

'You're not going anywhere. Not for a long time,' Grace insisted, yet even as the words left her lips she feared they were a lie. Madeline's lips were blue all the time now. Even the tablets the doctor left for her didn't seem to do her any good anymore.

'If . . . no, *when* anything happens to me, I want you to go and live with Aunt Gertie,' Madeline said.

'But what would happen to Father here all alone?' Grace said, shocked.

'He would hardly be alone, would he? He has a house full of friends for half the time now and Mrs Batley and Mabel are here to take care of him. You must do this for me, Grace. I can't bear to think of you here pandering to his whims and growing into an old maid. You're young with your whole life ahead of you and I want you to live it; to do the things I never did and enjoy yourself.'

'But I *do* enjoy myself.' Grace smiled. 'I'm quite happy staying in with you and reading and I love helping Mrs Lockett with the Sunday school children each week.'

Madeline sighed as she stared at the daughter she loved more than her own life. 'There is so much more to life than that, my love.' She traced a finger gently across Grace's smooth cheek. 'One day you will meet a young man and fall in love and then you'll begin your own family.'

'I won't!' Grace's chin came up. 'I don't think I'll ever want to get married. Some of the girls I went to school with are married already, some are having babies but that's not what I want.'

Grace had observed her parents' marriage and already she knew that this was not something she would want. Theirs was a very strange relationship, from what Grace could make of it. They lived together and yet they lived apart and neither of them seemed keen on spending any time together. No, she decided, she would rather live the life of an old maid than be treated as her mother had been. Thinking back, she couldn't remember a single time when her father had shown her even an ounce of affection. It didn't appear to bother Madeline. Truthfully, Grace suspected her mother was happiest when her father was away, which he was every single weekend now and sometimes for the odd night in the week too. She still questioned him occasionally about where he went but all he would tell her was that he visited a club and the friends he brought home with him were also members. Grace dreaded to think what type of a club it might be, for his friends were anything but gentlemen. They were crude and raucous and while they were there she did her very best to keep out of their way, even if it meant spending a lot of time in her room alone.

Now, seeing that her mother was growing tired, Grace drew the curtains. 'I'll let you rest for an hour then I'll bring you a nice tray of afternoon tea.' She kissed her brow and left the room quietly only to almost collide with one of her father's guests as she stepped out onto the landing.

'Oh, I'm so sorry,' she apologised. 'I didn't see you there.'

As he leered at her she smelled the alcohol on his breath. Her father was at work and his visitors were clearly taking full advantage of the fact, helping themselves to his finest whisky and cigars.

'Don't you be apologisin' to me, likkle lady,' he slurred, and if Grace hadn't found him so repulsive she might have found him amusing. He could barely stand straight let alone string a sensible sentence together.

'If you'll excuse me, I have things to do,' she said quietly, making to step past him, but he clearly had other ideas.

173

'Now don't be in such a rush,' he breathed as he placed his hand against the wall to stop her progress. 'Jacob said he 'ad a likkle daughter but I never reckoned yer'd be sho pretty. Why don't you come along to my room so we can shpend a likkle time together, eh?'

Grace was beginning to panic. 'I really don't think that would be such a good id—'

'Ah, Miss Grace, here yer are, I've been lookin' fer you.'

Grace glanced up and saw Mabel striding towards them with her lips set in a straight line and she could have cried with relief. She was glaring at the man and he seemed to shrivel before her very eyes.

'I, er . . . I'll get down to me friend, then,' he muttered and scuttled away like a frightened rabbit.

'*Scum!*' Mabel spat, not really caring if he heard her as she watched his retreating back. 'Was he giving you a hard time, pet?'

'Oh, I just think he's drunk and doesn't really know what he's doing.' Despite her brave words Grace was quaking inside and she wondered what might have happened if Mabel hadn't come along when she did.

'I was just takin' these clean nightclothes into your mam's room,' Mabel told her, then lowering her voice she hissed, 'Try an' keep out o' their way as much as yer can, pet.'

Grace nodded and hurried to her room, locking the door behind her. It seemed that she wasn't safe in her own home anymore but thankfully, after telling her father that she was sometimes nervous of his visitors, he had finally relented and let Harry fix a lock to her door.

Mabel meantime entered Madeline's room to find her sitting up in bed staring anxiously at the door. 'I heard a bit of a commotion outside on the landing,' she told her worriedly.

'Oh, it's nothing to fret about.' The last thing Mabel wanted to do was upset her mistress. The way she saw it the woman had enough to worry about what with the way her husband was carrying on. But Madeline was not going to be put off so easily.

'I heard one of Jacob's guests,' she said persistently. 'Who was he talking to? He sounded as if he was drunk.'

Mabel sighed as she tucked her mistress's clean washing away in the drawers. 'He just had a little spat with Miss Grace,' she admitted reluctantly and Madeline began to chew on her lip.

'I wish I could get her away from here,' she confided. 'I don't like the people Jacob is inviting into our home and I'm afraid that one of them will hurt Grace.' She had never forgotten Charlie Biggs. After Jacob had helped the police with their enquiries following his death, they had recorded a verdict of murder. But they had never apprehended the murderer and Madeline had her own thoughts on that score. Deep down she wondered if Jacob didn't know more about it than he was letting on.

'There ain't much chance o' that happenin' wi' me about,' Mabel said stoutly. 'Yer needn't worry, I keep me eyes peeled.'

'I appreciate that but even so I feel she's at risk.' Madeline lay back against her pillows. 'I think I might suggest that Grace goes to stay with Aunt Gertie for a while. She'd like that.'

'There wouldn't be any point, she'd never leave you,' Mabel sensibly pointed out.

Madeline sighed. 'I suppose you're right but I've just got this bad feeling that something is going to happen and I can't seem to shake it.'

Mabel smiled sympathetically before going about her business.

The next evening, Jacob's visitors all went off to the pub after supper and Jacob retired to his study with a bottle of whisky. It was quite late when Grace, who had been in bed for some time, became aware of the door creaking open allowing the light from the landing to flood into her room.

'Father!'

He was standing in the doorway with a silly smile on his face and even from the bed she could smell the whisky. She cursed herself silently then for forgetting to lock her bedroom door.

'What do you want?' She hopped out of bed and went to stand by the dressing table, wrapping her arms protectively about her chest.

'Jush a little cuddle from my favourite girl.' He was advancing on her, arms outstretched and she began to panic.

Before she could object further he had clutched her to him and as his slobbery lips sought hers she began to struggle and scream. She could feel his hands roving up and down her back then suddenly her mother was there too.

'*Get away from her.*' Madeline rushed forward and seconds later Grace watched the judge's heavy body topple to the floor.

Mabel rushed in and came to a skidding halt as she took in the scene before her.

'*What the hell . . .*' Mabel stared aghast from the judge's prostrate form to Madeline who was clutching Grace protectively to her with one hand while she gripped a bloody, heavy brass candlestick with the other. Both women seemed to be in shock.

'He . . . he was going to hurt her,' Madeline keened, on the verge of hysteria.

Mabel took control of the situation instantly and dropped to her knees. There was blood gushing from a gash on the judge's head and his breathing was ragged.

'Get into bed, Grace,' she ordered and the girl did as she was told. Her eyes were glassy and she was clearly in shock as she cowered beneath the bedclothes.

'Now you help me get the master into his own room,' she ordered Madeline. 'You take his legs an' I'll take his arms.'

But Madeline was trembling uncontrollably and couldn't move.

'*Now!*' Mabel snapped. The judge had taken a rare old wallop from what she could see but from where she was standing he'd got no more than he deserved. It was up to her now to protect the mistress and Grace.

Madeline sprang forward and with every last ounce of strength she had, she somehow managed to help Mabel lug the man's limp body along the landing and into his own room. Once he was on the bed, Mabel told her mistress, 'You get back to bed now. I'll see to the rest and not a word to anyone about what's happened mind!'

'But . . .'

'Just do as I say,' Mabel said bossily as she began to strip the bloodstained clothes from Jacob's body. 'When anyone asks what's happened we'll say we found him on the floor like this. He must have tumbled and banged his head. Now go!'

On legs that suddenly felt as if they had turned to jelly, Madeline stumbled from the room with her hand about her throat, feeling as if she was caught in the grip of a nightmare.

Once she was gone, Mabel washed the master and somehow got him into his nightshirt and under the bedclothes. She then scurried back to Grace's room and scrubbed the candlestick and every bit of evidence that could point to him ever having been there.

'You mustn't tell anyone that your father was in your room tonight,' she warned Grace but the girl was so shocked that Mabel wasn't even sure that she had heard her.

'I'm afraid he has had a seizure.' Dr Busby snapped the lock on his black bag and turned to Madeline with a grave expression on his face. He motioned towards the door.

Once they were out on the landing he stared questioningly at Madeline. 'Can you explain the gash and the bruise on his forehead and the large bruise on his chest?'

Leaning heavily on Mabel's arm, Madeline looked back at him nervously. 'It must have happened when he had the seizure,' she answered, licking her dry lips. 'Mabel found him on the floor of his room when he didn't get up for work this morning and she went to wake him. He must have fallen and cracked his head and his chest on the dressing table or something. She and Harry managed to get him into bed and I sent for you. But will he recover?'

He shook his head. 'It's far too soon to tell at present. But his condition is critical. He's too ill to even consider moving him to the hospital. Can you cope with nursing him here?'

'Yes, we can.' It was Mabel who nodded.

'Good, then for now all you can do is keep him as comfortable as possible and he must be kept quiet.'

Again, Mabel nodded as the doctor made to leave, saying, 'I shall call in again this evening after my surgery, but should you need me before then don't hesitate to contact me.'

As he clattered down the stairs, Madeline sagged against the wall.

'Come on, you look awful yourself. Let's get you back to your room and I'll fetch you a tray of tea,' Mabel said kindly, taking her arm.

But Madeline shook her head and drawing on every ounce of strength she had she pointed towards the stairs. 'No, will you help me downstairs, dear? There are things that I must do. Things that I should have done long ago. Where are Jacob's guests?'

'In the dinin' room fillin' their faces as usual,' Mabel said scathingly as she gently helped her mistress negotiate the stairs.

Outside the dining room, Madeline released her arm and drew herself up to her full height, straightened her skirt and took a deep breath before marching purposefully into the room.

The three men seated at the table all looked towards her, and with her face set, she told them, 'As soon as you have finished your meal I would like you all to pack your bags and leave immediately. Do not *ever* darken my door again!'

Mabel's mouth dropped open.

'What do you mean . . . *leave*?' one of the men said indignantly as he swiped a greasy hand down his waistcoat. There was egg yolk dripping in his beard and Madeline was repulsed at the sight of him, of all of them, in fact; they had less manners than pigs.

'It were Jacob invited us here an' we'll leave when he tells us to.'

'You will leave *now*,' Madeline said with authority. 'My husband, as you are probably all aware, is very ill and unlikely to recover for some time. In his absence I am requesting that you get out *right* now. Otherwise I shall have no choice but to bring the police in to have you evicted from my home. You have twenty minutes!'

The men glared at her but didn't argue and Madeline swept out of the room.

'Phew, yer were brilliant in there,' Mabel said admiringly. 'Do yer reckon they'll go?'

'Oh, they'll go all right,' Madeline said decisively. 'Otherwise I shall have Harry physically throw them out. Now I am going into the drawing room to watch the time. Would you see that they don't take anything that doesn't belong to them? I wouldn't trust them as far as I could throw them.'

'With pleasure!' Mabel was enjoying herself now and heading off to the men's rooms she began to stuff their belongings into their bags, which she tossed down the stairs where the men found them when they left the dining room.

'Jacob ain't going to be none too pleased when he hears how you've treated us when he gets better,' one of the men, a fat greasy little chap with rotting teeth, informed her indignantly.

Madeline eyed him calmly as Mabel held the front door open and Harry stood by in case there was any trouble. Madeline didn't

179

even bother to reply, she just watched as the men trailed out before Mabel closed the door resoundingly behind them.

'Good riddance to bad rubbish!' Mabel declared with satisfaction as she rubbed her hands together. Then side by side they went back upstairs to Jacob's room.

They found him awake and he glared at them. The left side of his face had dropped, making his features look quite grotesque, and the whole of the left side of his body appeared to be paralysed. But his eyes were burning with malice.

'Your visitors have left and I hope we never see them again,' Madeline told him coldly.

He grunted with effort as he tried to speak but all that came out was an unintelligible growl. Dribble was running down his chin and for the merest second Madeline felt pity for him but then it was gone. 'I shall be hiring a nurse to tend you, I'm quite sure you can afford it. Mabel and Mrs Batley already have more than enough to do. I shall also ensure that you are never alone with Grace again, you are despicable!'

Pain flashed in his eyes but she was beyond caring. Her respect for her husband had died a long time ago but at last she was in control and for now at least he could no longer hurt her . . . or Grace.

Chapter Twenty-Three

'But I don't *want* to go,' Grace sobbed later that day when her mother told her of her plans for her. She had decided it might be best for all of them if Grace went to stay at Aunt Gertie's for a while. 'I don't want to leave you.' She was still in shock from what had happened the night before.

'Don't be silly, darling. I have Batty, Harry and Mabel here to look after me,' Madeline told her softly. 'The nurse I have just hired to take care of your father arrives late this afternoon and it will do you good to get away.'

'She's right, pet,' Mabel added, her face strained. 'There's nothin' you can do here an' we'll see as your mam is taken good care of. If anythin' things will be better now that . . .' her voice trailed away but they all knew what she had been about to say. *Now that your father can no longer bully you all!*

'Very well then, I'll go. But I shan't stay for too long,' Grace whimpered. It appeared that the decision had been made for her. Her mother seemed to have summoned some new-found strength from somewhere and for the first time Grace could remember she seemed to be in charge of things.

'Good, then I think you should leave tomorrow,' Madeline said. 'I've already spoken to Aunt Gertie and as always she'll be pleased to see you. There's no sense in delaying. The sooner you are away from here the better, as far as I'm concerned. Now go up and pack whatever you think you'll need. I'll get Harry to go with you on the train.'

But at this Grace shook her head. 'I'm sixteen now, Mother, and hardly need Harry to accompany me.'

Madeline looked doubtful but she didn't argue. 'Very well. But I shall still get Mr Llewelyn to meet you off the train at the other end of the journey.'

Grace was agreeable to that at least and quietly went off to do her packing.

Madeline looked at Mabel helplessly.

'You're doing the right thing,' she assured her mistress. In fact, it had been Mabel's suggestion that Grace should go away for a time. 'She still can't remember anything after her father entered the room last night so it's far better that she's not here for now in case it all comes back to her. We need things to settle down so that you don't get into trouble.'

'But what if my husband improves and tells what happens?' Madeline answered anxiously.

Mabel shook her head. 'I doubt there's much chance of that happening so I should prepare yourself.'

Madeline nodded before heading for her husband's room again.

He was awake, and as she approached the bed he stared at her with reddened eyes full of hatred and grunted with frustration.

'Not so full of yourself now, are you?' Madeline eyed him with contempt and not a single ounce of pity. 'You have bullied me for years,' she went on, her voice little more than a whisper but his hearing appeared to be intact if nothing else, for his eyes stayed fixed on her and she knew that he had heard every word she said. 'But it all ends here. Grace is packing even as we speak to go and stay with Aunt Gertie and I intend to see to it that you never have access to her again. Furthermore, should you recover, I shall be joining her, so you will be free to entertain as many of your *friends* here as you wish without exposing our daughter to danger. *But*' – she leaned so close to him that he felt her breath on his cheek – 'I will tell you now, I hope with all my heart you *don't* recover!'

He tried to shake his head but the effort was too much and he groaned, an inhuman sound that touched her not at all. She had known for years that his feelings for his daughter were unnatural. He had kept the girl a virtual prisoner in her own home but now Madeline intended to make sure that Grace could have a life free from his strict rules. 'And so,' she said finally, 'now that I have hired a nurse to care for you, I shall not come in here again unless it is to see you being loaded into your coffin.' And with that she turned and left the room without so much as a second glance.

'Perhaps I should just go in and say goodbye to Father?' Grace suggested tentatively the next morning before Harry took her to the station.

'No, darling, there's no need for you to do that,' Madeline soothed, then they clung together, their tears mingling. Somehow, they both knew that because of what had happened their lives were never going to be the same again.

'Just always remember how much I love you,' Madeline choked, and then she pushed her towards the door where Harry was waiting with her case.

As promised, Aled Llewelyn was waiting for her at the station in Pwllheli and he greeted her with a hug, noting that Grace was not at all her usual self. It had been four years since she had last visited and he was shocked at the change in her. The child he so fondly remembered was gone and in her place was a girl on the verge of becoming a young woman.

Little was said on the way to Beehive Cottage despite Mr Llewelyn's best attempts to start a conversation so eventually he fell silent, leaving Grace alone with her thoughts. Her aunt and Cerys hurried out to greet her when they arrived and they too saw how subdued she was and put it down to the fact that she was concerned about her father's seizure.

As Aunt Gertie ushered her into the cottage the first thing Grace saw was a broad-shouldered young man sitting at the table plucking a chicken that was intended for their supper that evening. At first, Grace didn't recognise him but then he turned to look at her and her heart skipped a beat. He had Myfanwy's blue eyes and jet-black hair and she realised with a little start that this was Dylan, her brother. They had not seen each other since they were children and she was shocked at how much he had changed. He had grown considerably and was quite tall now. His shirt sleeves were rolled up to the elbows and she could see the muscles rippling in his strong arms as he methodically plucked the bird's feathers, sending them flying into the air to settle like snow on the flagstones. He in turn was noting the change in her and very much liking what he saw. Grace was still quite petite but she was slim and her red hair and green eyes were quite striking.

He inclined his head and smiled and she blushed.

'Now come along, Dylan,' Aunt Gertie scolded him in her usual forthright way. 'We'll be having that chicken for supper tomorrow night the time its taking you to pluck it.' Then turning to Grace, she said, 'We have some soup keeping warm for you until supper's ready.' Grace opened her mouth to tell her aunt that she wasn't hungry but Gertie held her hand up before she got the chance to speak. 'And I'll not take no for an answer, young lady. Even though you're almost grown up now you shall still do as you're told!' And so Grace dutifully took her place at the table as Aled whipped her case away to her room and Cerys carried her food to her.

'There we are, cariad.' She beamed at her. 'And it's right pleased we are to see you, though it's a shame it couldn't have been under happier circumstances. It's right sorry we are to hear how ill your father is.'

'Thank you,' Grace mumbled as she bent her head over her soup bowl. Aunt Gertie made no comment whatsoever. The truth of it was she detested Jacob Kettle with a vengeance and it wasn't in her nature to be a hypocrite and express sympathy that she didn't feel. As far as she was concerned he deserved all that was coming to him.

After forcing some of the soup down, Grace handed an envelope that her mother had sent for her to give to Aunt Gertie and the woman quietly read it, then crossing to a small bureau she put it safely away in one of the drawers.

The chicken was now well and truly plucked, and after cleaning it Cerys popped it in the oven while the cats chased the feathers about the floor causing mayhem.

'And to think I only gave it a good scrub this morning,' she grumbled as she chased the cats outside with a broom. She saw Grace stifle a yawn and suggested kindly, 'Supper will be a good couple of hours yet. Why don't you go up to your room and catch a quick nap while it's cooking? You look fair worn out after that long journey.'

'I think I will.' Grace smiled at her and hurried upstairs. As she stepped into the room where she had spent so many happy hours with the only true friend she had ever had, the memories came flooding back.

'Oh, Myfanwy, I wish you were here,' she whispered brokenly to the empty room. 'Everything is such a mess!' In her mind's eye, she saw again her mother standing over her father with the bloodied brass candlestick clutched in her hand. Her father had tried to rise and it was then that he had made the terrible gurgling sound and clutched at his chest before dropping back to the floor.

The rest of that night had passed in a blur as Grace lay trembling in her bed. And now she was banished to her aunt's, or at least that was what it felt like. Deep down she knew that it was for the best but she was desperately worried about her mother. What if the doctor realised that her father's seizure had been brought on by an attack? Would her mother be sent to prison? And would her father ever recover? Then there was the awful feeling of guilt that was weighing heavily on her. Shouldn't she be hoping that he would get better instead of wishing for him to die? It was evil to wish someone dead, the Bible told her so, but she couldn't help it.

Crossing to the window she stared out to the sea in the distance. The rain was lashing at the glass as if it was trying to gain entry and the landscape was wild and windswept and yet still it managed to look beautiful. Grace sighed and silently prayed for peace.

Chapter Twenty-Four

'So, how is my father?' Grace asked her aunt as Gertie placed the phone back on its cradle after speaking to her mother. She had been there for almost a week now and it was the longest week she could ever remember. As yet she hadn't ventured out of the house, not that the weather lent itself to venturing outside unless it was strictly necessary. The strong winds and rain had been replaced by freezing fog and frost and Aled had forecast there was snow on the way, which meant they might well be snowed in again if it fell thickly.

'There's no change,' her aunt informed her.

'None at all?'

Gertie shook her head. 'But your mother sounds well. Better than I've heard her for some long time, in fact, and she sends you her love and said to tell you you're not to worry about anything. Apparently, the nurse she has hired is very efficient and your father is receiving the best of care.'

Grace nodded and began to pace restlessly about the room. She loved her aunt and she loved staying with her, although the visits no longer held the same magic they'd had when she'd had Myfanwy to keep her company. But then she supposed it was also due to the fact that she had been just a child then. She was a young woman now and soon she would have to decide what she wanted to do with her future. She was still pacing when the door opened and Dylan stepped into the room admitting a blast of icy air which made the fire roar up the chimney.

'Shut the door, cariad, you're letting the warm out,' Cerys scolded. She was rolling out pastry to make a rabbit pie for dinner, but despite her scolding she smiled at him warmly before teasing, 'And what brings you back so soon? Two visits in one week, indeed, when we're usually lucky to catch a glimpse of you once a month.'

When Dylan blushed furiously, Cerys had to hide her amusement.

'Tad is doing some repairs to the boat today so we couldn't go out.' When he glanced towards Grace and blushed an even deeper shade of red, Cerys's suspicions were confirmed. If she wasn't very much mistaken her grandson was rather taken with young Grace and she was pleased with the idea. In her opinion, he could do far worse for himself than this sweet girl.

'Then in that case you can take this young lady out for a walk,' she told him with a wry grin. 'Afore she walks a hole in the floor. A breath of fresh air would do her good.'

Grace opened her mouth to object but seeing the determined look on Cerys's face she decided it might be simpler to do as she was told.

Shortly after, when Grace had wrapped up warmly, she and Dylan set off and headed in the direction of the cove. Grace was a little tongue-tied. She had never been alone with a young man before and was painfully aware that her father would have strongly disapproved of the fact.

'So how long will you be staying?' Dylan asked eventually.

Grace shrugged. 'I'm not too sure to be honest. My father is ill and . . .'

When her voice trailed away he glanced at her sympathetically. 'That must be very worrying for you.'

Grace flushed and chose not to answer. How could she without making herself appear very heartless? There was a strange expectant stillness everywhere, even the birds were not singing, as if the world was waiting for something to happen.

'So you fish in the winter as well as the summer, do you?' Grace asked, hoping to bridge the silence that had fallen between them.

With his hands thrust deep into his coat pockets, Dylan nodded as he kicked at a stone. 'Oh aye, we fish all year round, weather permitting. We would have been out today had we not had a problem with the boat. No doubt me dad will fix it and we'll be back out tomorrow.' He looked at her directly then and asked, 'And do you work?'

Grace shook her head. 'Not as yet. Funnily enough I was only thinking about what I might like to do this morning.'

'Any ideas?'

'I thought perhaps I might like to be a teacher. Or perhaps a governess, I haven't really had any training for any other sort of work but I have helped the local vicar's wife run the Sunday school and I enjoyed that.'

'I see. Will your father agree to you doing that sort of work? From what I've heard your aunt say about him he sounds to be quite strict.'

'He is,' Grace conceded. 'And if it were up to my father I wouldn't work at all. He says there's no need for me to work but I'd like to.'

'I can understand that.' Dylan grinned. 'Ever since I was a little lad all I've wanted to do was go to sea with me tad and I can't really see me ever doing anything else now. It can be a hard life, particularly in the winter when the sea is rough, and we've had more than a few close calls, I don't mind telling you, but I'm content and I suppose that's what matters.'

Grace glanced at him with a new respect. He was very open and honest, much as his sister had been, and thoughts of her brought a sudden lump to her throat.

189

'I . . . still miss your sister,' she told him falteringly and she saw pain flash briefly in his eyes.

'So do I . . . we all do,' he admitted. 'But me mam reckons as long as she lives on in our hearts she'll never be far away.'

They had reached the cliff top now and they stood side by side enjoying the view of the sheltered little cove far beneath them.

'Myfanwy brought me here once to peep at some baby birds in a nest on the face of the cliff,' Grace told him, and for the first time she smiled at the memory.

He chuckled. 'Myfanwy was a tomboy. Me mam allus said she should have been born a lad. She was always into mischief. Do you want to go down there?'

Grace nodded so they headed towards the steep path that led down the side of the cliff. It was a hard descent and by the time they reached the sand Grace's cheeks were glowing and she was out of breath. Frost had formed on areas of the beach and in the eerie grey light that had suddenly settled about them it shone like strands of silver ribbons.

They walked in silence for a time, listening to the waves lapping the shore, content in each other's company, but then Dylan suddenly sniffed the air and said, 'I think we should be heading back. It's going to snow any time now and the climb back up the cliff is bad enough without having to slip and slide all over the place.'

They hurried towards the cliff path. Grace had witnessed how quickly the weather could worsen in Wales and she had no wish to be stranded on the beach. They had almost reached the top when the first flakes of snow began to flutter down.

As Dylan took her hand to help her up the last few steps his heart began to race. There was something about Grace that attracted him as no other girl ever had. Since she'd arrived, he'd found that he was constantly thinking about her, and when he was with her he felt happy.

The realisation made colour flood into his cheeks and once

Grace was on safe ground he released her hand so abruptly she almost stumbled.

She glanced at him questioningly but he was striding towards the woods, keen to be back at the cottage. By the time they reached the back door the snow was already beginning to settle and Grace was breathless.

'Just in time,' Aunt Gertie commented as they stumbled into the kitchen.

Grace was shivering and after noting the way Dylan shepherded her towards the fire, Gertie glanced at Cerys and grinned.

'So, did you have a good walk then?' Gertie enquired as they all sat down to a meal. The rabbit pie stood steaming in the middle of the table smelling so appetising that it made Grace's stomach rumble with anticipation. There were also dishes full of buttery potatoes, carrots and peas and a big jug of thick gravy.

Grace nodded. 'Yes, we did, we walked down to the cove but it started to snow so we hurried back.'

'Just as well, the weather can catch you unawares here.'

The main meal was followed by one of Cerys's delicious jam roly-poly puddings, which she served with cream so thick that it stuck to the spoon.

'Oh, I'm so full I can hardly move,' Grace groaned as she clutched her stomach. It had been a long time since she had eaten such a big meal but she'd thoroughly enjoyed every mouthful. The fresh air had given her an appetite. 'I propose Dylan and I do the dirty pots. It's the least we can do after you've gone to all the trouble of preparing and cooking it.'

'I won't argue with an offer like that.' Cerys grinned. 'I might just sit by the fire and put my feet up for a while, though a nice cup of tea wouldn't go amiss.'

'We can do that too.' Grace hurried away to put the kettle on as Dylan began to clear the dirty pots onto the large wooden draining board.

Soon after Gertie and Cerys were sitting at either side of the fireplace with steaming cups in their hands while the young people washed and dried the dirty dishes.

'If I'm not very much mistaken, our Dylan is smitten with your Grace,' Cerys whispered.

Gertie glanced towards them and nodded. 'I reckon a blind man on a galloping horse could see that,' she commented with a wry smile. 'And I have to say he could do a lot worse. Grace has the temperament of an angel, just like her mother, and one day she'll make someone a very good wife.'

Once they'd finished the washing up, Dylan looked regretfully at the fading light outside. 'I suppose I ought to be heading off.'

'And when might we expect to see you again?' Cerys enquired as she handed him his muffler.

Glancing towards Grace, Dylan flushed. 'I'm not too sure but it will be soon, no doubt.' He moved towards the door, hoping Grace would follow him. When she did, his face broke into a wide grin. 'Till the next time then. Goodbye for now. Goodbye, Gertie.'

Cerys smiled at him and called, 'You mind how you go now, lad. You've a fair way to walk and it will be full dark afore you get home.'

At the door, Grace smiled at him and said, 'Thank you for the walk. I really enjoyed it. We shall have to do it again.' Then leaning forward, she planted a gentle kiss on his cheek and his heart began to race. Could it be that she felt the same way as he did? He hoped so.

'I did too,' he assured her. 'I'll be back just as soon as I can. Goodbye for now.'

He left and Grace excused herself and went to her room to read her Bible, feeling warm inside. In Dylan she felt she had found a friend.

The following Sunday, Grace decided to attend the service up at the convent. She hadn't ventured out since her excursion with Dylan, mainly because it had been snowing heavily ever since. So she set off early, unwilling to be late. She arrived just in time to see the young postulants streaming into the chapel, their white habits making them look pure and virginal. They were followed by the older nuns and behind them was Father Luke, who would lead the service. She remembered him from the last time she had visited.

Once inside the nuns took their places at the front of the chapel while Grace seated herself towards the back. Unsurprisingly, given the weather, there were no other worshippers from the village.

As always Grace felt at peace as she sang and worshipped with the nuns and when the mass was over she sat on when everyone else had left, feeling happy and content. A noise behind her made her start and she saw Father Luke hurrying down the central aisle.

'Oh, I'm sorry if I startled you.' He smiled apologetically. 'I forgot my Bible. I'm sure I'd forget my head if it wasn't screwed on.' He went to retrieve it then came back and took a seat beside her. 'Haven't we met before?'

Grace nodded. 'Yes, I always come to the services when I'm staying with my aunt at Beehive Cottage.'

'Of course.' His grin showed off his white teeth and made him look incredibly young. 'It's Grace, isn't it? You've grown up since the last time I saw you.'

She nodded thinking that he looked different too. He seemed more grown up than she remembered and she wondered how old he might be. Probably mid- to late twenties, she judged.

'Is something troubling you, Grace?' Father Luke had noticed the haunted look in her eyes.

'No . . . well . . . yes, my father is very ill back at home.' The words had spewed out before she could stop them but then she found him incredibly easy to talk to.

'Ah, I see, and you are concerned for him?'

Grace flushed a deep brick red as guilt flooded through her, but how could she tell him the truth, or anyone else for that matter. Instead she remained silent as she twisted her fingers together in her lap.

'Shall we pray for him together?' he suggested and she sprang up as if she had been burned.

'Er . . . no . . . thank you, I should be going now. My aunt will worry about me if I'm late.' She suddenly felt flustered. She could smell the scent of soap and incense oil on his clothing and she was finding it hard to tear her eyes away from him.

'Of course.' He too rose from his seat. 'Perhaps another time then? And I hope your father recovers.'

She inclined her head and raced out of the chapel, her cheeks flaming. For a few brief minutes back there she had found peace but now once again she was back in a living nightmare and she had no idea how to stop it.

Chapter Twenty-Five

Madeline stared down at the figure on the bed. Jacob had shown no signs of recovery in over two weeks and the doctor had grimly told her that it was possible he might never be the man he had once been. Now all her concerns were for Grace; how could she ever bring her back to live here when her father was in such a state? Thankfully the frequent phone calls she had with Gertie assured her that the girl was safe for now but what of the future?

'Do you have everything you need?' she enquired of her husband, for she knew Nurse Matthews expected it of her, which was the only reason she had ventured into his room again.

A loud grunt was her answer as Nurse Matthews appeared at her side to ask, 'Would you mind staying with him for a few minutes, ma'am, while I fetch his tea tray up from the kitchen?'

'Of course not,' Madeline answered graciously although her heart began to pound. Just the thought of being alone with him, even though he was now defenceless, made her break out in a cold sweat.

Seconds later the door closed behind the portly woman and Jacob's eyes bored into her, full of hatred and rage.

'I'm sorry it had to come to this, Jacob.' Her voice was little more than a whisper but she knew that he heard every word. 'But at least now I know Grace is safe from you and your friends.'

His one good hand began to thump the blanket in frustration and his head thrashed from side to side but she went on, 'I am seriously thinking of asking Aunt Gertie to keep her there indefinitely.'

The grunting became louder but it evoked no pity in her. As far as she was concerned he deserved everything he had got.

By the time the nurse entered the room some minutes later he was in such a state that the woman dropped the tray onto the bedside table and immediately began to prepare his medication. 'He has such rages,' she confided as she gently lifted his head and began to trickle the laudanum into his mouth but she had no sooner started than his hand came up and he slammed the glass out of her hand. It flew across the bed leaving puddles on the bedspread and she tutted. 'Now, now, sir. That's quite enough of that. Didn't the doctor tell you that it wasn't good for you to get agitated?' She turned to Madeline and suggested primly, 'It might be best if you were to leave, ma'am.'

Madeline nodded, only too happy to do as she was told. Once out on the landing she paused and took a great gulp of air as her hand pressed against her heart. It was beating wildly and she felt very unwell, even so she knew there were things that she must attend to so she cautiously made her way down to the kitchen where she found Harry sitting at the table enjoying a tea break.

'Ah, Harry. . . I wonder if you could go into town for me please and ask my husband's lawyer if he would be kind enough to visit me at his earliest convenience. Today if possible.'

Harry nodded and rose from his seat. 'May I tell him what you wish to see him about, Mrs Kettle?'

'Yes, you may. Tell him I wish to make a will.'

They had all noticed her pallor and the bluish tinge about her lips as she came in, and at her words, Mrs Batley looked very worried but she said nothing until her mistress had left the room. 'I don't like the sound o' that,' she commented. 'An' the mistress looks right poorly. Happen all this upset is takin' its toll on her, poor lass.'

Harry nodded in agreement as he shrugged his coat on. Outside the snow lay thick on the ground and he knew he would be quicker going on foot. Luckily, the judge's office wasn't that far away so he reckoned he could be there and back in half an hour if he put a spurt on.

'Make sure yer put yer muffler on an' all,' Mabel advised. 'You'll need it today. It's bitter out there.'

He paused to stare at her for a moment as if he was considering saying something, but then aware that Mrs Batley was present he nodded and slipped away.

That evening, Harry sat reading the newspaper till Mrs Batley went to bed then, blushing furiously, he motioned for Mabel to join him at the table.

'There's been something I've been wanting to say to you for a long time,' he began licking his lips and looking decidedly uncomfortable. 'An' I've no doubt when I've said it you'll laugh in me face . . . but the thing is . . . the thing, is I have feelin's for you, Mabel.' When she went to say something, he held his hand up to silence her. 'No, *please* let me finish, lass. This ain't easy for me. You see I know a girl like you could have your pick of any chap she fancied. You're kind an' beautiful whereas I . . . Well, basically I ain't much of a catch for anybody, am I, wi' me gammy legs an' nothin' much to offer you! But the thing is . . . I love you; I've loved you from the first second I set eyes on you, if truth be told but I was too afraid you'd laugh at me. I suppose what I'm sayin' is, I want you to be my girl but I'll quite understand if you turn me down.'

'*Turn you down?*' Tears were glistening in Mabel's eyes as she laughed and grasped his large hands in her smaller ones.

'Oh, Harry, you're the most handsome, wonderful man I ever

met and I'd live in a hut with you if need be! You'll never know how long I've longed for you to say that! You see, I love you too and I'd be proud to be your girl!'

'You *would*?' He looked shocked, then ecstatic. 'Just so long as you realise it could be some time before I have a home to offer you?'

'I don't care how long we have to wait.' And then their lips joined and all was right with the world.

At that moment Mrs Batley appeared in her dressing robe. She had forgotten to take her book to bed with her and had popped down to fetch it. The sight that met her eyes brought a wide smile to her face.

'An' about time too!' she commented wryly. 'I was wonderin' when you pair would finally see what was starin' you in the face. I was beginnin' to think I'd have to bang your heads together to make yer see a bit o' sense.'

'I'm Harry's girl now, it's official,' Mabel told her, her eyes never leaving his face and again Mrs Batley grinned and grabbed her book, chuckling. 'To my mind you've been that since the first time you clapped eyes on him.' And she scuttled out of the kitchen, leaving the love birds to it.

Madeline took to her bed again. Now that she knew Grace was safe and her affairs were in order she suddenly felt exhausted. After a few days of this Mrs Batley called the doctor.

'I fear the shock of all that's happened has taken its toll on her,' he told Mrs Batley.

'But surely there's *something* you can do!' Mrs Batley said.

Dr Busby shook his head. 'I'm afraid there's not,' he admitted. 'In truth with her heart being as weak as it is I'm shocked that she has survived this long. But don't give up hope. Mrs Kettle has been very ill before and she has rallied. We can only hope that she will do the same again.'

Some days later the phone in the hall rang and Mrs Batley's heart skipped a beat. Harry and Mabel were in town and Nurse Matthews was upstairs, which only left her to answer it. Usually she left it to one of the others as she hated the damned thing with a vengeance. She approached it gingerly, as if it might leap off the table and bite her. Tentatively she lifted the receiver and held it to her ear.

'He-hello,' she whispered nervously. She really didn't like these new-fangled things, as she considered them to be, not at all.

'Who is this?'

'It's Mrs Batley, ma'am. Mrs Kettle's housekeeper.'

'Then go and fetch her and tell her Aunt Gertie is on the phone.'

'I, er . . . can't do that, I'm afraid. Mrs Kettle is ill in bed.'

'Ill, you say? What is wrong with her?'

'It's her heart, ma'am.'

'I see.' Aunt Gertie sounded concerned now. 'And how long has she been like this?'

'For some days now.' Sweat had broken out on Mrs Batley's brow and her mouth was as dry as the bottom of a bird cage.

'And is her condition serious? What I mean is, should I be bringing Grace home to see her?'

'I reckon that might be a good idea,' Mrs Batley told her. 'The doctor told us there's nothin' else he can do fer her now so we can only hope that she rallies round again.'

'And her husband, Jacob, how is he?'

'The same.' Mrs Batley sighed. It wasn't easy having two invalids to run around after. 'There's been no change at all an' the doctor reckons the longer he goes on like this the less chance there is of him ever recoverin'.'

'Then in that case I think it might be wise if Grace and I paid a visit. The problem is, we are snowed in here. It could be days or even weeks before we're able to get to the station. In the meantime, I shall be in constant touch and will ring every day but if either of them get any worse please ring me immediately and please pass on a message to Madeline for me. Tell her that Grace is well. That will be at least one thing less for her to worry about.'

Mrs Batley nodded vigorously as if somehow Gertie could magically see her. 'I will, ma'am. Good day.'

The phone went dead and she hastily dropped the receiver back into the cradle before scuttling back to the sanctuary of her kitchen where she felt safe.

In Beehive Cottage, Gertie was worriedly chewing her lip. Should she tell Grace that her mother was ill or keep the news to herself until they were able to go to her? After a time she decided that Grace should be told, she was a young woman after all and Gertie was worried that should anything happen to Madeline and Grace realised that she hadn't been honest with her she would never forgive her. And so shortly after, she sat the girl down and relayed what Mrs Batley had told her. Grace sat silent for a time before bursting into tears.

'I should never have come,' she wailed. 'I knew she needed me.'

'She is being perfectly well cared for,' Gertie pointed out. 'And the second the weather improves we shall go to her.'

From that moment on Grace spent almost every minute gazing from the window praying for the weather to improve.

True to her word, Aunt Gertie phoned every single day for the next few days with Grace hovering anxiously at her side. Like Grace, she was desperately worried and felt frustrated because she couldn't go to her.

But then suddenly the calls stopped abruptly.

'Perhaps I should give her a ring just to make sure that everything is all right there?' Mabel suggested. Luckily, she didn't have a fear of the phone as Mrs Batley did. They all agreed that this would be a good idea but when Mabel tried the number she got nothing.

'The phone is dead,' she told Harry and Mrs Batley. 'I wonder if the snow has brought the line down or something?'

Harry nodded in agreement. 'That sounds the most likely. You'll just have to keep trying until you can get through again.'

It was a whole week later before Dylan finally managed to visit Beehive Cottage again to tell them that the train services had been resumed. The snow had finally stopped falling some days before and although it was still bitterly cold, the thaw had set in, making the lanes treacherously slippy.

Grace was so thrilled to hear the news that she threw her arms about Aunt Gertie and Dylan found himself wishing it was he that she had turned to for comfort.

'The trains couldn't run for over a week because of the snow drifts on the lines,' he told them as he sat with two hands round a steaming mug of hot chocolate.

'Hmm, I can quite believe it. We've had it drifting up the doors and windows here,' Gertie told him as she stroked Grace's hair. 'It brought the phone lines down as well and goodness knows how long it will be before anybody comes to repair them,' she grumbled. 'Still, if you say the trains are running again it isn't all doom and gloom. Me and Grace will catch one back to the Midlands tomorrow. I'm keen to check on how Madeline is. Hopefully we will find her on the mend when we get there.'

'Make sure you set out in plenty of time to get to the station then,' Dylan warned. 'The lanes are covered in ice.'

Gertie and Grace set off early the next morning and eventually boarded a train from Pwllheli and settled into one of the carriages. It had taken them twice as long as it normally would to get from the cottage to the train station, for just as Dylan had warned the roads were still treacherous.

The journey took two hours longer than it should have done and it was late afternoon by the time the train pulled into Trent Valley railway station in Nuneaton, it was getting dark. By then both Grace and Gertie were shivering with cold and stiff from sitting. They heaved the small bags they'd brought with them onto the platform and set off for Grace's home. All Gertie could think about was a nice hot cup of tea, while all Grace could think about was seeing her mother.

They entered the house by the back door and Grace instantly noticed that Mrs Batley's eyes were red and swollen. She was sitting by the fire sniffing into a large white handkerchief and the greeting that had been on Grace's lips died as she dropped her bag onto the floor and asked, 'Why, my dear Batty, whatever is the matter?'

'Eeh, pet . . . It's right good to see yer . . . But yer've come too late. Yer see . . . yer poor mam has passed away.'

Grace heard no more as the floor rushed up to greet her.

Chapter Twenty-Six

Grace sat numbly staring into the fire as her Aunt Gertie hovered over her with a bottle of smelling salts in her hand in case they were needed again.

'So what happened?' Gertie asked eventually. She was in shock herself but trying not to show it in front of Grace.

'I took her breakfast tray up as usual an' I couldn't wake her.' Mrs Batley started to cry again and great fat tears rolled down her plump cheeks. 'She must have gone peaceful in her sleep, which is somethin' to be thankful for I suppose, God rest her sweet soul.'

Grace felt as if the woman's voice was coming from a long way away. She was trapped in a nightmare, surely, and she would wake up in a minute and all of this would just have been a terrible dream. But it wasn't a dream and slowly it began to sink in. Her mother was gone, she would never see her again and she hadn't even been here to say goodbye to her.

'And how is Jacob? Does he know?' Gertie forced herself to ask.

It was Mabel who answered, Mrs Batley was crying too hard. 'He's the same, no change. And yes, he does know.'

'Right then, I suggest we get something hot into this young lady,' Aunt Gertie ordered. 'She's had a long journey and she's in shock.' So far Grace hadn't shed a single tear but her aunt had no doubt they would come later and the sooner the better as far as she was concerned. It would do her no good to bottle things up. Mabel scuttled away to lift the singing kettle from the range and make the tea as Gertie eased Grace's arms out of her coat. The girl just sat there and let her do it.

'I couldn't let you know we were coming because the snow brought the telephone lines down,' she told them. 'But I'd be grateful if you could get a couple of bedrooms ready for us. We will no doubt be staying for a while now. There will be things that need seeing to.'

Mrs Batley heaved a sigh of relief. Gertie was obviously thinking of the funeral. 'Miss Grace's room is just as she left it. It'll only need the fire lightin' an' a hot brick puttin' in the bed. An' it'll take us no time at all to get another room ready for you.'

'And where is Madeline now?' Gertie asked then with a catch in her voice. As painful as it was someone had to take control and get things organised.

'The undertakers came an' took her away to the chapel o' rest after the doctor had been an' issued the death certificate this mornin',' Harry told them grimly.

Gertie nodded. 'Right, it's too late to do anything else today. I suggest we all get a good night's rest and then I will speak to Madeline's solicitor first thing in the morning. Jacob is clearly in no state to do it. I assume she had a solicitor?'

'Oh yes, she did.' Mrs Batley sniffed and nodded vigorously. 'It was Mr Mackenzie from the master's law firm in the town. She had him out here not so long ago to make a new will an' me an' Nurse Matthews witnessed it for her. He's been back a few times since an' all for signatures an' things.'

'Good, then that should make things easier.' Gertie sank into the chair opposite Grace and gratefully accepted the tea that Mabel offered as silence settled on the room. Suddenly it seemed there was little left to say.

Sometime later Mrs Batley served dinner, hot jacket potatoes dripping with butter and a steaming cottage pie, but none of them seemed to have much of an appetite and they merely picked at the food. Grace didn't even attempt to eat hers at all and most of it was thrown away. The only one who did it justice was Nurse Matthews. As Mrs Batley confided later that evening, the woman had an appetite like a horse.

'So, how has Jacob taken the news of his wife's death?' Gertie asked the nurse, who was piling her plate high.

'It's hard to tell with him not being able to speak,' she answered with butter dripping down her chin.

'Hmm, well I dare say I should come up to see him.' Gertie didn't look overly enthusiastic. 'Although, as you say, I doubt he will be able to express his wishes regarding her funeral. I suppose there is no chance of him attending?'

The nurse shook her head. 'None whatsoever. He can't even get out of bed, he's completely paralysed down one side.'

Gertie nodded. 'Very well. Then unless she expressed any preferences in her will, Grace and I will have to do as we think she would have wished.' She leaned over and squeezed Grace's hand. That small action from her usually undemonstrative aunt was Grace's undoing, for suddenly the tears sprang to her eyes, sparkling on her long dark lashes before gushing down her cheeks.

Almost an hour later, Gertie stood outside Jacob's bedroom door with Grace at her side and steeled herself to face him.

'Ready?' She gave Grace an encouraging smile and when the girl nodded she tapped at the door and entered.

Jacob's head turned immediately in her direction and she tried hard not to let her shock show on her face. He was a wreck and it was hard to remember him as he had once been: upright and handsome.

'Jacob.' She inclined her head as his eyes bored into hers. They had never had any respect for each other and she hadn't expected things to be different now.

205

'I have asked Harry to request Mr Mackenzie to visit me first thing in the morning and then I will make the funeral arrangements for Madeline.'

His response was a grunt but his eyes had already left hers and were seeking Grace who stood close behind her. Grace nervously stepped into his line of vision and instantly his face softened and he held his hand out to her imploringly. Grace hesitated then took a step closer, clearly reluctant to touch him, and pain flashed in his eyes as he began to make guttural noises.

'Now, now, the patient is becoming agitated, perhaps it would be better if you came back later.' Nurse Matthews hurried to stand protectively at the side of the bed but he growled deep in his throat and lashed out at her as Grace retreated further back towards the door. Aunt Gertie ushered her out onto the landing, alarmed to see that the colour had drained from Grace's face and she was shaking.

'There's no need for you to go back in there if you have no wish to,' she told her niece. 'But now come along to your room. You've had a long tiring day. Everything will look a little better after a good night's sleep.'

Grace doubted that anything would ever look better again but she did as she was told.

The next day, Mr Mackenzie sat opposite Gertie in the drawing room as she stared back at him, her back straight and her hands folded primly in her lap.

'First of all, may I offer my condolences?' he said politely. 'Mrs Kettle was a genuinely lovely person and I'm sure that she will be sadly missed.'

Gertie inclined her head as he removed Madeline's last will from his bag and perched his steel-framed glasses on the end of his nose. He then cleared his throat and began, 'Ahem . . . it is usually customary to read the will following the funeral service but Mrs Kettle specifically requested that should anything happen to her I should share it with you right away. It is all very straightforward fortunately. She wishes you to now become Grace's legal guardian until she comes of age. I shall ensure that Grace has an allowance each month and also make an allowance to you to cover her board and keep should she wish to return to Wales with you for the foreseeable future. That, of course, will be entirely her decision. I have also promised to make sure that Mrs Batley has a sum of money each month to cover the running costs of the house, food, coal and the staff wages. However, should Judge Kettle recover sufficiently he will then take over control of his finances again, but Mrs Kettle did state that should this happen she would prefer Grace to stay with you.' He shook his head at this stage. 'Unfortunately, Dr Busby informs me that this is unlikely to happen. Indeed, the chances are that he could have another seizure at any time and it is unlikely he would survive it. The funeral arrangements Mrs Kettle was content to leave up to you and Grace. She thought perhaps Grace would wish to choose the hymns for the service, etc. Finally, should anything happen to the judge, the house, contents and any monies would all pass to Grace.' He peered at her over the top of his glasses and enquired, 'Is that all clear? Are there any questions you would like to ask?'

'None at all thank you, sir.' Gertie shook her head and he returned the will to his bag and took off his glasses.

'Then in that case I will wish you good day, ma'am. I realise you have arrangements to make but if I can be of any assistance in any way at all please don't hesitate to get in touch.'

'Thank you, Mr Mackenzie.' She rang the bell for Mabel who showed the lawyer to the door. Nurse Matthews was in the hallway and he stopped to have a brief chat with her so Mabel left them to it.

Gertie then went in search of Grace who she found sitting staring from her bedroom window. 'Ah, here you are.' After taking a seat, she carefully explained the contents of her mother's will to her and Grace nodded. It was just what she would have expected.

'If you don't mind, Aunt Gertie, I think I would like to come and live with you in Wales,' she said.

Gertie nodded. 'Of course I wouldn't mind,' she assured her.

At her kind words, Grace bowed her head and wept broken-heartedly. Gertie gathered the girl's shaking body into her arms and rocked her to and fro and Grace clung to her like a lifeline until the tears subsided slightly, then she frowned. 'The trouble is, I don't think my father will be very happy about me going,' she choked.

Gertie sniffed. 'Your father has *more* than enough people here to look after him so don't you get feeling guilty. You are far too young to be devoting your life to an invalid. When we get home we can perhaps think of something to fill your time so you don't get bored. Your father is actually a very wealthy man so there is no need for you to work if you have no wish to.'

'I want to do something but I don't quite know what yet,' Grace confessed miserably. All she could think about at that moment was the loss of her mother and what an enormous hole she would leave in her life. Without her, things would never be the same again.

Her aunt patted her hand. 'There's plenty of time for you to think about it; no rush at all. Meanwhile I have the vicar calling shortly to make the arrangements for your mother's funeral. Perhaps we could all sit down and plan it together?'

Grace gulped as tears started to her eyes again. It seemed that they were never very far away at present.

Two days later, Grace ventured into her father's room again and once more he became agitated at the sight of her, holding his hand out to her imploringly. Grace knew that she should take it but the thought of touching him made her shudder so she stood a safe distance from the bed.

'Mother's funeral will be on Friday, Father,' she informed him primly with her hands clasped tightly at her waist. 'And when it is over I shall . . . I shall be returning to Wales with Aunt Gertie.'

'*Ugh . . . ugh . . . ugh!*' His head began to thrash wildly from side to side and dribble oozed down his chin, but still Grace made no move towards him.

Seeing how distraught he was becoming, Nurse Matthews laid down the book she had been reading and hurried to the side of the bed.

'You'd best leave, miss.' The nurse was already pouring a few drops of laudanum into a glass of water. 'You're upsetting my patient.'

Grace stared at her father for a second longer. Then, only too happy to do as she was told, she left, closing the door quietly behind her. Once outside the bedroom she stood for a moment with her hand pressed over her mouth. The man she had just left holding his hand out to her was her father but all she had felt for him was revulsion.

On the day of the funeral the weather was abysmal. Rain lashed at the windows and the sky was low and grey. The service was conducted by Reverend Lockett, a long-standing friend of Madeline's, but Grace hardly heard a word of it. The church was full to capacity. Every one of the lawyers from the firm that Jacob had inherited from his uncle were there to pay their respects as well as many of his colleagues from the court. Word had spread of Madeline's death and, unfortunately, there were also some of the people Jacob had had staying at the house as his guests and Grace recognised one of them as the man who had waylaid her on the landing. He smiled at her lasciviously as she passed him in the church on her way to the front pew but she merely glared at him scornfully. And then came the interment but Grace didn't cry. The grief she was feeling went way beyond tears. As she watched the rain wash across her mother's fine mahogany coffin as it was lowered into the grave, and listened with half an ear as the reverend chanted the words of the burial service, she felt numb; the tears would come later.

Aunt Gertie was gently nudging her and she realised with a start that it was time to throw the handful of earth she was holding into the grave. It landed with a dull thud on the coffin and the rain instantly turned it to mud that smeared the brass name plate. And then at last it was over and Aunt Gertie took her elbow and led her away as the freezing rain stung their faces.

Back at the house Mrs Batley and Mabel had laid on a spread fit for a king and many of the mourners took full advantage of it, but Grace couldn't eat a thing. Instead she found a quiet corner and tried to hide away. People constantly approached her to offer their condolences but she could find no words so simply inclined her head, hoping they would soon go away. At last she heard the door close on the last guest and then Mrs Batley and Mabel were busy carrying the dirty pots to the kitchen. Normally Grace would have happily pitched in to help but today she sat on, locked away in her own little world of grief.

'Poor little lass.' Mrs Batley sighed as she emptied a tray full of dirty glasses onto the large wooden draining board. 'She don't even seem to be aware o' what day it is.'

Mabel nodded in agreement as she paused to throw some nuggets of coal onto the fire. 'Well they do say as grief takes different folks different ways. Perhaps she'll be better when she's away from here. It ain't exactly been a happy house fer some time has it?'

'Huh! How could it be wi' that evil bugger lyin' up there,' Mrs Batley snorted. 'Still, he's had his comeuppance now ain't he? They do say as what goes around comes around. I did think we might see an improvement in him once Grace was back home but if anythin' he's been worse. Nurse Matthews says his temper is somethin' terrible at the moment. Happen it's 'cos Grace won't go in to see him. I reckon the lass has made the right decision – about goin' to live wi' her aunt I mean, though I confess I'll miss her somethin' chronic.'

'We all will,' Mabel agreed. 'But I think she'll have a better life away from this place. Most lasses her age are out an' about havin' the time o' their lives but that poor little lamb ain't never been given no freedom. She ain't even been allowed to have any proper friends here. The only real one she had was the one that died in Wales, poor little mite. But hopefully that will all change when she's livin' in Wales again.'

The two women then went on with what they were doing and for now the subject of Grace's future was put on hold.

❧

'So, do you want to go into your father and say goodbye?' Gertie asked Grace on the day they were due to leave. The majority of Grace's clothes had been packed into trunks and were now stashed in the back of the car. Harry would be driving them to the station and Grace was pleased about that. Harry seemed to have changed since her father had become bedridden. He was more confident now that her father could no longer make him feel inferior and she was delighted to see that he and Mabel were now very close.

'I suppose I should.' Grace didn't look like she wanted to but she climbed the stairs all the same.

Jacob's eyes found hers the instant she set foot in the room and once again his one good hand reached out to her but she chose to ignore it.

'I'm going now, Father,' she informed him coldly.

'G . . . Gr . . . Gr . . .' Sweat broke out on his brow and his fist pummelled the bed in his frustration. 'N . . . no . . . no . . .'

Grace merely stared at him for a moment then she said quietly, 'I blame *you* for Mother's death. If you hadn't come to my room that night and . . .' She gulped deep in her throat as the painful memories came rushing back. Then suddenly all the hatred she now felt for him poured out of her. 'If it hadn't been for *you* and your sick obsession with me she might still be here. Her heart had never been strong and what happened that night was just too much for her. But you don't care, do you? You never loved her as she deserved to be loved. I wonder if you know how to love anyone, even me!'

His head wagged from side to side but he no longer had the power to move her.

'You treated mother no better than you treated the staff. Do you even care that not one of them likes you or has any respect for you? Well, it doesn't matter now. Your rule is over and I don't care if I never set eyes on you again. I'm only sorry for them having to stay here to take care of you.'

Somehow, he had worked his way almost to the edge of the mattress in his distress and he looked as if he might slide out of bed at any minute. But Grace made no move to help him, she felt nothing for him now, not even pity. 'I believe the saying goes, "what you reap you shall sow". Goodbye, Father.' And with that she walked away and didn't once look back. Deep inside she prayed that she would never have to look on him again. He was as dead to her now as her mother was.

212

As Harry drove them to the station they spotted Nurse Matthews heading purposely into town. It was her day off and Grace was surprised to see how different she looked out of her uniform.

'She's all dolled up like a dog's dinner,' Gertie commented. 'I wonder if she's got someone to meet?'

Grace shrugged, not caring much what the woman did with her spare time. She didn't care about anything at the moment, she was too locked in grief.

Chapter Twenty-Seven

'Why, Dylan, lad, I didn't expect to see you here,' Gertie said in surprise as she stepped from the train onto the platform in Pwllheli. Dylan, who was dressed in his Sunday best, blushed furiously.

'Me nan told me you were due home today so I thought I'd ride in with me grandad to meet you.' He twisted his cap in his hand as his eyes shifted to Grace, whose skin was waxen, but she didn't even look at him.

'Well, now that you're here you may as well help with the luggage.' Gertie waved to a porter and sent him off to fetch the boxes and trunks from the luggage van. 'I'll get Grace out to the trap while you wait for them,' Gertie said and shooed Grace ahead of her onto the cobbled street. The smell of the sea air met her and she breathed deeply, relieved to be home. Aled helped Grace climb up onto the back seat and tucked a warm rug across her legs as he glanced worriedly at Gertie.

'She looks right ill,' he commented in a whisper when they were standing beside the horse. 'Poor lass, she's clearly taken her mam's death badly.'

Gertie nodded just as Dylan appeared with the porter, dragging a large trolley with Grace's luggage piled upon it. The three men fell silent as they loaded it into the back of the trap.

'That's it then,' Aled said cheerfully. 'We're all ready for the off. Cerys has a lovely dinner all ready and waiting for you.'

Gertie had already climbed into the front seat to sit beside him and Dylan hopped lightly into the back next to Grace.

'It was right sorry I was to hear about your mam, cariad,' he said softly so that only Grace could hear but she merely nodded and stared ahead. Dylan made a few more attempts at conversation but when it became clear that Grace wasn't going to respond he fell silent and they sat watching the countryside pass them by. It started to rain halfway back to the cottage and, reaching into the back, Dylan got a canvas and flung it over their heads. It was the one that Aled usually used to cover the horse and it smelled, but as he was quick to tell her it would at least keep them dry. Normally Grace would have giggled but today she didn't even comment.

Aled and Gertie looked at each other, concerned. 'She just needs a little time to come to terms with what's happened,' Gertie muttered and Aled nodded.

For the next few days, Grace stayed mainly in her room only coming downstairs at mealtimes when Gertie insisted, although she ate little.

'You know the old saying,' Cerys told her. 'You can lead a horse to water but you can't make it drink. But she will when she's good and ready so stop fretting.'

There was nothing else Gertie could do so she went about her business. The weather was terrible and she had moved as many of her animals into the small barn as she could fit in there, separating them with bales of hay. Meanwhile, the wind continued to howl and the icy rain came down making them all wet and miserable and virtual prisoners in the cottage.

'I doubt our Dylan and his tad would have been able to go out in this for days,' Cerys fretted one day as she stood staring from the kitchen window. It had rained all the day before and overnight the puddles had frozen, turning the back of the cottage into a skating rink.

215

The words had barely left her lips when Grace appeared wrapped up for outside.

'Why, you're never thinking of going out in this are you, cariad?' Cerys was horrified.

'I thought a brisk walk might blow a few cobwebs away.' Grace tied a thick woollen muffler about her throat and pulled the matching hat well down over her ears.

'But it's blowing a gale out there,' Cerys pointed out. 'You'll be wet through in no time and you'll likely catch your death. Why don't you just wait until the rain stops at least?'

Grace shrugged as she headed for the door. 'I'll be fine and I shan't go far.' And with that she was gone, leaving Cerys to shake her head.

Once outside, Grace shielded her eyes against the rain, which was icy cold and sharp as needles, then she turned in the direction of the woods and began to walk, her head bent against the wind. It wasn't so bad once she reached the shelter of the leafless trees, although it was so cold that her teeth began to chatter despite the many layers of clothes she was wearing. She hadn't been sleeping well and was feeling exhausted, for every time she closed her eyes a picture of her mother standing with the bloodied candlestick in her hand flashed behind them. The guilt she felt was overpowering and sometimes she wondered if she could continue – if it hadn't been for her, her mother might still be here. Then her thoughts would turn to her father, lying in his bed a helpless cripple; it was a hard cross to bear. She moved on, locked in her morbid thoughts until eventually she emerged from the trees to see the convent spread out before her. She had never needed to feel peace as much as she did at that moment, so without even thinking she circled the gardens and headed for the tiny chapel. As she had hoped the door was open and she let herself in. The peace and silence met her as she walked down the short aisle and stood staring at the carved wooden image of Mary and baby Jesus. Puddles formed on the floor about her feet as the rain dripped from her clothes, and she hoped she wasn't making too much of a mess.

'Why . . . hello, Grace.'

The voice from behind her caused her to turn quickly and she felt colour flood into her cheeks as she saw Father Luke standing there smiling at her. She hoped he wouldn't be angry to find her there although in fact he looked pleased to see her.

'F-Father . . . I didn't expect anyone to be here.'

'I wouldn't be normally,' he admitted with a smile. 'But the inclement weather has made it impossible to visit some of my parishes so I've been staying here and catching up on some work.'

Grace nodded and sank down heavily onto the nearest pew and after a moment he sat beside her and gently took her hand. 'I was so sorry to hear of your mother's passing,' he said softly. 'But take comfort in knowing that she is now in a better place.'

The kind words unlocked the great blockage in Grace's throat and suddenly the tears came in a flood.

'That's it, let it all out,' he soothed as his arm slid around her shoulders and she leaned into him. Sometime later she straightened and smiled at him apologetically.

'I'm so sorry, father,' she muttered, taking the clean white hand-kerchief he offered and noisily blowing her nose.

'Don't be. It isn't healthy to keep grief locked inside.' He paused then as he stared into her haunted eyes before asking, 'But are you sure there isn't something else bothering you?'

She opened her mouth to deny it but then the temptation to confide in someone was too strong and she whispered, 'I am a *very* bad person. I feel my father's stroke and my mother's death are all my fault.'

He didn't pull away from her as she had expected but instead asked quietly, 'Is it something you would like to talk about? Perhaps you would like to take confession?'

Grace shook her head. 'I can't confess, I have been taking

instructions from a father at a nearby church back at home but I haven't fully converted to your faith yet.'

'Then perhaps you would like to share whatever is troubling you with me right here?' His eyes were kind. 'We are in God's house and He will listen, whatever faith you are.'

Grace thought about this for a moment then she began tentatively. 'When I was a little girl I was very close to my father and I realise now that he spoiled me shamelessly. But then, as I grew, I began to find his affection and restrictions oppressive. He wouldn't allow me to go out unless it was with him and I wasn't allowed to have any friends. It wasn't until I started at a local school at my mother's insistence that I realised just how isolated I was.' She gulped but forced herself to go on. 'A few years ago, Father began to invite guests to stay, men who I disliked intensely. They stared at me and made rude comments but I could bear that. And then Father started coming to my room at night.' She squirmed uncomfortably in her seat as she remembered. 'He . . . he began to want to touch me and fondle me and it made me feel uncomfortable. On the night he had his seizure he had been drinking downstairs . . .' Despite the bitter cold she found herself sweating and she licked her dry lips. 'Father came to my room and I remember asking him to leave but after that everything is a blur . . . the next thing I remember is my mother standing there. She was holding the candlestick that I kept on my bedside table and there was blood on it . . . Father was lying on the floor with a gash on his head and his face was a funny colour. I can remember Mabel, our maid, coming in and between them they managed to get Father back into his own room before sending for the doctor. So you see, it must have all been my fault. Mother must have thought Father was hurting me and attacked him but it's all just a blank.'

She was sobbing again now and when the young father's strong arms came about her she clung to him.

'I'm sure none of it was your fault,' he said firmly. 'It would have been a terrible shock seeing your father become ill like that and shock can do funny things to people, that's probably why you can't remember everything clearly. Your mind blocked it. By your own admission your mother had a weak heart. It could have given out at any time and they had probably rowed earlier on, which is what would have brought on your father's seizure. Furthermore, your father could have hit his head on the candlestick as he fell and it would have been your mother's automatic reaction to snatch it out of the way. You shouldn't blame yourself.'

She stared at him uncertainly for a moment feeling as if a great weight had been lifted from her shoulders. 'Really?'

'*Really.*' He nodded. 'Not all marriages are a bed of roses,' he said. 'And I should know. Believe me I have seen some things in my role as a priest . . . So you must put all this behind you now. You have your whole future ahead of you. Do you have any idea yet what you would like to do?'

'No . . .' she said uncertainly.

'There is plenty of time. But first you must allow yourself to grieve and then go on. The Good Lord will show you the way.'

She stared at him from her deep green eyes wondering how anyone so young could be so wise, and his stomach did a little flip. Quickly reverting to his role as priest he offered, 'I could continue to give you instruction if you wish, perhaps here once a week? And then when you feel ready you could be baptised into the Catholic faith, but only if you're quite sure that is what you truly want. Why don't you speak to your aunt about it? She's always seemed to be a very level-headed woman to me.'

'I will,' she agreed with the first smile he had seen from her that day. 'And thank you for listening to me, father.'

'That's what priests are for.' He returned the smile before rising. 'And should you feel the need to talk again, remember I am here for you. But now I really should be getting on. The Reverend

Mother is expecting me over in the convent and I don't want to get in her bad books.'

He left then and Grace watched him go feeling more at peace than she had since her father had taken ill. It was strange, she thought, that she always felt that way when she had seen him.

When she eventually left the chapel, she was surprised to find Dylan waiting outside with his coat collar turned up and his hands thrust deep in his coat pockets.

'My nan said you'd come up here so I thought I'd wander up and wait for you.'

Grace raised her eyebrow. It was hardly the weather for wandering anywhere but she was pleased to see him. They got on well and she found him easy to talk to, although she'd said little to anyone since returning to Wales this time, apart from Father Luke. She fell into step with him, telling him of Father Luke's offer to give her instruction in the Catholic faith, and Dylan frowned.

'My family are strict chapel-goers,' he muttered. 'Most of the Welsh people are, come to that.' Grace wondered why it should matter to him what religion she was but she was keen to get out of the biting cold now so they hurried on their way.

Both the Llewelyns and Gertie noticed the change in Grace the second she walked through the door.

'Hmm, it seems that walk did you some good after all,' her aunt remarked, looking up over the top of her glasses from the newspaper she was reading. 'You've actually got a bit of colour back in your cheeks.'

'Yes, an' a red nose and blue fingers to match, and yours aren't a lot better, our Dylan,' Cerys said drily as she finished kneading the dough for a new batch of loaves. 'Go and sit yourselves down by the fire and I'll get you both a brew. It'll be a bit stewed by now but it's wet and warm.'

'Aunt Gertie,' Grace said the second she had done as she was told. 'I've been speaking to Father Luke up at the convent chapel and he's offered to give me instruction once a week. Trouble is my father is in no fit state to give his permission.'

'That's not a problem,' Gertie said stoically. 'I have guardianship of you now until your father recovers – if he recovers that is – so if that's what you want I have no objections.'

'Oh, *thank you*!' Grace leaned over and plonked a sloppy kiss on her cheek before hurrying away to get changed out of her wet clothes.

'Can't see why it's so important to her, personally.' Gertie sniffed but she was smiling as she turned her attention back to the newspaper. It was nice to see Grace smiling again.

Meanwhile, up in the convent, Father Luke was deep in prayer in the chapel. Grace had awakened a feeling in him that he had never had before; a deep feeling of wanting to protect her and he had felt drawn to her. Although she wasn't pretty in the classical sense, there was something about her deep flame-red hair and those glorious dark-fringed green eyes, which seemed to be able to look right into his soul, that he found deeply endearing. But most of all, it was her nature that attracted him. She had a serenity and a grace about her that he found enchanting.

'Help me, dear Lord, for I should not have such feelings for a girl,' he prayed.

Down in Beehive Cottage, Grace was also thinking of him and looking forward to their next meeting. Father Luke was kind – *and handsome too*, a little voice in her head whispered – and at the thought, Grace bent her head to hide her blushes.

Chapter Twenty-Eight

In the early summer when the birds were singing in the trees and the sun was riding high in a cloudless blue sky, Grace was finally baptised into the Catholic Church. The Llewelyns and Aunt Gertie attended the service, even though none of them were particularly religious, and afterwards Aunt Gertie presented Grace with a silver rosary, which Grace said she would cherish for ever. Dylan was fishing out at sea that day otherwise Grace was sure he would have come too.

Whenever he was at home now he would visit and they would go off on long walks together. He had also taken her out to sea on a boat trip, and one Saturday evening he had taken her to a dance in the local village hall; it was a new experience for Grace and she had thoroughly enjoyed it. Over the last couple of years Dylan had developed into a very muscular, handsome young man and it had amused her to see the way the local girls' eyes followed him about the room. But he had not even glanced in their direction and didn't seem in the slightest bit interested in any of them.

Gradually Grace felt that she was returning to her former happy self, although she still had dark moments when she missed her mother terribly. Aunt Gertie phoned her home in Nuneaton religiously every week but still there was no change in her father.

'He's no better, but then he's no worse either,' she would tell Grace when she came off the phone.

On Dylan's next day off, Cerys packed a picnic hamper and Grace and Dylan set off for a day at the beach armed with their swimming costumes and two towels. Grace couldn't swim properly as yet but Dylan was teaching her and she loved to go into the sea.

Down in the little cove they favoured, Grace got changed discreetly behind a rock and as she rounded it with her clothes folded neatly across her arm Dylan shouted, 'Last one in is a rotten egg!'

Grace felt a sharp stab of pain as she thought back to the time when Myfanwy had said exactly the same thing to her. But then she pushed the thoughts aside as she dropped her clothes into a heap and chased after him, splashing into the waves. They spent a happy half-hour in the sea dipping and diving before emerging and dropping onto the towels Dylan had lain across the sand, and Grace poured them each a cup of lemonade from the bottle that she had left cooling in a small rock pool.

The hours spent in the sun had turned Grace's skin a ferocious red colour to begin with, which Dylan had teased her mercilessly about, although it wasn't so sore now. By contrast, Dylan was tanned and golden.

'I can't help it, it's because I'm a red-head,' she had pointed out.

Now, after a long cool drink, he sighed and turned onto his stomach, leaning up on his elbows to stare at Grace. Her normally deep red hair had golden highlights running through it from the sun and as it blew about her slim shoulders in the gentle sea breeze he had the urge to run his fingers through it.

'I was wonderin' if you might like to come to tea at my house on Sunday. I've asked me mam and she said you'd be welcome.'

Grace had been watching the seagulls as they dipped and dived into the sea looking for fish and his words took her by surprise. She had not visited Dylan's home since before Myfanwy's death and she was reluctant to accept but she had no wish to hurt Dylan's feelings so after a moment she answered, 'All right then. That would be very nice . . . thank you.'

They tucked into the fresh-caught sardine and tomato sandwiches that Mrs Llewelyn had packed for them.

Afterwards, they dozed in the sun for a while before going for another swim and eventually they set off back to the cottage. Dylan's father was taking the boat out fishing that evening and Dylan didn't want to be late.

'Dylan has asked me to go to tea at his house on Sunday,' Grace informed her aunt and the Llewelyns that evening as she helped herself from a freshly picked bowl of salad. There was cold ham, pickles and crusty bread to go with it and Grace was surprised at how hungry she was again. She was feeling much better, although she still had nightmares about her mother and father at times.

Gertie and Cerys exchanged a crafty little grin. Yes, Dylan was well and truly smitten with Grace. The trouble was, neither of them had any idea how she felt about him. She seemed to enjoy his company, but she had never hinted at any romance between them so Cerys fervently hoped that her grandson wasn't going to get his heart broken.

'That'll be lovely, cariad,' Cerys commented as she carved some more slices from the loaf and spread them with thick, creamy butter. 'You'll have to wear something nice.'

'Why?' Grace asked innocently. She didn't usually bother getting dressed up when she and Dylan went off on one of their jaunts.

'Oh, I, er . . . just thought you'd like to look your best when you go meet our Bronwen, that's all.' Cerys looked embarrassed and Grace frowned.

'But I've already met her. I went there with Myfanwy when we were children.'

'Ah, so you did but . . . I suppose I ought to warn you, Dylan's mam might have changed since the last time you saw her. She took our Myfanwy's death very badly, see? And if truth be told she has never been the same since.'

'That's sad.' Grace sighed. Strangely, although her friend had died some years ago, she only had to close her eyes to picture her as if they had been together only the day before. She still dreamed about her too and the dreams were so vivid that when she woke, it was hard to convince herself that Myfanwy hadn't really been with her. They finished their meal in silence and Grace didn't give the matter another thought.

Sunday dawned bright and clear and Dylan arrived to collect Grace shortly after lunch. She had chosen to wear a pretty cream cotton dress with sprigs of flowers all over it and she looked fresh and bright. Her red-gold hair was gleaming and there was a sparkle in her eye and Dylan's heart did a little flip. Grace was still quite petite, in fact her figure was almost boyish, but there was something about her that he found irresistible.

'Right, we'll be off then,' she told Gertie cheerfully as she slipped her feet into flat sandals.

'Have a nice time but mind you're back before it gets dark.' Gertie looked up from the lamb she was feeding. The mother had rejected the poor little thing. Cerys was busily washing up the dinner pots at the sink and Grace flashed them all a smile as she stepped out into the sunshine.

When they finally arrived at Dylan's home Grace didn't think it had changed a bit. Dylan's father was sitting mending some fishing nets in the sunshine and the garden was still scattered with shells, some of which she and Myfanwy had once collected from the beach.

'Afternoon.' Dylan's father inclined his head and Grace smiled at him as she followed Dylan down the path and in through the front door. After the bright sunshine, it took her eyes some time to adjust to the dimness as they went along the narrow hallway to the kitchen. They found Dylan's mother slicing a large, freshly baked loaf at the table and she glanced up, her eyes settling on Grace.

'Hello, Mrs Penlynn.' Grace smiled, noticing the pain that flared briefly in the woman's eyes. She was no doubt remembering the last time Grace had visited with Myfanwy.

'Afternoon. Sit yourselves down. Tea won't be long.'

It wasn't the warmest greeting Grace had ever received but she did as she was told, glancing at Dylan who smiled at her reassuringly.

'We've just been down to the harbour,' he told his mother.

'Oh ah.'

'It was quite busy,' he went on, hoping to draw her into a conversation but his efforts were in vain and his mother simply got on with what she was doing.

Grace began to feel slightly uncomfortable. Perhaps this hadn't been such a good idea after all? But she was there now so for Dylan's sake she determined to make the best of it. Things improved slightly when Dylan's father joined them and he began to tell her about his fishing trips.

'Ever been out on a fishing boat, have you?' he asked as he spread a thick layer of home-made bramble jam onto his buttered bread. There was also something called 'bara brith', which Dylan explained was a traditional Welsh bread made of sweet fruit and cold tea as well as a fine Caerphilly cheese and biscuits.

Grace shook her head. 'No, but Dylan took me on a boat trip once.'

'Ah, but that's not to be compared to the fishing boats. We go much further out to sea than them, which is why we can hit problems if a storm suddenly blows up.' He grinned. 'I've had some right close shaves, I don't mind telling you. The sea can be treacherous. Calm as a millpond one minute and towering waves the next. Still, I wouldn't be anything other than a fisherman. The sea is in my blood an' I reckon our Dylan takes after me.'

Dylan nodded in agreement and thankfully the rest of the meal passed comparatively comfortably, although Dylan's mother said very little and at times Grace could feel her eyes boring into her. She wondered if perhaps the woman blamed her for Myfanwy's death? After all, she had survived and her dear friend had not. The thought made her feel even more uncomfortable and she was relieved when it was over. Dylan's father moved to sit in a chair at the side of the fireplace to smoke his pipe and Grace stood up to help Dylan's mother clear the table.

'There's no need for you to do that,' the woman snapped ungraciously. 'Guests aren't expected to help with clearing up.'

'Oh, I, er . . . Sorry, Mrs Penlynn, I had no wish to offend you.' Grace flushed to the roots of her hair.

'Mam didn't mean to offend, *did* you, Mam?' Dylan stared pointedly at his mother before adding, 'But perhaps it's time we got off now, cariad.'

The older woman's lips set in a thin line at the term of endearment but she thankfully said nothing as Grace nodded hastily.

'Er . . . yes we should be off. Thank you so much for the lovely tea, Mrs Penlynn.'

The woman sniffed and began to carry the dirty dishes to the sink as Grace said her goodbyes to her husband before following Dylan to the door.

Dylan's face was dark as he marched down the path ahead of her and once out in the lane he told her, 'I'm sorry about that. I think Mam resents the fact that Myfanwy succumbed to the fever and you survived.'

'I can understand that.' Grace kicked at a stone. 'I feel guilty about it myself sometimes.' Then as a thought occurred to her she

227

suggested, 'Why don't we call into the churchyard on the way home. We could pick some flowers along the way.'

He nodded and they began to stoop and collect the flowers as they went. Once they were standing at the foot of Myfanwy's grave, Grace's eyes filled with tears.

'I still miss her so much,' she mumbled and Dylan nodded in agreement as he took her hand.

'I do too, but life goes on.'

She bent down to lay the flowers in front of the headstone then they picked their way through the graveyard to the lychgate still hand in hand. It was as they were meandering along the coastal road that Dylan suddenly said, 'There's been something I've been meaning to ask you.'

'Oh yes?'

'The thing is . . . I was wanting to ask you if you'd be my girl . . . officially.'

For a moment, Grace didn't know what to say. It had come as a complete surprise to her, for she had never looked on Dylan as anything more than a friend.

'But . . . aren't we a little young for anything like that?' she said eventually, suddenly conscious of his large, warm hand clasping hers.

'Not at all,' he denied. 'You're sixteen and I'm eighteen. There's lots of the fisher lasses your age who are wed already.'

'But I don't think I'm ready for something like that just yet,' Grace said in an attempt not to hurt his feelings.

To her relief, he smiled. 'It's all right. There's no rush. I just wanted you to know how I felt. Just say the word when you do feel ready and we'll take it from there because I know you're the girl for me, Grace. I knew it from the first second I clapped eyes on you.'

'But I don't know if I ever *will* be ready,' she said. 'I haven't decided what I want to do with my life yet.' The last thing she wanted to do was give him false hope.

Dylan laughed. 'Why, you're a girl. You'll get wed and have babies. That's what girls do.'

Grace frowned. 'Times are changing,' she whispered. 'Women are beginning to have careers now. I thought I might like to be a teacher but I haven't properly decided yet.'

'A teacher!' he scoffed and she felt a little flood of anger. Why shouldn't women have careers?

'Anyway, just think on what I've said,' he said, taking her silence as agreement.

Once they arrived back at the cottage her aunt immediately noticed how quiet she was and asked, 'Did you have a good time?'

'Er . . . yes, it was very nice.'

Somehow Grace's words didn't quite ring true and Gertie raised an eyebrow although she wisely refrained from asking any more while Dylan was there. She wondered if perhaps they'd had a tiff, although Dylan seemed happy enough.

Gertie waited until Dylan had left to tell Grace, 'I rang your home today and Nurse Matthews informed me that your father is slightly worse. Do you feel that you wish to visit him yet?'

Grace blinked. The answer to that question was no, she didn't wish to return home, but then perhaps she should if her father was deteriorating? A short time away from her aunt's would give her some space to think about what Dylan had said as well.

'Yes, I suppose I should.'

Her aunt heard the uncertainty and assured her, 'You don't have to if you don't want to, Grace.'

Grace smiled. 'I know, but I would have to live with my conscience if I didn't go and anything was to happen to him. I think I'll go for a few days at the end of the week, if that's all right with you. I shall be quite all right travelling on my own.'

She had already realised that if she went then, she would avoid Dylan's next visit. The trouble was she would also miss mass at the chapel with Father Luke but that couldn't be helped.

Chapter Twenty-Nine

'Eeh! Yer look grand, lass. The Welsh air must suit yer,' Mrs Batley greeted her when Grace arrived back home.

Grace gave her a hug, asking, 'Where are Mabel and Harry?'

'Oh, they've gone into town to do some shopping for me.' Mrs Batley grinned then as she leaned towards her and confided, 'They're like a pair o' lovebirds. More than ever since the master took bad, come to think of it. Harry seems to have more confidence an' him an' Mabel have been officially walking out together for some while. Not before time, eh? I was beginnin' to think they'd never get together properly but now I have high hopes that a weddin' might be in the offin' afore too long. But that's enough about them, how are you, lass?'

Grace forced a smile. Just being in this house brought memories of her mother flooding back and it was painful. 'I'm all right. I still miss my mother, of course, but I dare say that's something I shall have to learn to live with. I came back to visit because Aunt Gertie told me that Father had taken a turn for the worse.'

Mrs Batley nodded. 'He has, although he hasn't had another turn nor nothin'. He just seems to have lost the will to live. Happen he's missin' you an' seein' you will perk him up again.'

Grace secretly doubted that, but she didn't say anything. Instead she lifted her small case. 'I'll just take my case along to my room and pop in to see him. Then I'd love a cup of tea, if it's not too much trouble.'

'Nothin's too much trouble fer you, pet,' Mrs Batley assured her. 'This place ain't been the same wi'out you an' yer mam.'

Upstairs Grace dropped her case onto the floor and stared around at the familiar room. Strangely it didn't feel like home anymore and she knew then that she would never return on a permanent basis. Her home was with Aunt Gertie now – until she decided what she wanted to do with the rest of her life, that was. She had been plodding along nicely but Dylan's suggestion that they should get wed had added urgency to making the decision now. She went along to the bathroom to wash and tidy herself, thinking how luxurious this all was compared to Beehive Cottage. The toilet there was located at the end of a long cinder path at the bottom of the garden and the bath was a tin one that they carried in from the yard and filled with hot water from the boiler. Yet Grace realised she hadn't missed all the modern conveniences her father had had installed, probably because she was happier at her aunt's. Here there was electric lighting at the flick of a switch but now Grace was accustomed to gasoliers and candles lighting her to bed.

She straightened her back and after another glance in the mirror that hung above the sink to make sure that her hair was tidy, she took a deep breath and set off for her father's room. She may as well get it over with.

She tapped at his bedroom door and stepped inside. Nurse Matthews was sitting in a chair by the window reading a book and her father was lying in bed staring sightlessly at the ceiling. Grace was surprised to see that the nurse had started to take a pride in her appearance. She had lost a little weight and had her hair cut into a more fashionable style. However, her father seemed to have shrunk to half his original size and looked vastly older. Grace supposed she should feel sympathy for him, yet she still felt nothing as she approached the bed. His mouth was still grotesquely twisted down at one side and his eyes when he turned to her were dull and listless.

'Hello, Father.' He raised his one good hand to her but she could see that even that was weak now and merely hovered inches above the counterpane.

She knew that she should take it but couldn't bring herself to. Even being close to him made her cringe. 'I thought I would pay a visit to see how you are,' she said. 'And I thought perhaps I'd stay for a couple of days.' She wanted to make sure that he knew from the start that she had no intentions of returning permanently. He shook his head and Grace wondered how he was managing to cling to life. He looked so old and frail that it was hard to remember the man he had once been.

'He's been a bit under the weather, haven't you, judge?' Nurse Matthews smiled a greeting as she laid her book aside. This had turned out to be one of the best jobs she had ever had so she made sure that Jacob received the best care she could give him. He might not have much of a life but the longer he lived the longer she could stay there.

'So I heard, that's why I've come back,' Grace answered. It certainly appeared that the woman was doing a good job. A silence stretched between them then until she told him, 'I'm very contented living with Aunt Gertie and I love living in Wales. I attend the chapel at the convent there every Sunday morning and recently I converted to the Catholic faith.'

'*N-no . . . come h-home.*' The words came out as a gurgle and clearly cost him an enormous effort.

Grace eyed him coldly. She supposed she should treat him with more compassion but remembering how he had treated her mother she found it impossible.

'I shall *never* return home, not to stay,' she informed him. She could see that Nurse Matthews was becoming alarmed at how agitated her father was, so, having done her duty as far as she was concerned, she excused herself, leaving Nurse Matthews to try and calm her patient, who had worked himself up into a rare old state of distress.

The kettle was singing on the hob and Mabel and Harry were back by the time she got downstairs and they were delighted to see her.

After tea, Grace rose from her seat. 'I think I'd like to visit the churchyard and take some flowers to my mother's grave. It's far too nice an evening to be stuck in the house.'

Mrs Batley nodded her agreement. 'You do that, pet, an' by the time yer get back I'll have a meal ready for yer.'

Thankfully, on the way, Grace found a little flower shop still open so she purchased a large bunch of red chrysanthemums and hurried on. The churchyard was deserted and there was nothing but the birds to be heard as she weaved amongst the tombstones. She was pleased to see that a fine marble headstone bearing her mother's name had been erected at the head of the grave, no doubt by Mr Mackenzie, and a bunch of roses that were just beginning to droop were placed in a pot in front of it. Mrs Batley had promised her before she left for Wales that she would tend the grave and she saw that she had kept her word. After quickly removing the drooping flowers, Grace replaced them with her own, then sitting back on her heels she said quietly, 'I miss you *so* much, Mother. I'm so sorry for what happened. But I've accepted that you've gone now and I know I have to get on with my life. I think that's what you would have wanted. I recently converted to the Catholic faith. I don't suppose that will surprise you. You know I was always fascinated with it. I just told Father but he got in a lather about it. He always begrudged the time we spent together at church, didn't he?'

She gently laid her hand on the mound of grass in front of the headstone and she could feel her mother's gentle presence rising

233

up from the ground beneath. 'I like living in Wales with Aunt Gertie. She's nowhere near as hard as she appears; in fact she's a big softie underneath, but then I suppose you know that, don't you? I've been spending a lot of time with Dylan there. He is Myfanwy's brother. You know – my best friend who died. We have a lovely time together but now I'm worried because he . . . he says he wants to marry me. The trouble is, I don't love him like that, I love him more like a brother, and I don't want to get married. And then there's Father Luke.' She smiled as she thought of him. 'He's the priest who conducts some of the services up at the chapel. He's not at all as you'd imagine a priest to be – he's young, probably less than ten years older than me, which is young for a priest, isn't it? I feel so peaceful when I'm with him and the nuns. All the worry and the stress seems to float away when we're together and we talk about anything and everything.' She sighed then. 'The trouble is, I feel that it's time I did something now. Something to give my life a purpose, but I don't know what. I wish you were here to advise me. I just need some sign so that I know what I should do.'

Her only reply was the sound of the birds singing in the trees, and she sat, with tears streaming down her face, basking in the peace of the place. It was funny, she thought, how the only time she ever felt truly happy was when she was in or close to a church. Suddenly it came to her like a bolt from the blue. Perhaps her mother was sending her a sign after all! She would enter the church and devote her life to God rather than marry a man she didn't love. She slowly climbed to her feet and smiled down on her mother's resting place, feeling that she was suddenly very close to her. She would go back to Wales tomorrow and go and speak to Father Luke and the Reverend Mother at the convent about her decision. Rising to her feet she planted a gentle kiss on her mother's headstone. 'Thank you,' she whispered. 'Sleep tight until we meet again.' And as she turned and walked away, she felt as if she was leaving a little piece of her heart behind.

She felt quite light-hearted as she set off for home and Mrs Batley noticed her serene expression the second she walked back into the kitchen.

'I've decided that I'm going back to Wales tomorrow, Batty,' Grace informed her. 'There's nothing I can do for Father if I stay here. Between you all he's getting the best care he could ever have.'

'But you only just got here,' Mrs Batley objected.

Grace crossed to give her ample waist a little squeeze. 'I know but I've finally decided what I want to do with the rest of my life and I want to get back and put my decision into action.'

Mrs Batley raised an eyebrow and paused in the act of stirring the gravy on the top of the range. 'Oh yes . . . and what will that be then? Teaching? I know you always had a yen to do that.'

'I did,' Grace admitted. 'But I've finally realised where my true vocation lies. I want to be a nun.'

'*A nun!*' Mrs Batley was so shocked that the spoon she was holding clattered onto the top of the range splashing gravy everywhere. 'But you can't be serious? You're just a young lass with your whole life ahead of you. Why would you want to shut yourself away from the world?'

'I wouldn't be,' Grace assured her. 'The order I am hoping to join are working nuns. They work out in the world doing all sorts of things.'

Mrs Batley plonked heavily onto the nearest chair as she shook her head. 'But if you do that we will never see you again,' she muttered brokenly and Grace smiled.

'*Of course* you will. You don't just become a nun overnight. It takes years before you take your final vows and during that time you're allowed to visit your family.'

'I see . . . then I dare say if that's what your heart is telling you to do you should try it. But promise me you'll give it proper thought first?'

'I will.' Grace kissed her cheek.

Pulling herself to her feet, the older woman continued putting the finishing touches to the meal, although deep inside she felt that Grace was taking the wrong path. In her opinion, the girl was far too young to be thinking of locking herself away from the world but all she could do was hope she would have a change of heart.

True to her word, Grace was ready to leave early the next morning.

'Will you be goin' up to say goodbye to your father?' Mrs Batley tentatively questioned and Grace paused. It might be some long time before she came here again, if ever.

Slowly she climbed the stairs and once outside her father's room she paused, a lump forming in her throat. She raised her hand to knock but then stepped away with tears streaming down her cheeks. She was well aware of how seriously ill her father was and that she may never see him again, but even that couldn't force her to say a final goodbye. She hated him – detested him, in fact – and yet he was still her father and so her emotions were mixed. As she stood struggling with herself, she finally reached a decision and turning about she walked away.

There were tears from both Mabel and Mrs Batley as she left, but she promised them she would keep in touch and by the time she set off for the station with Harry carrying her case, she felt lighter than she had for some long time.

'Mabel told me what you were planning,' he said tentatively when they had walked for a while. 'Are you sure this is what you want, pet? I mean you've had a lot to deal with lately an' I wouldn't want you to make the wrong decision.'

'It's nothing to do with anything that's happened,' she told him. She knew he was only speaking out of concern. 'I suppose deep

236

down it's always been what I've wanted but I've only just realised it.'

They were at the entrance to the station now and there was a catch in his voice as he handed her the case. 'Then if that's what you really want, pet, I wish you well. But just remember we'll always be here for you. Keep in touch, won't you?'

Grace nodded, too full of emotion to speak, then watched him walk away on his poor bandy legs before heading for the ticket office.

'I see,' Aunt Gertie said later that evening as they sat in Beehive Cottage sipping cocoa.

Grace held her breath, waiting for the objections, but surprisingly they didn't come.

'I see no harm in paying a visit to the Reverend Mother. None of this will happen overnight and it will give you valuable thinking time. But I know someone who will be heartbroken when he hears of it. It's as clear as the nose on your face that young Dylan is smitten with you, and had you felt the same I think you could have done far worse for a husband. But there you are, you must be true to yourself. I always have been despite what people have said.' She gave a cynical little laugh. 'When your uncle died and I sold up to come here everyone thought I'd gone stark staring mad. They said that I was far too young to never consider marrying again, but why would I do that when I had already had the best? So I went ahead with my plan, and do you know what? I've never regretted a second of it, so you follow your star.'

When Grace retired to bed, she stood at the open window gazing out at the garden. It was washed in moonlight and beyond it the sea looked as if it had been painted silver by some huge unseen hand. A new chapter of her life was about to begin and she could hardly wait.

Chapter Thirty

'And have you given what you are suggesting a lot of thought, my child?'

Grace nodded eagerly as she stared into the serene face of the Reverend Mother. She had waited three long days for this appointment and during that time she had become more determined than ever that this was what she wanted to do.

'Oh, yes,' Grace told her eagerly.

The woman stared at her closely for what seemed an eternity before nodding. 'Very well, I see no reason why you shouldn't have a trial period here. During that time, you will learn to let go of earthly attachments to family and friends and material possessions and see if this is the life you truly feel ready for. If after six months you are still of the same mind you may join our postulants. But I must warn you, it may not be as easy as you think. Your time will be spent reading the Bible and in prayer. Then, should you still be of the same mind when you join the postulants, you will be trained for a job of work. Teaching or nursing, perhaps? Finally, when you are considered ready, you will take your final vows and become a bride of Christ, but that will be some time away in the future. This is not a vocation that you enter into lightly.'

'Oh, I realise that, mother,' Grace gushed.

'Very well then, I am prepared to let you enter the convent.

When would be suitable for you? I understand you have an ailing parent?'

'I have,' Grace admitted. 'But he has a full-time nurse caring for him so I'm not needed.'

When Grace left some time later she had a spring in her step. Her new life couldn't start quickly enough but she knew already that she would miss her aunt and the Llewelyns, although the Reverend Mother had agreed that during her trial period she would be allowed to visit them for one hour each month.

Her aunt took the news well when she arrived back at the cottage, although the same couldn't be said for Cerys.

'A young girl like you locking herself away in a convent,' she grumbled with a shake of her head. 'And our Dylan is going to be heartbroken! Still, it's your life at the end of the day.' And with that she turned her back and got on with what she'd been doing.

That night Grace had a very vivid dream. She and Myfanwy were standing together at the open window gazing at the sky. 'You must follow your star,' Myfanwy told her as she pointed to the brightest in the sky. The dream was so real that when Grace started awake it took her some time to realise that it hadn't been real, although she could have sworn she could sense Myfanwy close by. Perhaps she should take it as a sign that she was doing the right thing?

She had agreed to join the order the following week so it was inevitable that she would have to see Dylan one more time before she left and she was proved to be right when he wandered in on the following Sunday with a broad smile on his face.

'What's wrong? Has someone died or something?' he asked Grace as he noted the anxious expression on her face.

'No, nothing like that but there is something I need to tell you. Shall we go for a walk?' Grace suggested nervously.

Dylan frowned but nodded as he followed her out of the door.

'So . . . what is it?' he asked when they were some way from the cottage. It was then that Grace noticed he was carrying a small bunch of flowers and she gulped.

Slowly she began to tell him what she was planning to do and as she talked she saw the colour drain from his face.

He looked bewildered. 'But why would you want to be a nun?' he gasped. 'I thought our future was mapped out for us.'

'That's the problem . . . *you* thought it was.' Grace hated to hurt him but there was no alternative. 'I don't *want* to get married, Dylan . . . not to anyone. I feel that becoming a bride of Christ is my destiny and I'm sure you'll meet someone else in time. Someone who will love you as you deserve to be loved.'

'No, I bloody well won't!' he spat as his face turned ugly. 'I love *you*, damn it! Isn't there anything I can do to change your mind?'

Grace shook her head. There was nothing left to say and with a snarl he tossed the flowers at her feet and stormed off. Tears stung her eyes. She had hated to shatter his dreams but it was time to follow her own dream now. She watched until he was out of sight, then with a heavy heart she turned and made her way back to the cottage.

'It's time for you to go,' Aunt Gertie said the next morning. 'But just remember there's always a home here for you should you change your mind.' Gertie always found it hard to express her feelings but they showed in the tears that were spangling her eyelashes.

Grace nodded as she stood clutching the small bag that was all she was allowed to take with her. It contained a nightdress and a small selection of underwear. Anything else she needed would be supplied by the convent.

The Llewelyns both looked upset but Grace was not about to be swayed from her decision by anyone.

Grace kissed her aunt then did the same to the Llewelyns before walking quietly away. This was the bit she had been dreading but she could see no point in prolonging the agony.

'I'll be back to see you in a month's time. Meanwhile you know where I am if there is any news from home.'

Gertie nodded as Grace set off with her eyes straight ahead.

Once up at the convent she was shown to the Reverend Mother's office. 'Ah, Grace,' she greeted her. 'Sister Agnes will show you to the postulants' quarters, although as I explained you will not be classed as a postulant straightaway. You are very young so I wish to make sure that this is what you truly want before we move on to that stage. You will spend the next six months in prayer, taking instructions from Father Luke and working about the convent.'

'Yes, mother.'

'Good, then off you go. Sister Agnes will supply you with sufficient clothing. There is no need for your hair to be shorn until you take the veil but from now on it must be discreetly tied back at all times. The only toiletries you will be allowed to use is unperfumed soap, which again we will supply. Is that clear?'

'Yes, mother.

The elderly nun nodded and Sister Agnes led her to a small wing attached to the back of the convent. Inside there were a number of small cell-like rooms, one of which she allocated to Grace. It was somewhat bleaker than she had expected it to be and was so tiny she could touch the walls if she extended her arms. All it contained was an iron-framed bed and a tiny chest of drawers on which stood a plain white pottery jug and bowl for washing. The walls were whitewashed and completely bare save for a crucifix above the bed. The floor was tiled and the single blanket a dull grey colour. It was a far cry from the luxurious bedroom she had back in her home town, or the pretty little room with the chintz curtains she had made her own back at Aunt

Gertie's, but Grace didn't mind. Even so it felt cold, despite the warm temperature outside, and she wondered what it would be like in the winter.

'You may put the things you have brought with you in there. ' Sister Agnes pointed to the small chest of drawers. 'And while you are doing that I will go and find you two dresses and some suitable shoes.'

By the time she had returned, Grace had finished her unpacking.

'There is one dress to wear and one to wash. You will take your turn in the laundry each week with the postulants who are responsible for the convent's laundry. And you will change the sandals you are wearing for these. Those you have on are most unsuitable.' She glared disapprovingly down at Grace's pretty sandals and placed a clunky, ugly, leather-strapped pair onto the bed along with two plain light-grey shift dresses that turned out to be completely shapeless and very unflattering.

'There is no place for vanity in the House of God,' the nun told her primly as she saw Grace looking at the dresses. 'The next six months will be spent teaching you to let go of the material world.'

'Yes, sister.'

The sister nodded. 'Good, now get changed and when you are ready I will take you to the chapel for Bible study. You will then join the postulants for lunch, and this afternoon will be spent in prayer. Tomorrow you will be given duties.'

Grace flushed when she realised that the woman had no intention of leaving the room. Noticing her hesitation, the nun snapped, 'There is no room for modesty in a nun's life.'

Grace hastily cast off her skirt and blouse and tugged the ugly dress over her head. It was far too large for her but Sister Agnes merely handed her a length of string to use as a belt. Another shorter length was used to secure her unruly curls at the nape of her neck, and finally she slid her feet into the cumbersome sandals.

They were clearly well worn and very heavy but Grace made no complaint. She followed the sister to the tiny chapel that she loved where she was given a Bible to study and left to her own devices. For the first hour she sat quietly, content to read, but then she found her eyes constantly straying to the stained-glass window above the small altar. The sun was shining through it casting rainbows across the walls and she suddenly had a yearning to be outside. She quickly turned her attention back to the book in front of her. What sort of nun was she going to make, she wondered worriedly, if she couldn't even spend a morning studying the Good Book?

At lunchtime, she joined the postulants for a meal in a small dining hall. They were each given a small dish of lamb cawl, a popular Welsh stew, but it was watery and the meat was so gristly that Grace could barely chew it. It was nothing at all like the delicious cawl that Mrs Llewelyn made. On top of that, it was almost cold by the time they had said lengthy prayers but Grace was hungry so she forced it down anyway. They were given water to drink, then after more prayers Grace was sent back to the chapel to spend the afternoon in yet more prayers. For the first hour, she was quite content. Outside she could hear the other postulants working in the garden but as the afternoon progressed she found her concentration slipping. She had always enjoyed praying but she was fast discovering that to have to pray for a whole afternoon was not as easy as she had thought it would be. By teatime she had to admit that she was bored and already she was beginning to wonder if she was cut out for this life. By the time Sister Agnes came to collect her for her evening meal, Grace was close to tears.

She expected the sister to be angry with her but in actual fact she was quite the opposite. 'Did you find it difficult?' She smiled as she noted Grace's glum expression. 'Don't worry, my child. It takes time to leave the outside world behind. That's what this period is for. Believe me, it will get easier and one day you will come to enjoy the time you spend in prayer.'

Grace felt slightly better as she blinked back tears. She was actually missing her aunt and the Llewelyns and feeling quite isolated and she felt guilty for that too, as she admitted to the elderly nun. The whole day had been nothing like she had expected. Nanny Donovan had taught her that bathing and the changing of clothes should always be a private affair and so she had found changing in front of the nun very uncomfortable.

'That too is natural in the early days,' the woman assured her. 'You have chosen a new path in life, vastly different to the one you have known, which is why the Reverend Mother is giving you this trial time to decide if it really is the one you wish to take. She is very wise. But now come and have your evening meal and be aware that this evening we have taken a vow of silence for the duration of the meal, apart from the prayer that will be said before.'

After lengthy prayers, everything was unnaturally silent in the dining room – the only sound being that of the cutlery that the postulants were laying on the tables. After a time, they all rose and formed a queue and were served with their meal, which Grace discovered was the main meal of the day. There were jugs of milk on the table, which she supposed was better than the water they had been given at lunchtime, and the meal was slightly better too, although it still left a lot to be desired and the portions were meagre. Thankfully Grace was petite so she didn't have an enormous appetite which she supposed was just as well. They were each given a spoonful of boiled potatoes which she soon discovered were still slightly hard in the middle, along with cabbage that had been boiled almost to death. Added to this was a spoonful of peas and a pork chop that was surprisingly tasty. Grace ate most of the peas and all of the chop but she struggled with the cabbage and potatoes and left most of it. For dessert they were served half a roast pear with a spoonful of cream each and Grace quite enjoyed that, although she found the silence eerie. At last the meal was over and Sister Agnes descended on her.

'I shall now show you where the bathroom is.'

Grace sighed with relief. She was positively bursting to use the toilet but hadn't dared to ask directions.

'And then you may either spend a quiet hour in the grounds or retire to bed. Lights out is at nine o'clock sharp in the summer. Eight o'clock in the winter.'

Grace was escorted to the toilet block, which turned out to be a crude wooden building at the back of the convent. Inside was a large bucket over which a piece of wood with a hole in it was placed. But then she supposed she shouldn't have expected anything luxurious. What was it Sister Agnes had told her earlier? *There is no room for modesty in a nun's life.* The nun left her then and when she had finished, Grace wandered out into the beautifully kept gardens. A number of the postulants in their white habits were there enjoying the last of the sunshine and they beckoned her to join them.

'How have you found your first day?' a young woman who looked to be in her mid- to late twenties, asked kindly. She was very tall with a hooked nose and Grace thought ungraciously that she would never have won any beauty contests, then instantly felt guilty for having such uncharitable thoughts. As she glanced around Grace noted with a little shock that she was easily the youngest there.

'It's been . . .' She wondered how best to describe it. 'Unlike I'd imagined it to be,' she eventually admitted.

The woman nodded understandingly. 'I think we all felt like that for the first few days,' she admitted. 'But it does get easier eventually.'

At that moment, if Grace had been honest with herself, all she wanted to do was run back to the shelter and security of Beehive Cottage, although she didn't admit it, of course. Instead she sat back and listened to the chatter until the women began to drift away, at which point she entered the building and made her way to her own room. She lit the candle on the chest of drawers, for it was already gloomy inside although it was still light outside, and hastily washed in the cold water in the jug and dried herself on the scratchy, threadbare towel that had been provided. Finally, she knelt at the side of the bed to confess her sins to God before she slept.

'Forgive me, Father, for I have sinned,' she whispered and went on to confess all the impure thoughts she had had throughout the day, which was a considerably long list. Then she gave her a hair a hundred strokes of the brush, as her mother had taught her, and slid into bed. The mattress was lumpy and uncomfortable and the blanket scratched her skin and she tried hard not to think about the comfy bed back in Beehive Cottage. Eventually she fell into an uneasy sleep which was riddled with nightmares. It was the night her father had had his seizure and she was back in her room at home fighting him as he tried to kiss her. Again, she could feel his hands on her skin and then suddenly she saw her mother standing there clutching a candlestick smeared with his blood and he was lying on the floor jerking convulsively. That's when she woke up in a cold sweat and a tangle of damp sheets. So much of that night was still a blur. Somehow, she knew that there was something her mind had blocked from her memory and much as she longed to put that terrible night behind her, she knew that she never would until she remembered what it was.

Down in Beehive Cottage, Gertie was also lying awake thinking of her niece and wondering how she was coping with her new life. Poor girl, she had led such a strange life. She remembered the letter Madeline had sent to her with Grace shortly after the girl had come to stay following her father's seizure. She had read it late the same night after Grace had retired to bed and it was clear that all Madeline's concerns were for her daughter.

She seems to have no recollection of what really happened so please never tell her unless she ever remembers, Madeline had implored. *The only other person who knows is Mabel and I would trust the girl with my life.*

Gertie had read the letter with a heavy heart and then tucked it away in the bureau. 'It's all right, Madeline, she'll never learn the truth from me,' she whispered to the empty room, then turning on her side she tried to sleep but it was a very long time coming.

Chapter Thirty-One

'I believe you have found the first few days difficult?'

Grace sighed and nodded before lowering her eyes from Father Luke's. Difficult was an understatement. She had been at the convent for four days now, four days that felt like four months. On her second day, she had been assigned to the laundry for the afternoon where she had managed to drop a whole basketful of clean clothes onto the floor as she carried them outside to hang them up. Every item had had to be washed all over again, which hadn't pleased the rest of the staff and had made her late for prayers in the chapel, which hadn't pleased the Reverend Mother. On the third day, she had fallen back to sleep after being woken by Sister Agnes, which had resulted in her being late for prayers yet again. The trouble was, Grace had never been taught to do housework and six o'clock in the morning felt like the middle of the night to her. Later that day she had been sent to work in the kitchen garden and was soon in trouble again for pulling up a whole row of lettuces that she thought were weeds. She had also been scolded for speaking when the nuns were observing a rule of silence and for being sick when she had been relegated to toilet cleaning.

'There is no favouritism here,' the Reverend Mother had told her firmly as Grace stood before her desk with her head bowed in shame.

'No, mother,' Grace had muttered miserably. And now here she was with Father Luke who would read her scriptures with her. The Reverend Mother had given her a list of them that she wanted Grace to be able to recite by heart by the weekend.

'I just can't seem to do anything right,' she confided to him as tears pricked at the back of her eyes. She was tired and hungry and her hands were sore from the time spent in the laundry. Her knees ached too from the many hours she had spent kneeling in prayer.

She had never thought becoming a nun would be so hard.

'It is early days and you have much to learn and forsake.' The sympathy in his voice was the last straw, and the tears started to roll down her cheeks.

Father Luke meanwhile was perplexed. There was something about Grace that he found very endearing and worrying all at the same time. He felt tempted to put his arm about her and comfort her, although he didn't of course. He tried to tell himself that he was merely being kind. After all, he was a priest and as such he shouldn't allow himself to become overly involved . . . but she looked so sad and vulnerable.

'I don't think I quite realised what was involved in becoming a nun,' Grace confided in a choked voice. 'And I'm beginning to understand now what a privileged life I've led. At home I had maids to wait on me and things continued much the same way when I went to Aunt Gertie's. I'm afraid I must be a very selfish person.'

'Of course you're not, you're a *lovely* person,' Father Luke blurted before he could stop himself and instantly wished that he could bite his tongue out. It had been a very unprofessional thing to say but that was the effect she had on him. Sometimes, when he was with her, he forgot that he was a man of the cloth and spoke to her about things that had nothing at all to do with religion. He knew she loved white roses and toffee; that she had learned to swim in the sea since coming to live in Wales and that she loved animals. None of these things had anything to do with the path they had both chosen to take in worshipping the Lord and the Holy Mother, and yet the more he saw of her the more he wanted to know about her. It was very unsettling.

'Perhaps it would be better if I left you to study the scriptures alone today,' he suddenly said as he rose abruptly.

Grace blinked with surprise. This wasn't the first time he had cut their meetings short and she wondered if he was annoyed with her. She watched as he gathered his things together and strode away without another word. Once he was gone she lay her head on her arm and wept, feeling more alone and abandoned than she had ever felt in her life.

By the time Grace's first visit to her aunt was due, she was feeling much better. Being the newest and the youngest member of the convent meant being responsible for the most menial jobs and Grace had done plenty of them by then. She had scraped potatoes and peeled vegetables with the elderly nun who did the cooking until her fingers were so sore they tingled from being immersed in cold water. She had scrubbed toilets and mopped floors, scrubbed laundry until her hands were red raw and worked for long hours digging vegetable plots in the kitchen garden until she was sure her back would break. Then there was the ironing: mountains of sheets and pillow cases that she never seemed to come to the end of. And between these chores she had spent her time on her knees in prayer or learning parts of the Bible by heart. More and more she realised what a pampered life she had led. Back at home, Mrs Batley and Mabel had waited on her hand and foot and when she went to live with her aunt, Mrs Llewelyn had continued to do the same. She had never known what it was like to have to prepare or cook a meal, her clothes had always been washed and ironed for her and she hadn't even known what it was like to have to make her own bed, let alone clean toilets.

The whole experience had been a huge change for her but now that she was becoming more accustomed to the nun's way of life Grace was sure that eventually it would make her a better person. Admittedly there were things she missed. Sweet-smelling shampoo for a start, rather than the coarse soap the nuns used, and soft towels and tasty meals, but then she accepted that going without these things would be worth it in the end, so she endured everything without complaint. Now at last she had permission to leave the convent with strict instructions that she should be back within two hours, so she set off immediately, determined not to miss a precious minute with her aunt. As she made her way down the hillside through the forest she breathed deeply. That was another thing she had missed; being able to wander where she wanted to at will.

Soon the cottage came into sight and Grace hurried her steps. Her aunt was in the garden feeding the goats and she raised her hand in greeting as Grace approached although she raised her eyebrows when she saw what she was wearing.

'Well, you'll certainly win no fashion contest in that get-up,' was her greeting and Grace had to stop herself from laughing. This from someone who was clad in big boots and men's breeches. One of the dogs ran to greet her, his tail wagging furiously and Grace bent to stroke his silky ears as her aunt asked, 'So how is it going?' She thought Grace had lost a little weight; worrying, considering she was already thin as a beanpole.

'Fine.' Grace gazed about appreciatively. The garden was a blaze of colour with every sort of flower she could think of growing closely together. There were hollyhocks, foxgloves, roses of every hue, tall Michaelmas daisies, all giving off a heady scent that made a lovely change from the smell of disinfectant and carbolic soap she had become accustomed to at the convent.

251

Her aunt glanced at her reddened hands then and commented, 'It looks like you've been working hard?'

'Yes, all the nuns have to. We have a rota so I'm probably doing something different every day between masses and learning the Bible. But have you heard how my father is?'

'Still the same according to Nurse Matthews. I still ring every week and should there be any change I'd get word to you.'

Grace made to go into the cottage to see the Llewelyns but her aunt caught her sleeve gently and warned, 'Dylan is in there, just so you know.'

Grace nodded and moved on. She had hoped she would avoid seeing him but she supposed they were bound to bump into each other at some point so she may as well get it over and done with.

He was sitting at the table sipping some of Mrs Llewelyn's excellent home-made lemonade when she entered the kitchen.

'Hello, Dylan.'

He nodded but made no attempt to speak, and just for a moment she felt a pang of regret. What an easy life she could have had compared to the life at the convent had she married Dylan, but the trouble was she didn't love him. Luckily she got a much warmer welcome from Cerys, who hurried over to give her a hug.

'Why, I swear you've got thinner,' she declared as she looked disapprovingly at Grace's shapeless dress and the string in her hair. 'There's some dinner left in case you haven't eaten. Will you have it now? I've got it keeping warm in the oven.'

Grace had eaten but the thought of one of Mrs Llewelyn's lovely dinners was too much to resist so she nodded.

'Yes, please.' Grace sat next to Dylan at the table but he instantly rose.

'I'd best be off,' he said to his nan. 'I promised me dad I'd help him do some work on the boat this afternoon.'

'Right you are, cariad. I'll see you the same time next week, shall I?'

He nodded and left the kitchen without even glancing in Grace's direction, which hurt her more than she had thought it would. She had hoped that they could remain friends but it appeared that it was all or nothing with Dylan.

'Don't mind our Dylan,' Mrs Llewelyn soothed, seeing Grace's glum expression. 'He was fair taken with you and you've dashed his hopes but happen he'll come round in time. A handsome young chap like him won't be on his own for long. The girls will fair queue up for him.'

Grace hoped that she was right. Dylan was a lovely young man and she wanted him to be happy. She then went on to tell Mrs Llewelyn all about her first month in the convent as the woman darted about getting her a drink and fetching the dinner she had saved for her from the oven. Grace's stomach rumbled in anticipation at the sight of it. Thick, juicy slices of roast beef, cauliflower and carrots fresh from the vegetable patch, and roast potatoes cooked just the way she liked them all awash with thick, creamy gravy.

'That was delicious,' she said when she had cleared every morsel from her plate. She thought gloomily of the tasteless meals she would be eating when she returned to the convent.

Mrs Llewelyn smiled. 'Good. I've heard the meals aren't up to much up there. Is that right?'

'The food is very plain,' Grace admitted. 'To be honest I left a lot of it for the first week or so. I'm afraid old Sister Mary who does the cooking believes more in quantity than quality, bless her, but then I got so hungry that I would have eaten anything and I always clear my plate now.'

'So why don't I make you a nice hamper of food to take back with you?'

Grace giggled. 'I don't think that would go down very well with the Reverend Mother. But thank you for the thought. I have quite enough to eat, it just isn't as tasty as your food, that's all.'

The time she spent with them seemed to pass in the blink of an eye and before she knew it, it was time to go back to the convent.

Aled Llewelyn had come in by then and he offered to walk back with her but Grace told him she would be fine.

'So, will you rest for the remainder of the day now, it being the Sabbath?' Mrs Llewelyn asked her at the door. She thought that Grace looked worn out and there were dark shadows beneath her eyes.

'No, I shall be going to a mass in the chapel when I get back, then after the evening meal myself and the postulants will be studying the Bible.'

Cerys thought it all sounded very boring but she kissed her lightly and made no comment as Grace left to spend a few minutes with her aunt in the garden before she set off.

Aunt Gertie kissed her soundly on the cheek and when Grace left her there were tears in her eyes.

That evening, Father Luke joined the sisters for supper and once or twice his eyes locked with Grace's but they both hastily looked away from each other.

It was the young priest who was supposed to take Grace and the postulants for Bible study that evening so she was somewhat surprised after they had all entered the chapel to find Sister Mathilda waiting for them.

'Father Luke had matters to attend to down in the village,' she explained as they all settled into the pews. Grace seemed to have a permanent ache in her backside nowadays from sitting so long on the hard wooden seats. But she missed Father Luke. He always managed to inject some humour into the lessons whereas Sister Mathilda was very straight-faced. Now that she came to think of

254

it, the priest had missed quite a few lessons with her lately and she wondered if she had offended him in some way. Perhaps I should ask him the next time I see him, she mused. But then the lesson began and soon she was immersed in it.

※

Back in Nuneaton Mrs Batley was still struggling to come to terms with the way of life Grace had chosen. 'Why would a young lass like that choose to lock herself away from the world in a convent, eh?' she asked Mabel. 'I mean she had everything going for her. Admittedly she ain't had the happiest of lives, but I reckon when him upstairs pops his clogs she's going to be a very wealthy young woman.' She paused then as something occurred to her. 'An' have you noticed what a frequent visitor Mr Mackenzie's become?'

Mabel put her head to one side and thought about it for a moment before saying, 'Aye, he has been calling round a lot now you come to mention it. To be honest, I don't reckon he's ever had much time fer the judge, although he always had a good word to say fer the mistress, God bless her soul. But then now he's in charge of all the master's finances, I dare say he has to keep him up to date.'

'Huh! Finances, me arse!' Mrs Batley scoffed. 'I reckon it's Nurse Matthews is the draw. Think about it, she's goin' to great lengths to look her best nowadays, ain't she?'

'I suppose she is,' Mabel admitted thoughtfully.

'We were as thick as thieves till lately but I've noticed she ain't comin' down to keep me company so much anymore. Happen she's worried that I'll disapprove but if they were to get together it would be no bad thing, if you ask me,' Mrs Batley went on. 'Mr Mackenzie was widowed young and to my knowledge Nurse Matthews has never been married. But they're the right age for each other so good luck to 'em that's what I say. A bit o' romance never hurt anybody, to my mind.'

255

Mabel blushed then and glanced towards Harry who had been reading the paper but whose ears had now pricked up. He smiled and gave her an almost imperceptible nod so, gulping, Mabel said quietly, 'Actually, Batty . . . there's somethin' me an' Harry have been meanin' to tell yer.' This seemed as good a time as any.

'Oh yes?'

'Well the thing is . . . we were thinkin' it were about time we took the plunge . . . got married like . . . what do yer think?'

'I think it's about bloody time,' Mrs Batley said with a grin. 'I thought yer were never goin' to get round to it. When is the happy day to be?'

'We thought round about Christmas.'

'Right, well we'd best put the plans in motion then. It's been some time since this house had anythin' to celebrate. I shall do a slap-up spread fer you an' yer family the like o' which this place ain't seen for a long time an' sod him upstairs. He can hardly object, can he?'

She saw Harry and Mabel exchange a smile that melted her heart. They were clearly meant for each other. I wonder if the young mistress will be allowed to come home fer the celebrations? she wondered. She decided she would ask Gertie to pass on the news the very next time she rang. Meantime, there would be lots of organising to do – there were the flowers to think of and the dress of course, and a hundred other things.

Seeing the dreamy look on the older woman's face, Mabel seemed to read her mind and told her hastily, 'We're only plannin' on havin' a quiet do, Batty. Me mam an' dad ain't that well off, as yer know.'

'Quiet do, me foot!' Mrs Batley frowned. Over the years she had come to look on Mabel as the daughter she had never been blessed with and she intended to give her and Harry a day to remember. She would use a little of the money the old master had left her to do it and gladly. 'You'll have a weddin' fit fer a princess,' she told her firmly and now it was Harry who was grinning. Knowing Mrs Batley as he did, there would be no use arguing with her once she had made her mind up about something. She could be as stubborn as an old mule so he was happy to sit back and leave all the arrangements to the women.

Chapter Thirty-Two

Before everyone knew it, Christmas was almost upon them. Grace and the postulants had been allowed to go out and gather holly and ivy and now it decorated the chapel and the usually bare corridors of the convent. The shiny green leaves and rich red berries on the holly made the otherwise bare corners look homely, although, as Grace had discovered, it was almost as cold inside as it was out. At night, her small cell was so bitter that her breath hung in the air in front of her as she hastily changed into her coarse nightgown, and she would lie beneath her blankets for a long time, shivering.

One cold, frosty night as she tried to get warm, her thoughts turned to Christmas Day. She and the postulants had been given permission to visit their families for dinner. It would be a very different Christmas to the ones that had gone before, however. There would be no exchanging of gifts this year, for Grace was not allowed to bring material possessions with her. Even so, she was still looking forward to it. Thinking about Christmas inevitably brought back memories of her old home, where preparations would be under way for Mabel and Harry's wedding. They were to be wed the week before Christmas and though she was sad that she wouldn't be able to attend, part of her was glad that she wouldn't have to face her father again. Aunt Gertie reported that he was still clinging to life, although no one knew how. She still missed her mother dreadfully too, and from time to time had terrible nightmares about the night her father had had his seizure, but thankfully not as often now so she was grateful for that at least.

Life at the convent was getting better, although she still struggled with certain things. She missed being able to wander at will up and down the valleys. She missed swimming in the sea and picking wild flowers, but then she supposed these were small things to forsake if one day she was to become a true nun. Some of the other postulants were almost ready to take their final vows and she envied them, for most of them seemed to be able to leave the outside world behind with ease.

But despite her difficulties, Father Luke had informed the Reverend Mother that he felt Grace would be ready to become a postulant in the New Year and she was excited about it. She would then wear the white veil and have to dedicate even more time than she did now to prayer. She didn't mind the thought at all. Her main concern, though, was her feelings for Father Luke. An image of his face would flash in front of her eyes when she should be praying, and just the sight of him could make her heart skip a beat. Sometimes she felt as if she was just living for the times they spent together, and it confused her.

Eventually she slept and dreamed of Father Luke, as she often did.

On Christmas Day, after some hours spent praying in the convent chapel, Grace set off to spend some time with the Llewelyns and Aunt Gertie. She wished she had a small gift for each of them. But then, as the Reverend Mother had told her, Christmas was not about gifts, it was a day when everyone should be celebrating the birth of their Saviour, the baby Jesus.

'Ah, here you are then,' Aunt Gertie said when Grace stepped into the kitchen bringing an icy blast of air with her that made the fire roar up the chimney. 'Shut that door, do! We've only just managed to get the room warm.'

After the biting cold of the convent, Grace felt as if she was walking into an oven but she didn't comment as she hurried across the room to kiss her aunt. 'Merry Christmas, Aunt Gertie.'

'The same to you, dear. Now take that ugly old cape off and come and get warm by the fire. You can tell us what you've been up to then.'

Grace giggled. 'Truthfully, there isn't much to tell: I've prayed, scrubbed floors, prayed, done the laundry, prayed, helped in the kitchen and prayed, and that's about it. But Father Luke thinks I may be almost ready to become a proper postulant soon, possibly in the New Year.'

'Huh, it's a waste of a young life, if you were to ask me,' Mrs Llewelyn grumbled and Grace and her aunt grinned at each other.

Grace was relieved to see that Dylan wasn't there, she would have felt awkward, although from what she had gathered during past visits he was well and truly over her now. In fact, Cerys had told her that he'd had more girlfriends than hot dinners in the previous months. Grace could only hope that one of them would be right for him as she still felt guilty for not being able to return his feelings.

'Mrs Batley was full of Mabel and Harry's wedding when I rang her the other day,' Aunt Gertie informed her. 'It went off really well, apparently, and when it was over she paid for them to have four days' honeymoon in Skegness as her present to them.'

'I'm so pleased, and how nice of her.' Grace threw her cloak over the back of the chair and sat at the table with her aunt to help her finish preparing the Brussel sprouts. There was a nice fat goose cooking in the oven and the delicious smell made Grace's stomach rumble. 'And did she mention how my father was?'

'No better no worse, apparently, but there is one more little bit of gossip. Mrs Batley reckons that something is going on between Mr Mackenzie and Nurse Matthews.'

'Really?' Grace was surprised but pleased for them if that was the case. 'Then there could be another wedding in the offing.' She chuckled. 'Mrs Batley will be in her element.'

Mr Llewelyn, who had been outside feeding the chickens, joined them and after giving Grace a kiss he settled down next to the fire to smoke his pipe.

By the time she left later that afternoon, Grace was feeling happy, despite the bittersweet memories of Christmases spent with her mother. The Christmas dinner had been delicious and she wasn't looking forward to going back to her cold, bleak room in the convent at all.

I'm so ungrateful, she scolded herself. The postulants all seemed so content with their lot, so much so that some of them had preferred to stay at the convent and spend Christmas Day in prayer.

Already the light was fading from the afternoon and a thick frost was forming so Grace quickened her pace. It would be darker still under the trees and she didn't want to get lost in the forest. She had only gone a few yards into the woods when something suddenly shot across the path in front of her and she yelped with alarm before realising that it was only a fox. Taking a deep breath, she moved on again until a voice saying her name startled her yet again.

'Who is it?' She spun around quickly to see Dylan step out from behind a tree. He looked perished – his nose was glowing red and his unmittened hands were blue. She realised that he must have been waiting for her and didn't know whether to be angry or sorry for him.

'Hello, Grace,' he said timidly. He'd dreamed about this meeting but now it had come he felt humiliated and embarrassed. Over the last months, he'd sown his wild oats with any lass that was willing, and there'd been no shortage of them. The trouble was, none of them could hold a candle to Grace in his eyes, so he'd waited here to see her, praying that she'd had a change of heart and was ready to give up this stupid idea of becoming a nun. 'I, er . . . thought I'd just stop by an' wish you a Merry Christmas.' The words sounded inane even to his own ears. She must have known he'd been purposely waiting for her but she didn't blink as she answered, 'And the same to you, Dylan.'

They stared at each other for a while, neither quite knowing what to say, until Grace broke the silence. 'I ought to be getting back. Sister Mathilda will be angry if I'm late.'

'Would you like me to walk with you?'

She heard the hopeful note in his voice and sadly shook her head. 'Thanks, but it might be best if I go on my own.'

Seeing his downcast expression her gentle heart softened. 'I . . . I often think of the happy times we spent together,' she said softly. 'And I'm sorry I couldn't be what you hoped, but you deserve someone who will love you with all their heart. I will always look upon you as a true friend and remember you with fondness, so be happy, Dylan. Goodbye.'

He watched until she disappeared into the gloom before ramming his hands into his coat pockets and slowly turning in the direction of Beehive Cottage. He may as well call in and get a hot drink inside him. It felt like he'd been standing out in the cold for hours and what good had it done him? He cursed himself. For days he'd been practising what he would say to her and what had he said when it came to it? Practically nothing!

Grace meanwhile was hurrying towards the dim light beyond the trees ahead. She had seen the pain in Dylan's eyes and it had hurt her more than she cared to admit because she cared for him but she could never imagine loving him as a woman should love her husband. She could never imagine loving any man in a physical way if it came to that. Every time she even thought of it she remembered the feel of her father's hot, sweaty hands on her body and broke out in a cold sweat. The only man she felt truly safe with was Father Luke and she supposed that was because he was a priest and had taken a vow of chastity so would never think of such things. Why does everything always have to be so complicated? she wondered. But she had chosen her path in life and there was no veering away from it now, so she walked on with her head down. Suddenly some of the joy had gone from the day.

In the New Year, Grace took the white veil of the postulant and her life changed yet again. She was still allowed to visit her aunt but not as frequently, for now she was preparing herself for when she became a bride of Christ. Oddly enough, she didn't see quite so much of Father Luke now. He and Sister Eileen shared the postulants' Bible classes between them and the priest had put Grace into the elderly nun's group, which, much to her surprise, had hurt her. She shouldn't really have cared who tutored her, she supposed, and yet she found that she missed him and still thought of him constantly. She saw him occasionally going to and fro to the chapel and he always inclined his head and smiled at her, but he never stopped to speak anymore, so with that she had to be content.

She was still expected to do the back-breaking jobs she had done before along with the other postulants and sometimes when she listened to them she felt envious. They seemed so committed and excited about the life they were about to embark on and appeared not to have any regrets about their families or the things they had left behind. So why do I? she asked herself in an agony of guilt. She was still frequently sent before the Reverend Mother like a naughty schoolgirl for things she had done wrong or things she had failed to do and sometimes she wondered if the serene-faced woman was losing patience with her. The last time was when she had been caught standing on her bed gazing out of her window at the balmy night sky after lights out when she should have been kneeling at the side of her bed in prayer.

'Do you still truly feel that this is the path you wish to follow, Grace?' the Reverend Mother had asked and Grace had nodded vigorously.

'Oh, *yes*, mother . . . It's just that sometimes I get distracted. It was such a lovely evening, I just wanted to look at the stars. But I will try harder, *really* I will.'

The woman had smiled at her. It was very hard to be annoyed with Grace, she so wanted to please everyone, although she didn't always succeed.

'Very well. I can understand that you love nature, but in future your prayers must come first. Now go, child, and try harder.'

By the time Grace celebrated her eighteenth birthday, some of the girls who had been postulants with her had already taken their final vows, but Grace feared she was still a long way from taking that step and she knew the Reverend Mother wouldn't even contemplate it for her just yet. It had been a bitterly cold winter and some of the nuns, including Sister Eileen, had come down with chills that confined them to bed.

One day, the Reverend Mother called her into her office and told her, 'I am going to ask Father Luke to give you some one-on-one time.'

So on a cold and frosty morning in early January 1911, Grace sat face to face with Father Luke in the chapel. It was freezing in there and yet she was so happy to see him that she didn't feel it.

Some time ago, she had hacked off her beautiful red hair to shoulder length. She saw no point in keeping it too long – it would be shorn when she took her final vows anyway and it was so much easier to manage at the length it was – although already it had sprung into curls again. Her figure had filled out slightly too, although she was still petite, and now Father Luke saw a young woman rather than a girl sitting before him and his throat felt dry. What was it about this girl that made him ache to know her better? he wondered. It was a sin for a man of the cloth to have such thoughts and yet he couldn't seem to stop himself, which was why he had suggested that Grace should join Sister Eileen's group.

'How are you?' he asked awkwardly. When she smiled he felt his legs turn to jelly.

'I am well, father . . . and yourself?' Grace could feel the colour flooding into her face as it suddenly hit her like a blow: she, who was preparing to offer herself to Christ, had fallen in love with Father Luke! It was ridiculous, preposterous and yet deep down she finally realised it was true. That was why she always felt safe in his presence . . . she loved him, but up until now she had not allowed herself to admit it.

Confusion made her gasp and put her hand to her mouth, then suddenly she was gathering her things together and making to rise.

'Grace . . . where are you going?' The distress in his voice made tears spring to her eyes and she looked at him helplessly. Their eyes locked and she saw mirrored in his what she felt for him. He cared for her too, she realised with a jolt of pleasure, but then the reality of the situation hit her full force and she knew that it was hopeless. Their love must never be allowed to blossom. What they felt for each other was a sin.

'I . . . perhaps I should go,' she breathed, but his hand was on her arm sending tingles all down it.

'No . . . not yet . . .' Father Luke looked as confused as she did as he too battled with feelings he had desperately tried to ignore. He had hoped that if he avoided her company he would

265

stop thinking about her but it had all been in vain. Her face would pop into his mind when he least expected it and he had found himself looking for a glimpse of her at every opportunity.

And then suddenly they were both standing and as he pulled her into his arms she didn't try to stop him. Neither of them could fight what they felt for each other anymore. It felt right and in that moment, she knew that this was meant to be. Her head was against his chest as he stroked her hair and she could hear his heart pounding in time with her own.

'Oh, my *darling* girl . . . this is so wrong, we should stop,' he said in a strangled voice. 'I've tried so hard for so long to ignore the feelings I have for you but I just can't seem to help myself.'

'Nor me,' she whispered as she stared up into his wonderful deep blue eyes. They were so full of emotion that they seemed almost black today. And then suddenly his lips were on hers and she had the sense of coming home. This was where she was meant to be.

He kissed her lips, her eyes, her throat and somewhere along the way her white veil slid off and fell to the floor unnoticed. Then he gently took her hand and led her unprotestingly to a small room tucked away at the side of the chapel. It was seldom used and old, long-discarded habits hung on pegs on the wall. Reaching across her he snatched some of them and threw them down on the floor before gently lowering her onto them. Once more his lips were on hers and they might have been the only two people left in the whole world. She clung to him as if she might never let him go as his hand began to gently stroke her breasts through the rough material of her habit, and then he was gently pulling it over her head and gazing in wonder at her tenderly. His hands began to wander over her breasts making her nipples tauten with desire and setting off powerful emotions and feelings that she had never known before. Their hands explored each other's bodies on the uncomfortable floor but it didn't matter where they were anymore. They were oblivious to anything but each other.

His hand was stroking her thigh now and she sighed with desire as her passion rose to match his. He was whispering endearments and she wished that the moment could go on for ever. And then suddenly he too was flinging off his clothes and she gazed at his perfect body in wonder.

'I . . . I should stop,' he groaned.

She shook her head. 'No . . . no.' He was astride her now and she arched her back to meet him. She felt a brief sharp pain that lasted for no more than a minute and then she was clinging to him as their passion rose and they moved together as one until at last stars exploded behind her eyes and she writhed in ecstasy.

'Oh, my darling girl, I'm *so* sorry,' he choked as he lay on top of her, catching his breath, sometime later. 'I've done the unforgivable and taken advantage of you.' She could feel his tears on her cheeks and she gently wiped them away as she smiled serenely up at him.

'No,' she assured him softly. 'I *wanted* you to do it.'

Despite her assurance, he sat up abruptly and, deeply distressed, ran his hand through his thick blonde hair. The magical time they had shared was suddenly over. Grace began to yank her clothes back on and tidy herself, suddenly confused as the enormity of what they had done came home to her. They had committed the cardinal sin! A priest and a postulant, it was like something Cerys Llewelyn might read in one of the romances she was so fond of borrowing from the free lending reading room in Pwllheli!

And yet still she couldn't regret what they had done. 'What will happen now?' she asked tentatively.

He shook his head as he hastily dressed. 'I don't know, Grace. Forgive me. We must pray to God for an answer.' He rose then and walked away without giving her a backward glance and she sat staring at a statue of the Sacred Mother as she tried to put her thoughts into some sort of order.

The next few days passed in a blur. Many of the nuns were still down with sickness so those that were well spent most of their time caring for them, running two and fro, mopping fevered brows and emptying chamber pots. Grace had always thought of the nuns as beings apart so it was a shock to find that they were merely women beneath their dark habits. The illness raged on for almost a month before everyone slowly started to recover and some sort of normality returned to the convent.

It was round about then that Grace began to feel unwell and thought that perhaps she too was coming down with the illness. And yet, strangely, her symptoms didn't seem to match those of the others. It was only first thing in the morning that she felt unwell and would have to rush off to the toilets to be sick.

It's just a sickness bug, she told herself and tried to go on as normal, although for every minute of every day her thoughts were on Father Luke. She hadn't set eyes on him since the day in the chapel and longed to be able to speak to him, but suddenly another elderly father had appeared to take the services and the Bible class and life went on much as it had before.

Chapter Thirty-Three

'Where is Father Luke?' she hissed to the young postulant sitting next to her, one day early in February as they took their places in the chapel and waited for the service to begin.

'I heard he asked to be sent to another parish,' the young woman whispered back, and Grace's stomach did a cartwheel. Did this mean that she would never see him again? Had he lied when he told her that he loved her? Her heart broke at the thought. She was still feeling unwell and for the last week she had noticed a slight change in her breasts. They were swollen and sore, but then she had been working very hard while the other nuns were ill so she supposed that she had just overdone it. Now it was all she could do to concentrate on the singing and the prayers. Why would Father Luke ask to be moved after what had happened between them? Had it meant nothing to him? She blinked to stop the tears from falling and somehow managed to get through the mass. The misery she was feeling did not go unnoticed and two weeks later she was summoned to the Reverend Mother's office. She made her way there on feet that felt like lead, looking deathly pale.

'Are you feeling unwell, Grace? You look very pale,' the Reverend Mother asked when she saw Grace.

'I'm all right, thank you, mother. Just a little under the weather, that's all,' Grace muttered. She felt as if her world had fallen apart.

She had thought that her life was mapped out for her but those few precious minutes she had spent with the priest in the chapel had made her question if she was really cut out to be a nun. How can I be? she constantly asked herself. She was wicked, evil even, in the eyes of God, surely? How could she offer herself to him as his bride now? She had been soiled by human hands.

'Would you like me to call the doctor in to take a look at you?'

The Reverend Mother's words brought her thoughts sharply back to the present and she shook her head. 'No really . . . I shall be fine.'

'Then I'm going to recommend a few days' bed rest. You have worked diligently caring for the sisters that were ill. Don't think your efforts went unnoticed,' the kindly nun told her. 'I shall have your meals delivered to your room for the time being and if you are no better in a few days' time I shall insist that the doctor sees you. You may spend the time in meditation and reading your Bible. Go along, child.'

Grace nodded and miserably made her way back to her room. She knew that the Reverend Mother had only been trying to be kind but she would have preferred to stay busy. At least she didn't have time to think when she was working. Now the next few days stretched interminably ahead of her.

Grace stayed in bed for four days but the rest didn't seem to do her much good. Her breasts were still tender and the sickness continued in the mornings, but all the same she was relieved when she was allowed to return to her normal duties.

It was the middle of March when she was hanging over the lavatory being violently sick early one morning that Sister Mathilda found her.

'Goodness me, my child. Whatever is the matter?' she asked.

Grace glanced up at her, her face waxen and her eyes sunken from lack of sleep. 'I . . . I think I've got some sort of stomach complaint but I can't seem to shift it,' she responded innocently.

'Right, well it's back to bed for you,' the old nun told her firmly. 'The doctor is calling in later this morning to see Sister Mildred and I shall get him to take a look at you while he's here. Come along now.'

Grace reluctantly dragged herself back to bed where, much to her surprise, she instantly fell fast asleep. She was woken much later that morning by Sister Mathilda who had shown the doctor to her room.

'I shall leave you now,' the nun said and glided silently away as the doctor smiled at Grace.

'Right then, young lady, let's have a look at you, shall we? The sister informed me that she found you being sick this morning. Has this happened before?'

Grace nodded. 'Yes, it's being going on for about two months now . . .' She blushed. 'And my breasts are sore too.'

He took his stethoscope from his bag and, after asking her to lift her nightdress, he gave her a thorough examination before straightening. Grace noticed that he looked solemn and asked in a timid voice, 'Is there something seriously wrong with me?'

'Nothing that you're going to die from,' he assured her. 'I'll get the Reverend Mother to explain what's wrong to you.' He returned his stethoscope to his bag and snapped it shut before turning on his heel and leaving without another word.

Shortly after, Sister Mathilda came to say that the Reverend Mother was ready to see her and Grace followed her through the corridors with her heart in her throat. What if the doctor had been lying and she was seriously ill? Perhaps this was her punishment for being so wicked.

'Come in, Grace, and shut the door behind you, please.' The Reverend Mother was standing in the window looking out over the grounds of the convent with her arms tucked into the sleeves of her habit, and she looked very concerned.

Grace stood in front of the desk and eventually the nun said quietly, 'I don't quite know how to tell you this, Grace. But after his examination the doctor is fairly certain that you are going to have a baby.'

Grace's eyes almost popped out of her head, and for a moment the floor rushed up to greet her and she had to grip the edge of the desk.

'B-but I *can't* be!' she gasped.

'The doctor is quite certain that you are.' The woman eyed her calmly. She was almost as shocked at the news as Grace was. Grace had always seemed to be so innocent and naive, but perhaps that was the problem? Perhaps someone had taken advantage of her?

'Has some man' – the nun chose her words carefully – 'forced himself upon you?' she ended and was further shocked when Grace shook her head.

'No, mother,' she said in a small voice.

'Then would you like to tell me who the father of the baby is?'

Grace reeled with shock. She was carrying Father Luke's baby, but how could she tell the nun that? She shook her head mutely and the nun sighed.

'Then I'm afraid you must realise what has to happen. The situation is impossible and you can no longer remain here.'

Grace had been standing with her head bowed in shame but now it snapped up as she stared at the nun in disbelief. 'You're sending me away?'

'I have no choice, do I?'

Grace saw the sense in what she was saying. Who had ever heard of a pregnant postulant?

'I would like you to go and change into the clothes that you arrived in and leave immediately. You may leave the dress you are wearing on the bed.'

Grace nodded numbly. There was clearly no more to be said so she turned and left without another word so she didn't see the tears that rolled down the nun's cheeks.

Once back in her room, she stared around her. This small, cell-like space had become her home and it was strange to think that she would never see it again. She removed the clothes she had arrived in so long ago from the small chest of drawers, folded her white veil and dress and placed them neatly on the end of the bed. She then slipped on her skirt, blouse and sandals, surprised at how strange it felt to be wearing them again. It took only a matter of minutes to pack her rosary and the few items that she had brought with her into her bag and she was ready to leave. After one last glance about her room, she stepped out into the familiar corridors and made her way to the front door. The nuns she passed on the way kept their heads bowed and she flushed with shame. There was no one to say goodbye to her; it was as if the last years had never been and she let herself quietly out of the front door. Glancing back as she walked away she thought she saw the Reverend Mother standing at her window, but the figure quickly vanished and she couldn't be sure. Some of the postulants were working in the kitchen garden but Grace hurried on with her head down. She didn't want to talk to anyone just yet; she wasn't even sure where she was going.

A short time later when she reached the shelter of the forest, she sat down heavily on the grass with her back to a stout tree trunk. Everything had happened so fast that her mind was spinning. She was going to have a baby! *A baby!* And it was Father Luke's baby! Her hand dropped to her stomach and she stroked it absent-mindedly as her heart broke. He must have regretted what had happened between them, otherwise why would he have asked to be moved? But she didn't regret it and at least now she would have a part of him to keep for ever.

She swiped at a tear as she remembered the look of disappointment on the Reverend Mother's face. It must have been such a shock to her when the doctor told her and she would have felt that Grace had let her down. But it was done now and she was

273

going to have to get on with things. At least I shall be all right financially, she found herself thinking as she tried to be practical. Mr Mackenzie would have continued to send her allowance to her aunt each month so there should be a tidy amount amassed by now. But where should she go? She shied away from the thought of returning to her home town. How could she face her father with an illegitimate child growing inside her? She doubted that Aunt Gertie would be too pleased about it either, but hopefully she would give her shelter until she had found somewhere reasonable for herself and the baby, when it came, to live.

It felt strange to be sitting there with nothing to do and for a moment she enjoyed the sense of freedom. But Grace was a practical person at heart and she knew that she would have to go and face her aunt and give her the shocking news sometime, so she may as well go and get it over with. She rose slowly and picked her way through the trees. She hadn't been allowed to visit her aunt for almost three months now so she would be surprised to see her, especially wearing ordinary clothes. When the cottage came into view, Grace stood for a moment admiring it and realised that she had missed it. She could see Mrs Llewelyn hanging freshly washed sheets on the line with her mouth full of wooden clothes pegs and Mr Llewelyn was digging in the vegetable garden. Grace took a deep breath and ploughed on.

It was Cerys Llewelyn who saw her approaching first and as she took in Grace's attire, her mouth gaped and the pegs dropped to the ground.

'Why, cariad, whatever are you doing here and dressed like that?'

'I'll explain later, Mrs Llewelyn,' Grace told her calmly. 'But I need to speak to my aunt first. Where is she?'

'She's inside on the phone . . . but I ought to warn you—' The last part of the sentence was lost on Grace as she stepped into the cottage and quietly closed the door behind her.

Gertie paused with the phone receiver still to her ear when Grace entered. She showed no surprise whatsoever to see her, but then Grace knew that it took a lot to shock Aunt Gertie.

'I'll call you back,' her aunt said shortly to whoever it was she was speaking to, her eyes still trained on her niece.

She dropped the phone back into the cradle and Grace took a deep breath. It was best to get it over and done with. But she had no chance to say anything, for Gertie told her, 'My dear girl, that was Mrs Batley and I'm afraid I have some very bad news for you . . . your father passed away early this morning.'

Grace just stared at her. This was the second shock she had received today and she just couldn't take it in. But one thing was for certain, now was not the time to tell her aunt about the baby.

Chapter Thirty-Four

'Eeh, what a day this has turned out to be,' Mrs Batley commented as she poured boiling water onto the tea leaves in the teapot. The undertaker had just left with the judge's body, which would now lie in the chapel of rest until his funeral. The words had barely left her lips when Nurse Matthews walked into the room looking very smart indeed in a little hat that she wore at a jaunty angle and a smart two-piece suit. She had lost a lot of weight over the last few months and out of uniform she looked quite attractive. She was carrying the small suitcase she had arrived with and as they caught sight of it both Mabel and Mrs Batley raised their eyebrows.

'I'm leaving,' the nurse informed them. 'There is no need for me to be here now my patient has gone but I wanted to say goodbye before I went.'

'But what about the wages that are due to you?' Mrs Batley said. 'Mr Mackenzie hasn't had time to come and sort everything out yet.'

'Oh, don't worry about that.' Nurse Matthews smiled. 'I shall send my address through to him and he can forward them on to me. I thought I might go and stay with my sister in Ledbury for a while before I take up another post.'

'Well, yer deserve a rest,' Mrs Batley conceded with a little catch in her voice. She had grown fond of the nurse during the time she had been there. 'The judge weren't the easiest o' patients. But are yer sure yer up to travellin' today? None of us got much sleep last night after the judge had another seizure. Why don't yer wait until tomorrow?'

Nurse Matthews's face softened but she shook her head as she drew on her gloves. 'Thank you, but I'd rather get off, if it's all the same to you. I rang my sister this morning to tell her to expect me and she'll be worried if I don't show up.' She crossed the room and shook Mrs Batley's hand then turned and did the same to Mabel. 'Goodbye. I hope everything works out well for you.' She suddenly looked quite tearful. But then she had been with them over two years now so Mrs Batley supposed it was quite natural; she was feeling a little tearful herself.

'Goodbye an' take good care o' yerself, Edith,' Mrs Batley responded, and minutes later they heard the front door close behind the woman. Mrs Batley sighed, it was the end of another era. Then glancing at the clock, she commented, 'Grace's train should be arrivin' any time now. Gertie said she'd caught the first one after bein' told the news this mornin' so I dare say we'd best get a meal on the go.' It was late afternoon by then and as she fetched some potatoes from the pantry, she frowned and said, 'It's funny that Mr Mackenzie ain't been yet, ain't it? I rang his office to tell 'em what had happened first thing this mornin'. I thought he'd be straight round here. Still, he was perhaps busy wi' other business. No doubt he'll be here tomorrow.' She set Mabel to work peeling the potatoes while she arranged some lamb chops in a baking tin and added chopped onions and peppers before popping it in the range. 'There,' she said, wiping her hands down her apron. 'A few veg to go with that an' the mash an' it'll make a nice dinner. I've got an apple pie I made yesterday that'll do fer the puddin'.' She briefly thought of going up to strip the bedding from the master's bed but decided it could wait until the morning. She couldn't face going into his room at present.

Grace arrived an hour later looking tired and strained.

'Eeh, pet, I'm so sorry,' Mrs Batley said as she gave her a cuddle.

'It's all right, Batty.' Grace sighed. 'We weren't that close towards the end, as you know.' That was an understatement, she thought. She had hardly been able to bring herself to stay in the same room as him since her mother's death, but now was not the time to say it. Her mother had taught her that it was wrong to speak ill of the dead and he had been her father, after all. In fact, she could remember a time when she was little when she had thought the sun rose and set for him, so her emotions were mixed.

'Has Mr Mackenzie been yet?' she asked.

'No, luvvie, I were sayin' to Mabel earlier on that it were strange he hasn't been but happen he'll be here tomorrow.'

Grace frowned. 'My aunt informed me today that Mr Mackenzie hasn't been sending my allowance through for some months now. Has he been paying you the household expenses?'

Mrs Batley nodded. 'Aye on the nose every first o' the month. Per'aps he overlooked yours, you'll need to address it wi' him when he comes. Although everythin' will change now anyway. I've no doubt yer father has left you a very wealthy young woman.' And then for the first time she noticed that Grace was dressed in ordinary clothes and her mouth gaped like a goldfish's as she asked, 'But why are yer dressed like that?'

'I have left the convent,' Grace said shortly.

'Well, I never!' Then a smile spread across the woman's face as something occurred to her. 'Does this mean that you'll be livin' here now?'

'I haven't decided what I want to do yet.' Grace sank onto a chair. Her head felt as if it was spinning. So much had happened in just one day and now she was so tired she felt she could have fallen asleep standing up.

Harry came in then covered from head to toe in coal dust. He had recently taken a job at the local pit. There wasn't really enough work to keep him going in the house now that he had it tip-top and he wanted to feel he was earning his wages.

After he had greeted Grace, Mabel instantly shooed him away to get out of his sooty clothes and have a bath while the women sat at the table drinking yet more tea. Tea was Mrs Batley's cure for everything.

'Harry is doin' really well down the pit,' Mabel told Grace proudly. 'An' there's a pit cottage comin' vacant in the next couple o' weeks in Stockingford that he's been told we can have if he wants it.'

'Oh, so won't you be working here either, then?' Grace asked. She could never remember a time when Mabel hadn't been there. She and Mrs Batley were like family to her.

'Oh aye, I shall still walk here every day,' Mabel promised and blushed. 'Till our first nipper's on the way anyway. Me an' Harry are keen to start a family as soon as you like.'

Grace was happy for her, she was positively glowing and married life clearly suited her.

The meal when it was served was tasty but Grace found that she didn't have much of an appetite and excused herself soon after to retire for an early night.

As she lay tucked up in bed, the enormity of everything that had happened that day struck home and tears began to course down her cheeks. This time yesterday she had been training to be a nun with her future mapped out for her. Today she had discovered she was going to be a mother, had been sent away from the convent in disgrace and then discovered that her father had died. It seemed incredible that her life could have changed so completely in just a few short hours, but it had and now Grace knew that she had no choice but to get on with things.

Grace rang the lawyer's firm in town the next morning only to be told by Mr Blenkinsop, one of the junior lawyers, that Mr Mackenzie hadn't turned up for work that day. It was most unlike him.

'Perhaps he's unwell?' Grace suggested but the man disagreed.

'No, Miss Kettle. I sent the clerk round to his house first thing and it was all locked up with no one there. We can't understand it.'

A little niggle of unease rippled through Grace but she told him calmly. 'Very well. Please keep trying to contact him, would you? And let me know immediately you find him.'

'Of course, Miss Kettle. Good day to you.'

The following day, with still no sign of Mr Mackenzie, Grace was forced to organise her father's funeral. It would take place the following week and she was dreading it.

So towards the weekend, when the kitchen door opened and Aunt Gertie breezed in unexpectedly, Grace was sure she had never been so pleased to see anyone in her life. Her whole world had collapsed and she had dreaded the thought of facing the funeral on her own. Her father's solicitor's firm in the town was in chaos without Mr Mackenzie to organise them and she needed to find out what was going on.

The very next day Grace and Gertie set off to see Mr Hibberd, the other partner in the judge's law firm.

'What exactly is going on?' Grace demanded when they had been shown into his office. The poor man was as jumpy as a cricket.

'We have no idea as yet,' he admitted nervously. 'Although it does appear that Mr Mackenzie has gone.'

'Gone? What do you mean *gone*?' said Gertie, glaring at him.

The poor man quaked in his boots. 'Yesterday we took it upon ourselves, with the landlord's permission, to gain entry to Mr Mackenzie's house,' the man explained. 'We were worried that he might be lying inside ill, you see, and unable to get help . . .'

'*And?*' Gertie demanded impatiently as Grace fidgeted at the side of her.

'And we found that all his clothes and personal possessions were gone. The landlord also informed us that he had only paid his rent up until the end of this week.'

Gertie frowned as she strummed her fingers on his desk. There was something fishy going on here, if she wasn't very much mistaken.

'So, he's done a moonlight flit, has he? Right then, I think it's time we gave you permission to look into my niece's finances. There's something not quite right here.'

'We were going to ask if we might do just that this very day,' he explained hastily and after fetching a form, which gave Grace's consent to look into her late father's affairs, Grace and Gertie left the office leaving strict instructions to be kept up to date with what was going on.

'I reckon that nurse who cared for your father has had something to do with this,' Gertie commented as she strode back to the house.

'Nurse Matthews?' Grace was shocked.

'Don't you find it strange that she left immediately your father died? I reckon her and Mackenzie have run off together. I think they've been planning it. Mrs Batley mentioned that they'd been seeing a fair bit of each other.'

Grace wondered if perhaps her aunt hadn't been reading too many novels but decided not to say anything until Mr Hibberd got back in touch to tell her the state of her affairs.

They didn't have to wait long. He arrived at the house late that afternoon looking weary and sick.

'I'm afraid I am the bearer of bad news,' he told them after being shown into the drawing room by Mabel. 'It appears . . .' He licked his dry lips, there was no easy way to tell them what he had found out so he decided he may just as well get on with

281

it. 'It appears that Mr Mackenzie had been spiriting your father's money into Nurse Matthews's bank account a little at a time for some long while. Ever since your father became ill, in fact. They had even remortgaged this house. I can only assume one of them faked your father's signature.'

'So, stop fiddle-faddling, man,' Gertie snapped impatiently. 'Where does this leave Grace financially?'

The poor man gulped as he took off his spectacles and began to nervously polish them with a clean white handkerchief. 'I'm afraid it means that there will be very little money left after funeral expenses, etc. He has taken everything, even the clients' money that we kept in the safe in our office. It is going to have terrible implications on the business. I fear it may have to be sold. But there is the . . .' He shrugged helplessly. This was as much of a shock to him as it clearly was to Grace and Gertie. He had worked side by side with Mr Mackenzie for years and would never have believed him capable of such deception.

'It's as I feared,' Gertie muttered. 'Have the police been informed?'

He nodded. 'Oh yes, they are trying to locate the couple even as we speak but they suspect they may have already left the country. It would seem that they have been planning this for some time between them.'

Gertie slammed her clenched fist onto a small table making the figurine on it jump.

'It's *disgraceful* that a man in his position should do such a thing, and what about my niece?' she stormed. 'She should be in a wonderful financial position now, instead of which she is almost penniless. Her poor mother would turn in her grave if she knew!'

Grace had paled. When she had been told that she was to have a child she had at least known that she would be able to support it, but if what Mr Hibberd was saying was true, how would she manage now?

Mr Hibberd rose, looking almost as shaken as Grace. He hated to be the bearer of such bad news so soon after her father's death, but what choice had he had?

'Keep us informed,' Gertie told him shortly as he gathered together his papers, and with a nod he left the room, his shoulders stooped.

'Oh, Aunt Gertie, what am I going to do?' Grace asked tearfully.

Gertie squared her shoulders. 'You will come home with me, of course. You will always have a home there. But now we must go and break the bad news to the staff.'

Mrs Batley sat down heavily on the nearest chair when she was told what had happened, while Mabel clung to Harry's hand.

'Well, we'll be all right won't we, Harry?' Mabel muttered. 'But what about Mrs Batley?'

'Don't worry about me, pet.' Mrs Batley gave her a reassuring smile. 'I'm no spring chicken anymore and I'd have had to retire sometime. Thanks to the old master I've got a nice nest egg tucked away so I reckon it's time I looked about fer a nice little cottage where I can live out me life in peace.'

Grace let out a little sigh of relief. They had all taken the news far better than she'd expected but she was still reeling. How could Mr Mackenzie have done such a thing? He had always seemed to be so genuine, as had Nurse Matthews. It just went to show, you never really knew anyone. That thought brought an image of Father Luke to her mind and a lump formed in her throat. She had thought she knew him. She had given herself to him, heart and soul, but it seemed she had meant nothing to him, despite him telling her that he cared for her. It was a bitter pill to swallow. And now she had her father's funeral to get through, before planning on how she could support herself and her baby. It was a daunting thought.

Chapter Thirty-Five

The heavens opened on the day they buried Judge Kettle. Very few people had turned up at the church – just some of the people from his law firm, and Mrs Batley, Mabel and Harry were there. Gertie wasn't surprised. He had never been the nicest of men. But even so, she felt for poor Grace, who stood woodenly beside her, clinging to her arm as if it was a lifeline.

Once the service was over, Grace watched her father's coffin being lowered into the ground as the rain lashed down on them. She hadn't expected to feel anything, but in fact she was overcome by so many different emotions and she found herself thinking back to happier times when she was small and her father was everything to her. Harry had told her of the hard life her father had endured as a child and she wondered now if this was what had made it so hard for him to show genuine affection. She would never know now but she was sad that he had died with no one to care for him at the very end.

'That's about it then.' Mrs Batley looked around at the empty drawing room and sighed as she thought back to the happy times she had spent there. Grace had given Mabel and Harry some of the furniture for their cottage, the rest had been taken to the local auction house early that morning. Mrs Batley had managed to find a tiny cottage that was just right for her in the parish of Attleborough and now she was looking forward to being a lady of leisure, although it would be hard to walk away from the house she had called home for so many years. Her bag was packed and ready to go at the side of the door, Harry had taken the rest of her things to her new home the evening before, so now all that was left were the goodbyes.

'You take care o' yerself now, pet.' There were tears in the woman's eyes as she gently stroked Grace's smooth cheek. 'An' be sure to keep in touch an' come an' see me sometimes. Oh, an' don't forget to hand the house keys in to Mr Hibberd on the way to the station.'

'I will,' Grace promised in a wobbly voice as she saw her to the door, where she suddenly broke down and hugged the woman to her. 'I shall miss you so much, Batty,' she whispered brokenly.

'Aye, an' I shall miss you an' all, pet,' the woman replied in a choked voice. Then with an enormous effort she pulled herself together and set off. Grace watched her walk away and raised her hand just before the woman turned a corner, then she went back inside to collect her own bags. She had said her tearful goodbyes to Mabel and Harry the night before.

Knowing how difficult this must be for her, Gertie gave Grace's arm a little squeeze. 'I'll go and wait outside for you while you have a last look around. But don't be too long, mind. The cab I ordered will be here shortly.' She stepped outside into the sunshine. It was a beautiful day, a complete contrast to the day before, and she hoped this was a sign of better things to come for Grace, who had endured so much over the past few weeks.

Inside Grace wandered from room to room, lingering in her mother's old room. It was hard to believe that she would never come here again. She chose not to enter her father's room, instead she walked straight past it, moving briskly down the stairs and out of the front door to join Aunt Gertie outside.

The cab had just arrived and Gertie was helping the driver to load their luggage into the boot. They were taking away considerably more than they had arrived with as Grace had wanted to keep some of her mother's things as mementos, which Gertie supposed was quite understandable. As they pulled away, Grace looked back just once then kept her eyes straight ahead. Her future was so uncertain now and she felt afraid. Admittedly, Aunt Gertie had assured her that she would always have a home with her, but she didn't know about the baby yet. Would she have a change of heart when she did?

They stopped off briefly for Grace to hand the keys to Mr Hibberd, who looked worn down with worry, then they went on to the station. Gertie had phoned to arrange for Aled Llewelyn to meet them in Pwllheli later that day, so once they had got the porter to stack the luggage in the baggage van at the back of the train, they climbed aboard and settled back in their seats.

The journey was uneventful and passed mainly in silence. Grace was lost in her thoughts. Once or twice she opened her mouth to confide her secret to her aunt but then lost her courage and clamped it shut again. She would wait for the right moment, she decided.

It was evening before they arrived back at the cottage and Cerys Llewelyn was waiting to greet them with hot, sweet tea and a meal she had been keeping warm in the oven.

'I can't believe what's happened. Have they caught the thieving varmints yet?' she asked.

Gertie shook her head. 'Not so much as a sniff of them. I reckon they caught a boat the same day the judge died. They could be anywhere by now.'

'It's shocking,' Cerys said angrily. But then she was secretly pleased that Grace would be staying with them, and Dylan had been over the moon when she'd told him that Grace had left the convent. Perhaps now she would see sense and realise what a good catch he was?

It took three days before Grace found the opportunity to tell her aunt about the baby. Gertie was cleaning out the hut where she kept the goats and Grace volunteered to help.

'Th-there's something I need to tell you, aunt,' she said timidly as Gertie threw a pitchfork full of clean hay into the shed.

'Oh yes, go ahead then!'

Grace took a deep breath and nervously licked her lips. 'The fact is . . . I left the convent because . . . because I'm going to have a baby.'

She waited for her aunt to explode but surprisingly she calmly went on with what she was doing.

'And is the father prepared to stand by you?' she asked eventually.

When Grace shook her head, Gertie sighed. 'I see. Well, as I said you're more than welcome to stay here.'

'But I can't now.' Grace's voice was choked. 'I'll be the talk of the village when people find out. Can you imagine what they'll say about a postulant that ended up pregnant? And if you're sheltering me they'll gossip about you too.'

'So?' Gertie paused to lean on the handle of the pitchfork and stare at her. 'Let them talk! While they're gossiping about us they'll be leaving some other poor bugger alone.'

'But it's not quite as simple as that,' Grace pointed out. 'The baby will suffer too if I stay here because it's illegitimate. It would be better if I were to get a job and move away somewhere where no one knows me. I can say that I am a widow and work until the baby's born.'

'Hmm, and then what will you do? How will you live when you have a baby to care for? And furthermore, *where* will you live?'

Grace blinked. Everything seemed so complicated at the minute and sometimes she wished she could just go to sleep and never wake up, although she felt better now that she had told her aunt the truth. She had taken it far better than Grace had expected her to.

'Do you want to tell me who the father is?' Gertie asked.

Grace shook her head.

Gertie shrugged. 'Fair enough, it's none of my business at the end of the day. You're not the first girl to find yourself in this predicament and I can guarantee you won't be the last. But now I'd best get on. I don't want it to rain until I've got all this dry straw into the shed.' And with that she continued with what she was doing.

❀

The following weekend, Dylan visited all dressed up in his Sunday best. 'I brought you these,' he said self-consciously as he held out a rather dilapidated bunch of daffodils to Grace.

She blushed as she took them off him and, heartened, he hurried on, 'I was sorry to hear about your father, and about what happened with the solicitor. You wouldn't believe that someone in a position of trust could do something like that, would you?'

Grace shrugged. She was sick of thinking about it and worrying about her and the baby's future and she really didn't want to go over it all again. The Llewelyns had no idea about the baby as yet – Gertie clearly thought that it was up to Grace to tell them when she felt ready, for which Grace was grateful. However, she knew that she wasn't going to be able to hide it for much longer. This morning she had noticed the slight swell of her stomach and the waistbands on her skirts were becoming tighter, so it was only a matter of time before they guessed anyway.

Throughout the afternoon, Dylan constantly tried to start a conversation with her but she wouldn't be drawn and wished that he would just go home. He had made it more than obvious that he still had feelings for her but Grace doubted he would feel the same when he learned the truth.

'Fancy a little walk?' he suggested late in the afternoon.

Grace's nerves were stretched to breaking point by then, so she politely refused saying she had a headache and went and locked herself in her room. Anything was better than having to sit there listening to Dylan rattling on.

It took two more weeks before Cerys discovered her secret. Grace had risen early and rushed to the toilet at the end of the cinder path. Thankfully the morning sickness was much better now but she still suffered from it occasionally and it seemed that today was one of those days. Cerys heard her as she was collecting the chickens' eggs and when Grace emerged she found Cerys waiting for her with a frown on her face.

'Got something to tell me, have you, cariad?' she asked. Grace was still clad in her thin cotton nightgown, which revealed the gentle swell of her stomach quite clearly. She shrugged helplessly, there was no point in trying to conceal it any longer. Cerys Llewelyn was no fool and she was bound to have guessed before very much longer anyway.

'Good lord above!' Cerys sagged against the wall of the toilet clutching the basket of eggs. 'You're going to have a baby, aren't you? Is that why you left the convent? Or were you sent away in shame?'

'I was sent away,' Grace admitted miserably.

'Well . . . this is a fine state of affairs! I bet our Dylan won't be interested in you now!' the woman snorted. 'And you with barely a penny left to your name. What will you do now and does your aunt know?'

'I haven't decided what I'll do yet, and yes she does.'

Cerys softened then as she said, 'Oh, cariad, how could you have been so stupid?' But she was confused. She knew what a confined life the nuns led so how on earth had Grace managed to get pregnant? When Grace merely hung her head, Cerys sighed. 'You'll have to tell our Dylan. You know that, don't you? He's still carrying a torch for you, though I doubt he will when he knows about . . .' Her voice trailed away as she stared pointedly at Grace's stomach.

'Don't worry. I'll tell him this weekend if he calls,' she promised, then she walked away leaving Cerys staring after her.

Dylan turned up on Sunday afternoon. He'd been as regular as clockwork since Grace had been back and he was heartened when Grace said, 'Shall we take a stroll down to the beach?'

He nodded eagerly, unaware of the look on his nan's face as he and Grace stepped out into the sunshine. They had gone some way before Grace finally said, 'Dylan . . . I have something to tell you.'

His heart skipped a beat. Was she going to tell him that she still wasn't interested? He knew that he wouldn't be able to bear that. She was the first person he thought of on waking and the last person he thought of at night. To prevent her from speaking, he stopped suddenly, drawing her to a halt with him. Turning her to face him, he said quickly, 'No, *you* listen to me first. This needs to be said.' She was staring up at him from her wonderful green eyes as he stumbled on. 'You *must* know that I still have feelings for you, Grace? They never went away, not even when you were up at the convent. Oh, I *tried* to forget you, admittedly. I went out with a lot of lasses for a time but none of them meant a thing. What I'm trying to say is . . . I love you and I want to marry you. Will you be my wife, Grace, and make me the happiest man on earth?'

'Oh, Dylan!' Seeing how earnest he was made tears spring to her eyes and she reached her hand out to stroke his cheek. 'I'm flattered that you've asked, but I can't marry you or anyone else for that matter.'

'*Why* can't you?' There was an edge to his voice now as he stared back at her, and shame washed through her.

'I can't marry you because . . .' She gulped. 'Because I'm going to have a baby.' There, it was said and she watched the different emotions flit across his face. Shock, horror, disbelief and finally . . . disgust!

'*No!*' He stepped away from her as if she was carrying some highly contagious disease. And then his face twisted in anger. 'Whose *bastard* is it?' he spat.

Her hand automatically flew to her stomach to protect her unborn child. There was a wild look in Dylan's eyes and she was afraid of what he might do.

She shook her head and refused to answer, starting as he suddenly grabbed her arms and began to shake her until her teeth rattled.

'*Whose is it*? *I asked.*' His voice echoed along the empty path and some seagulls who had been relaxing ahead of them flew off flapping their wings and squawking.

And then as suddenly as his temper had risen it seemed to desert him and he released her and pushed her roughly away from him.

'Forget what I said.' His voice was a growl that came from deep within him. 'I wouldn't marry you now if you were the last girl left on God's earth. You're nothing but a slut and a whore!' With that he turned and strode away, his hands clenched into fists as she stood there shaking with grief, shame and fear. After a time, she forced herself to turn and retrace her steps, trying hard not to think of the future that stretched bleakly ahead of her.

Chapter Thirty-Six

'Our Dylan's gone then, has he?' Mrs Llewelyn asked as Grace walked back into the kitchen.

'Yes, he's gone,' Grace answered miserably.

Cerys glanced at her husband who had his head buried in the paper and sighed. Grace had obviously told Dylan about the baby if her glum expression was anything to go by and he'd probably reacted badly. But then, surely Grace had expected that? There weren't many men who would be prepared to bring up another man's child. The problem was, Dylan had set Grace on a pedestal and now she had well and truly tumbled off it, poor lass.

'Happen he'll come back when he's had time to think on it,' Cerys told her optimistically as she poured her a glass of freshly made lemonade. 'But come and sit down and have this. There's no use upsetting yourself, it's not good for the baby.'

Grace obediently took a seat but her mind was working overtime. Now more than ever she realised that she couldn't stay here. If Dylan were to mention that she was having a baby her name would be mud in the village and she would never be able to hold her head up again. They would brand her baby a fly-blow and the poor little mite would grow up with the stigma of being illegitimate: shunned and scorned. Then there was her aunt. The people thereabouts already regarded her as eccentric but would they turn against her if they knew she was giving shelter to what they would regard as a fallen woman? No, Grace decided, she couldn't allow that, it was time to move on. But where could she go?

That evening when the Llewelyns had retired, she asked tentatively, 'Aunt Gertie, how much of my allowance did you manage to save up before Mr Mackenzie stopped sending it?'

Her aunt rose to fetch a tin from the end of the mantelshelf and tipped the contents onto the table.

'There's quite a few pounds there if you'd care to count it but it won't go far if you're still thinking of moving away. There'll be rent to pay, coal and food to buy, not to mention the things you'll need to get ready for the baby. Just think on before you do anything rash. I've told you I'm quite happy for you to stay here so stop worrying about what people will say, it will just roll off me like water off a duck's back. I've never been conventional and I'm too long in the tooth to change now.'

Grace managed a smile as she counted the money in front of her. There was almost thirty pounds which seemed like a fortune, but Grace knew that her aunt was right. It wouldn't go far. Even so she decided that over the next couple of weeks she would travel to villages some way off from Sarn Bach and make enquiries about properties to rent. Perhaps she could try Llanengan or Rhydolian slightly further along the coast? They weren't too far away but far enough that no one would know her there. And she would have to do it soon before the baby really started to show.

With her plans made, it was somewhat of a shock when Dylan turned up again three days later looking repentant.

'Can we go somewhere where we can talk?' He looked so sad that Grace didn't have the heart to refuse him. She had been feeding the chickens who were clucking about her feet, but she nodded as she untied her apron and followed him in the direction of the sea, hoping that he wasn't going to get angry with her again.

Once they reached the clifftop, they stood gazing out to sea at the fishing boats bobbing on the waves until she said quietly, 'I thought you'd be out there today with the weather being so nice.'

'I should be,' he answered shortly. 'But I needed to see you so me dad went out without me. You see . . . the thing is, I've been doing a lot of thinking and I want to apologise for how I reacted when you told me about the baby.'

'You don't need to,' she told him dully. 'I suppose I deserved all I got.'

'Is there any chance at all that the father of this baby will stand by you?' he asked and she shook her head, staring straight ahead as colour burned into her cheeks, but her heart was crying 'if only!'

'Right, in that case my offer still stands.'

Grace's head snapped towards him and she stared at him in shock.

'The thing is, if we get married straightaway, no one will know that the baby isn't mine and I'll bring it up as my own.' He grasped her hands. 'I will, Grace, *honestly*. You and the baby will want for nothing and I'll do my very best to make you happy, *truly* I will. I love you, you see? That's why I'm offering again. I can't bear to be without you.'

'But, Dylan . . . I don't love you, not in that way,' she said as tears spilled onto her cheeks. 'It wouldn't be fair to you.'

'Huh! Don't get worrying about that. Love will come in time and until then I'm prepared to wait for as long as it takes, for . . . you know? The only thing I will ask is that we let people believe that the baby is mine, at least then I won't have fingers pointing at me.'

Grace blushed and lowered her eyes. It was a tempting offer, she had to admit. At least this way the baby would have a name and a father. 'B-but where would we live?' she faltered. 'And how would your parents feel about you marrying someone from another faith? I know they are strict chapel.'

'Ah well, happen you would have to convert to chapel,' he admitted. 'And for a while we'd have to live with my parents . . . just until I could find us somewhere of our own. Me tad has just bought another fishing boat and I could use that to earn our own living and pay him back as we could afford it. So, what do you say? You must see it makes sense?'

Still Grace hesitated so he said then, 'How about I leave you to think on it tonight and I come back for your answer tomorrow? If it's yes, we can go and see the pastor straightaway and set the ball rolling. We could be man and wife in two weeks' time if we get the banns read this coming weekend.'

'All right, I'll sleep on it,' she promised and without another word he nodded, rammed his cap on his head and walked away. She walked back to the cottage in a daze. Mrs Llewelyn saw her coming and Grace instantly blurted out what had happened and told her of her grandson's change of heart.

'Hmm, well it would solve a lot of problems and our Dylan is a good lad. You could certainly do a lot worse,' the woman pointed out. 'It would be nice for your aunt too, if you were to stay close by. Gertie isn't the best at showing her feelings but I know she's been fretting about you and this way she would still get to see you.'

Grace nodded and slunk away to spend some time by herself. She knew that it would solve all her problems and yet her heart still yearned for Father Luke. She also knew that she would probably never see him again, so should she think of the baby's well-being? Dylan was solid and reliable and she did like him. Not in the way he liked her, admittedly, but as he had said, love might grow in time.

She spoke to her aunt about it later that evening and Gertie said much the same as Mrs Llewelyn had.

'But that's not to say that you have to do anything you don't want to,' she ended stoically. 'Only you can make this decision, Grace. This is the rest of your life so you have to be sure.'

That night she tossed and turned as she struggled to reach a decision. Eventually she got up and stared out of the window at the view, which was washed in moonlight.

'Oh, Myfanwy what should I do?' she whispered. A large owl suddenly glided out of the trees to swoop on some poor unsuspecting rodent in the grass. The time was ticking away and in just a few short hours Dylan would be back for the decision which could change the course of her life for ever. The trouble was she was no nearer to making it!

There were dark smudges under her eyes when she rose the next morning and yet Gertie noticed that she seemed incredibly calm. Dylan arrived mid-morning and the two of them instantly set off for the cliff face again.

'Well?' he asked eagerly when they were out of earshot of the cottage. 'Have you decided?' He was turning his cap in circles between his two hands.

'Yes, I have. And, yes, I will marry you, Dylan, and thank you for asking.'

He let out a whoop of joy and threw his cap into the air as he caught her to him but when he tried to kiss her lips she turned her face away.

'It's all right, I'll not force you to do anything you don't want to do. It'll be in your time. But come on now, there's not a moment to waste, we'll be away to see the pastor and set the wheels in motion. We'd best call in and tell me mam an' all. Me tad is out fishing so he'll have to wait for the news till this evening.'

Grace allowed him to grasp her hand and tow her along, but inside her heart was breaking, for she knew that once Dylan had put a ring on her finger her chances of ever being with the man she truly loved would be gone for ever. But then she was forced to acknowledge that Luke had chosen God over herself. They had committed a sin and now it would be her that paid for it for the rest of her life.

She was breathless by the time they approached Dylan's parents' cottage and apprehensive about facing his mother. The last time she'd visited, she'd made it more than obvious that she no longer had any time for her so Grace could only imagine how she would react to the news that she was about to marry her son.

Bronwen was gutting fish for their evening meal when Dylan burst into the cottage dragging Grace behind him, and the smile on her face died as her eyes settled on Grace.

She nodded before saying shortly. 'I heard your dad passed away – my condolences.'

'Mam, we have something to tell you,' Dylan said proudly, clasping Grace's hand and smiling from ear to ear. 'Me and Grace, we're getting wed.'

'You're *what*!' The colour drained from the woman's face as she stared at her son in disbelief. She had suspected for some long time that he had a soft spot for the girl and she had heaved a sigh of relief when she heard that Grace had entered the convent. The likes of her wasn't for them; Grace was a toff, well spoken and soft. Dylan needed a village lass, but now here he was telling her that they were going to get wed! Had he taken leave of his senses?

'But . . . but you can't!' she said weakly as her fingers plucked at the large pinafore she was wearing.

Dylan chuckled and drew Grace further into the room, and as the light from the tiny leaded window shone on the girl, Bronwen saw the slight swell of her stomach and gasped. 'Dear God . . . you're with *child*!'

Dylan's face was grim now as he nodded. 'Aye, she is, Mam. That's why we need to get wed.'

'And where were you planning on living?' Two spots of colour glowed on the woman's cheeks as she faced her son.

'Why here of course . . . just till I can find us somewhere of us own!'

Bronwen's shoulders sagged as she saw that he meant every

word he was saying, and Dylan snapped, 'And I don't know why you're taking on so. Wasn't I born six months after you and me tad were wed?'

Bronwen turned away abruptly as Dylan snatched Grace's hand and hurried her outside.

Grace was feeling humiliated and ashamed but Dylan smiled reassuringly. 'Take no notice of me mam. It's just come as a bit of a shock to her. She'll come round, you'll see.'

Grace doubted that, if the way his mother had glared at her was anything to go by, but she followed him meekly without a word. She had made her decision for the sake of her unborn child and now she must stand by it.

Grace and Dylan were wed in the tiny Methodist chapel in Pwllheli on the first Saturday morning in June. It was a very quiet affair, as Grace had insisted upon, with only a handful of people attending, but Dylan didn't stop smiling throughout the ceremony. Grace wore a pale blue dress and cream shoes. She'd had to let the waist of the dress out slightly to accommodate her fast-growing bump, but as she walked down the aisle on Aled Llewelyn's arm everybody, apart from Dylan's mother, remarked on how beautiful she looked. Cerys had surprised her just before they left the cottage with a bouquet of lily of the valley and her kindness was almost Grace's undoing.

'Who ever heard of a bride without a bouquet?' Cerys said as she fussed over Grace's hair and the girl had to swallow the tears that threatened.

Her life was about to change yet again and she wasn't looking forward to moving in with Dylan's mother at all. Still, she consoled herself, Dylan had promised that it wouldn't be for long so she clung to that.

Aled drove them to the chapel and once the short service was over they went on to a public house in nearby Penlan Street for the wedding breakfast that Gertie had treated them to. The meal was delicious, but Grace found that she couldn't eat a thing. The thin gold band on her finger felt wrong and she just wanted to run away and cry, although after a time her face ached from forcing smiles. Dylan, on the other hand, was beaming from ear to ear and halfway through the meal he whispered, 'How are you feeling, Mrs Penlynn?'

Mrs Penlynn! Grace forced yet another smile. She couldn't answer for fear of bursting into tears and all the time her heart was crying, Oh, Luke, where are you? It should have been *you* I married!

At last it was over and the party assembled in the street outside to say their goodbyes. 'Now, you come and see us often, mind,' Cerys said before clambering up into the trap.

It was Gertie's turn then and she pecked Grace on the cheek, saying in a low voice, 'You know where we are, pet.'

Grace nodded mutely and watched as the trap rattled away.

'Right then, lad. We'd best go and get ready to get the boats out. Time and tide wait for no man, eh?' Griffen, Dylan's father slapped him heartily on the shoulder as he winked at Grace. He seemed friendly, at least. He tugged at the starched white collar of his shirt and laughed. 'Eeh, it'll be a relief to get this darn shirt off and get back into me fisherman's outfit.' Taking his wife's arm, he walked ahead as Dylan took Grace's hand. She had laid her small bouquet on Myfanwy's grave when they left the chapel and now she moved mechanically as panic threatened to overwhelm her. She wished Dylan didn't have to go to sea, not today anyway, but as she was to learn, fishermen had to take full advantage of the weather. But what would she do when she was left alone with Dylan's mother? Would Bronwen make her feel unwelcome? She was soon to find out.

Chapter Thirty-Seven

The minute they entered the tiny two-up two-down cottage that was Dylan's home, his mother nodded scornfully towards the trunks that were piled up at the side of the door. They contained Grace's clothes and possessions and Aled had delivered them earlier that morning.

'I suggest you get that lot put away, that's if you can find somewhere to put them!' Bronwen sneered. 'I don't want them left down here where I'll be forever tripping over them.'

'I'll carry them up now for you.' Dylan smiled at his bride reassuringly. He didn't want anything to spoil this special day so he chose to ignore his mother's unpleasant tone, although he vowed he wouldn't allow her to continue to talk to Grace that way. The poor girl looked terrified and this was her wedding day. Grace followed him upstairs without a word as he heaved the first heavy trunk up the steep narrow staircase. There was a tiny square landing at the top of the stairs with two doors leading off it and Dylan turned into the one on his left. Grace blinked with surprise when she followed him in. The room was very small, barely big enough for one person let alone two, but she supposed they would manage. Her eyes were drawn to the iron bed and she felt herself blushing as she imagined herself lying in it next to Dylan.

'We'll stack these trunks in the corner for now,' he told her.

'Then when you've unpacked them I'll try and find room out in the shed for them. It'll give us a bit more space.'

Grace nodded as he set off down the stairs to fetch another trunk and soon they were all neatly stacked in the corner.

'There, that should keep you busy for a while.' He nodded towards an old chest of drawers. 'I've made some room in there for you and I've knocked some nails in the back of the door so that you can hang some of your clothes up.'

She managed a faint smile then blushed an even deeper shade of red as he began to undress.

'Best get changed then,' he said cheerily. 'Me dad hates to be kept waiting but he's promised we'll finish for dark this evening. We fish right through the night sometimes if the conditions are favourable.'

He threw his shirt onto the bed and reached for a thick old jersey that he wore on the boat as Grace quickly averted her eyes and hurried across to the window, where she made a great show of looking at the view. There wasn't much to be seen, if truth be told. Just the small yard that they shared with the next-door neighbour and the long, narrow gardens stretching down to the privies at the bottom of them. Tin baths were hung on the walls at the back of the cottages and she noted that most of the garden was planted with vegetables. Eventually she turned to find Dylan fully dressed in his work clothes and she took a closer look at the room. Apart from the bed and the old chest of drawers, the only other furniture was a rather dilapidated washstand on which stood a plain chipped jug and bowl. There wasn't room for anything else and Grace began to feel claustrophobic. The curtains hanging at the window were so faded and thin that she wasn't sure what colour they might once have been and the only concession to comfort on the floor was a small clippie mat at the side of the bed to cover the scrubbed wooden floorboards. Even so, she had to admit that everywhere was spotlessly clean, including the sheets and blankets on the bed, but already she was longing for when Dylan found them somewhere of their own to live.

'Right, I suppose I'd best be off then. I have a wife to support now,' Dylan teased as he crossed to put his arms about her waist. 'How about a kiss for your husband to see him on his way?' He could feel Grace tense but then she raised her head and kissed him on the cheek. It wasn't quite what he'd been hoping for but he kept his smile in place anyway as he told her, 'Don't get doing too much now. I'll see you later,' and with that he turned and clattered away down the stairs as Grace chewed on her fist in an attempt to stop the tears that were threatening.

'Oh dear God, what have I done?' she moaned silently as she sank onto the side of the bed. But common sense told her that it was done, there could be no going back now. She had made her vows, till death us do part, and from this moment on she must try to stop thinking of Luke. He was her past, Dylan was her future.

'How much longer are you going to be up there?' Bronwen shouted up the stairs sometime later. 'There's vegetables waiting to be peeled down here. Come and make yourself useful. I've got enough to do with two men to look after so don't think I'm going to skivvy for you an' all.'

Grace had been sitting on the side of the bed steeped in misery but at her mother-in-law's words her head snapped up, she swiped the tears away with the back of her hand and straightened her back. Perhaps it was time to get a few things straight.

She sniffed then walked down the steep, narrow staircase and into the kitchen with her head held high. 'I'd like to make it clear that I am *more* than prepared to pull my weight and I don't expect you to wait on me, I am used to hard work after the time I spent up at the convent,' Grace said in a clear voice. 'All you have to do is tell me what needs doing and I'll do it. And I'd like to know how you wish me to address you. Will it be Mrs Penlynn, Bronwen or Mam? I'm quite happy to go along with your preference.'

The woman looked slightly taken aback. It appeared that the girl had spirit after all. She nodded. 'Then I dare say, for our Dylan's sake, you'd best call me Mam.'

'Very well . . . Mam.' The word felt strange on Grace's tongue but she forced herself to say it. 'Now where are these vegetables you want me to peel?'

At teatime, the meal the women had prepared was placed over pans of hot water on the hob to keep warm for when the men came in from fishing, and they dined on bread and cheese. As soon as it was over, Grace washed and dried the pots before Bronwen had a chance to ask her and then asked, 'Is there anything else you'd like to me to do?'

Bronwen had settled in a chair by the open back door to work on the new jersey she was knitting for her husband and she shook her head. 'No . . . thank you,' she answered grudgingly.

'In that case, if you don't mind, I think I'll go for a walk and familiarise myself with the area a little more.'

Bronwen nodded but didn't answer, so Grace slipped past her and headed for the harbour.

They had hardly said a word to each other since Grace had come down to the kitchen early that afternoon and now she just wanted to escape the tense atmosphere. Dylan's mother had made it more than clear through her actions that Grace wasn't welcome in her home and already Grace's nerves were stretched to the limit. After taking a deep breath, she slowly wandered through the cobbled streets and it was as she was going that she suddenly felt a movement in her stomach. It resembled the feeling she had felt when Mr Llewelyn had once driven the trap over a humpback bridge too quickly. Her hand moved to her stomach as a smile spread across her face. It was her baby moving. She'd felt flutters before but never anything so strong as this and suddenly she knew that she had done the right thing in marrying Dylan. She didn't love him but he would be a good father and provider for her baby, who she loved already. In just a few months' time she would meet him – it was funny how she always thought of the baby as him – but who would he look like? Grace half hoped that he would take after her and have red hair. If he was blonde like his father it would take some explaining, but then she would cross that bridge when she came to it. Feeling slightly brighter she moved on. She had her wedding night ahead of her but for now she tried not to think about it.

'Would you mind if I went to bed?' Grace asked her mother-in-law that evening as the sky was darkening.

'No, you go up, I'll see that the men get their meal when they come in,' Bronwen answered. Grace had a feeling that the woman just wanted to get rid of her but she said goodnight politely and made her way upstairs. Once in the room her heart began to pound again as she thought of the night ahead. She quickly undressed and washed herself from head to toe with the cold water in the jug that she had taken upstairs earlier, then after pulling the fine lawn nightgown trimmed with lace, which had been a gift from Aunt Gertie, over her head, she quickly slid into bed. At some stage, she must have fallen asleep because the next thing she was aware of was the bedroom door creaking open and someone entering the room. It was dark with only the light from the moon filtering through the thin curtains, so Grace lay very still.

'Grace . . . it's me. Are you awake, cariad?' Dylan's voice penetrated the darkness but still she lay as if she had been turned to stone. In the darkness, she could hear him fiddling with his clothes as he undressed. Then the bedclothes were lifted and he slid in beside her. The next minute his arm snaked about her waist. With a little shock, she realised that he was naked but she forced herself to breathe evenly, praying that he would believe she was asleep. His body was curled into her back and she could feel the heat of him as he tenderly kissed the back of her neck.

'Sleep tight, my lovely,' he whispered. 'You've had a big day.' Soon after she felt his arm relax, his breathing became regular and she knew that he was asleep. He had promised that the physical side of their marriage needn't happen until she was ready and for now it appeared that he was prepared to keep his word.

Over the next month, Bronwen softened slightly, more, thought Grace, at the prospect of her first grandchild than anything to do with her. Each week she walked to Beehive Cottage to visit her aunt but now that she was growing bigger she was finding it increasingly difficult and wondered how much longer she would be able to make the trek.

It was early in July as Grace was getting ready for her weekly visit that Bronwen suddenly said cautiously, 'I've been thinking. You must have been still up at the convent when you fell for this baby.' As she eyed Grace suspiciously, the girl flushed scarlet. 'And our Dylan was sowing his wild oats with the village girls round about then,' she went on, her eyes fixed on Grace.

Grace kept her mouth firmly shut as Bronwen narrowed her eyes. 'So how did you and my lad manage to come together?'

'I . . . I'd rather not talk about it,' Grace muttered as she pulled her shoes on. Bronwen clearly suspected that the baby might not be Dylan's, but how could Grace tell her the truth? She knew that her mother-in-law didn't approve of her and should she ever

305

discover that the baby wasn't Dylan's, Grace had no doubt that she would make her life hell. 'I'm going now,' Grace said, and she scooted out of the house at a speed that surprised even herself.

On the way to her aunt's, Grace fretted about what she should do. She hated deceiving anyone, even Bronwen, but she had promised Dylan faithfully that she would let everyone believe that the baby was his.

'Ooh, cariad, happen this walk is getting too much for you,' Mrs Llewelyn greeted her when she finally arrived all hot and bothered. 'You look all in. Come and sit down and I'll get you a nice cold drink. I'll call Gertie an' all to let her know you're here. She's out the back cleaning out the pigsty.'

Grace sank gratefully down at the table and looked around as Mrs Llewelyn pottered away. This place still felt like home, unlike where she was living now. Still, she supposed she was lucky. Most men wouldn't have touched her with a bargepole once they knew she was carrying another man's baby. Dylan had kept to his word too, apart from the odd peck on the cheek and a cuddle in bed, his demands had gone no further. So why then, she questioned herself, am I so very unhappy?

❧

One night in mid-September Grace woke with a dull ache in her back in the middle of the night. Dylan was fast asleep at her side and through the thin dividing wall that separated the bedrooms she could hear his father gently snoring. Slowly, so as not to disturb her husband, she inched to the edge of the bed, then grabbing her dressing robe she draped it around her shoulders and crept downstairs. Perhaps if I walk about a bit it will go off, she thought. But an hour later, after countless walks about the kitchen, it was worse if anything. She was still pacing when Bronwen appeared early the next morning and the woman raised an eyebrow. Bronwen always rose early to prepare the men's breakfast and pack the food they would take with them when they went to sea.

'You're an early bird,' she commented as she raked the embers in the fire and threw some wood on them. 'Didn't you think to put the kettle on?' Then seeing how pale Grace was she asked, 'Is something wrong?'

Grace shook her head as she stroked her back. 'No, it's just this pain in my back. I thought if I got up and walked about it might go off but it's getting worse, if anything. I must have laid funny.'

Bronwen sniffed. 'I don't think any amount of pacing is going to take this away. It sounds to me like the baby is on its way. I'll call our Dylan and get him to fetch old lady Gower before he goes to sea; she delivers all the babies hereabouts!'

Grace looked shocked. It had never occurred to her that this might be the start of the baby coming and suddenly she was afraid.

'Sh-shouldn't a doctor be here too?' she asked in a small voice.

'Huh! Why would you want to waste money on a doctor? You're young and healthy so there shouldn't be any problems.'

Grace could only pray that she was right. Strangely, she didn't care so much about herself. But she knew if anything were to happen to Luke's baby she would be heartbroken. This baby would be all she would ever have of him and suddenly she couldn't wait to meet it.

Chapter Thirty-Eight

Dylan pounded down the stairs the second his mother woke him, his face the colour of bleached linen. He had pulled his trousers and shirt on, although the shirt was unbuttoned as he snapped his braces over his shoulders and asked fearfully, 'Is the baby coming?'

'Well, of course it is! Why else would I wake you? You daft ha'p'orth,' his mother snapped. 'Now get yourself round to old lady Gower and tell her we need her as soon as possible.' Bronwen sniffed then for all the world as if Grace had committed a sin by going into labour at such an early hour. 'She'll no doubt be miffed by being wakened at such an ungodly hour but tell her there'll be an extra sixpence in it if she gets a shufty on.'

Dylan needed no second telling, he was already pulling his boots onto his bare feet, then he shot off, his shirt tails flapping behind him.

'And you, young lady, need to get yourself upstairs,' Bronwen ordered. 'I'll get Griffen up and you can do the birthing in our bed. There's more room in there. I'll go up and rouse him and get everything ready, then you can come up.'

Grace nodded as she bit on her lip. She wished her mother was there. She wished Luke was there, but this was no time for self-pity. Soon she would meet her new baby and she tried to concentrate on that. She had no idea what to expect, although

308

the horrific tales she had heard the fisherwomen whispering about what they had endured during childbirth had struck terror into her heart.

Griffen came down the stairs shortly after, fully dressed and bleary eyed but his voice was kindly as he said, 'So, the little one's about to make its appearance is it, cariad?' Then seeing the look on her face, he gently squeezed her hand. 'Don't be frightened now. God will never send us more pain than we can endure.'

Grace gulped, praying that he was right, and shortly after Bronwen came back down to tell her, 'Everything is ready, go and get into my bed. Old lady Gower shouldn't be too long.'

'But what if she doesn't get here in time?' Grace croaked.

Bronwen laughed. 'First babies have a habit of taking their time so don't get worrying about that. Now be off with you while I get some water on to boil and get some towels ready.'

Grace did as she was told and once in the front bedroom she glanced around nervously. It was considerably bigger than the room she shared with Dylan, admittedly, but all the same she felt strange in there and would have preferred to stay in her own space. She saw that Bronwen had positioned the small wooden cradle that had once been Dylan's and Myfanwy's at the end of the bed and she smiled as she thought of her friend. Myfanwy would have been so excited at the prospect of a new niece or nephew. But then, Grace reminded herself, it wouldn't have really been her relative and guilt stabbed at her yet again.

When Bronwen mounted the stairs some short time later with a pile of freshly washed towels across her arm, Grace was lying on top of the pile of old sheets the woman had laid across the mattress to protect it. The backache had turned into a dull nagging bellyache, although as yet it was bearable. Bronwen laid the towels down without a word and Grace wondered if she should ask Dylan to fetch her Aunt Gertie for the birth. At least then she'd have someone she felt comfortable with. She suggested it when he burst back into the room, but Bronwen shook her head. 'There's no time for you to go haring off to Sarn Bach! You need to get to sea and do your job.'

Dylan opened his mouth to protest but she glared at him. 'Go on now. The birthing room is no place for a man and she'll be hours and hours yet most likely. The last thing I need is you flapping about the place an' all!'

He looked uncertainly from his mother to Grace, who raised a reassuring smile. 'Your mother is right, Dylan,' she said softly. 'You just get yourself away and don't worry about me. Hopefully it will all be over by the time you get back this evening.'

He bent to kiss her cheek then walked out of the room and soon after she heard the door of the cottage open and shut as the men left for their fishing trip. They'd been gone no more than a few minutes when she heard the door open yet again and the sound of someone labouring up the stairs. Seconds later a very old woman appeared in the doorway and grunted, 'I don't know what all the panic is about. First babies are known for taking their time. I could have had me sleep out.'

Grace could only stare at her in horror. Her grey hair, which was pinned into a straggly bun at the back of her head, was thin and wispy, and her clothes looked as if they hadn't been washed for some long time. The fingernails on her gnarled hands were filthy too and Grace silently prayed that she would at least wash them before she touched her. She had a clay pipe dangling out of the corner of her mouth but Grace was relieved to see that at least it wasn't lit . . . for now, anyway!

The old woman removed her grimy shawl and threw it across the foot of the bed, saying, 'Right, now I'm here I may as well have a look at how far on you are. An' you, Bronwen, away an' put the kettle on. Oh, and when the tea's made put a drop o' gin in mine.'

She rolled the sleeves of her blouse up and without another

word hoisted Grace's nightgown above her waist and began to feel none too gently about her swollen stomach. Grace lay there, her cheeks burning with embarrassment, when suddenly she felt a gush of warm liquid between her legs.

'I . . . I think I just wet myself,' she whispered, mortified.

'No, you ain't. Your waters have just broken,' the old woman cackled. 'That's good. Things should start to speed up a bit now.'

She drew the nightgown back down and sank into a chair at the side of the bed as Grace stared up at the ceiling wishing she were a million miles away.

It was almost half an hour later when the first contraction came and it took Grace's breath away. Old lady Gower had slurped her way through three cups of tea by then and she nodded with satisfaction.

'That's it,' she told Grace. 'Now we have to time 'em to see how far apart they are.'

As the contractions slowly began to mount, the morning wore on and they were into the afternoon.

'Wi-will it be much longer?' Grace gasped weakly. This was turning out to be so much more painful than she'd expected.

'Probably another couple of hours or so at least.'

Bronwen had brought the baby clothes Grace had stitched into the room and laid them in the crib along with a lovely shawl that Cerys Llewelyn had knitted for her, and Grace just wanted it to be over so she could see her baby wearing them.

'You're doing well,' Bronwen encouraged. Her attitude to Grace had softened somewhat as the day wore on. To give the girl her due, she hadn't made a fuss and despite the fact that she was in terrible pain she had barely made a whimper. And, of course, added to that was the fact that Grace was about to present her with her first grandchild. For all she hadn't wanted Dylan to marry her, she couldn't deny that the girl wasn't afraid of hard work. Whenever she saw a job that needed doing she got on with it

311

without being asked and even when she was asked she did it uncomplainingly. Perhaps I've been a little harsh with her, Bronwen thought as she dipped a cloth in cold water, wrung it out and mopped Grace's sweating brow. It was only minutes later that Grace moaned deep in her throat and brought her chin to her chest so Mrs Gower once more pulled up her nightdress to see what was going on.

'I reckon you're almost there,' she told Grace. 'Now when the next pain comes I want you to pant. Do you understand? Don't push till I tell you – just pant!'

Grace nodded, and as the next sharp pain ripped through her she couldn't hold back a strangled cry as she tried desperately to do as the old woman had told her. The trouble was, the urge to push was overwhelming and it was easier said than done. She felt as if she were being rent in two and, in that second, she wished she could die. But then she pulled herself together to face the final hurdle. If she died, her baby might too and she couldn't bear to think of that happening.

'Right . . . on the next pain, push, girl, *as hard* as you know how,' the old lady urged as she leaned across her.

Grace felt the pain mounting and pushed with all her might, biting her bottom lip so hard that she tasted blood.

'Good, good, and *again* on the next one!'

Once more, Grace did as she was told and this time she was rewarded when the old lady cried, 'The head is crowning! I can see the head. Come on now push *harder*.'

At some stage, she had grasped Bronwen's hand and now her mother-in-law urged her on too. 'Come on, Grace, not much longer now. You're almost there. One more time now!'

And so, with a last superhuman effort, Grace pushed with all the strength she had left and seconds later she felt something warm slither out of her and her mother-in-law crowed with delight.

'It's a little lad. A fine little lad! You have a son, Grace! And

312

my, he's a bonny little chap. Big too, just like his dad! Although he looks nothing like him!'

A mixture of emotions tore through Grace. She was relieved and delighted that the birth was over but now the fear she had harboured – that her mother-in-law might suspect the child wasn't Dylan's – reared its head again.

The old woman snorted as she deftly cut the umbilical cord. 'It's too soon to say who he looks like,' she said, and after wrapping the baby in a towel that Bronwen held ready, she laid him on his mother's chest.

As Grace stared down at him in awe, all her fears fled. She knew in that moment that she would love this child unreservedly for the rest of her days no matter what transpired in the future. He was howling lustily, his little arms flailing at the indignity of being propelled from the warm, safe place he had grown in, but after a few seconds he opened his eyes and Grace's heart did a little flip. They were a deep blue, exactly like his father's. It was impossible to tell what colour his hair was as yet. It was plastered to his head, but as the midwife delivered the afterbirth Bronwen whisked him away for a bath. When she returned him, all clean and scrubbed in the tiny nightgown that Grace had laboriously stitched, her heart sank. His downy hair was a silver blonde.

'I don't know where he got his blonde hair from,' Bronwen commented as she passed him back to his mother. 'Both Myfanwy and Dylan were dark at birth and he certainly doesn't get it from you!'

'That will probably change an' all,' Mrs Gower said as she straightened and wiped her bloody hands down the front of her grimy apron. 'But that's me done now so how about you get me and the new mother a nice cup of tea? I reckon she's earned it. Then you can pay me and I'll be on me way.'

As Bronwen bustled away, Grace smiled at the old lady. 'Thank you so much,' she said gratefully.

'Think nowt of it. I've done this countless times, though I have to say not all first-time mothers are as brave as you've been. I'll leave your mother-in-law to clean you up. Goodbye, cariad.' And with that she shuffled away.

Left alone with her beautiful new son, Grace wondered what Luke would have thought of him. He clearly hadn't cared about her and regretted what had happened between them, otherwise why would he have run away with not a word? It still hurt to think of him so she pushed him from her mind and concentrated on getting to know her baby.

Soon after, Bronwen arrived and washed Grace. The girl didn't object at all, after the indignity of childbirth she doubted she would ever be embarrassed again. Once she was clad in a clean nightgown with her hair brushed, Bronwen showed her how to hold the baby to her breast and he latched on and suckled instantly.

'He's going to be a greedy little beggar,' the woman teased and Grace stared down at him feeling more content than she had for a very long time. Even so, as the day wore on, she couldn't help glancing nervously at his hair. Would Dylan comment on him being so fair? All she could do was wait and see. Up to now he had shown her nothing but kindness and had stuck to his promise about not forcing her into the physical side of their marriage. But Grace was wise enough to know that now the birth was over he might expect more from her and she dreaded it. Still, this was a special day and she decided that she would face that when it arose.

'Have you thought of any names yet?' Bronwen asked, dragging Grace's thoughts back to the present.

Grace flushed. She would have liked to call him Luke but daren't suggest it. 'Not really. I thought I'd ask Dylan if there were any he preferred.'

Bronwen nodded then pottered away leaving Grace to rest.

It was growing dark when Dylan arrived home and he instantly pounded up the stairs. His mother was just leaving the bedroom with an empty tray in her hands and she smiled at him.

'Is it over . . . has she had the baby?'

'She has that. You have a son, Dylan.'

He nodded, then without another word he entered the bedroom and stared towards the bed.

Grace was propped against the pillows with a serene expression on her face and a look in her eyes that he had never seen before. The baby was suckling greedily at her breast and dragging his cap off he slowly approached the bed, wondering what to say. Things would have been so different had the baby been his, he thought. As it was, he felt a little flicker of jealousy. Grace had never once looked at him the way she was looking at the baby.

'It's all over then,' he said rather unnecessarily.

She smiled. 'Yes. It's a boy.'

He stepped closer then frowned when he saw the halo of silver-blonde hair.

'I was wondering if you had a preference for his name?' she said and he nodded.

'I was thinking Aiden. It was me grandad's name.'

Grace nodded. 'I like that. And could we have Luke as his middle name? I, er . . . always liked that name.' She held her breath as she watched his face, afraid that he might associate it with Father Luke but he merely nodded.

'I don't see why not if that's what you want. The Welsh version is spelled Luc.'

She gave a little sigh of relief. 'Then Aiden Luc it is,' she agreed and they both fell silent as they stared at the newly named member of the family.

Chapter Thirty-Nine

'What's this?' Aiden was one month old when Dylan came across an envelope in the chest of drawers as he was searching for some clean socks. They had moved back into their own bedroom shortly after Grace had given birth and now with the crib placed at the end of the bed they barely had room to move.

'Oh, my aunt gave it to me before we got married.' Grace was in the middle of changing Aiden's binder on the bed. 'It's the allowance that my father's solicitor used to send each month. There's some there too from the sale of the furniture that went to the auction house when my father died. Mrs Batley forwarded it on to me.'

'How much?' His eyes were like cold hard pebbles.

'A-almost fifty pounds, I think,' she answered nervously. Dylan always seemed to be in a bad mood nowadays and would snap her head off at every opportunity.

'*Fifty* pounds! And you didn't think to mention it? Meanwhile we stay here under me mam's feet where there's barely room to swing a cat around.' He shook his head angrily and rammed the envelope into his pocket. 'I'm your husband and what's yours is mine,' he told her in a voice that brooked no argument. 'We've more than enough money here to pay for a place of us own. I can't believe that you'd try to hide it from me.'

'I didn't try to hide it,' Grace protested weakly, although deep down she knew that she had. Somehow that money had been her safety net. A means of her and Aiden to escape should things go wrong. 'I . . . just didn't think about it.'

'Well, it's a good thing I found it then, isn't it?' Dylan's voice was cold. 'I shall be out looking for somewhere this very day, happen then you won't be able to come up with the excuse that me mam and tad might hear us through the wall each night.' He stamped out of the room then without giving either her or the baby so much as another glance.

Grace bit her lip and bowed her head in shame. Dylan had become impatient to consummate their marriage but she had always managed to put him off, saying she was too afraid they would be overheard. Soon now, by the sound of it, she wouldn't be able to make that excuse. She scooped her son into her arms and sank onto the side of the bed with tears in her eyes. Dylan had changed dramatically since Aiden had been born. He had never so much as once held the child and now it was becoming increasingly obvious that he resented him despite the promises he had made before they got married. Even Bronwen had noticed how distant he suddenly was, but if she thought it was anything to do with the baby she hadn't commented.

He would walk out of a room when she fed the child and if Aiden woke during the night he would burrow beneath the bedclothes and pretend he hadn't heard him. Now she wondered what the future held in store for her. Should Dylan find them a home of their own to rent she would have to allow him to have his marital rights. Still, she tried to console herself, Dylan had made an honest woman of her and given the baby his name so she supposed that would be a small price to pay for respectability.

'You two had a row, have you?' Bronwen asked when Grace had settled the baby into his crib and gone back downstairs.

'No, no. I think he's just keen for us to get our own place now,'

Grace answered sheepishly. 'After all, it's not fair for you to have us under your feet all the time.'

Bronwen nodded but Grace suspected she hadn't believed a word she'd said.

The following Sunday afternoon, Dylan came home after being out for a few hours and informed her, 'I've found us a cottage.' Grace frowned. Dylan smelled of drink. He'd taken to going to the local inn lately, something she'd never known him do before. 'It's a bit out of the way,' he went on, 'and it needs some work doing on it but it was dirt cheap so it'll do for now.'

'Oh, can I come and see it?' Grace asked.

'There'll not be time. I'm having a day off work tomorrow and we'll be moving in.'

'So soon?' Grace was shocked. 'But what about the things we'll need? A bed, pots and pans, curtains and things?' She was dismayed at the speed with which things were happening, although she vowed she would do her best to make it into a home for them. Dylan deserved that at least.

'You can go round the market and the second-hand stalls in the morning and get the basics and I'll get a cart to take the things to the cottage in the afternoon.'

'I'll watch Aiden while you go,' Bronwen volunteered and Grace nodded. It seemed she didn't have much choice in the matter.

'So whereabouts are you going?' Dylan's mother asked.

'It's that row of three terraced cottages just beyond the edge of the harbour,' he told her shortly and Bronwen looked horrified.

'Not that row of old tin miner's cottages?' she gasped. 'But they're almost derelict! I thought they'd have been pulled down by now. I know old lady Gower lives in one of them.'

'Well they haven't been pulled down and they're not that

318

bad! A bit of spit and polish and it'll be as comfy as old boots.'

Bronwen clamped her mouth shut. She very much doubted that and she dreaded to think what Grace would say when she saw them. Still, she didn't want to instigate yet another row, there seemed to have been too many of them of late, so she bent her head back to the net she was repairing.

The next morning bright and early, Grace was at the market. Griffen had sorted out an old wooden trolley from the shed for her and soon it was full of pots and pans and any essentials that she could think of. In the second-hand shop, she found an old brass bed that was badly tarnished but strong, along with a clean second-hand mattress and a table with three mismatched chairs. They weren't very elegant but they were sturdy so she decided they would do for now. She also found some drawers, an old washstand and two fireside chairs that she would attempt to re-cover. After paying for them she arranged for Dylan to pick them up later in the day with the horse and cart and continued with her shopping. She found a good length of pretty flowered cotton on another stall, along with a length of thicker material that would hopefully be enough to re-cover the chairs with, and added them to the trolley. It would make nice curtains when she found time to sew some. Eventually, she was running out of money and time. Aiden would be screaming for a feed soon so she dragged the trolley back to the cottage.

'Good gracious!' Bronwen was amazed when she saw how much Grace had bought, although a lot of it was cleaning materials.

'From what I heard you say I think I'm going to need it,' Grace told her with a rueful grin, then she lifted Aiden from his crib and started to feed him.

Soon after, Dylan arrived with the horse and cart he'd borrowed for the afternoon. He had already picked up the furniture that Grace had bought that morning and now he started to load the smaller items onto the cart while Grace flew about collecting their clothes together. At last they were ready to go and once Grace had clambered onto the hard bench seat next to Dylan, Bronwen passed Aiden up to her. Griffen, who was going along to help them unpack, clambered into the back.

'Be sure to keep in touch now,' Bronwen told them. Strangely, despite her feelings when they'd first married, she'd grown fond of Grace during the time she'd lived there. 'And take these with you an' all.' She placed a large, covered pot at Grace's feet. 'I doubt you'll have much time for cooking tonight so I made you a nice lamb cawl. You'll only need to warm it up, and there's a fresh loaf there as well.'

'Thank you.' Grace smiled at her as Dylan picked up the reins and soon they were on their way.

Once they had passed the harbour Dylan turned the cart up what was little more than a dirt track and the cart swayed from side to side. At times, Grace was fearful they were going to lose the furniture off the back of it and they seemed to be going a very long way out of the town, although she didn't voice her concerns.

Some way further on, she spotted a huddle of three old terraced cottages nestling in front of a copse and her stomach sank as she realised that this must be where they were going. There was smoke pouring from the chimney of the middle cottage but the two on either side looked unoccupied and almost derelict. Dylan drew the horse to a halt in front of the furthest one and she tried not to show her dismay as she looked at it properly. There was a small garden at the front, which was completely overgrown, surrounded by an old picket fence that was falling down in places. She saw that some of the tiles were gone from the roof. The windows were so filthy that she couldn't see through them and the whole place looked completely neglected. How am I ever going to make this place into a home? she wondered but she forced a smile as Dylan helped her down from the cart.

'Right then, boyo, I'll have a little look round inside, then I'm going to repair the roof,' Griffen said positively.

Dylan led them up the path to the front door, which was swinging open drunkenly.

'I'll fix that afore I go as well,' Griffen declared as Grace choked back tears.

Clutching Aiden close to her she picked her way along the path through the weeds, which were almost waist high in places, to the door. Dylan had gone ahead and as she entered what appeared to be a kitchen-cum-sitting room, she couldn't stop herself from gasping with dismay. It was even worse than she had feared. Leaves had blown in and were piled in every corner and she was just in time to see a long tail disappear into a hole in the skirting board. Wild animals had entered at various times and left faeces about the floor and the place reeked of stale urine, but Dylan didn't seem to notice the mess and was beaming from ear to ear.

'So, what do you think?' he asked as if he had brought her to a palace.

'It's, er . . . going to need a lot of work to make it habitable.' Grace was so distressed that her voice came out as a squeak.

'Rubbish, we'll have it shipshape in no time,' he declared confidently, throwing open another door that led into what she assumed was a small parlour. Various bits of furniture had been left in there but it was so gloomy she couldn't really see what there was or if it was salvageable.

'Let's look upstairs,' Dylan said as he sprinted over to a small staircase in the corner of the kitchen.

Grace followed him up and found herself on a small landing with two doors leading off, not dissimilar to his parents' cottage. The first was quite small and smelled musty, although she was forced to admit that it would be a perfect size for Aiden when he got a little older. The second bedroom was somewhat bigger with a large wardrobe standing in one corner. It was very dusty and grimy but after giving it a quick examination Grace hoped that it would be worth saving. It would certainly come in very handy for their clothes. Back downstairs in the kitchen she saw that there was a range – it was desperately in need of black leading but at least she would have something to cook on. The deep Belfast sink and wooden draining board looked to be in good order as well, although they, too, were coated in layers of dust.

'There's a well at the back of the cottage that will provide us with water,' Dylan told her. 'And the privy is at the end of the garden.' They were at the back of the cottage out in the weak sunshine and Grace noted that there was a tin bath hanging on the outside wall. 'Oh, and old lady Gower has a goat. Look, you can see it in her garden and she said she'll sell us some milk every day to save you having to walk into the town to fetch it.'

Grace merely nodded. Dylan was clearly taken with the place and she didn't want to spoil it for him. There was no alternative but to roll up her sleeves and get stuck into the cleaning.

Over the last weeks, the weather had turned colder and now she shivered as she went back into the cottage.

'I'll need to light a fire before I do anything else,' she told her husband. She could already hear her father-in-law hammering away as he fixed the fallen tiles back onto the roof.

'I thought of that.' Dylan smiled. 'I bought a sack of coal with me, it's on the cart. Though once we get settled we can use the wood from the fallen trees in the copse behind us. I bought a brush too that I borrowed from the chimney sweep. The cottage has stood empty for some time so the chimney will have to be swept afore we light anything.' He darted away to return seconds later with Aiden's crib and the brush.

Grace settled the baby into the crib in the bedroom and covered

322

him with a thick blanket before making her way out to the well to collect some water. Thankfully there was a bucket at the side attached to a long rope so she managed to draw some up without too much trouble. By the time she got back inside out of the biting autumn wind, the air was full of soot and there was a pile of it in the hearth, along with a couple of dead birds and Dylan looked as if he had done a shift down the pit.

'That should do it,' he said, eventually removing the brush. 'I'll get us a fire going now.'

Within an hour, Griffen had made the repairs to the roof and was working on the door and with a bright fire now blazing in the hearth things didn't look quite so bad. With the first bucket of water, Grace gave the windows a thorough wash and was heartened to see the light stream in. The windows were actually quite nice, with small leaded panes and Grace tried to imagine what they would look like with pretty curtains hanging at them. The afternoon was drawing in by then so Griffen and Dylan carried the rest of their things in from the cart.

'I ought to be getting the horse and cart back now,' Griffen told them. 'Unless there's anything else you need me to do afore I go?'

Grace smiled at him. 'You've already done more than enough. Thank you for your help.'

He blushed and hurried away.

Aiden was snuffling by then and Grace had to stop what she was doing to feed him, while Dylan manhandled what furniture they had into the rooms. As soon as Aiden was settled again, Grace started on the floor. She swept out all the leaves then mopped it thoroughly twice over until she began to see the colour of the flagstones. She then warmed up some of the cawl that Bronwen had sent them in a large pot on the fire while Dylan went to buy a jug of goat's milk from Mrs Gower. They sat on the mismatched chairs at the kitchen table to eat it, listening to the wind howling outside.

'At least we're warm and cosy in here,' Dylan said, grinning. Grace could only nod. In actual fact, it didn't look quite so bad now and she silently prayed that they would be happy here and that she would be able to turn it into a home. She also hoped that now that they had a place of their own Dylan might begin to show Aiden a little more attention. Only time would tell.

Chapter Forty

For the first month after they had moved into the cottage, Grace spent every single day scrubbing and cleaning. When he wasn't out fishing, Dylan tackled the outside. He scythed down all the overgrown grass and weeds and made a start on digging the garden ready for planting in the spring, and very slowly, between them, the tiny home was transformed.

'I have to admit you've done wonders with the place,' Gertie commented when she came to visit one cold and blustery November day. The last of the leaves that were left on the trees were clinging to the branches while the ones that had already fallen flew about in the wind like confetti in colours ranging from russet to gold.

Grace smiled as her eyes followed her aunt's to the pretty curtains that now framed the tiny windows. With the left-over fabric, she had made cushions for the chairs, and the week before Dylan had arrived home with a horsehair sofa that he'd bought for a snip, which now stood before the fire. The black-lead grate gleamed as did the copper pans that hung above it and the floor was so clean Gertie declared she was sure she could have eaten her dinner off it. The rest of the cottage was just as spruce. Grace had scrubbed the floorboards in each room until they were almost white, and warm blankets covered the old brass bed, which now shone. The wardrobe had also been polished to a high shine and had proved to be very useful indeed, and the curtains, which

Grace had sat up night after night laboriously stitching, shut out the cold night.

Despite her initial reservations, Grace had enjoyed doing it. She found that while she was kept busy cleaning and caring for Aiden she didn't have so much time to think of Luke, although whenever he did flash into her mind the hurt still cut deep. Thankfully, Dylan still hadn't demanded his rights but Grace knew that it couldn't be put off for ever, especially now she could no longer use the excuse that his mother and father were only feet away from them. On the days when he went to sea he'd taken to coming home late, often the worse for drink, which she had never known him to do before. She always tried to be in bed feigning sleep when this happened, although most times he never even made it up the stairs. He would stagger in and fall asleep on the sofa in front of the dying fire.

Now Gertie brought her thoughts back to the present when she told her, 'I spoke to Mrs Batley on the phone the other day. She's enjoying her retirement and asked me to give you her love. Oh, and she said to tell you that Mabel and Harry are now expecting their first child. They're over the moon about, it so she says.'

'How lovely!' Grace was thrilled for them.

'Do you ever feel a bit isolated here?' Aunt Gertie asked then.

After thinking about it for a moment, Grace shrugged. 'Not really, although I thought I would when I first saw it. It's no more isolated than Beehive Cottage. There's always Mrs Gower about in her cottage and she's actually quite nice when you get to know her. A bit eccentric, perhaps, but harmless.'

'Hmm.' Aunt Gertie took a sip of her tea as she stared at Grace over the rim of her cup. She seemed to have taken to motherhood like a duck to water and it was clear to see that Aiden was thriving. He was a plump, happy baby who smiled the instant you looked at him and Grace adored him. If truth be told she was never happier than when it was just her and the baby alone in the cottage. Yet for all that, Gertie suspected that Grace wasn't truly happy and if the rumours that were flying about were anything to go by, she wasn't surprised. She'd heard via Aled that Dylan was now a frequent visitor to the inn in the town. Tact had never been Gertie's strong point, so she suddenly blurted out, 'Aled mentioned that he saw Dylan coming out of the inn in town one night last week and he looked like he'd had more than enough to drink. Is everything all right?'

'Of course it is,' Grace said defensively as colour burned into her cheeks. 'He's entitled to enjoy a beer when he's been at sea all day, isn't he!' Then, instantly repentant, she muttered, 'Oh sorry, Aunt Gertie. I didn't mean to snap your head off.'

Gertie airily waved her apology aside. 'You don't have to say sorry to me . . . But you know, Grace, you shouldn't spend your life wondering about what might have been if Aiden's father had stood . . . Oh, just forget I said anything. You know my mouth is always running away with me. Of course you're all right. But just remember, if ever you should need me . . .'

'I know, and I appreciate it.' Grace sighed as she stared down at Aiden who was fast asleep in his crib with his thumb in his mouth. He looked nothing at all like her and certainly nothing like Dylan, which she sensed was the problem. Every time Dylan looked at him he must wonder who the baby's father was. His eyes were still a startling deep blue, and his hair, now that it was growing, was so fair that it was striking. Bronwen had commented on it yet again only the day before when she'd visited.

'I can't recall any of my family ever having hair that colour, or Griffen's for that matter.' There had been a questioning look on her face and Grace had known that she was still deeply suspicious as to the paternity of the child but she would rather have died than enlighten her. She knew Aunt Gertie was curious too, but she remained tight-lipped.

That evening, as always, she had Dylan's meal ready shortly before it got dark. The fishermen worked shorter hours in the autumn and winter, but by seven o'clock he still hadn't appeared so she placed the meal over a saucepan of boiling water on the stove to keep it hot for him.

At ten o'clock there was still no sign of him. The meal was ruined by then so she threw it away and placed a crusty loaf of fresh-baked bread and a block of cheese on the table. He would have to help himself when he got in. She felt far too tired to wait up for him. Leaving the oil lamp burning on the table she took herself off to bed by the light of a candle. Aiden was already fast asleep and soon she was too.

A large thud and a muttered curse downstairs startled her awake. It sounded like someone slamming the back door. The candle had burned down and she had no idea what time it was. Grabbing her robe, she slipped it on, grateful that Aiden was still fast asleep, then she crept to the top of the stairs and peered down them. Dylan had flung himself onto one of the fireside chairs so she quietly made her way down, her bare feet making no sound on the wooden stairs.

'I left you some food on the table. Your dinner dried up and I had to throw it away,' she told him testily. He turned bloodshot eyes towards her and grinned.

'Never mind about me dinner. Come over here and give your husband a kissh.'

Grace stared at him in dismay. He was clearly very drunk as he staggered up from the chair and came towards her with his arms outstretched.

'I think the best place for you is bed. You need to sleep it off,' she scolded him but he grabbed her around the waist. The smell of ale on his breath made her gag and she tried to push him away. In the tussle one of the kitchen chairs overturned and hit the floor with a clatter and Grace began to panic.

328

'*Stop it* now, Dylan! You don't know what you're doing!' She had never seen him this bad before.

'Ah, but I do.' He raised his hand and tweaked one of her breasts painfully. 'I'm doin' what I should have done a long time ago. Ashertin' me rights as your husband!'

'No . . . not like this!' Her head wagged from side to side. 'At least come upstairs to bed.' She'd always known this day must come but had never imagined it would be like this. But Dylan didn't seem to hear her.

'I don't *wanna* go upstairs in that room with the little bastard!'

'Dylan! How *could* you say such a thing!' There were tears in her eyes now as she renewed her efforts to push him away, but suddenly he tripped her and she fell in a heap on the cold flagged floor.

He was on her in a second and grabbing the frilled neckline of her nightgown he yanked on it and it tore to the waist, exposing her bare breasts.

What followed was a nightmare. Dylan fastened his mouth around her nipple and bit cruelly and she shrieked with pain.

'Hmm, you don't complain when him upstairs is fastened to it, do you?' he sneered as his hands raked up and down her bare thighs.

She struggled frantically as her worst fears were realised. Dylan resented her son although he had promised that he would bring him up as his own.

'*Please,* Dylan . . . not like this,' she sobbed, but he was panting now and she gasped with pain as he suddenly thrust his finger into her. It had been nothing like this with Luke. He had been gentle and tender but Dylan was behaving like an animal. Then suddenly she felt him struggling with the buttons on his trousers. She was powerless to stop him, for he had all his weight on her, then he thrust into her and she screamed as pain tore through her, but Dylan was oblivious to anything but satisfying himself.

Upstairs Aiden began to cry. She tried to push Dylan off her but he brought his hand back and gave her a blow across the cheek.

'*Lie still*, you bloody little whore!' he grunted. 'I bet you didn't object to the fly-blow's father doin' it to you.'

All she could do was lie there as he bucked and grunted, and pray it would be over soon. She wished that she could just curl up and die as pain and humiliation washed through her. This wasn't the man she had agreed to marry; the man who had always shown such kindness and gentleness to her. She didn't even recognise him anymore and wondered how she was going to live with what he had done to her. She could feel blood trickling down her chin from a split in her lip and her eye was already closing. It seemed to go on and on as Aiden's cries rang in her ears but at last he let out a shuddering gasp and flopped on top of her. She lay motionless, afraid that if she moved he might do it again. A few minutes later, she was relieved to hear his breathing become regular and he began to snore loudly. He was fast asleep! Very, very gingerly she rolled him off her and staggered to her feet, then pulling her ruined nightgown about her bare breasts she raced upstairs to see to Aiden.

At some stage during that long night she managed to fall asleep with the baby clutched in her arms. She woke at first light, fed and changed her little son then, when he was happily settled in his crib and fast asleep again, she ventured back downstairs.

Dylan was exactly where she had left him on the floor and she stepped over him as she went to fill the kettle at the sink.

He grunted and leaned up on one elbow to stare across at her. Then as memories of what had transpired the night before rushed back to him and he saw the state of her face he looked mortified. Her eye was black and blue and her lip was swollen.

'Oh, Grace, *forgive* me,' he choked as he staggered to his feet. 'I . . . I don't know what came over me . . . I would never hurt you, cariad, *never*! It'll never happen again, *I promise*. I think I was just frustrated because you'd made no move towards me.'

'In case you've forgotten, you said before we were wed that that side of it could come in my time,' she answered coldly.

He lifted the chair that had been overturned the night before in the scuffle and dropped heavily onto it, burying his face in his hands. 'I know and what I did was unforgivable. But I love you so much and all you seem to care about is the baby.' He shook his head and she saw there were tears in his eyes. 'Oh, you wash and iron, and cook and clean for me, admittedly. But never once have you kissed me without me making the first move and I suppose I was feeling frustrated.'

'But I was always honest with you,' she pointed out, suddenly feeling guilty. 'I was hoping that I would grow to love you in time but if this should happen again—'

'*It won't*,' he interrupted her.

She shrugged as her anger ebbed away. Perhaps she should have tried to be a little more loving towards him at least. 'Well, happen you need to get ready for work. Your father will be wondering where you are. I'll make you something to eat,' she said dully.

Looking deeply ashamed, he slunk away to have a wash and when he returned Grace had bacon and eggs on the table ready for him. However, his face was the colour of lint and he clearly had no appetite.

'I'm sorry,' he muttered. 'But I don't feel very hungry.'

'I'm not surprised.' Grace snatched his plate away. 'You've got a hangover and serves you right.' She pointed to the other end of the table where she had wrapped some food in a cloth for him to take with him. 'There's your snap. Now you'd best be off.'

Humbly he lifted the small parcel and headed for the door, where he paused to look back and ask fearfully, 'You *will* still be here when I come home tonight, won't you? I'll be on time, honestly.'

She nodded but kept her back to him. 'I'll be here.'

It was only when she heard the door close softly behind him

that she allowed herself to sag against the sink as the tears came once more. *What have I done?* she wondered, but the sound of the bird's dawn chorus in the trees outside was her only answer.

After a while she boiled some water and washed herself from head to toe but still she felt dirty. She felt as if she had been violated and despite her promise to Dylan to be there when he got home, she wondered if she would ever be able to look at him in the same way again. She'd seen a side of him that she didn't like.

That day she struggled through the household chores – things that she usually enjoyed doing – and early in the afternoon she carried a wicker basket full of clean washing out into the garden and began to peg it to the line.

She had been there for some minutes before she became aware of someone watching her and whirling about she saw old lady Gower eyeing her over the fence.

'That's a good shiner you have on you there,' she commented.

Grace flushed with embarrassment as she lifted her hand to cover her eye. 'I, er . . . fell over in the kitchen last night and cracked my face on the floor,' she mumbled, although even to her own ears she didn't sound very convincing.

'Mm . . . I heard you scream when it happened.'

Grace cringed. The old lady obviously knew that she was lying, she'd probably heard the whole disgusting episode.

'Stay there and I'll go and make you a fresh parsley poultice, it's good for bruises,' Mrs Gower said and pottered away.

Grace was happy to try anything. Her eye was sore and her head throbbed and she knew that old lady Gower was renowned for her herbal cures as well as being used by the local women as a midwife. The path to her door was trodden almost daily by folks from the surrounding villages who came seeking one of her cures. And so when she returned, Grace gently pressed the poultice to her eye without a qualm.

'You could try this for your split lip an' all.' Mrs Gower handed Grace a tiny pot. 'It's only camomile but you'll find it will soothe it.'

'Thank you, Mrs Gower.' Grace accepted the pot, cringing with humiliation. The old lady turned and walked away without another word, leaving Grace to stare after her.

❧

True to his word, Dylan was home early that evening and he instantly began to set the table as Grace silently dished up the dinner. He even made her put her feet up while he washed and dried the pots when they were done, but Grace found that she couldn't bring herself to look at him. Instead she sat staring into the fire, her heart heavy as she thought of the future with a man that she could never love now.

That night for the first time in some while she had a nightmare and once again it was about her father. She was back in her bedroom once more on the fateful night he had had his seizure, but this time instead of seeing her mother standing there holding the candlestick she saw herself holding it and she started awake in a cold sweat as realisation slowly dawned. It hadn't been her mother who had hit him . . . it had been *her*. Shock coursed through her like iced water as it finally all came flooding back. She could remember her father trying to push her back onto the bed and her reaching out blindly for anything to use as a weapon that might stop him. Her hands had closed around the heavy brass candlestick and she had struck out blindly, bringing it down on the side of his head as hard as she could. He had shrieked and reeled away from her as her mother rushed into the room and took the weapon from her. And then he had dropped to the floor and Mabel had come rushing in. But why had they let her believe that it was her mother who had caused him to have a seizure rather than herself?

She glanced at Dylan to check he was still asleep before gingerly lying down again. The last thing she needed now was for him to wake up, but thankfully he slept on while she lay there with her mind racing.

As soon as her lip and eye were healed, she determined to go and speak to Aunt Gertie about what she'd remembered. She was the only one Grace felt she could confide in now.

As it was, Aunt Gertie turned up out of the blue the very next day. She often popped in unannounced but this time she frowned when she saw the state of her niece's face.

'Walk into a door, did you?' she asked sarcastically and Grace lowered her head.

'Er . . . something like that.' And then before Aunt Gertie could say any more she rushed on, 'I've remembered . . . what happened on the night my father had his seizure.' Before Gertie could comment she hurriedly told her the rest. When she had finished the woman sighed.

'I feel awful,' Grace told her as tears welled in her eyes. 'It was *me* who was responsible for his seizure. Why did my mother let me think it was *her* that had hit him?'

Gertie sat on the sofa and patted the seat at the side of her and Grace went to join her.

'I already knew,' Gertie confessed. 'Do you remember your mother gave you a letter to give to me just after it had happened when you came to stay? Well, she told me what had really occurred but begged me not to tell you. She didn't want you to feel that what happened to him was your fault.'

'But it *was* my fault!' Grace said miserably.

'Oh, Grace!' Gertie shook her head. 'If he hadn't come into your room none of this would have happened.' And then making

334

a decision she went on, 'I think it's time you learned a few facts about your father. Did you ever find out where he went to each weekend?' When Grace shook her head, she went on, 'He went to brothels. And worse yet they were no ordinary brothels. These were places that sold little girls and boys to men with fetishes. Men like your father. The so-called house guests that your mother hated so much were part of the crowd he mixed with. How could he say no to them if they said they wanted to stay? His reputation would have been in ruins if ever any of them had made it known publicly where they went. Why do you think it took Harry so long to make a commitment to Mabel? It was because he knew where the judge went and he was so ashamed that he thought Mabel would never want him if she ever found out that he knew.

'They had a heart to heart when your father was confined to bed and he told Mabel everything. I already knew because I made it my business to make enquiries about your father when I knew your mother was going to marry him. Why do you think I disliked him so much? And now you're telling me that you're going to punish yourself for hitting someone like that? Huh! If you ask me you did the world a favour. He was hardly coming into your room for a game of tiddlywinks at that time of night, was he? Just think what might have happened if you hadn't stopped him. Furthermore, with the life he lived – his drinking and debauchery – there was every chance he would have had that seizure anyway.' Her face grew sad then as she squeezed Grace's hand. 'Your mother loved you more than life itself, that's why she was praying that you would never remember. I think she was worried that the police might become involved when they saw his injuries and if that had happened she was prepared to take the blame for it and protect you.

'But now that you have remembered, I think you should know the truth and put it all behind you. Your father brought the situation about by coming into your room and all you were trying to

335

do was defend yourself – anyone in that position would have done the same. Anyway, from the state of your face I think you have more pressing things to worry about at the moment, my girl. Let the past go, and remember if the present ever gets too hard for you there will always be a home for you and Aiden with me.'

Suddenly everything fell into place: the way her father would come into her room and try to fondle her, the way he would watch her. It was just too horrible to think about and with a muffled cry Grace buried her head in her aunt's shoulder and sobbed, wondering if she would ever find peace.

Chapter Forty-One

'Aunt Gertie called in earlier and asked if we'd like to go over to Beehive Cottage and have Christmas dinner with her.' Grace told Dylan early in December.

He looked up from the paper he was reading and scowled. 'Why would we want to do that when we have our own place?'

Grace shrugged. 'I suppose she just thought it would be nice . . . being family, you know?'

'She's not *my* family,' Dylan pointed out and turned his attention back to the newspaper. He had been true to his word and since the night he had attacked her he had returned home every evening without visiting the pub, but over the last few days Grace had noticed him growing restless. The hours he could work were severely restricted now due to the dark mornings and evenings and it was so cold that there was nothing he could do outside either. Grace had taken to drying the wet washing over a line that she had strung up in the kitchen. It was no use hanging it outside, it merely froze, but Dylan complained about it constantly.

'Those binders of his stink!' He never referred to the baby by his name.

'How can they when I've boiled them?' Grace would retort. Now she saw the frown she had come to dread cross his face and she shrank inside. Some minutes later Dylan tossed the paper down. 'I reckon I'll go into town and pay me mam a visit. All this sitting about doesn't suit me.'

Grace glanced towards the window. He'd been in less than an hour but already a thick frost had formed and the smell of snow was in the air. Added to that the wind was enough to cut you in two, as she had discovered when she had made a dash down the garden to the privy. He saw her looking and barked, 'Object to that, do you?'

He seemed intent on starting an argument so Grace shook her head. 'Not at all, but it's bitter out there so wrap up warmly.'

'Such *wifely* concern.' His voice was laced with sarcasm as he shrugged his arms into his coat but Grace chose to ignore it. She just wanted him to go now. When he set off she went to the window to watch him and felt a pang of guilt as she saw his stooped shoulders. They were living as a married couple and Grace never denied him his rights when he turned to her in bed, but he'd obviously picked up on the fact that she didn't enjoy it. She would just lie there woodenly and pray for it to be over. Unbidden a picture of Luke flashed before her eyes and she screwed them tight shut to rid herself of it. The sooner she stopped thinking about him the less it would hurt, she scolded herself, but she couldn't seem to stop it. With a sigh, she went to the sink and began to wash some baby clothes.

Just as Grace had feared, Dylan went to the inn that night after visiting his mother and it was late when she heard him crash into the kitchen. Chewing her lip she stared towards the bedroom door wondering what sort of a mood he would be in. Hopefully he would drop into the chair and sleep till morning. Aiden suddenly woke and let out a lusty yell and she hopped out of bed and flew to his side hoping to quieten him before Dylan heard. He always got so annoyed when he cried, which wasn't often, thankfully, as he was a very good baby. With him tucked in her arm she sat on the end of the bed and quickly bared her breast to feed him, but it was too late and seconds later she heard the sound of Dylan's unsteady footsteps on the stairs. The door flew inward and he glared at her.

'Spoilin' him *again*, are you?'

She smiled at him hoping to lighten his mood. 'He just needs a feed before I settle him down for the night. Why don't you go back downstairs in the warm? As soon as I've finished I'll be down to make you some supper.'

He glared at her before reeling about and doing as he was told and Grace let out a sigh of relief. Hopefully by the time she'd settled the baby back down in his crib, Dylan would be asleep. Almost half an hour later she tiptoed down the stairs to find Dylan, as she had hoped, spread out fast asleep in the chair with his mouth gaping open. Yet strangely she felt no relief, only utter despair as she stared down at the man she had married. Too late she had realised what a terrible mistake she'd made but she couldn't undo it. She was tied to Dylan for life for better or for worse and in that moment, she didn't know who she felt the sorriest for: herself or him.

Over the last weeks, she had thought on her aunt's words and had come to terms with what had happened on the night her father had had his seizure. As her aunt had quite rightly pointed out, she hadn't planned to hurt him and he could well have had the seizure at any time. It had been awful to discover how depraved her father had been, though. Whenever she thought of the many children he must have abused it made a cold shiver run up her spine. But he was gone now and she had Aiden to think about, so she tried to go from day to day as best she could. There could be no changing the past; what was done was done.

Aiden was almost six months old when in mid-March, Grace started to feel ill and realised very quickly that she was with child again. She remembered the symptoms all too well.

Soon after, she broke the news to Dylan, not at all sure how he might take it, but she needn't have worried, he was thrilled.

'Oh, my love.' Rising from the table he tenderly placed his arms about her. 'What wonderful news. A baby . . . of our own.'

His words stabbed at her heart like a knife. She'd hoped that with time he would grow to love Aiden but now she knew that it wasn't going to happen and she kept the baby out of his way as much as possible. The trouble was, it was getting more difficult to do that as Aiden grew and demanded more attention. Still, she chided herself, happen he'll be a little softer when this one comes along. She could live in hope.

The pregnancy progressed well and after the initial morning sickness wore off, Grace felt as fit as a fiddle and blossomed. Her skin had a glow to it and her eyes and hair shone, although she quickly grew so huge that she almost forgot what her feet looked like and had to take to waddling like a duck.

'You'll have a little lass this time,' old lady Gower predicted as Grace was pegging the washing to the line early in September. Aiden was almost a year old by then and the baby was due in weeks.

Grace giggled. 'Will I now? And how would you happen to know that?'

The old woman tapped the side of her nose and winked. 'I just do and it ain't often I'm wrong. You just mark me words, it's a lass, I'm tellin' you.' And with that she pottered away.

Grace quite hoped that she was right. It would be nice to have one of each. Her eyes went to Aiden who was tottering about on the only small patch of grass that wasn't taken up with growing vegetables in the garden. Just days before, he had taken his first tentative steps and it seemed now that there was no stopping him.

340

He was chasing a butterfly and laughing and as always when she looked at him, Grace felt a surge of love. Her hand dropped then to the swell of her belly where the baby was wriggling about. Very soon now she would have yet another child to love and she could hardly wait. Dylan had been surprisingly kind to her during the months of her pregnancy and never tired of stroking her belly and speaking of their unborn child.

'Will you be wanting a boy?' she asked him once.

Dylan had shaken his head. 'I don't mind what it is, if truth be told, just so long as it's healthy,' he'd told her and she'd felt comforted.

Now, however, she was aware that there was dinner waiting to be prepared and cooked, so lifting the wash basket she waddled into the kitchen to start it, keeping a watchful eye on Aiden from the window the whole time. Very soon the potatoes were scrubbed and the vegetables had been peeled. She'd made the pastry for the meat pie earlier in the morning so she decided that it was time for a cup of tea. Keeping an eye open for Aiden through the open kitchen door she had just poured the boiling water into the teapot when Dylan's mother came puffing into the room laden down with a heavy basket. Bronwen had taken to doing some of the heavier shopping for Grace over the last few weeks and Grace was grateful to her.

'Eeh, I don't know if that hill is getting steeper or it's me getting older,' the woman breathed as she dropped onto a kitchen chair. 'And it's hot as hell out there, I tell you!' Taking a large white handkerchief from her pocket she mopped her sweating brow as Grace grinned.

'Well, you timed it right. I've just made a pot of tea. Or would you rather have a cold drink?'

'Tea will be fine,' her mother-in-law informed her, then glancing around she asked, 'The little 'un in bed, is he?'

'No, he's playing out in the garden.' Grace's smile froze as she

341

saw Bronwen frown and she suddenly realised that she couldn't hear him.

'I didn't see him,' Bronwen commented but her words fell on deaf ears. Grace was already racing towards the open door. A glance at the empty lawn proved her visitor to be right. Grace's heart sank and she felt as if she'd had all the breath sucked out of her.

'B-but he was here just minutes ago,' she gasped as panic set in.

'In that case, he can't have gone far, now calm yourself down. It's no good for the baby getting yourself all worked up.' Bronwen had come to stand behind her. 'You just stay where you are,' she advised, 'and I'll go and look for him.'

But Grace was already heading into the garden, her feet barely touching the ground as her head swung from side to side for a sight of her tiny son. 'He . . . he can't have been gone for more than five minutes, ten at most.' She was crying now and the commotion brought old lady Gower out of her cottage to see what was going on.

'So what's to do then?' She raised a questioning eyebrow at Bronwen. She could see at a glance that she'd get no sense out of Grace.

'Aiden's gone missing,' Bronwen informed her worriedly.

'Right then, we'd best go and find him. You go on up the lane' – she gestured to Bronwen – 'I'll walk down towards the village, an' you, Grace, you go and see if he's headed for the trees at the back of us.'

In her mind's eye Grace was picturing the large pond that stood in front of the trees. If he'd managed to make it there . . . Then lifting her faded serge skirt, she was off like a hare, regardless of her swollen stomach.

'Aiden! Aiden! Are you there?' As she ran she called and called repeatedly but there was no answer and not a sign of him. Eventually she came to the edge of the pool where she paused to press her hand into her side and catch her breath. Her heart was hammering and she felt sick but the surface of the pool was as calm as a millpond.

What if he's fallen in and the weeds have pulled him under? she wondered. And without stopping to think, she splashed into the water and began to feel about frantically beneath the surface. Very soon only her chin was above the water level and she knew that she could go no deeper. Sobbing, she turned about and painstakingly waded back towards the bank as Bronwen suddenly appeared.

'Whatever are you doing?' she scolded as she reached down to help Grace up the slippery bank. 'Aiden is safe and sound back at home. He'd not gone far along the lane. Mrs Gower found him. But come out of there now. Getting yourself into such a state is no good for neither you nor the baby.'

Crying with relief, Grace dropped onto the grass, her clothes clinging wetly to her and her hair hanging in rats' tails. The pain in her side was getting worse but she didn't care now that she knew that Aiden was all right.

Dylan's mother tutted. 'Just *look* at the state of you. Let's get you back home and into some dry clothes.' She helped Grace to her feet and Grace leaned on her as they made their slow way back to the cottage. Grace felt strangely light-headed and they were almost halfway back when suddenly she doubled over.

'*Oh no,*' she panted. 'I think the baby's coming and it's too soon.'

Bronwen looked horrified. 'Now see what you've done haring off like that,' she snapped. 'But if the baby *is* on its way we're lucky we have old lady Gower to hand. Come on, there's no time to lose, we need to get you home.'

They limped on and when the cottage came into sight, Grace heaved a sigh of relief to see Aiden sitting on Mrs Gower's lap on a chair outside the kitchen door.

'Help me get her inside,' Bronwen shouted. 'I think the baby is on its way.'

343

Mrs Gower lifted Aiden to the ground then hobbled towards them and took Grace's other arm.

'We'll get her straight upstairs where I can have a look at her,' she ordered.

Somehow, between them, they managed to manoeuvre her up the steep, narrow staircase.

'Right, firstly we'll get you into a clean nightgown and out of those wet clothes,' the old lady told Grace. 'And you' – she nodded towards Bronwen – 'go and watch the young feller me lad. We don't want him wanderin' off again.'

Grace bit down on her lip as another pain tore through her. Mrs Gower meantime was busily stripping the wet clothes from her and rubbing her hair with a piece of huckaback that was folded on the end of the bed.

'It . . . it's too soon for the baby to come yet. I still have another six or seven weeks to go,' Grace groaned. Her teeth were chattering and she felt sick from all the pond water she had swallowed.

'You should 'ave thought of that afore you went throwing yourself into that dirty pond,' Mrs Gower grumbled as she slipped a clean nightgown over her shivering frame. 'Everyone knows that water is stagnant. God alone knows what germs are lurking in there.'

With a strength that belied her small frame she swung Grace's legs up onto the bed and Grace flopped back against the pillows like a rag doll.

'Now then, let's see what's going on with this baby!' Mrs Gower rolled her grimy sleeves up and without ceremony hoisted Grace's nightgown up above her waist and bent to examine her.

'Hmm!' She clucked as she shook her head. 'I'm afraid this little 'un is well an' truly on its way now.'

'No . . . *please*, you *mustn't* let it come yet,' Grace fretted as her head swung from side to side. 'Dylan is so looking forward to this baby . . . if anything should go wrong now . . .'

Mrs Gower could only shake her head as she turned to go and fetch hot water and towels. 'I'm afraid it's all in God's hands now,' she muttered as she disappeared through the door but Grace was in the grip of another contraction and didn't even hear her.

Chapter Forty-Two

It was almost dark when Dylan came whistling merrily up the lane that night. He and his father had had a good day fishing and the money he'd made from his catch was nestling in his pocket. It was only when he reached the little picket fence that surrounded the cottage that he noticed there were lights shining from every window. That's odd, he thought. Grace was usually very frugal with the oil for the lamps. The second he entered the kitchen he saw his mother sitting at the table and he frowned.

'What's this then?' he queried. His mother rarely ventured out of an evening, even to visit him and Grace.

She nodded towards the ceiling. 'It's Grace. The baby is coming.'

He frowned. 'But it's too soon, surely?'

She nodded in agreement. 'Aye, it is, but there were a bit of bother early on. Aiden went wandering off so she went looking for him and ended up in the pool beyond the trees. She thought he might have fallen in.'

'But that pool is *filthy*,' he exclaimed. 'You used to tell me an' Myfanwy that you'd skelp our backsides if ever you found out we'd even been near it.'

'So I did,' she agreed. 'But Grace was panicking. Anyway, the long and the short of it is the shock brought on early labour. Mrs Gower is up there with her now. I thought she'd have had it be now but she ain't having an easy time of it apparently.'

Dylan scowled as he began to pace up and down before asking, 'And Aiden?'

'Right as ninepence, he'd wandered off down the lane. He's fast asleep in the other room now. I took his cot through there so as Grace wouldn't disturb him.'

He ground his teeth together as he pushed his hand through his thick hair. At that moment Mrs Gower clattered down the stairs and when she saw Dylan she looked relieved.

'Ah, you're back then – good! Now get yourself into town quick as you know how, boyo, an' tell the doctor he's needed here.'

Dylan looked worried. 'Is something wrong?'

Evading the question, she answered, 'Let's just say this little 'un should have been here by now. But don't waste any more time standing there, get yourself away!'

Dylan sprang towards the door sensing that something was seriously amiss.

'Oh, and call in and tell your dad I'll be staying here tonight else he'll be worrying,' Bronwen called after him.

As he disappeared off down the lane, Mrs Gower wearily made her way back upstairs to Grace. It had been a long day and there was still no sign the birth was in sight as yet.

It was almost an hour later when Dylan and the doctor returned and wasting no time the doctor went straight upstairs to Grace leaving the father-to-be to pace the floor. Soon it was deepest night and Dylan and Bronwen began to think the baby was never going to put in an appearance, but then suddenly the sound of a newborn baby's cry echoed down the stairs and Dylan sprang to his feet with a joyous smile on his face.

'It's here . . . the baby's here!' He shouted as he caught his mother about the waist and danced her around the room. 'I'm a father!'

Bronwen stared at him with a frown on her brow. 'What do you mean, son? You already have a son asleep upstairs. You've been a father for some time.'

347

'Oh, er . . . yes . . . I know,' he blustered. 'What I meant was I'm a father *again!*'

The little seed of doubt that had always been in the back of Bronwen's mind about Aiden's paternity was growing again. She had always wondered why Grace had wanted the child's middle name to be Luc but this wasn't the time to address it so she merely nodded as they stared upwards waiting for Mrs Gower to come and inform them whether the child was a boy or a girl.

Thankfully they didn't have long to wait. Shortly after, the old woman appeared with a tiny bundle wrapped in a towel in her arms.

'Here you are then.' She held the baby out to Dylan who took it with a rapturous expression on his face. 'You have a little daughter, but I should warn you, she's very tiny.'

Dylan didn't seem to hear her, he was too intent on studying the tiny miracle in his arms.

It was his mother who asked, 'And how is Grace?'

Lowering her voice Mrs Gower told her, 'Not good. She had a bad time of it an' she's feverish and delirious now. Will you be staying to see to her and the babe?'

Bronwen nodded as Mrs Gower stifled a yawn with the back of her hand.

'Good, then I'm away to me bed. I'm getting too old for all of this.' And with that she took her leave.

'Eeh, just look at her, Mam, she's right bonny.' Dylan was smiling from ear to ear as Bronwen went to meet her new granddaughter. She was indeed a tiny little thing and she looked so weak that the first sight of her filled Bronwen with foreboding. How could anything so tiny survive? she wondered. She didn't express her concerns to Dylan, though.

Instead she said, 'Right then, we'd best get the child bathed and fed, eh?'

After fetching the tin bowl from the sink, she filled it with warm water from the kettle and washed and dried the infant. She had very little hair but already it was obvious that when it grew she was going to be dark like her father. The clothes they had laid ready swamped her but once she was clean and wrapped in a warm shawl that Bronwen had knitted, she handed her back to her doting father and fetched some goat's milk to warm on the range. The doctor was still upstairs with Grace and if what Mrs Gower had said was right then it was doubtful that Grace would be up to feeding her that night. Instead, Bronwen attempted to drip the warm milk into the baby's mouth, although most of it dribbled down her chin.

'Shouldn't she be hungry?' Dylan asked anxiously.

'Don't forget she's only just been born. No doubt she will be in a few hours' time.' She smiled at him reassuringly although she was deeply concerned.

Sometime later the doctor came down the stairs with a grave expression on his face. 'I'm afraid your wife is very ill,' he told Dylan, who was still cradling the baby in his arms. 'She seems to have developed a fever. No doubt caused by swallowing some of that filthy water in the pond. You'll need to watch her closely throughout the night and I shall call in tomorrow to see how she is.'

He then beckoned Bronwen towards the door and once out of earshot of her son he told her in a hushed voice, 'I'm concerned about the baby too. She's very small and weak. Keep her warm and try to get some milk into her.'

'Do you think she'll survive, doctor?'

He frowned. 'To be honest, I wouldn't like to say at the moment. It could go either way for both mother and baby but rest assured I shall do all I can. Now, I'll wish you goodnight.'

Bronwen paid him his fee from the tin tea caddy on the mantelpiece, thanked him profusely and quietly closed the door behind him. With a very heavy heart she hurried away upstairs to check on Grace. Shortly after, Dylan joined her and bending to his wife he took her hand and whispered, 'We have a lovely little lass, Grace? Can you hear me?'

But Grace was beyond hearing as she lay with beads of sweat on her brow, muttering unintelligibly.

'You go down and keep an eye on the baby,' his mother ordered as she took a damp cloth from the bowl of cool water at the side of the bed. She proceeded to mop Grace's brow. 'I'm going to stay up here and try to get this fever down. Call me if the baby cries and I'll come down and try again to get some milk into her.'

Dylan nodded and after glancing worriedly at his wife he went to do as he was told. He had been gone no more than a few minutes when Grace's head started to thrash from side to side on the pillow.

'L -Lu . . .' she mumbled.

Bronwen leaned closer. 'What's that you're trying to say, pet?'

'L-Luk . . .'

Bronwen frowned. What was Grace saying – look, luk . . .? And then suddenly it came to her, the girl was crying for someone called Luke! Could it be that this Luke was Aiden's father? Was that the reason she had wanted Aiden to have his middle name? Bronwen suspected it could be because after seeing the newborn she was fairly sure now that Aiden wasn't Dylan's child. Even so, for now she put her suspicions to one side and concentrated on trying to get Grace well again.

Grace hovered between life and death for the next twenty-four hours but then after Bronwen dripped one of Mrs Gower's remedies into her mouth, the fever finally broke and she slipped into an exhausted sleep.

'She'll recover now,' Mrs Gower said with satisfaction. 'Though I have me concerns about the baby. Is she still not taking any milk?'

Bronwen shook her head. 'Not so much as a drop, though I've tried to feed her every hour or so. Our Dylan is beside hisself with worry about her.'

Mrs Gower took a deep breath. To her mind the baby didn't stand a chance of surviving although she couldn't say that, of course. She had fetched Aiden to her house early that morning and kept him there all day to give Bronwen and Dylan time to concentrate on the invalids, and not once had either of them asked after him. She too had wondered from time to time if Aiden were Dylan's son. He certainly didn't favour either Grace or Dylan for his looks, and now she was fairly certain that he wasn't Dylan's, which would explain his coldness towards Aiden, the poor little mite. He hadn't asked to be born after all, whoever his father was. On the other hand, Dylan was clearly quite besotted with his new baby daughter and had hardly put her down all day. He'd sat rocking her and cooing over her and had even changed her binders – admittedly, somewhat clumsily, but he'd managed it.

'I'm sure she just smiled at me,' Dylan told her when she went downstairs and she smiled indulgently.

'It were probably just a bit o' wind, lad. But has she still taken no milk?'

Worried again now, he shook his head, his eyes never leaving his daughter's face. 'We'll have to name her when Grace wakes up,' he told her. 'But I'm hoping that Grace will agree to Myfanwy after me late sister. She and Grace were best friends when they were little before Myfanwy died.'

'It's a lovely name,' old lady Gower muttered before heading back to her own cottage where Aiden was fast asleep. She felt cold inside, for as she'd stared at the sleeping baby she had sensed death close by. She had inherited this sense from her mother, who had always told her that she had 'the gift'. The old lady sometimes wasn't sure if it was a gift or a curse, for over the years she had spent many a sleepless night over it. And now she knew with utter certainty that the lovely baby next door was not destined to stay on this earth and no amount of her potions would change it.

Grace woke up properly the next day and immediately asked

to see her baby and Aiden. Dylan carried the child upstairs to her while Bronwen rushed around to fetch Aiden from Mrs Gower's, where he was happily playing with a tin cooking pan and a wooden spoon on her kitchen floor and making enough noise to waken the dead.

'I . . . want to hold her,' Grace croaked when Dylan appeared and he reluctantly handed the child to her. Grace was still incredibly weak and he had to support her as she stared down at her tiny daughter.

Grace's eyes filled with tears as love for this helpless little infant flooded through her.

'She . . . she's just beautiful,' she murmured as she stroked the soft skin on her baby's cheek. 'But she's so tiny.'

'Aye, well that's because you brought her birth on too early by chasing after *him*!' Dylan snapped, unable to conceal his anger, but then seeing the tears slide down Grace's cheeks he softened. 'Anyway, she's here now and she's a little beauty,' he went on in a gentler tone. 'I was thinking we should name her and wondered how you'd feel about calling her Myfanwy?'

Grace smiled through her tears, never taking her eyes off this precious child. 'I think that would be lovely,' she muttered. 'It suits her and she has a look of Myfanwy about her, don't you think? I reckon she'll have her dark hair and blue eyes.'

He nodded in agreement but then Aiden exploded into the room and the close moment they had just shared was gone.

'*Babba!*' he said excitedly, struggling to clamber onto the bed next to his mother and sister. Grace saw the closed look come down in Dylan's eyes but he gave the little boy a leg-up just the same. They made a pretty picture, the three of them, and Dylan smiled.

'We'll be a proper family now,' he whispered and Grace prayed that he was right.

Over the next two days, as Grace grew steadily stronger, the child weakened. She refused to take any milk even from her concerned mother and eventually Dylan, who had still not gone back to work, sent for the doctor.

'I'm afraid there's nothing I can do,' the doctor told him sadly after examining her. 'You must understand she was born very prematurely, which put her at a terrible disadvantage. We can only pray that she will start to rally.'

But she didn't rally. Dylan took to sleeping downstairs in the chair with her in his arms. Bronwen stayed on to help, for Grace was still too weak to get out of bed, and then one morning Grace was startled awake by a piteous scream from the room beneath her.

'Mam, Mam, come quick. I don't think Myfanwy is breathing!'

It was Dylan's voice, and full of dread, Grace dragged herself from the bed. For a moment, her legs turned to jelly and the floor spun up to meet her, but somehow she managed to drag herself down to the kitchen.

Bronwen was just rushing out to fetch Mrs Gower and Dylan was frantically rocking the baby to and fro, his eyes bloodshot from lack of sleep. 'She's barely breathing and I don't know what to do!' his voice caught on a sob as Grace wobbled over to him, but as she reached for her daughter he clutched her possessively to him.

'Leave her alone,' he spat. 'Haven't you done enough? If it weren't for you haring off after *the bastard* this wouldn't be happening!'

Grace dropped onto a chair as tears spilled down her cheeks, for she knew deep down that what he said was right. It was her fault that Myfanwy had been born too soon and somehow, whatever happened, she was going to have to live with that. Seconds later a breathless Mrs Gower panted into the kitchen with Bronwen close behind her, only to skid to a halt as she stared towards the corner of the room.

'It's too late,' she said woodenly. 'She's already gone to be an angel.' She watched then as the ebony-haired girl standing in the corner of the room, who was clutching the baby to her with a beautiful smile on her face, melted away like mist in the morning.

'No, no she *can't* be.' Dylan was sobbing broken-heartedly as he stared down at the lifeless infant in his arms.

'Give her to me,' Mrs Gower said gently, and as Dylan handed her over he looked like a broken man.

Little Myfanwy was laid to rest in the tiny churchyard two days later in the same grave as her namesake, and as Grace watched the tiny coffin being lowered into the hole she felt as if her heart was breaking. But the worst was yet to come.

When they got back to the cottage Dylan began to drink and by teatime he was so drunk he could no longer stand.

'This is all your fault, you *whore*!' he spat. 'You sacrificed *my* child for yours. Why should your bastard live while *mine* died?'

Grace bowed her head. 'I'm *so* sorry this has happened,' she muttered. 'I loved her too, you know!'

Dylan glared at her, hatred shining from his eyes. 'You *will* be sorry for what you've done. By God you will afore I've finished with you!'

'Now then, son. We know you're upset, we all are, but you mustn't say such things,' Bronwen scolded, hoping to keep the peace.

Gertie and the Llewelyns had come back to the cottage for a small tea following the funeral and now all Grace wanted was for everyone to leave so that she could grieve in peace.

'What did you mean anyway?' Bronwen questioned. 'About Aiden being *her* child?'

Grace held her breath, all too aware that any moment now her shame would be public knowledge.

'Didn't I tell you?' he laughed as he took another swig of whisky. 'She was already pregnant when I married her an' the bastard's not mine! I married her to give it a name an' look how she's repaid me!'

Suddenly Bronwen remembered back to the night when Grace had been delirious and everything fell into place. She had been calling for someone called Luke. More than ever now she was convinced that this must have been the name of Aiden's father. A hush fell on the room as Bronwen rose and gathered her things together without another word, then turning to her husband she said, 'Come along, we're going and I'll not darken this door again, so help me.'

Grace shuddered as she bowed her head in shame.

Chapter Forty-Three

August 1914

As Grace made her way from stall to stall in the marketplace she began to feel uneasy. Little clusters of women were huddled together discussing the assassination of the Archduke Franz Ferdinand and his wife in the streets of Sarajevo by a teenage Serbian nationalist back in June, and they were all saying that this could well lead to the outbreak of war. Grace had heard Dylan saying the same thing to Aled Llewelyn but found it hard to believe that something that had happened so far away could affect them. It frightened her just to think of it and she was glad when her shopping was done and she could hurry home.

'Aiden, come away in now, pet,' Grace called later as she stood at the open kitchen door. She smiled as she saw her son playing with the small goat she had purchased some time ago to supply them with milk. But the sun was fading and she knew Dylan might be home soon so she hoped to get Aiden into bed before he arrived. Dylan had never forgiven her for the death of their daughter, or Aiden for that matter. Many a time she'd had to step between Dylan and the boy when Dylan went to take a swipe at him, so now she found it easier to try and keep them apart.

Mrs Gower was in her own garden picking a lettuce from her

vegetable patch and she raised her eyebrow, although she didn't comment.

Since Grace's baby had died, she had been round to Grace's many a time with ointments and potions for Grace following one of Dylan's drunken tempers, but never once had either of them spoken of how Grace's bruises had appeared. In the beginning, Grace had found it humiliating. She was all too aware that Mrs Gower must know that Dylan beat her; how could she not? Their cottages were joined so she no doubt heard everything through the wall.

There had never been another child and sometimes Grace wondered if this was a good or a bad thing. Either way, she tried not to think of it. Dylan had changed almost beyond recognition over the last years. He often had days off work following a drinking binge and some time ago Grace had been forced to do whatever work she could to make ends meet. Even when he did go out fishing now, Dylan spent most of the money he earned in the inn and if it wasn't for Grace growing their own fruit and vegetables and being as frugal as she possibly could she knew that there would have been times when they might have gone hungry.

Each Monday morning now, hail or shine, she would walk to the larger houses on the outskirts of the town and collect dirty washing in an old trolley that Aled Llewelyn had made for her. She would then wash, dry and iron it before returning it to the owners. The small amount she earned made all the difference. It meant that at least twice a week she could afford to buy meat, not the best cuts admittedly, but Grace had become adept at producing a meal from almost nothing, and thankfully there was always an abundance of fish. It was just as well, for ever since the day of her baby's funeral her mother-in-law had refused to have anything more to do with her and she certainly had no time for Aiden.

'She tricked my son into marrying her while she was carrying someone else's bastard!' she would tell anyone who would listen to her, and despite Grace doing her best to explain that this hadn't been the case, Bronwen merely turned a deaf ear.

Now, seeing that Aiden was still playing with the goat, she scolded, 'Come away in I said, young man! Your dad will be home anytime.'

Aiden immediately scooted towards her. He didn't like his dad at all and young as he was he knew that his dad didn't like him, though as yet he had no idea why.

'Will I get washed?' he asked as he took his mother's hand and entered the kitchen and Grace's heart filled with love for him. He was such a lovely little boy, a bit on the skinny side, admittedly, but his glorious mop of blonde hair and his startling blue eyes made people give him a second glance. He was so like his father that sometimes it hurt Grace to look at him and she was fiercely protective of him.

'The water's in the bowl waiting for you,' she told him, pointing towards the sink. 'And your pyjamas are laid out for you as well.'

The child instantly stripped out of his dirty clothes and Grace thought how lucky she was to have him. He was such an undemanding little chap and good as gold into the bargain, although sometimes she felt as if he were two different children. When they were alone together he was playful and smiling but when he was in Dylan's presence, he was quiet and had developed a nervous tick in his eye. It broke Grace's heart but there was nothing she could do to change it apart from strive to protect him as much as she could.

Once Aiden was washed and changed she sat him at the kitchen table and sliced a large wedge from the fresh-baked loaf before smothering it in blackberry jam.

'Aunt Gertie brought this over for you,' she told him as he hungrily licked his lips. 'She said to tell you the next time we go to Beehive Cottage you and Aunt Cerys can go blackberry picking and she'll make us some more.'

He nodded as he greedily bit into his treat. He loved Aunt

Gertie and Uncle Aled and Aunt Cerys too. They were always kind to him and one or another of them often turned up with little treats. Never while his father was there, though, he'd noticed. Not since the night he had laid in bed listening to his dad shouting at his mum when he came back from the inn.

'Tell them to stay away!' Dylan had warned. 'We're not bloody charity cases just yet. I'll see to me own family!'

'But, Dylan, you've brought no money in for almost two weeks now,' his mother had answered and then Aiden had heard the sound of something crashing over and his mother cry out. He'd burrowed down in the bed then and tried not to hear any more. He always did that when he heard his dad shout. Once, he'd ventured down the stairs only to find his mum's nose pouring with blood and when he'd gone to run to her his dad had hit him.

'It's all right, pet. I knocked the chair over when I tripped and hurt my nose,' she'd told him as she'd glared at Dylan. She always seemed to be hurting herself, Aiden thought, so now Aunt Gertie or the Llewelyns only visited when they knew that he was out.

Soon his belly was full of bread and jam and milk from the goat and he yawned.

Grace smiled. 'Come on, young feller me lad, let's get you tucked in,' she said and Aiden willingly followed her upstairs. She was kind, was his mam, and she never shouted at him, not like his dad.

Within minutes of his head touching the pillow he was fast asleep, so Grace went back downstairs to tackle the huge pile of ironing that never seemed to get any smaller.

She was still ironing by the light of the oil lamp when Dylan got home and she glanced at him warily, trying to gauge what mood he was in before rushing away to fetch his meal. She had been keeping it hot over a saucepan of boiling water on the range for over an hour and prayed it wouldn't be dried up so that he had something to complain about.

'Did you have a good day?' she asked cheerily, hoping to put him in a good mood. He'd clearly been drinking, she could smell the ale on him, but he seemed to be calm enough.

'Aye, I did till I got to the inn this evenin'.' He stared at her for a moment before asking, 'So have you heard the news?'

When she stared at him blankly he lifted his knife and fork and shook his head. 'As of today, we are officially at war; the men in the inn were on about it. Didn't I tell you it was coming?'

Grace rubbed her throat as a cold hand closed about her heart. She hadn't seen a newspaper for some days now, Dylan didn't always bring one home anymore. He was always too intent on getting to the inn when he finished his day's fishing nowadays, but she knew that war had been on the cards for some time. And now it had finally happened. It was a frightening thought.

'So how will it affect us?'

He shrugged as he took a mouthful of the cod and sliced fried potatoes on his plate. 'Time will tell, I dare say. They're saying that there'll be recruitment centres springing up all over the place and most of the young men will be gone in no time.'

'And will you have to go?' she enquired.

Another shrug. 'Who knows? It's bound to affect the fishing industry even if I don't have to,' he answered. 'If the enemy boats start to come into our waters the men reckon we'll be restricted as to how far we'll be allowed to go out to sea.'

'I see.' Grace chewed on her lip. She'd been dreading this. Still, she told herself, whatever happens we'll just have to make the best of it.

Over the next two weeks, the world seemed to go mad. Young men queued at the recruitment centres and went off to the training camps like conquering heroes, as if they were embarking on some wonderful adventure.

'They'll rue the day, the silly buggers, you just mark my words,' Mrs Gower said gloomily over the garden fence one day. 'I don't mind betting half of 'em won't come home!' She pottered away, leaving Grace to peg the rest of the washing to the line with a heavy heart.

Things had been quiet in the cottage for the last couple of weeks. Dylan still went to the inn but came home reasonably sober, but that night everything suddenly changed.

He was so late coming in that Grace eventually turned off the heat beneath the saucepan that was keeping his meal warm and wearily made her way to bed. She had been washing and ironing all day and was so tired that she fell asleep almost instantly. It was the sound of the kitchen door slamming against the wall as it was flung open that made her start awake and she groaned. It could only mean one thing – Dylan was drunk. She lay for a moment listening to him crashing about the kitchen, muttering and cursing. She hoped that he would drop into the chair and fall asleep but her hopes were dashed when he came to the bottom of the stairs and screeched, 'Where are you, woman! I wantsh me dinner!'

Grace sighed as she slung her legs over the edge of the feather mattress. Much as she didn't want to face him if he was in a state, she would have to or he would wake Aiden up and the child was nervy enough as it was.

She found him sprawled in the chair when she reached the bottom of the stairs and he instantly began to rant at her. 'Whass the idea o' clearin' off to bed! Ain't a man entitled to a meal when he'sh done a hard day's graft?'

'I can warm your dinner up again in no time,' she said, hoping to placate him. 'Though I can't promise what it will be like. I've been keeping it warm for hours.'

He narrowed his eyes as he glared at her. 'Oh, sho I have to ask your permishion to go for a drink now, do I?'

361

'Of course not,' she assured him as she placed the saucepan back on the heat. 'I was just sayin—'

'Well, *don't* bloody say, you whore,' he rasped. 'Just get that food on the table *now*!'

'But it won't be hot again ye—'

'*Now!*' he roared and Grace began to tremble as she carried the meal to the table. Hopefully he was so drunk that he'd just eat it.

But he didn't. After one mouthful he spat the food all over the table then threw the plate at the wall where it smashed, depositing pottery and food all over the place.

'You're bloody *useless*!' he ground out. As he approached her with his fist clenched she could do nothing but raise her hands to try and protect her face. The thump when it came was full on into her stomach and she groaned as the air left her lungs and she doubled over.

'P-*please*, Dylan, I haven't done anything,' she pleaded but he was incensed now and the blows began to rain down on her thick and fast until she tumbled to the floor and rolled herself into a ball. 'Y-you'll wake Aiden,' she sobbed and he laughed – a cruel laugh that made the hairs on the back of her neck stand on end.

'I've a good mind to fetch that little bastard down an' give him a thrashin' too,' he grunted and from that moment on Grace said not another word. Far better she took the beating than risk her son. At some time during the frenzied attack, he began to kick her and one of the kicks connected with her mouth. She felt the blood spurt and a tooth loosen at the back of her mouth but still she managed not to cry out. And then as quickly as it had erupted, his temper was done and he slouched away to drop into the chair again. Waves of pain were washing through her, but Grace lay as still as a statue in case he came back to start on her again, but within seconds he was snoring loudly. Slowly she tried to drag herself to her feet but a shooting pain in her chest made her drop to the floor like a stone and she knew no more.

'*Mammy, Mammy*, wake up.' A small hand shaking her arm made her open her eyes groggily to find Aiden standing over her. Tears were running down his face as he stared at the bloody state of her but she managed to smile weakly at him. Daylight was streaming through the kitchen window and she wondered what time it was.

'It's all right,' she soothed, although it hurt to talk and she dreaded to think what she must look like. 'Mammy had a nasty fall but I'll be fine if you help me up.'

Aiden did his best and she had managed to get to her knees when Dylan suddenly snorted in the chair and opened his eyes. He stared towards them and she saw a look of horror dawn in his eyes as he saw her.

'Oh, good God above, what have I done?' he groaned as he dragged himself out of the chair and lurched towards her.

Grace initially shrank away from him, but when she saw that he meant her no more harm, for now at least, she allowed him to help her to her feet.

'Sh-shall I fetch Mrs Gower?' Aiden whimpered his eyes never leaving his mother's face.

'No!' Dylan and Grace said together and the child watched as Dylan helped Grace to the nearest chair. One of her eyes was completely closed and both of them were black with bruises. Blood from her split lip had stained the front of her nightgown and when she opened her mouth she spat out a tooth.

Dylan looked truly repentant as he saw what he had done. 'I'll fetch a bowl with some water and a cloth in it,' he told her but Grace shook her head.

'N-no, you just get yourself off to work, I can clean myself up,' she told him weakly.

He shook his head. 'I'll have missed the tide be now anyway. Please let me help you.'

When he returned with the bowl he began to gently wash her wounds.

Once she raised her hand to stop him and pain lanced through her again. 'I . . . I think one of my ribs is broken,' she muttered and he bowed his head in shame.

'I'm so, so sorry.' In that moment, she almost believed he was . . . until the next time. There was always a next time with Dylan and sometimes she wondered where the kindly man she had married had gone to.

'You'll have to help me bind my chest,' she gasped. 'Tear up one of my petticoats into strips and bind it as tightly as you can, otherwise I won't be able move about.' Every breath was painful but Grace was determined to appear as normal as she could for Aiden's sake. And then the child shocked them and both heads turned towards him as he suddenly said to Dylan, 'I *hate* you! You're naughty, Dada. Go away!'

Grace hardly dared to breathe. She was in no state to protect him if Dylan were to turn on the boy now.

The silence lay thick between them as Dylan stared back at the lad and then in a shaky voice he told them, 'Well, happen you're about to get your wish, boyo, cos while I was drunk late yesterday me an' some o' the other lads off the boats went an' signed up for the army. I'm going to war!'

Chapter Forty-Four

Two weeks later, as Aiden hid behind her skirts on the doorstep, Grace asked, 'Are you sure you have everything you need?'

Clutching the small bag she had packed for him, Dylan shrugged. 'I dare say I won't need much. They'll be issuing us with uniforms when I get to the training camp.'

They stared awkwardly at each other. There was so much he wanted to say but the words seemed to lodge in his throat.

'Well, take care and be sure to write.' Like her husband, Grace was struggling for words.

'We were told we'd get a few days' leave when the training is over, but happen I'll just let them move me on to wherever it is they're sending me.'

When Grace didn't argue, he bowed his head in shame. Only now did he realise what a terrible fool he had been, and all because he had loved her so much that he hadn't been able to bear thinking of her giving birth to another man's child. But it was too late to do anything about it now. Worse still, he must leave knowing that she would have no wages coming in for a time until his army pay kicked in. Her broken ribs were slightly easier now and the swellings on her face had gone down, but she still was in no fit state to collect the washing that usually brought in a few extra pennies each week.

'Are you sure you'll manage, cariad?' he asked as his conscience stabbed at him.

She nodded. 'We'll be all right. We have eggs from the chickens and milk, and there's enough vegetables and fruit in the garden to see us fed for a while till I'm ready to work again.'

He nodded. 'Right then, I'd best be off.' He leaned towards her hoping for one last kiss but she turned her cheek. He didn't blame her really, he'd been a real bastard.

His eyes dropped to Aiden then as he swung his bag onto his shoulder. 'See you, boyo. Take good care of your mam, now.'

Aiden stared up at him with frightened eyes, and with a huge lump in his throat, Dylan turned and walked away, tears blinding him.

He turned just once at the end of the lane to see Grace and Aiden still standing there and he raised his hand. She waved back and then he was gone and she suddenly felt guilty. She knew that she should be feeling upset. After all, her husband was going to fight for his king and country and could very well be killed and never come back, and yet all she could feel was relief. Admittedly the first few weeks were going to be difficult until she was healed enough to earn again but at least she wouldn't have to live in fear of what state Dylan would be in when he came home each night now. Thankfully, what had remained of her inheritance had bought the cottage outright so she didn't have to worry about paying rent and as she'd said, the garden was well stocked so no doubt she and Aiden would muddle through. She had briefly considered moving back to Nuneaton. Mrs Batley and Mabel still wrote to her regularly and she knew that one or either of them would have taken her and Aiden in. Alternatively, she knew that she could go back to Beehive Cottage. But pride forbade her from doing that. She had made her bed and now she must lie in it.

'Right then, how about we go and milk Nanny and then you can have a nice cool drink?' she suggested. Aiden smiled up at her. As always, now that his father was gone he was like a different child.

'I'll go and see if the chickens have laid any eggs an' all, shall I, Mammy?' As he skipped away, she smiled and leaned heavily against the door post. It still hurt to breathe and although the swelling on her face had gone down a little, it was a kaleidoscope of colours and her split lip kept reopening every time she smiled.

'You do that, sweetheart,' she murmured. 'The basket is in the pantry. Mind you don't break any, though!'

Mrs Gower appeared at the back door later that afternoon to ask, 'Get off all right, did he?'

Grace smiled. It was funny to think that when she'd first moved there she'd been slightly afraid of the old woman and yet now she found she enjoyed her company.

'Yes, he did.'

'Good, then let's have a look at that chest o' yours. I've got summat here as you can rub on it that should ease the pain an' then I'll bind it again for you. I reckon you could have a couple o' cracked ribs there!'

Grace knew better than to argue and nodded as she painfully began to remove her worn cotton work blouse, which had been washed and repaired so many times that it was almost see through. She couldn't even remember the last time she'd had something new to wear and when she thought back to the expensive London clothes her father had always insisted she wore, it seemed like a lifetime ago.

She sat patiently as the woman applied a salve to her bruises, failing to see the look on her face. Mrs Gower was fuming to see what he'd done to her. As far as she was concerned, she was glad he'd gone. He'd probably have killed the poor lass if he'd stayed, but as usual she didn't comment.

Once she was done she bound Grace's chest tightly again, saying shortly, 'There, that should give you a little relief when it starts to work. Oh, an' by the way, I've got a chicken round home you can do for you and the lad's dinner. I had a couple that had stopped laying so I wrung their necks earlier on.'

Feeling embarrassed, Grace frowned. 'It's very kind of you but really we—'

367

Mrs Gower held her hand up. 'I won't take no for an answer. I'll never eat two on me own now, will I? You'll be doin' me a favour if you take it off me hands.'

'In that case, thank you very much,' Grace muttered. It would be the first meat they'd had for over a week and even after making a roast dinner for them there'd be enough left over to do a stew that would last them for at least another couple of days if she used some of the vegetables from the garden.

It was another three weeks before Grace was well enough to wheel the handcart into town to collect the dirty washing but she was sadly disappointed when many of her customers told her she was no longer needed. Most of their sons or husbands had gone away to war and already people were tightening their belts and cutting down on their outgoings wherever they could.

'I've got to do something to bring some money in,' she mused to her Aunt Gertie when she called in later that afternoon.

Gertie nodded. 'Well, I don't know what truth there is in it but I heard when I was at market that the nuns are preparing to turn the convent into a nursing home for injured soldiers for the duration of the war.'

Grace raised an eyebrow. 'But how would that help me? I'm not a nurse.'

'Maybe not, but they'll need cleaners, won't they? They'll also need VADs.' Seeing Grace's puzzled look she went on, 'Voluntary Aid Detachment nurses, they're not trained but they help out with changing bandages, emptying bedpans and such, leaving the trained nurses to do the more professional stuff.'

'Hmm, I suppose it's worth giving it some thought,' Grace admitted. 'Although everyone is saying they think it might be over fairly quickly.' It was hard to believe there was a war on at all, because except for all the local men who had gone away to fight nothing had changed in their part of the world.

'You do that,' Gertie urged. 'You could always drop Aiden off to us, it's on your way and one of us could easily look after him till your shifts were finished.'

❧

The following morning, the postman brought the first letter from Dylan and Grace settled down at the kitchen table to read it.

Dear Grace,

I just wanted to let you know that I have finished my training. I don't mind admitting that I've found it hard although I always considered myself to be reasonably fit! Me and some of the other chaps are being shipped out to the front next week although no one will tell us exactly where we are going. It's all very hush-hush although me and the other chaps reckon we'll be sent to —! (This part of the letter was censored.)

I hadn't realised just how comfortable you had made the cottage until I saw the barracks I have been living in here. They're actually tents and while it's pleasant enough to sleep in them in the summer I'm not so sure it will be in the winter, but who knows where I might be by then. The food leaves a lot to be desired as well, though I suppose I shouldn't grumble. I hope you are well and managing. As of now you will receive a part of my wages each month, I hope it will be a help. I have been told that if you wish to reply to me you may send the letters to this address and they will be forwarded on to me. I have no idea when I might see you again but until then I remain,

Your loving husband,

Dylan xxx

Grace snorted. Loving husband, indeed! And even now he hadn't been able to bring himself to ask after Aiden and it hurt. She hadn't missed him at all, and already there was a marked difference in Aiden. The nervous tic in his eye had disappeared and he seemed happier and more content. Even so, Dylan was her husband so she supposed she should reply to him. She felt guilty because she had never been able to love him as she should, so in fairness she couldn't lay all the blame on his shoulders. With a sigh, she set the letter aside. She would reply to it later.

❧

Over the next few weeks, Grace walked into town at least twice a week to buy a newspaper so that she could follow the progress of the war. She'd heard no more from Dylan so she could only assume that he had been posted abroad somewhere. On one particularly busy market day, for the first time in ages, she came face to face with Bronwen and their meeting wasn't pleasant.

Grace usually went to market late in the afternoon. There were bargains to be had then when the stallholders were about to pack up and she usually managed to buy some cheap cuts of meat if she timed it right. She was just paying for a piece of brisket when a voice right behind her made her jump and whirling about she came face to face with her mother-in-law.

'It's a wonder you've the nerve to show your face round here,' Bronwen ground out. 'It's because of you my son is away fighting. Have you read in the papers what the men out there are having to endure? Filthy trenches and rats squirming about their feet!'

'Bronwen, I had nothing to do with it,' Grace said reasonably. 'Dylan and some of his friends joined up when they'd had too much to drink one day and once it was done there was no going back.'

'Huh! Is *that* what he told you,' the woman sneered. 'Well, I know different. He went to get away from you and your whoring ways and that bastard he's had to keep for all this time!'

Grace blushed crimson. People were stopping to stare and she just wished the ground would open up and swallow her. Turning back to the stallholder, who was watching open-mouthed, she hastily paid him, dropping some coins in the process in her embarrassment. It seemed pointless trying to speak to Bronwen, she was clearly in no mood to be reasonable so she was keen to get away as quickly as possible. She had left Aiden with Mrs Gower, and she was relieved that he hadn't been here to hear it. The poor little soul had suffered enough at the hands of this woman's son.

After hastily stuffing her purchase into her deep wicker basket, she began to hurry away but Bronwen's raised voice followed her, 'That's it, *walk away,* you little *slut*. Got customers waitin' back at home for you, have you?'

Grace's cheeks were burning as she mustered what dignity she could and sped away and she didn't slow her steps till the town was far behind her. Only then did she stop to lean heavily against the trunk of a tree and allow the tears to spill down her cheeks. Even with Dylan away it seemed that there was to be no peace for her and she wondered where it would end.

Chapter Forty-Five

As autumn approached, the newspapers reported that the British Expeditionary Force had been forced to abandon their position in Mons and retreat with the French to the Somme, where they hoped to halt the German advance on Paris. As had been rumoured, the convent had been adapted to care for the injured and now the first casualties began to arrive.

Life still went on much the same for Grace, although the days were turning colder now and she had to spend more time in the woods each day collecting fallen branches that she could chop into firewood to keep the cottage warm. She spent her days collecting the remaining fruit from the apple and pear trees in the garden and making enough jam to hopefully last them through the winter. She also pickled whatever vegetables she could and made sure that she had a good supply of flour in, reasoning that she would always have enough to bake their own bread. Even so it was getting harder to make ends meet now that the food supply in the garden wasn't so plentiful, so one day when Aunt Gertie was paying her weekly visit she asked, 'Would you mind very much taking care of Aiden for an hour or so tomorrow for me? I'm going up to the convent to see if there are any jobs going and I could drop him in on the way.'

'It'd be no trouble at all,' Aunt Gertie assured her. Grace was very proud and had declined all her offers of help up to now so she was pleased that Grace was looking ahead. If what people were saying were true, certain things would become harder to get before very much longer now that the boats were no longer bringing in so many supplies from abroad.

And so, the next morning bright and early, Grace and Aiden set off. She dropped him off at Beehive Cottage where she knew he would be spoiled shamelessly by Cerys Llewelyn and began the long trek up the hillside. As she passed beneath the canopy of trees she was reminded of all the times she had walked that way during her time as a postulant and she felt sad. She had been so sure of what she wanted when she had first arrived in the convent. But all that had changed when she met Father Luke and now she wasn't even sure if she believed in God anymore. If there truly was a God how could he allow such awful things in the world to happen? She was breathless by the time she emerged from the trees and she stood for a moment in silent contemplation, staring at the convent. It looked much the same as it always had apart from the fact that there were a number of military vehicles parked outside the front doors, which she assumed were ambulances.

Eventually she took a deep breath, patted her hair into place and moved on. After approaching the front doors, she came upon a scene of organised chaos. Men on stretchers lay on the floor as nuns and nurses milled around sorting out what wards they should be admitted to. She stood back not wishing to disturb them and eventually when all the injured had been whisked away she cautiously approached the Reverend Mother's door and nervously tapped on it.

'Come in,' a voice she remembered so well commanded and when Grace entered a smile spread across the older woman's face.

'Why, Grace, my dear girl. How lovely it is to see you.' The nun rose, coming round her desk and taking Grace's hands in hers. 'But how may I help you?'

'Actually, I was rather hoping that I might be able to help you,' Grace said, returning her smile. 'I was wondering if you're in need of cleaners or VADs to help with the patients?'

'As it so happens we are in urgent need of both.' The smile slid from the elderly nun's face and she shook her head sadly.

'The wounded are just trickling through to us but I fear before long we will be packed to the rafters so we will need all the help we can get. Come, I will show you around.'

As they moved from room to room around the convent, Grace reflected that although it appeared the same from the outside it was vastly changed inside. The dining room now had two rows of neatly made beds down either side of it, as had most of the other rooms. In fact, the only places that seemed to have remained the same were the kitchens, the Reverend Mother's office and the chapel. As they walked round, the patients were efficiently being lifted from the stretchers into the prepared beds by nurses in starched white caps and cuffs.

'So,' the Reverend Mother said when they'd finished their tour. 'Do you still think this is something you might like to do, Grace? I should warn you, the hours will be long and tedious and you will see some horrific sights. We already have men here who have lost limbs, others are suffering with horrific burns to name but a few of the injuries. I'm afraid it isn't a job for the faint-hearted. If you join us as a voluntary nurse, part of your job would entail emptying bed pans – not the nicest of jobs – and also administering bed baths to the men.'

Grace drew herself up to her full height. 'I can do it,' she declared with conviction.

'In that case, we shall go back to my office and discuss your wages, which will be paid by the war office, and your start date.'

Half an hour later, Grace skipped out of the convent with a smile on her face. She was to start first thing the following Monday morning so now she had to make sure that Aunt Gertie didn't mind looking after Aiden for so long each day, although she didn't envisage that would be a problem. Her aunt and the Llewelyns had already offered to help in any way they could.

She found that she was looking forward to it. For a long time she had been confined to the cottage and it would be nice to feel that she was doing something useful again. Aiden's reaction to her news was everything she could have hoped for. He was delighted to discover that he would be spending more time at Aunt Gertie's with her and the Llewelyns.

So, first thing on Monday morning, Grace dropped Aiden off at her aunt's as planned and Aiden skipped into the cottage. 'Bye bye, Mammy,' he called cheerfully, not bothered at all that she was leaving him, and Grace laughed, not sure whether to feel happy or upset.

On arrival at the convent she was shown to what had formerly been the boot room, but was now used for storing linen and uniforms, by a stiff-faced sister. After glancing at Grace, the nun handed her a mid-blue coloured dress.

'Try that on for size,' she told her and Grace and did as she was told.

'Hmm, near enough, I should say,' the woman commented. She began to go through the pile again and handed Grace another identical dress. 'You'll need two of everything,' she informed her. 'Also, flat black sensible shoes but it's up to you to purchase them.' She then gave her two huge white aprons with a large red cross on the front of each of them and two sets of white cuffs along with two white collars and two starched caps, saying, 'You can get ready in there then come to Ward Three and report to me.'

It was quite difficult without a mirror but Grace was eventually ready, she just hoped she had fixed her cap on properly.

When she finally found Ward Three, formerly the day room, she was shocked to see that all the beds had filled up over the weekend. 'You'll do,' the sister told her after looking her up and down.

'But remember, I expect you to look clean and smart at all times. You will be responsible for keeping your own uniform clean. I won't tolerate shoddiness on my wards. Your dinner time will be from twelve thirty until one, when you can be spared, and your shift will finish at six o'clock. Is that all clear?'

'Yes, sister.'

The woman nodded approvingly before beckoning to a nurse, who was dressed in a dark blue dress – the uniform of the trained nurses.

'Nurse Mayoll, I shall put Nurse Penlynn with you so that you can show her the ropes and tell her what you wish her to do.'

The woman nodded and when the sister departed she smiled. 'Right, we'd best get started. But you might like to take your cuffs off and roll your sleeves up for the first job. I'm afraid there are a number of dirty bed pans waiting to be washed in the sluice. You'll find another apron in there that you can put over your clean one. Then, when you've done that, you can help with the bed baths. After that I shall need you to mop the floors while I change any dressings that need doing.'

'Yes, nurse.' Grace's head was swimming already. It sounded like she was going to be kept very busy indeed, but it didn't trouble her, she was well used to hard work. Even so, she found her stomach rebelling at the first job. The stench in the sluice room was appalling and more than once she thought she might be sick as she emptied one disgusting mess after another. Finally she was finished and after making sure that the room was clean, she went to rejoin the nurse in the ward.

'Ah,' a fresh-faced young nurse said, smiling at her. 'Sister sent you to help me with the bed baths, did she? Good, you're just in time.' The young woman was pushing a trolley which had a bowl of hot water, clean towels and toiletries on it, and approaching the first bed, she pulled the curtains around it and smiled at the man lying in the bed. His head and eyes were heavily bandaged so it was hard to gauge how old he was.

'Right, Mr Johnson,' the nurse said cheerfully. 'We've just come to freshen you up. Just relax now, this shouldn't take long.' Then without further ado she whipped his pyjama bottoms down, making Grace flush to the very roots of her hair. As she began to wash his most private parts she instructed Grace to wash his top half and Grace felt sorry for him. If she was feeling embarrassed how must this poor soul be feeling? she wondered. Perhaps it was just as well that he couldn't see what they were doing.

'Your wife is coming to see you today, isn't she, Mr Johnson?' the little nurse said.

He nodded. 'Aye, she is but I wish she wasn't. I don't want her to see me like this,' he said piteously. 'What use am I going to be to her now if my eyesight doesn't come back?'

'Now, we'll have none of that silly talk,' the nurse scolded him gently. 'I dare say your wife is just relieved that you're still alive. And didn't the doctor say that there's every chance you might regain some of your sight once the burns start to heal? You just have to be patient. You're doing very well. I'm going to change your dressings in a minute and then you'll feel a lot more comfortable.'

After they'd washed him from head to toe, Grace helped the nurse change him into clean pyjamas and once he was settled against his pillows, the nurse trotted away to return minutes later with a second trolley with dressings of various types.

'You should stay and watch me,' she told Grace as she carefully began to unwind his bandages. 'This is one of the jobs you may have to do if we get really busy.'

Grace gulped. She didn't fancy that at all. In fact, she thought she'd rather be emptying the bed pans, but she didn't say so, she merely stood and watched. Her heart went out to the man once all the soiled dressings were removed. The top half of his face was terribly burned and she could only begin to imagine how much pain he must be in. His eyes looked as if they had been welded shut and it was already apparent that even when he healed he was going to be hideously scarred. Seeing the horrified look on Grace's face the nurse smiled at her sympathetically as she gently and deftly placed clean dressings over the wounds.

'There, that's better, isn't it?' She patted the man's hand and swished the curtains aside instructing Grace to go and refill the bowl with clean water for the next patient. And then they slowly and methodically worked their way about the ward.

'All the men in here have suffered varying degrees of burns,' the nurse informed her. 'In the ward next door are the patients with missing limbs. That's pretty grim, I don't mind telling you.' She shook her head and sighed sadly. 'And it's so frightening the way they are arriving now. More and more of them every day. The nursing nuns tend to stay on Ward Five. That's where the patients who aren't expected to survive are put.'

Grace shuddered at the thought and hoped that she wouldn't be expected to work in there. Not for a time at least. What she had seen up to now had been bad enough.

At last all the patients were washed and Grace was instructed to start the cleaning. She fetched a mop and bucket and slowly cleaned the ward from top to bottom before washing all the tops of the lockers down. It was already past her lunchtime by the time she'd finished and the ward sister told her that she might go and take half an hour.

After collecting a cup of tea from the large kitchen, Grace carried it outside with the sandwiches she had brought. There was a distinct nip in the air and the wind had blown up but Grace settled on a bench, glad to feel the breeze on her face as she reflected on her first morning at work. It had been a lot harder than she'd expected, but she wasn't daunted. And surely it will get easier? she thought.

The Reverend Mother stopped her as she was just about to leave that evening. 'The ward sister tells me that you've done really well today. You're a hard worker, Grace, and I think you'll be an asset to us.'

'Thank you.' Grace smiled and hurried on her way.

By the time she arrived at her aunt's to pick up Aiden she was feeling worn out but satisfied.

'I bet you're feeling dead on your feet,' Cerys Llewelyn greeted her. 'Sit yourself down. I've saved you some hotpot so you don't have to cook when you get home. Aiden's already had his. He's outside with Aled and your aunt putting the chickens in the coops for the night.'

'Oh, but you shouldn't do that,' Grace said in dismay. 'It's more than enough that you're willing to have Aiden for me without having to cook for us as well.'

'Rubbish, it's no harder to make a little extra when I'm cooking for us anyway,' Cerys assured her.

Grace was secretly relieved. Her feet felt as if they were on fire after rushing about all day.

Shortly after, she and Aiden set off for home. He was clearly happy with the new arrangement and skipped almost all the way back.

When she reached the cottage she found a nice fire burning merrily in the grate. Mrs Gower must have come round especially to light it for her. Grace smiled. Some people were kind, there was no doubt about it, and for the first time in some long while she felt slightly more optimistic about her and Aiden's future.

Chapter Forty-Six

'Not *more* patients?' The ward sister groaned as she looked wearily around at the rows of full beds on either side of the room.

'Don't worry, I'm sure we can fit another couple of beds in,' Grace told her.

'Perhaps you could ask the porter to fetch another two from the store room and get them made up for me, Nurse Penlynn? Meanwhile I'll go and see if there's any room in any of the other wards. I have a horrible feeling we're going to need it, although thankfully some of the patients will be going home this week. That will free another few up.'

'Of course, sister.' Grace had been working at the convent hospital for over two years now and there was little that could shock her anymore. She was highly regarded by all the staff, for she managed to remain calm in the direst of circumstances. During that time, she had held the hands of young men until they died. She had mopped the tears of men who'd had limbs blown off and written letters to the loved ones of those who'd been blinded. She'd become used to the cheeky ones who flirted with her and could now give as good as she got without flushing crimson, and she was loved by patients and staff alike.

Aiden was now five years old, leggy as a colt, and a constant source of joy to her. Over the last couple of years, she'd received the odd letter from Dylan, but she never showed them to her son. He was clearly happier with Dylan out of his life and she sometimes wondered how he would react when the war was over and Dylan came home. But then, she told herself, she would face that bridge when they came to it; there was nothing to be gained in worrying about it for now.

Within half an hour the two extra beds had been squeezed into the ward and Grace had them neatly made up. Minutes later they were full. The two new patients were young men who had been the victims of the deadly mustard gas and Grace sighed when she saw them. The effects of the gas on its victims was horrendous. It not only caused horrific burns to the skin but it also affected their lungs, making breathing difficult, and it also made them nauseous. Sometimes, it even left them blind. She very soon saw that these two men had been badly affected and hurried away to find the doctor.

'Oh, Nurse Penlynn, were you looking for Dr Shaw?' the ward sister asked. 'I meant to tell you, he's been transferred to another military hospital further along the coast but his replacement arrived this morning. He's in with the Reverend Mother but I just left word for him to come and examine the two new patients in Ward Four as soon as he's able to. May I leave you to ensure that he has everything he needs?'

'Yes, sister.' Grace turned back to the ward. The last months had been hellish, ever since the endless battle at the Somme, which was being described in the newspapers as a bloodbath. The soldiers there were forced to live in horrendous conditions and reported having to tramp through mud that was so deep it actually drowned the injured who were unfortunate enough to fall into it. Thousands upon thousands of young men were being slaughtered each day and Grace despaired at the thought of it. But all she could do was her best for the ones that filtered through to the hospital and, like everyone else, pray that there would be an end to it.

Now she hurried back to the two new patients. One of them,

a young boy who looked to be no more than seventeen or eighteen, was crying piteously.

'Is me mam comin', nurse?' he asked croakily. The gas had affected the muscles in his throat and he was having difficulty in breathing. Grace had seen others like him and doubted very much whether he would survive.

'She will have been informed where you are so I'm sure she'll be here very soon,' she soothed, lifting a glass of water and holding it to his swollen lips. Yellow blisters had erupted all over his body and she felt heartsore for him, poor little soul.

'Ah, good morning. I'm Dr Hughes. So, who have we here?'

Grace heard the doctor lift the clipboard from the end of the bed and gently laid the patient back against the pillows. And then she turned and just for a moment the floor seemed to rush up to meet her.

'Luke!'

As his eyes flew to hers she watched the colour drain from his face like water from a dam.

'Grace!'

They stood as if they had been turned to stone for what seemed like an eternity but then Grace noticed that the young patient had picked up on the tense atmosphere and was plucking at the bedclothes and she croaked, 'I . . . I'll leave you with the patient, doctor.'

She hurried away and when she came to the sluice room she ducked inside to try to compose herself. Her heart was hammering so loudly she was sure he must have heard it and she felt sick. Seeing him again had brought back all her old feelings and she knew without a shadow of a doubt that she still loved him, despite the way he had treated her. But she was married to Dylan now, till death did them part, and it was useless!

The last time she had seen him he had been clad in his vestments and now here he was a doctor, which had been yet another shock.

Somewhere along the line he must have left the church. But why? she wondered.

It was some minutes before she had pulled herself together enough to venture out into the ward again and she was relieved to see that Luke had gone. With a sigh, she returned to work but she found it hard to concentrate.

It was late afternoon when she saw Luke again as she was taking some medical records down to the Reverend Mother. They came face to face on the stairs. There was no way she could avoid him without looking like some lovesick schoolgirl so she raised a weak smile and made to pass him.

'Grace . . . Please, we need to talk.'

He had placed his hand gently on her arm and she stopped reluctantly. 'I don't think we really have anything to talk about.' Her voice was composed, giving no sign of her inner turmoil.

She saw the hurt on his face. 'But we do.' As he ran his hand through his wonderful thick hair, her heart gave a little lurch. 'Perhaps you could spare me just a few minutes at lunchtime?'

She shrugged. 'I might have to work through it but I'll see what I can do.' And then she shrugged his hand from her arm and clattered away down the rest of the stairs while he stood staring sadly after her.

She managed to avoid him for the next two days but on the third day, as she was snatching a hasty sandwich in the staff rest room, he quietly slipped inside.

'At last,' he breathed as he closed the door behind him and she instantly stiffened as he came to sit beside her.

'I think I have some explaining to do and also some apologies to make.'

She dropped the half-eaten sandwich into her lap, thinking what a state she must look. She'd just been working in the sluice room and was sure that she must smell.

'The thing is . . .' he began. 'Firstly, I should apologise for what I

383

did to you, it was unforgivable. And also for the cowardly way I ran away.'

'It was a long time ago and we were both to blame for what happened, you didn't force me to do anything.' But then her curiosity got the better of her and she blurted out, 'But how come you are a doctor now?'

He grinned. 'Actually, I'd already done half my medical exams before I decided to join the Church. But then after you and I . . . Well, as you probably know I requested a move to another parish but the damage was done and I had to question if I was really cut out to be clergy. After a lot of soul searching, I was forced to admit that I wasn't, so I left the Church and went back to my medical training. I suppose the rest is fairly self-explanatory and here I am. But I want you to know that I *did* come back to try and see you about a year after I left. The Reverend Mother told me you'd gone so I went into the village to find you. While I was there making enquiries, a woman in the marketplace told me you were married and had just had a baby so I thought it best I kept away from you. I'm glad you met someone who could make you happy, Grace.'

Grace bit her lip to try and stem her tears. *Happy!* If only he knew the truth. And yet she felt elated to think that he'd taken the trouble to try and find her. Perhaps he had cared for her after all? But even if he had, that was all in the past now.

'I hope you're happy too in your new vocation,' she said quietly. 'But now I really should get on. You know what Sister Marsh is like. She'll have my guts for garters if I'm late.'

Rising quickly, she made for the door but his voice stopped her once again when he asked, 'Did you have any more children, Grace?'

She nodded. 'Yes, I had a daughter . . . but she died. Just the one now, a son . . . We called him Aiden.' And then she slipped quietly away.

In December, there was yet another influx of patients and as the ambulances arrived the nurses and the VADs stood on the steps waiting to tell the stretcher-bearers which wards to take them to.

Half a dozen had already gone in when yet another stretcher stopped in front of Grace.

'Another one with burns,' the stretcher-bearer told her and as Grace opened her mouth to tell him where to go she gasped with shock. It was Dylan lying on the stretcher and he looked in a bad way.

Seeing her distress one of the nuns hurried to her side to ask, 'Is everything all right, Nurse Penlynn?'

'Th-this man is my husband,' Grace stuttered.

'Oh dear.' Taking control of the situation, the nun quickly told the man where the patient was to go, then gripping Grace's elbow she told her firmly, 'And you can come to the kitchen with me. You've had a nasty shock. A good strong cup of sweet tea is what you need.'

Grace's legs seemed to have developed a life of their own as she followed the elderly nun but once in the kitchen she began to pace.

'I ought to go and find out how bad my husband is!'

'Not until you've drunk this and given the doctor time to look at him,' the nun insisted.

So Grace sat down and drank the tea as quickly as she could.

Ten minutes later she entered the burns ward and the sister there raised her eyebrows enquiringly. 'Hello, I didn't think you were on my ward today,' she said, glancing at the staff rota on her desk.

'I'm not.' Grace's eyes were fixed on the curtains drawn around one of the beds. 'But the man who was just admitted here is my husband.'

'Oh!' The sister looked alarmed. 'The doctor is in with him now . . . but I feel I should warn you, he has severe burns and it doesn't look good.'

'I . . . I see. I'll wait to speak to the doctor, if I may.'

'Of course you may.' The sister patted her arm sympathetically and sighed. When was this terrible war going to end?

Aunt Gertie and the Llewelyns were shocked when Grace told them the news that evening.

'We ought to let our Bronwen know,' Cerys said quietly. 'Especially if he's as bad as you say he is.'

Grace nodded numbly. 'I'll go and see them.'

'No, cariad, there's no need for you to do that. I'll go,' Cerys volunteered. She knew how vicious Bronwen could be with Grace. 'I'll get Aled to walk me there this very evening. They're bound to want to see him as soon as they can just in case . . .' Her words died away but they all knew what she meant. *Just in case he died*, which was a very real possibility at the moment. The doctor had gently explained that, as well as the burns to his skin, his lungs were badly affected by the mustard gas.

'Thank you,' Grace said quietly, then calling Aiden to her she set out for home.

As they walked she tried to explain to him as gently as she could what had happened and he stared up at her with frightened eyes. 'Does that mean that me dad will be coming home?'

'He might be . . . if he gets better.' Grace found that she couldn't lie to him and was dismayed to see him start to blink nervously. He hadn't done that for so long now that it broke her heart to see him doing it again.

Over the next few days, Griffen and Bronwen were almost constantly at Dylan's bedside and Grace kept out of their way, only visiting him when they were gone. And then one day, when she had popped into the ward to check on him before going home, he suddenly opened his eyes and looked at her.

A doctor came running and hustled her out and minutes later he joined her to tell her, 'He's fully conscious now.'

'Does that mean he'll recover?'

He pursed his lips and sighed. 'I really couldn't say. It's all in God's hands. We can help the wounds on the outside to heal but who knows what's happening on the inside? What I will say is, if you are willing to have him back at home when he's slightly better, and nurse him yourself, he probably stands a better chance. There's no place like home when you're ill.'

Grace's heart sank. If she did what he suggested it would mean giving up her job. But then Dylan *was* her husband.

'Very well,' she told him. 'I'll do that.'

Chapter Forty-Seven

'I'll be sorry to lose you, Grace,' the Reverend Mother told her when she handed in her notice later that week.

'I shall be sorry to go,' Grace admitted. 'But with things as they are . . .'

'I quite understand.' The nun smiled at her kindly. 'Dylan is your husband and it's right that you should put him first. May God be with you, my child, and your husband.'

Grace left the office with a heavy heart. She would have to tell Aiden that Dylan would be coming home soon – she hadn't dared to as yet but it was only fair that he should be given warning.

Pausing in the corridor, she rubbed her hand across her eyes, seeing again the look in Dylan's eyes when she had first gone to see him in the ward. He had stared at her as if he hated the sight of her and that look had struck terror into her heart. Of course, she sympathised with the position he was in. His hands and face were horrifically burned and the doctors had warned that his insides could be just as bad, but it was as if Dylan thought it was all her fault. With a sigh, she pulled herself together and made her way to the doctor's office to make the arrangements for Dylan to return home. The doctor had promised that one of the medical staff would visit regularly to check on his progress and Grace prayed that it wouldn't be Luke. They had avoided each other as much as possible since he had been at the hospital but it was inevitable that their paths would cross from time to time, and each time they did it only brought home to Grace just how much she still loved him. She was terrified that if Dylan saw Luke and Aiden together he would guess that he was the boy's father. But she would have to cross that bridge when she came to it. For now, she must concentrate on getting her husband home.

Soon after, she returned to the ward with all the arrangements in place. She would work her week's notice, then the following day an ambulance would deliver Dylan back home. She realised that his mother would probably be a frequent visitor and that was yet another thing to dread. But Grace couldn't see how she could deny her access to her son, so somehow she would have to try to make the best of it. They all would.

She was just about to leave that evening when Luke hurried towards her in the foyer and she felt the familiar flutter in her stomach at the sight of him.

'Ah, Gra— Mrs Penlynn,' he corrected himself. 'I'm told that your husband will be coming home to you shortly.'

'Yes, doctor,' she answered woodenly.

He nodded, avoiding her eyes. 'Right, I'm sure you will be more than capable of dressing his wounds. You've certainly had plenty of practice, but I just wanted to let you know that one of us will visit you at least twice a week to check on his progress and it goes without saying that if you have any concerns whatsoever you only have to let us know and someone will be there as soon as possible.'

'Thank you.' She managed a weak smile before hurrying on her way but she could feel his eyes burning into her back.

Later that evening when she and Aiden had had their evening meal she told him, 'I have something to tell you, sweetheart.'

He looked up at her with his amazing blue eyes. 'Really? Is it something nice? Something to do with Christmas?'

'N-not exactly.' She licked her dry lips. 'The thing is, your daddy will be coming home soon.'

She watched his face fall but forced herself to go on cheerfully, 'I'm afraid Daddy got hurt, his poor face and hands have been badly burned so we'll have to look after him between us until he gets better, won't we?'

'Can't they do that in the hospital?'

Grace swallowed. 'He is in the hospital at the moment but you know they really need as many beds as they can get because of all the poor men who are being injured in the war, so they are sending as many home as possible, and Daddy is one of them.'

He nodded, his face solemn, then went back to the jigsaw he had been playing with although Grace could see he wasn't happy with the news at all. She supposed she couldn't blame him. He'd been so happy while Dylan was away and now she could only pray that Dylan would try harder with the lad.

Just over a week later, Grace stood at the door of the cottage to welcome Dylan home when the ambulance pulled up outside. She had cleaned the cottage from top to bottom and there was a cheery fire roaring in the grate. She'd also managed to manoeuvre Aiden's bed downstairs so that Dylan wouldn't have to try and climb the stairs. Aiden could sleep with her for the time being.

The two ambulance men carefully carried the stretcher inside and helped Dylan into the bed she had made up with fresh sheets before asking, 'Anything else we can do for you, missus?'

'No thank you, we shall be fine now.' She smiled and saw them to the door before turning back to Dylan and saying cheerfully,

'Welcome home. I've got a nice pot of tea all ready for you and I've done us a stew for dinner, just the way you like it. We'll have it when Aiden gets home from school, shall we?'

She was tucking the blankets around him as she spoke and all the time his eyes were boring into her.

'H-have you . . . missed me?' His voice came out as a croak. His throat was burned too and she could only imagine how painful it must be for him to talk.

'Of course we have,' she assured him lightly, avoiding his eyes. 'But now let me go and get you that drink.'

She was just pouring the tea into the cups when Mrs Gower marched in and went to stand at the side of the bed.

'I see you're back then,' she said rather unnecessarily. 'And how are you feeling?'

'How . . . would you expect me . . . to feel?' He raised his bandaged hand in the direction of his face.

She shrugged. 'Lucky! At least you came back,' she stated in her usual forthright way. 'That's more than can be said for most o' the men an' boys from the village, God bless 'em. There's telegrams arrivin' for their families thick an' fast.'

Dylan glared and turned his head away as she pottered over to Grace who had added another cup to the table. She filled them all and handed one to Mrs Gower before carrying one over to Dylan. He took it awkwardly and sipped at it, keeping his eyes on the two women. They seemed to have become close during the time he'd been away and he was none too pleased about it.

'Now, you know if I can help in any way you only have to ask,' Mrs Gower told Grace and the younger woman smiled at her gratefully.

'Thank you but I'm sure I'll manage.'

'*Hey!* I am in the room you . . . know?' Dylan snapped and started a bout of coughing which resulted in his tea sloshing all over the clean sheets.

Mrs Gower rolled her eyes. From the little she'd already seen of him, poor Grace was going to have her work cut out, but then he'd turned into a right nasty piece of work before he left so there was no change there.

Aiden cautiously inched into the room that afternoon after school and as Dylan's eyes settled on him he frowned. The lad had grown, and filled out an' all from what he could see of it.

'Come and say welcome home to your dad,' Grace encouraged, but before he got the chance Dylan butted in.

'I *ain't* his dad! . . . An' it's about time he knew . . . it!'

'Dylan, *stop* it!' Grace was horrified as Aiden stared at the man in the bed. She had always known that Aiden would find out one day but surely it needn't have been done so callously?

'Why don't you pop next door and see if Mrs Gower needs you to collect her eggs for her,' Grace suggested, trying to keep her voice light.

Aiden hovered uncertainly before shooting off like a bullet from a gun and when he was gone, Grace turned back to Dylan, her hands on her hips and her eyes blazing. 'Did you *have* to tell him quite so heartlessly?' she spat.

He sneered. 'He . . . had to know he's a bastard . . . sometime!'

Grace clenched her hands into fists as she fought to control her temper. She could take whatever Dylan cared to throw at her but she'd be damned if she'd let him hurt Aiden. He was the innocent in all this and didn't deserve it.

'I'll do all I can for you,' she told him quietly. 'I'll nurse you, wash you, feed you or do whatever you need doing, but if you *ever* speak to my son like that again I shall pack our bags and we'll be gone. *Do* you understand?'

Dylan looked slightly taken aback at her reaction. It seemed she'd gained some confidence in the time he'd been away but he'd soon knock that out of her. Although his hands were heavily bandaged, his fingers were free, so reaching out he spitefully

392

pinched the skin on her arm making her cry out as a bruise instantly began to appear.

'I'm master . . . in me own home,' he breathed and with a sigh of disgust Grace turned about to go and fetch fresh sheets as she rubbed at her arm. He'd only been back for a matter of hours but already she could see how it was going to be and she dreaded the future.

'What did he mean? What he said earlier about him not being me dad?' Aiden asked that night in bed as he cuddled into his mother's side.

Grace swallowed the tears that were threatening before she said gently, 'Before I married your . . . Dylan, I loved somebody else but we couldn't be together so I married Dylan instead.' She knew that she had no alternative but to be honest with the child. If she didn't tell him no doubt Bronwen or somebody else would and it was far better that he heard it from her.

He lay silent for a moment, digesting what she had told him then he surprised her when he said quietly, 'I'm *glad* he ain't me dad. I don't like him.'

'Shush now and try to sleep,' Grace soothed and shortly after his gentle snores echoed around the room.

But there was no sleep for her as she realised what a terrible mistake she had made. Already she had noticed the nervous tic returning to Aiden's eyes and her heart bled for him. If only she hadn't agreed to have Dylan home. But it was done now.

She had no sooner got Aiden off to school the next morning than the kitchen door opened letting in a blast of icy air and Bronwen stormed in glaring at Grace with contempt.

'I've come to change me son's dressings,' she stated. 'I don't trust you to do it without hurting him!'

'It's already done and I've changed his sheets,' Grace informed her coldly, pointing to the pile of soiled bandages she had placed to soak in a bucket, but the woman merely swept past her to lay a gentle hand on her son's arm.

'How are you feeling, boyo?' she asked softly as if Grace wasn't even in the room. 'I was saying to your tad, you should have come home to us and let me nurse you.'

'I'm quite capable,' Grace snapped. 'I've certainly had enough practice while I was working up at the hospital.'

But Bronwen was crooning to Dylan and completely ignored her.

A few nights later, following a visit from one of the doctors, Aiden asked her, 'Are we going to have a Christmas tree this year, Mam?'

Grace blinked and paused in the act of rolling the pastry for the pie she was making for their evening meal. Dylan was asleep. She'd noticed that while he was awake Aiden rarely spoke.

'I'm so sorry, darling. I hadn't given it a thought,' she admitted. She'd been so busy looking after Dylan that she hadn't realised Christmas was almost upon them. Now, though, she was reluctant to spend what wages she had managed to save on such an extravagance. Every penny would have to count from now on. 'I'll tell you what,' she said brightly, 'why don't we go into the woods and cut some holly tomorrow after school instead? We can dot it about and it will look just as festive as a tree.'

Aiden looked disappointed but nodded in agreement. And she decided that no matter how tight money was, she would buy him a small present to open on Christmas morning. Bronwen was an all too regular visitor now so she could pop into the market one day while she was there and leave her to look after Dylan. She found that she was looking forward to getting out of the house for a while.

When the doctor made his next visit and examined Dylan he looked grave.

'I think he's got fluid on his lungs,' he told Grace. 'And his throat is still badly blistered. It doesn't appear to have improved at all. Is he managing to eat anything?'

'Not a lot,' Grace admitted. 'Although I do try to tempt him.' She glanced towards Dylan as she spoke. He was almost skeletal now.

'Then I'll leave you this medicine. It might help his appetite.' He dived into his bag and handed her a small bottle.

Grace thanked him and once he'd gone she fetched a spoon and poured some of the medicine onto it. Dylan took it meekly enough but then suddenly lashed out catching her a glancing blow on her eye.

'What was *that* for?' Grace screeched as she reeled away from the bed. Dylan seemed to be getting more violent towards her with every day that passed. She supposed it was frustration and tried to make allowances for him but it was getting more and more difficult.

'I . . . felt like it,' he gasped.

With tears in her eyes Grace fled outside and stood shivering. She had thought it was hard working at the hospital but that had been nothing compared to her life now. Dylan didn't even tell her when he wanted to use the bedpan anymore and she seemed to spend half her time washing him and the soiled sheets. It was so cold that if she hung them out they simply froze and flapped stiffly on the line so she had no alternative but to string lines up and down the length of the kitchen to dry them there, which she knew he hated. Some Christmas this is going to be, she thought glumly as she gingerly raised her hand to her swollen eye. It was beginning to close already and she knew she would have a right shiner on her by the next morning. But I'm as trapped as a fly in a spider's web, she thought sadly. The only blessing was that Aiden hadn't been there to see what had just happened.

Chapter Forty-Eight

'So what did you do this time? Trip again, did you?' Aunt Gertie asked wryly when she visited the next day.

Grace flushed and said nothing. She knew her aunt could read her like a book so there was no point in lying.

Aunt Gertie sighed but said no more. She felt sorry for the predicament Dylan was in but the way she saw it he shouldn't take his frustration out on Grace. All she was doing was trying to help him. She was just thankful that Grace had old lady Gower close by. She'd proved to be a real godsend to her niece and Gertie happened to know that Aiden spent more time with her now than he did in his own home. She couldn't blame the poor little mite. Dylan didn't have a kind word for him and although she knew it was wrong, Gertie sometimes wished Dylan hadn't survived the war. He was making her niece's life hell and there was not a thing Gertie could do about it. She had never interfered in her niece's marriage and she didn't intend to start now.

'I don't suppose there's any point in inviting you and Aiden for Christmas dinner, is there?'

Grace shook her head regretfully. 'I'd love to come, and I'm sure Aiden would too, but it wouldn't be right to leave Dylan alone.'

'Couldn't Bronwen come and spend the day with him?'

Grace raised an eyebrow. 'I'm sure she could but can you imagine what she'd say? She hasn't got a good word for me as it is and if I were to clear off and leave him on Christmas day, well . . . Although, I suppose Aiden could come. I'm sure he'd be far happier there with you than here. I'll bring him over on Christmas morning, shall I?'

Gertie shook her head. 'No need for that. I'll get Aled to fetch him first thing. He reckons we're going to have snow so he's making Aiden a sledge. He can tow him home on it if it has snowed by then, he'll love it.'

Grace perked up a little. At least Aiden might have a good day even if she couldn't. Just before Gertie left to go into the market, Bronwen arrived and the two women eyed each other with dislike.

'Is there anything you need fetching?' Gertie asked as she pulled her gloves on and wrapped her thick woollen scarf about her neck. As usual she was dressed in men's trousers and the colours she wore clashed violently but Gertie didn't care. She had stopped worrying about what people thought of her years ago and as long as she was comfortable she was happy.

'No thanks, I think we have all we need,' Grace assured her and once her aunt was gone she hurried to the sink to put the kettle on.

'Bumped into a door again, did you?' Bronwen leered as she glanced at Grace's eye, but Grace chose to ignore her. She'd found it was easier that way.

Aiden woke early on Christmas morning and he and Grace crept downstairs. For the child's sake, she had filled vases with holly to try to make the room look festive and with the fire glowing in the grate the cottage looked warm and cosy. Money was tight but she had still managed to buy a few little presents for Aiden, which were now hanging in a stocking above the fireplace. He leaped on them gleefully and Grace watched with a smile as he drew them out one by one. There was a little tin soldier that she had bought from a stall in the marketplace. A new pair of woollen mittens that she had painstakingly knitted herself and a warm woollen scarf to match. There was a bag of marbles and a tiddly-winks game and finally two barley sugar sticks that made his mouth water.

'But I'll save these till after dinner,' he promised and as he flung his arms about her neck Grace thanked God for him. Meanwhile, Dylan watched from his bed but thankfully he said nothing to spoil it for the child.

Once Aled had come to collect him, Christmas Day passed much like any other day for Grace, although she was thrilled that Aiden at least had a wonderful time at her aunt's.

Before she could blink, they were into a new year and Aiden was back at school although she wasn't sure how long it would be for. It had been snowing heavily and she feared that if they had much more of it the lane leading to the cottages would be impassable.

Then one day she answered a knock at the door to find Luke standing on the doorstep looking so handsome that her heart did a cartwheel in her chest. It was what she had feared the most since she had left the hospital. Just for a second their eyes locked and it was all Grace could do to force herself to look away from him.

'Dr Evans is off sick,' he told her, kicking the snow from his boots and looking away. 'So I've come in his place to see your husband. How is he?'

'No better, no worse, I don't think,' Grace muttered raising her hand to hide her split lip, but she wasn't in time, Luke had already spotted it and he frowned, although he didn't say anything. He was concerned to see that she had lost weight and there were dark circles under her eyes.

'Hello, Mr Penlynn, I'm Dr Hughes. How are you feeling?' he said as he approached the bed.

As Dylan stared up at him his eyes seemed to stretch and in that moment Grace knew that he had seen the likeness between Luke and Aiden and her heart sank.

'I-it was *you*,' Dylan croaked as he tried to raise himself from the pillow. '*You're* the bastard's father!'

Luke looked completely bewildered as he tried to calm his patient. 'I'm sure I have no idea what you're talking about but lie back now, there's a good chap, and let me have a look at you.'

Dylan's arms flailed out in front of him and Luke stepped back from the bed, alarmed. 'Does he often get this agitated?' he asked with a frown.

'Er, sometimes,' Grace answered in a wobbly voice.

'Get out . . . Do you hear me . . . *get out!*'

The door banged open then and Mrs Gower appeared. 'So, what's all the commotion about?' she asked. 'They must be able to hear you for miles.' And then she stopped dead in her tracks as she stared at Luke. It was like looking at a grown-up version of Aiden and in that moment, she too guessed the truth. Recovering herself, she approached the bed and told him sharply, 'Calm yourself down now, man. You're getting yourself into a rare old state.'

'I think it might be best if I left.' Luke snapped his bag shut and backed towards the door with Grace close on his heels.

'I'm so sorry,' she told him. She bowed her head in shame and he felt like snatching her into his arms and running as far away with her as he could get. He couldn't, of course, so he merely nodded and strode away through the snow with his lips set in a narrow line. What the hell had the man been ranting about, *the bastard's father*? He could only assume that he was delirious. He felt sorry for Grace, though. Dylan's wounds had embittered him and it was more than clear that he was giving his wife a hard

400

time. However, he knew all too well that he couldn't interfere between a husband and wife, and Grace must love him to put up with it. Pushing the sudden surge of jealousy aside, he went on his way.

Back in the cottage, old lady Gower was trying unsuccessfully to calm Dylan. 'You're going to make yourself really ill,' she warned and then gave a wry smile as she realised what she had said. The chap already was very ill. Yet strangely it wasn't him that she felt empathy for at that moment, but Grace. The poor young woman looked to be just about at the end of her tether. The weight had dropped off her and with her bruised eye and split lip she was a pitiful sight. She always made excuses for her injuries but the old lady was aware of exactly what was going on. How could she not be when only a wall divided her kitchen from theirs? Every day she would listen to him ranting and raving at her, or listen to the sound of pots smashing when he churlishly flung them across the room. It was a wonder the poor girl had any pots left at all!

She looked down at Dylan and said, 'If you'll not take the medicine the doctors are prescribing for you, happen you'll never get better. It'd serve you right if we all turned us back on you. So are you goin' to take it or not? Makes no difference to me either way but I'll tell you now, the next time I hear you've knocked it out of Grace's hands again, that'll be it. I'll wash me hands of you!'

She raised an eyebrow and after a minute he nodded. 'I dare say I will then!' he said grudgingly.

'Just try it, Dylan,' Grace cajoled as she held the mug with the medicine in it out to him. 'It can't do any harm and it just might do you good.'

He sniffed and nodded so she lifted his head from the pillow and held it to his lips. Once or twice he retched as he sipped at it and some of it trickled down his chin but at last he managed to swallow it before knocking the mug away.

'You can get away from me now, *whore*,' he cursed.

Mrs Gower shook her head. Her biggest fear wasn't for him, it was for Grace because she was sure that one of these days he was going to do her a real injury. Even in his weakened state he could land a cruel blow. 'Ungrateful bugger,' she grumbled as she made for the door and Grace silently agreed with her. 'I'll be round to make sure he takes more of the same at this time tomorrow. Happen he'll behave better towards you if I'm here. Meantime send Aiden round to have his tea with me an' if you need me just hammer on the wall.'

Grace nodded. Sometimes she didn't know how she would cope without Mrs Gower but it hurt to know that her son was happier round at her cottage than he was in his own home. Sometimes he didn't venture home until it was almost time to go to bed because he was so afraid of Dylan and his cruel tongue. She supposed it was for the best but she missed him and wondered if life would ever get back to any sort of normality.

They were into March when one of the doctors from the hospital pulled her to one side one day after examining Dylan to ask her, 'How long has he been being sick for?'

Grace shrugged. The smell of vomit hung on the air despite all her scrubbing and cleaning. 'Ever since he came home but I do think he's getting worse instead of better.'

The doctor nodded in agreement. 'I'm afraid he is. His lungs still have fluid on them as well as being badly blistered and I ought to warn you that I think his chances of recovering now are very slim indeed.'

'I see.' Grace felt numb as she stared towards the bed where Dylan had fallen into a doze, his laboured breathing echoing around the room. 'Is there anything more I can do for him?' she asked woodenly.

The doctor shook his head. 'I think you're already doing all you can,' he told her sympathetically. 'And I'm just trying to prepare you, not upset you, my dear. You've done an excellent job of nursing him.'

She managed a weak smile as the doctor snapped his bag shut and left, then she sat down wearily on the nearest chair to have a few minutes rest while she could. She was still sitting there when Mrs Gower arrived with her tin mug and instantly the old lady's eyes were drawn to the large bruise on Grace's arm. Grace hastily pulled her sleeve down to cover it before saying with forced cheerfulness, 'Ah, here you are. I'll put the kettle on and make us a nice cup of tea while Dylan is asleep. Aiden is going straight to Aunt Gertie's for tea after school today so you can have an evening off.'

'I don't mind having the boyo,' Mrs Gower said as she placed the tin mug on the table. 'And what did the doctor have to say about him?'

Grace shook her head, stemming the tears that suddenly threatened. 'He said it isn't looking good,' she whispered.

'Hmm.' Mrs Gower stared towards Dylan. 'Then you'd best prepare yourself. It could be any time now.'

Dylan stirred at that moment and snatching up the mug, Mrs Gower approached the bed. 'Come on then, lad. Get this down you.'

She held the mug to his lips and slowly and painfully Dylan swallowed it a dribble at a time. He seemed to be getting weaker by the day and Grace secretly wondered if there was any need for Mrs Gower to go to all this trouble every day anymore.

'Right, we'll have that tea now,' Mrs Gower said when she'd wiped his chin with the edge of her apron and dropped the tin mug into her pocket.

❦

That evening Dylan developed a fever and began to toss and turn on the bed.

'You go on up, pet, and get tucked in,' Grace encouraged Aiden, who as always was keeping a safe distance. Bronwen had only left a short time before. She'd taken to coming for a couple of hours each day in the late afternoon now and Grace almost wished she had stayed so that she could nurse her son through the night. She was so tired that her eyes felt as if they were full of grit but even so she filled the tin bowl with cool water and by the light of the oil lamp she sat patiently sponging Dylan's face to try and get the fever down.

By the time Bronwen arrived the next day Grace was actually relieved to see her. Dylan was still being violently ill and so Mrs Gower had agreed to let Aiden stay with her for a few days.

Taking one look at Grace, Bronwen told her sharply, 'Go up to bed for a few hours. You look dead on your feet. I'll see to Dylan.'

Grace knew that Bronwen was only offering to get her out of the way so she could have Dylan to herself but she was so tired that she did as she was told. Once upstairs she was too tired to even bother undressing. She had spent almost twenty-four hours sponging and changing Dylan and washing soiled sheets so the second her head hit the pillow she was fast asleep.

Grace was brought back from a lovely dream where she and Myfanwy had been paddling in the sea by Bronwen shaking her arm.

'You'd best come down.' Bronwen was crying and Grace felt

404

a cold hand close about her heart as she struggled from the bed.

'Is he worse?'

Bronwen merely nodded and Grace shot past her and charged down the stairs. Dylan was propped against the pillows, his eyes feverishly bright and sweat standing out on his forehead, but when he saw her he managed a weak smile and held his hand out to her.

'G-Grace . . .'

'Don't try to speak,' she urged as she stroked his burning skin. He felt as if he was on fire.

'But th-there's things I have to say . . .'

For the first time in weeks she saw a glimpse of the old Dylan, the one she had once cared for, and it affected her deeply.

'I-I need to say . . . I'm sorry. For the way I've treated you. I-I thought I'd be able to handle seeing . . . you with another man's child . . . but I couldn't and I've treated you very badly.' As a tear slid down his cheek, Grace bowed her head.

'Please s-say you'll forgive me.'

She was too full of emotion to speak so she merely nodded and gently squeezed his hand.

He smiled again as he looked beyond her to the dark shadows in the corner of the room. 'I-I have to go now. Myfanwy is waiting for me . . . But remember, Grace . . . I did love you . . . too much. Did you ever love me . . . j-just a *little*? I can die happy if I can just hear you say it . . . just the once.'

Grace sniffed back her tears and told him softly, 'Yes, Dylan. I did love you.' Then leaning forward, she gently kissed his burning lips.

He stared at her for a moment longer, as if he were trying to memorise every inch of her face then his grip on her hand relaxed and with a sigh and a final gentle smile he closed his eyes.

After becoming accustomed to the sound of his laboured

breathing, the silence was suddenly deafening but then she heard a sob behind her and found Bronwen close to her shoulder.

'Me lovely boyo has gone,' she wailed.

Grace nodded as she gently raised her hands to close his eyes. 'Yes, he has,' she whispered brokenly. 'And may he rest in peace.'

Chapter Forty-Nine

'I'll lay him out,' Mrs Gower offered a short time later. She had heard Bronwen sobbing through the wall that divided the cottages and hurried round, guessing what had happened.

'Y-you don't have to do that,' Grace said in a wobbly voice, but the old lady shook her head. Bronwen was clearly in no state to do it and Grace didn't look much better. 'I bring 'em into the world and I sees 'em out,' she stated. 'Just give me a couple of pennies for his eyes then you walk into town and ask the doctor to call and the undertaker to come and collect him.' She looked towards Bronwen then and snapped rather harshly, 'And you'd best calm down. You must have seen this coming. At least he's out of pain now.'

Bronwen continued to sob as the old lady went to put the kettle on for some hot water to wash Dylan with. He'd been sick so many times over the last few days that the smell of vomit clung to him, despite Grace's best efforts to keep him clean, so no doubt he'd need a clean shirt too.

When the kettle had boiled she made them all a strong cup of tea and put plenty of sugar in Bronwen's.

She then watched as the woman drank it before telling her, 'You may as well walk into town with Grace and get yourself home. I dare say your husband will want to know what's happened and there's nowt else you can do here.'

Seeing the sense in what she said, the woman nodded. She was too distressed to argue for a change and shortly after, she and Grace set off into the brand-new morning. It seemed strange that it looked set to be a fine day after what had happened but it just went to show that life went on.

As soon as they'd gone, Mrs Gower slipped round to her own cottage to check that Aiden was still asleep before returning to do as she'd promised. Once Dylan was washed from head to toe she crossed his arms over his chest and placed the pennies on his eyes before opening the window as far as it would go – not only to dispel the sickroom smell, but to let his spirit fly free. Finally, she stood looking down at the corpse, for that was all he was now. She had watched him walk away some time ago, hand in hand with his sister, a fine-looking little lass with ebony black hair and a smile that could move mountains.

And now there was one last job she had to do but that could wait until later in the day, so she settled herself in Grace's chair and helped herself to another cup of tea.

The doctor had been and issued the death certificate and the undertaker had called and taken Dylan's body to the chapel of rest. It was now mid-afternoon and Grace was cleaning the house like someone possessed. Up to now Mrs Gower hadn't seen her shed so much as one tear but no doubt they'd come in time. To her mind, Dylan's passing was a good thing. If he hadn't gone when he had she feared he'd have inflicted serious injuries on the poor girl. But it was over now and she had a long trek ahead of her.

Slipping from the cottage she set off through the woods and as she climbed she began to huff and puff. It was a steep climb but she plodded on. The buds on the trees were a delicate green and already bluebells were peeping through the earth. She was almost halfway up the hill when a large badger ran across the path in front of her and Mrs Gower smiled. Wildlife held no fears for her, she had an affinity with all creatures, great and small. At last the convent came into sight and leaning against the trunk of a tree the old woman stopped to get her breath back. Eventually she moved on and once inside the foyer, which smelled strongly of disinfectant and sickness, she stopped a young nurse who was hurrying by and asked to see the Reverend Mother.

'Do come in,' the nun invited when Mrs Gower knocked on the door.

The old lady closed the door firmly behind her and began to tell her what she had come for.

She left within minutes feeling deflated. It was really the handsome young Dr Hughes she had wished to see but the kindly nun had informed her that he had left only the day before. He had been transferred to another military hospital further along the coast but she had no idea which one.

Mrs Gower was not one for showing her emotions but once out in the sunshine again she could have wept. She was no fool. She'd seen the spark between Grace and the young man when he had called at the cottage and she had also immediately guessed, just as Dylan had, that he was Aiden's father. But now he was gone once more and it seemed that yet again Grace was to be cheated of her chance at happiness. Moving on, she comforted herself that at least she had done what she thought was right. But Grace . . . poor Grace.

The funeral was a dismal affair. Bronwen insisted on seeing to all the arrangements herself, right down to choosing the coffin, which was one of the most expensive the undertaker could provide. She still expected Grace to pay for everything though, and Grace did so without complaint, although it would mean that the small amount of money she had left was sadly diminished.

Bronwen also informed her, just days before the service took place, that she would be entertaining any mourners that wished to return after the service at her own cottage and that Grace could attend if she wished to. But from the way she extended the invitation Grace knew she would not be welcome, so she decided that she would say her goodbyes to her husband at the chapel and then return home.

The temporary truce that had seemed to exist between them while they were nursing Dylan was over and Bronwen hoped that after the funeral she need never set eyes on Grace or her bastard ever again.

After the interment, Grace and Aiden walked home to their cottage. Aiden had been unusually quiet but, clutching his mother's hand, he suddenly asked, 'Do you think I might get to meet my *real* father one day?'

He had never mentioned anything since the day Dylan had informed him that he wasn't his father but now Grace realised that it must have been preying on his mind.

'I don't know, love,' she answered truthfully. 'I hope you do but if not we'll be fine on our own.'

'Will you go back to work at the convent again now?' Aiden asked and Grace realised with a little jolt that she hadn't really considered what she might do. She knew that she would have to do something and supposed that it wouldn't be a bad idea, although she dreaded to think how she would feel if she was close to Luke again. All the love she had always felt for him was still there, simmering away beneath the surface.

'I might,' she told him. 'But let's just get today over with and then I'll make a decision.'

Aiden nodded before letting go of her hand and skipping ahead in the bright sunshine. It seemed wrong that someone should be buried in the dark earth on such a lovely bright day somehow, Grace mused. She had noted that Aiden hadn't shed a single tear since the day Dylan had died, but then, why should he?

Mrs Gower was waiting for them when they reached the cottage with the kettle already singing to make a pot of tea.

'So how did it go?'

Grace shrugged. 'As well as could be expected, I suppose.'

'Hmm.' Mrs Gower lifted the kettle and poured the boiling water over the tea leaves she had measured into the teapot. 'And what will you do now?'

'Aiden just asked me the same thing,' Grace told her as she removed her bonnet and placed it on the end of the table. She hadn't been able to afford a new one but she had trimmed it with black ribbon as a mark of respect. 'He asked if I was going to go and work back at the convent and I suppose it isn't a bad idea. That is, if you'd be prepared to keep your eye on him after school each day until I got home? I would pay you, of course.'

'You don't need to ask and I won't want paying,' Mrs Gower told her smartly. 'But what you have to remember now is, you're still a young woman. Life can't be all about work and caring for your son. Happen there'll be some nice young chap out there who'll treat you as you deserve to be treated.'

Grace gave a wry grin. 'I think it's rather soon to be thinking of getting married again on the day I buried my husband, don't you?'

Mrs Gower sniffed. 'All the same, it's something for you to think on.'

Grace shook her head as she sank into a chair. She felt she could be honest with Mrs Gower. 'I should never have married

411

Dylan,' she admitted with a catch in her voice. 'You obviously know that Aiden wasn't his. I married him to give my baby a name and I hoped in time that I'd grow to love him. But then when Aiden was born, Dylan couldn't take to him and the rest you know.'

'And do you still have feelings for the lad's father?'

Grace nodded miserably.

'Hmm, I thought as much. They do say that we only ever know one true love in a lifetime and happen it's right. But who knows, your paths might cross again one of these days and now that you're free . . .'

Grace shook her head. 'That isn't likely to happen. Aiden's father doesn't even know he exists.'

'All the same, stranger things have happened and I'm a great believer that what will be will be,' the old lady said as she pushed a cup of tea towards her.

Grace sighed. If only, but she had discovered long ago that happy ever afters were not for the likes of her. From now on she would earn her own living and Aiden would be the centre of her world.

Chapter Fifty

November 1918

'It's over! The bloody war is *finally* over!'

Grace paused as she passed the day-room door to see the men inside leaping about with joy, or at least those of them who were able to. Even those in wheelchairs were smiling and shaking the hands of the people closest to them.

She had started working back at the convent shortly after Dylan's death and the time since had been some of the most peaceful she had ever known. Aiden was now seven years old, a fine boy who had suddenly become all gangly arms and legs. He was going to be tall like his father one day and she was reminded of Luke every time she looked at him. As she watched the patients now she found that she too was smiling. The war was over at last! But at what cost? There had been so many thousands of young lives snuffed out like candles in the wind, so many men maimed. Just the day before she had sat for hours at the bedside of a young man with horrific injuries who had cried pitifully for his mother. She had held his hand and soothed him as best she could, and when he finally drew his last breath she had felt relieved. At least his suffering was over. But she wouldn't think of that now. Today was a day to rejoice.

Within seconds, people seemed to be pouring out of every

413

doorway, kissing the nurses and shaking the hands and clapping the backs of the men nearest to them. Even the Reverend Mother had come out of her office and was beaming like a Cheshire cat.

'Nurse Penlynn.' She beckoned to Grace excitedly. 'Run to the kitchen, would you, and ask the cook if she can organise a little party fare? I think we should celebrate.'

Grace was only too happy to oblige and the rest of the day passed in a pleasant blur. It was only as she was wending her way home across the frosty ground through the woods that evening that she gave a thought to her future. No doubt the casualties would continue to pour in for a time, and it would take even longer for the patients to be well enough to recover and leave. But then, she supposed, the convent would revert to being a place of worship, and what would she do for a job then? It was a sobering thought. She had enjoyed working there despite the heartbreaking things she'd witnessed. Still, she was determined not to worry about it just yet. That was a long way in the future. For now, she just wanted to rejoice like the rest of the country.

'Heard the news, have you?' Mrs Gower asked the second Grace walked through the door.

Aiden raced across the room and flung his arms about her waist before she had the chance to reply.

'The war is over, Mammy,' he told her joyously as she fondly ruffled his thick blonde hair. 'The teacher at school told us an' we've been allowed to play all day. No lessons nor nothin'. An' tomorrow we're having a party with jelly and everything.'

Grace smiled indulgently. 'And quite right too. I think the whole country is happy today.'

Mrs Gower, meanwhile, ladled one of her delicious rabbit stews into a bowl and plonked it unceremoniously on the table. 'Get that down you. It's freezing cold out there and you look perished through, girl! But this'll warm you up.'

They had fallen into an easy routine some time ago. On the

414

days when Grace was working, Mrs Gower cooked an evening meal for them and at weekends Grace cooked for the old lady. It had worked very well and over the last few years they had grown even closer. They talked of what peace would mean for them as Grace ate but eventually she told Aiden, 'Come along, young man. Happy day or not, it's time you were getting ready for bed.'

The old woman watched them go then sat in her rocking chair with a smile on her face. She had ventured into the market that day, a rare occurrence for her arthritis always seemed to get worse in the cold weather, and quite by chance she had overheard two women talking about the handsome young doctor who had taken over the old practice in the nearby town of Porthmadog.

'Eeh, they reckon he's a dreamboat,' one of the young women had sighed. 'Blonde hair and eyes as blue as the sea by all accounts. I think his name is Dr Hughes . . .'

Mrs Gower had hobbled on to the next stall, her mind in a spin. The description and the name. Surely it had to be the same young doctor that had visited Grace? There was only one way to find out. She decided she would catch the bus to Porthmadog the very next day and pay this dishy new doctor a little visit.

Before they knew it, Christmas was almost upon them once more and one evening, Grace came home to find Aiden holding a small metal toy bus.

'That's nice,' she commented. 'Where did you get that from?'

'Me friend,' he told her smugly with a broad smile. 'I often see him on me way home from school.'

'Oh, he's not one of your school friends then?' He had mentioned his new friend on a number of occasions now and until today Grace had assumed he was from school.

Aiden chuckled as if she had said something really funny. '*Of course* he ain't. But you'll like him when you meet him.'

'I'm sure I will,' she answered, feeling vaguely uneasy. Who *was* this friend? But then she scolded herself, he was clearly no threat to the child, and Aiden wouldn't take kindly to it if she tried to mollycoddle him.

'Do *you* know who he is?' she asked Mrs Gower the next evening when she collected Aiden after work. It had been preying on her mind, Aiden mixing with strangers.

Mrs Gower widened her eyes innocently. 'Can't say as I do but I know he's rare kind to Aiden, so I'm sure you have nothing to fret about.'

That weekend, Grace took Aiden to collect holly from the woods and when they got back to the warm little cottage they filled every vase they had with it and placed it about in the downstairs rooms.

'*There!*' Grace rubbed her hands down her skirt and smiled with satisfaction. 'That looks Christmassy, doesn't it?'

'It'll look better still when me friend brings the Christmas tree he's promised me,' Aiden spouted.

Grace's eyes widened with shock. '*What* Christmas tree?' she demanded and Aiden grinned.

'You'll see.' He laughed and scampered away before she could ask any more.

Grace was preparing their tea on Sunday evening when a tap came on the kitchen door and before she knew it Aiden was flying across the room to answer it. Mrs Gower, who was sitting in the chair at the side of the roaring fire, grinned as Grace raised her eyebrows.

Aiden flung the door open letting in a blast of icy cold air and whooped with delight. 'I *knew* you'd come,' he gabbled, leaning forward to yank the caller into the room. Whoever it was was momentarily hidden behind the enormous Christmas tree they were holding in front of them.

And then they set the tree aside and suddenly Grace felt as if everything was happening in slow motion.

'*Luke!*' Her voice came out as little more than a squeak as he gave her the smile that she still dreamed of.

'Hello, Grace. It's been a long time.' As he came towards her with his cold hands outstretched she kept expecting to wake up. This must be some sort of lovely dream, surely?

'Right, mister' – Mrs Gower stood up and grasped Aiden's hand – 'me and you should have our tea round at my house this evenin'. I reckon your mam and Luke have a lot of catching up to do.'

Aiden went off happily enough and only then did Luke lead Grace to the table where he sat down beside her.

'I'm sorry if this seems a little underhand and it's come as a shock to you,' he told her. 'But I wanted to get to know my son a little before I came to see you.'

She stared at him wide-eyed. 'You *know*? About *Aiden*? But *how*?'

He sighed and tapped the side of his nose. 'Let's just say a little dicky bird visited to have a word in my ear.'

'And would that little dickey bird happen to be a little old lady who lives not a million miles away?'

He grinned and then becoming serious again he admitted, 'It might have been but *why* didn't *you* tell me that we had a son?'

She lowered her eyes as tears glistened on her long dark lashes. 'I didn't know myself that I was having a child until after you'd gone and when I did find out I didn't know what to do. The Reverend Mother sent me away from the convent. Then Dylan offered to marry me to give the baby a name so I took the easy way out. But I wasn't fair to him. I should never have married him.' She shook her head sadly as the tears slid down her cheeks. 'I never loved him as I should have and he knew it.'

Luke tenderly brushed the tears away with his fingertip before delving into his jacket pocket and extracting a small velvet box.

'I shall never forgive myself for leaving you as I did,' he said gravely. 'I was a coward and didn't know how to handle my feelings so I ran away. The trouble was, I couldn't forget you, you were always there everywhere I looked. But I hope that now you'll let me try to make it up to you and my son. I love you, Grace. I've *always* loved you. That's why I ran away again after I'd come to visit Dylan. I couldn't bear to see you married to another man and I didn't want to make the situation worse for you. But that's all in the past now, so I'm asking most humbly . . . will you marry me?' He sprang the lid on the box and Grace stared down at a pretty emerald and diamond ring that winked in the light of the fire and once again the tears gushed as she nodded and fell into his arms. Tenderly he placed the ring on her finger and at last, for Grace, the war was well and truly over.

Next door, Aiden was looking very pleased with himself as he sat watching Mrs Gower saw slices off a fresh-baked loaf.

'I think me mam likes me new friend, don't you?' he asked cautiously and when Mrs Gower smiled he shocked her when he said, 'But he ain't *really* me friend, is he? He's me dad.'

'What makes you say that?' she replied, trying to keep her voice steady.

Aiden gave a sly little grin. 'Well he looks just like me, we've got the same colour hair and eyes and everything. And he's kind. I'd *like* him to be me dad.'

'Well, you'll have to ask him and your mam about that.' Mrs Gower didn't feel it was her place to tell him although she couldn't have been happier at the way things had turned out. She paused to stare into the corner for a moment as her mind slipped back to when Dylan had died. He hadn't known that the magic potion she gave him to drink each day was actually arsenic. She'd told him that it was one of her herbal remedies that would help him sleep and after a lot of grumbling he had finally agreed to try it. After that it had been easy to make sure he took it each day. She felt no guilt whatsoever for what she had done. The way she saw it, he would have died sooner or later anyway. She had merely released him from his pain and suffering a little sooner than anyone had expected, and by doing so she had saved Grace from any more vicious swipes.

It was sad to think that yet more years had been wasted after his death because Dr Hughes had left but at least it was all turning out for the best now. It was perhaps as well, she thought as she glanced towards the corner again. She had been feeling very tired lately and all too often she had glimpsed Myfanwy standing there patiently waiting for her. Over the time they had lived close to her, Mrs Gower had come to look upon Grace and Aiden as the daughter and grandson she had never had. But hopefully she wouldn't have to worry about them anymore. Luke would look after them now and at last she could go on to a better place.

'Soon . . . very soon now,' she whispered to the young girl in the corner and with a happy smile she got on with making Aiden his tea.

Epilogue

As the guests streamed into the little church perched high on the hill in Sarn Bach they were all smiling. Outside the sun was shining in a cloudless blue sky. It was a perfect day for a wedding. Mrs Batley, was feeling very smart in a new blue two-piece costume and matching hat, while Mabel who waddled in at the side of her with her husband's hand protectively on her elbow, looked fit to burst. Her third baby was due any day now and she had jokingly told Harry only that morning, 'I hope he or she can wait till after the ceremony before putting in an appearance.' They had left their two younger children, Daisy and Timothy, at home with Mabel's mother as they intended to return to Nuneaton by train that evening, hopefully in time for the expected new arrival to be born in their own bed.

Close behind them was Cerys and Aled Llewelyn. Even the Reverend Mother and Sister Mathilda were there, as well as a number of Luke's friends and extended family. Next came Aiden, clutching the hand of a beautifully dressed lady wearing a hat that was the envy of every woman there on one side of him, and on the other, he held the hand of a tall, upright gentleman who looked like an older version of Luke, his son.

'Will Mam be here soon, Granny?' Aiden asked and the woman smiled down at him.

'Yes, cariad, very soon now,' she promised. It had come as something of a shock when Luke's parents had first learned that not only was their son getting married but that they already had a grandson but Aiden had them eating out of the palm of his hand and they hoped that he would be the first of many. Once inside the church they walked down the aisle to take a seat in the front pew and on spotting Aiden, Luke winked at him.

'You're looking very smart in your new suit, son,' he teased and Aiden preened, feeling very grown up.

Meanwhile Mrs Batley, Mabel and Harry had also taken a seat and leaning towards Mabel while they waited for the bride to arrive, Mrs Batley whispered, 'Hey, did you hear about the police catching up with Nurse Matthews and Mr Mackenzie then, eh? They'd been in France, apparently, living the life of Riley but they came back on a visit to see Nurse Matthews's elderly mother who is seriously ill. One of the neighbours spotted them, by all accounts, and reported them to the police and they were apprehended on their way back to the docks. According to the newspapers they're in custody now awaiting trial so they'll finally get what's coming to them.'

'And will the police be able to retrieve any of the money they stole?' Mabel asked, always one to enjoy a bit of gossip.

'Some of it, but Grace says Luke won't touch a penny of it. It's going to be put in a trust fund for Aiden and any more children they may have for when they're older.'

The church was full by then and buzzing with conversation but that stopped abruptly when the organist suddenly started to play the wedding march.

All eyes turned towards the door and there was Grace looking absolutely radiant on the arm of her Aunt Gertie, who had happily agreed to give her away. Grace was dressed in a smart, cream lace two-piece that showed off her slim figure to perfection. A tiny hat trimmed with a small veil was perched at a jaunty angle on her head and she was carrying a posy of lily of the valley and freesias. But it

421

wasn't her outfit that everyone noticed, it was the look of pure happiness on her face as she walked down the aisle with her eyes firmly fixed on the groom who was staring back at her adoringly.

'Now *there's* a love match if ever I saw one,' Mrs Batley sighed dreamily, mopping at her eyes with a scrap of lace hanky. Mabel and Harry nodded in agreement as they each thought back to their own wedding day. And then Grace reached Luke's side and the service began.

'Dearly beloved, we are gathered here today in the sight of God to witness . . .' The priest's voice echoed up to the rafters loud and clear as the happy couple stood before him at last. Eventually Gertie and James, Luke's younger brother and best man, stepped aside as Grace and Luke took their vows and there was barely a dry eye in the church, for the love the couple clearly had for each other was so tangible that the congregation felt that they might almost be able to reach out and touch it. And then it was over and as the happy couple left the church they were showered with rice and rose petals.

'So how are you feeling, Mrs Hughes?' Luke asked with a twinkle in his eye and Grace giggled. She still often thought of him as Father Luke.

'Like a very old married woman,' she replied as he planted a kiss on her lips. Then they were surrounded by friends and family all wishing them well until it was time to climb into the trap for the short drive to a hotel in the town where Luke's parents had generously arranged a lavish reception for them.

But first there was something that Grace wished to do so taking Luke's hand she skirted the church and crossed the grass to stand before the grave of her dear friend Myfanwy and her tiny namesake who had been taken from her far too soon. There was also another person she was missing that day, for sadly Mrs Gower had died soon after Luke had come back into her life, peacefully in her own bed as she would have wished.

'I hope you can all see me today and know how happy I am,' she whispered as she bent to lay her posy on the grave with tears in her eyes. And it was then that she saw them. Myfanwy was standing in the shade of a tall yew tree with the baby held tenderly in her arms and Mrs Gower was standing close beside her and they were both smiling. Grace blinked and they were gone and she felt a deep sense of peace as her husband led her to the waiting pony and trap.

The meal at the reception was delicious, followed by dancing to a full band and as the day wore on everyone let their hair down and thoroughly enjoyed themselves. Just once, Grace thought briefly of Dylan and her smile faded. His parents had moved away from Sarn Bach shortly after his death and she hoped that wherever they were they had finally found peace. But today was not a day for being sad and soon she was waltzing in her husband's arms and smiling again, amused to see Aiden attempting a waltz with his new grandmother. He would be staying with them that night at their beautiful country house in Porthmadog and she knew that they would spoil him shamelessly. Luke's father was an esteemed surgeon at a hospital in Wales so he was delighted that Luke had now taken over the local general practitioner's surgery in Sarn Bach and was following in his medical footsteps.

Mabel and Harry left early to catch the train home and Grace grew quite tearful as they said their goodbyes. Mrs Batley was staying on with Aunt Gertie for a few days' holiday.

'Promise to let me know immediately the little one arrives,' she pleaded and Mabel nodded.

'Aye, I will, have a good evening now.' She bestowed Grace with a wicked little wink then Harry whisked her away leaving Grace to return to the party. But first she and Luke took a minute to just stand and enjoy the quiet. The hotel was on the edge of the village and as she gazed at the hedgerows and saw the daffodils and primroses peeping from beneath them and the soft green buds on the trees unfurling, it came to her that everywhere looked as if it was slowly coming back to life after a long cold winter. Just like me, she thought as she nestled her head contentedly on Luke's shoulder.

Some hours later, Grace and Luke left the party in yet another flurry of rice as the guests waved them away to spend their first evening in their new home. It was a beautiful house up on a hill overlooking the sea and surrounded by a pretty garden and Grace knew that she would never tire of the view. She and Luke had spent the last few months furnishing it and now it was time to make it into a home.

'So, here we are, home at last, Mrs Hughes,' Luke joked as he placed his key in the door and unlocked it. Then turning about, he swept a giggling Grace up into his arms to carry her across the threshold.

'Stop it, put me down, you'll hurt your back,' she laughed. 'And I'm hardly a virgin bride. In fact, I ought to warn you, you're actually carrying two of us.' She had saved this piece of information for this special day.

Luke dropped her to her feet abruptly. 'What you mean you're . . . we're going to have . . .'

She nodded. 'Another baby, yes. I thought I'd wait till we were married before I told you.'

Happy tears shone in his eyes as he hugged her to him. 'Do you know,' he said softly, 'I didn't think today could get any better but it just did.'

'And this is only the beginning,' she answered, staring up into his eyes and then his lips came down on hers and they might have been the only two people left in the world. It was the first day of the rest of their lives.

THE END

Acknowledgements

Once again, I would like to thank Eli, my editor, and the wonderful team at Bonnier Zaffre for all their help, support and encouragement. Not forgetting of course, my brilliant agent, Sheila Crowley, and her lovely assistant, Abbie Greaves, at Curtis Brown. I am so lucky to have you all behind me, thank you all so much xx

Welcome to the world of Rosie Goodwin!

Keep reading for more from Rosie Goodwin, to discover a recipe that features in this novel and to find out more about what Rosie Goodwin is doing next . . .

❧

We'd also like to introduce you to MEMORY LANE, our special community for the very best of saga writing from authors you know and love, and new ones we simply can't wait for you to meet. Read on and join our club!

www.MemoryLane.club

Dear Readers,

It doesn't seem like any time at all since I was writing to you for the release of *The Little Angel* and here I am again with book three of my Days of the Week collection being published! I'm happy to share with you that this is a very special book for me because it is my 30th published novel. Something of a milestone! Little did I realise back in 2004, when my first book was released, that I would still be tapping away and bringing my characters to life! I have all of you to thank for that, because if it wasn't for all your lovely comments, support and enthusiasm I would probably not have continued, so thank you all very much. Since I last wrote we have also celebrated my sales passing one million, so I'm thrilled about that, too!

This book is about Tuesday's child, who we know is 'full of grace'. In this one we meet Grace, aptly named for the day of the week she was born on. Once again this is a completely different story, I do like to keep you all guessing, and I'm afraid as usual I do rather put her through it! I think the dark side must come out of me when I'm writing but then as we all know, life for many isn't all roses around the door. Even though this is another stand-alone story you may all recognise some of the characters that were mentioned in *Mothering Sunday* and *The Little Angel*. I hope you'll all enjoy reading *A Mother's Grace* as much as I enjoyed writing it.

I have now just finished book four, which will be out in November. It is going to be called *The Blessed Child*. Keep reading for a snippet to whet your appetite. And so now it's time to put my thinking cap on for the fifth book! I promised myself I'd have a little break but already I'm champing at the bit to get started on a new one. Thursday's child 'has far to go' and I think I already know the direction she may be taking. Let's just say for now that it may well involve a very long sea voyage!

On a more personal level, I'm pleased to report that my lovely new granddaughter, Poppy, is thriving and all is well here. I've had quite a busy time with lots of events across the country where I got to meet some of you, and that was lovely. It's nice to escape from my office now and again.

Meanwhile it's time to get out the gardening tools again as the weather improves. Can't wait!

Do keep your messages on Twitter and Facebook coming, please. I do love to hear from you all. And also do keep your eye on the Memory Lane website

where you'll be kept up to date with everything that's happening and have the chance to win some smashing books and prizes! You can join at www.MemoryLane. club.

Take care and much love,

Rosie
xx

Turn over for a sneak peek at Rosie Goodwin's next novel in the Days of the Week collection:

The Blessed Child

Nuneaton, March 1863

Nancy Carson loaded the last of the clean washing into a small wooden cart and laid a white sheet neatly across it. A fine drizzle had started to fall and the last thing she needed after all the effort she had put into the washing and ironing, was for it to be ruined. It had been a long, hard day and there was nothing she would have liked more than to put her feet up at the side of the fire, but needs must. At least now that she was taking washing in and Reuben, her seventeen-year-old son, had started work, they were managing to make ends meet a little. Wednesday, her daughter, who was two years younger than Reuben, had recently started work too, at the local corner shop so at last the future was beginning to look a little brighter. Not before time, she thought ruefully as she wrapped a shawl tightly about her slim shoulders. The last six months had wrought so many changes in their lives that sometimes Nancy felt dizzy just thinking about it.

Much of this had been caused by the birth of little Joseph, who was fast asleep beside the fireplace in the wooden cradle that Reuben had carved for him. Her husband had not been at all pleased to know that there was to be an addition to the family and had walked out on the lot of them shortly before the child had been born. They had not seen hide nor hair of him since and Nancy still missed him at times. Admittedly he had been no saint but he was her husband so his leaving had cut deep.

Nevertheless, Nancy was a survivor and when, soon after Joseph's birth, it became clear that they could no longer afford to live in their smart little cottage in Bedworth, she had moved them all, lock, stock and barrel, to a cheaper cottage in Stockingford in the neighbouring market town of Nuneaton.

Turning to Marcie, her youngest daughter, she told her, 'You'll have to watch Joseph for me until Nessie gets home. I'm delivering this clean laundry to Biddy Spooner. Goodness knows we need the money this week.' Biddy Spooner ran a lodging house in nearby Haunchwood Road and was well known for being somewhat eccentric and putting on airs and graces, but she was a good payer and one of Nancy's regular customers.

Marcie pouted. She hated their new home and constantly blamed her mother for bringing them there. She also resented the new baby and had as little to do with him as she could. Babies were dirty, smelly little creatures as far as she was concerned.

'It's no use pulling that face, my girl!' Nancy scolded as she dragged the cart towards the door. 'I'll not be gone long, so it won't hurt you to make yourself useful for a time. Nessie should be back soon.' With that she hauled the cart over the step and set off into the bitterly cold late afternoon.

No one would think we were into March already, Nancy thought, as she began to shiver. The weather had hardly improved since Christmas and soon her teeth were chattering and her threadbare shawl clung damply to her shoulders as the cart bumped across the rough ground behind her. Already it was dark and she had to pick her way carefully to avoid the bumps and hollows in the field. Still, she thought, at least coming this way would take a good ten minutes off her journey and then she could hurry back to the warmth of her fireside.

She was passing a small copse when she had the strangest feeling that someone was behind her. She wheeled about to peer into the darkness.

'I... Is anyone there?' Only the howling of the wind in the leafless trees answered her, so after a moment she grabbed the handle of the cart and set off again, but she had taken no more than a few steps when suddenly something hit her hard between the shoulder blades and she sprawled on to the muddy ground, winded. Somehow, she managed to turn on to her side and as she gazed up, a face slowly swam into focus.

'*You bitch!*'

Nancy's eyes stretched wide with shock. 'But... what are *you* doing here? What do you want?' she rasped as she struggled to catch her breath. And then she saw the cudgel of wood hurtling towards her again and felt a searing pain in her shoulder as she tried to raise her hand to defend herself.

'S... *stop*!' she pleaded, but her attacker was beyond reasoning, his face twisted with hatred. Again and again the blows rained down on her as she struggled to rise from the muddy ground.

'Please... *no more!*' But her pleas fell on deaf ears and if anything, the attack became more frenzied as the man grunted with exertion. Soon, realising that her pleas were useless she curled herself into a ball until at last a comforting darkness rushed towards her, and she knew no more.

Once he saw her take her final breath, the shadow stopped, staring down at the woman's inert form until his breathing returned to some sort of normality, then, with not an ounce of remorse, he slipped away into the night, leaving her lifeless body exposed to the cruel winter air.

September 1864

'Mr Grimshaw is at Ma Baker's, Nessie. Shall we hide under the table and pretend we're not in?' fifteen-year-old Marcie asked fearfully.

'No we will *not*!' her sister, Wednesday, affectionately known as Nessie, replied proudly. 'I've never hidden from the rent man yet and I'm not about to start now. Just sit down at the table and leave him to me.' Seeing the frightened look on her younger sister's face, her expression softened. 'It'll be all right, love,' she assured her. 'I've got some of the rent for him, he'll wait for the rest.'

Despite her brave words, Nessie's stomach was in knots. It was a well-known fact that their landlord was not a man to be messed with, but what alternative did she have? Before her horrific death some eighteen months before, her mother had always insisted that all of her offspring were out of the way when the landlord called and somehow, she had always paid him. But now, with only Reuben's wage coming in, things were going from bad to worse and some days, Nessie, as the oldest girl, struggled to even feed them all, let alone pay the rent.

She felt a moment's resentment as she thought of her father who had abandoned them all two years before when he had run off with the landlady of the local inn close to where they had lived. They'd not seen him since and in some ways, it had been a blessing. At least now they didn't have to live in fear of him rolling in drunk and aggressive from the pub. Compared to where they used to live, the rent on this cottage was much cheaper but it was reflected in their living conditions, which were sparse to say the least. 'But needs must,' their mother had told her brood cheerfully and somehow, she had managed to hold the family together, bless her.

Blinking back tears as she thought of her mother and the unthinkable way in which her life had come to an end, Wednesday smiled at her sister. 'Take Joseph out into the back yard for a few minutes, Marcie. The fresh air will do him good.'

Joseph was now almost twenty months old with light brown hair and hazel eyes. He was small for his age and had never been a robust child, but the whole family, with the exception of Marcie, adored him and spoiled him shamelessly. Nessie watched as her sister swept him up into her arms and hurried away with a resentful look on her face. Then taking a deep breath, Nessie squared her slight shoulders and waited for the knock on the door.

It came soon enough and with what she could muster of the rent money gripped tight in her hand, she went to answer it.

'Mr Grimshaw.' Her voice was icily polite and he grinned lasciviously at her as his eyes swept over her.

There was no doubt about it, this little filly was turning into a head-turner. Admittedly she wasn't beautiful in the classical sense. Her hair, which was unfashionably straight, hung almost to her waist like a shimmering copper cloak streaked with gold and her nose was a little too upturned to be deemed pretty. Her cheeks were deeply dimpled when she smiled and her mouth was just a fraction too wide. Even so, her lips were full and red and her skin like peaches and cream. But it was her eyes, easily her best feature, that fascinated him. They were fringed with dark, gold-tipped lashes and were a deep tawny colour that could change to darkest brown if she was upset. They were quite unlike anything he'd seen before. At sixteen years old, her slim figure was filling out nicely and Seth Grimshaw desperately wanted to own her.

'So, me beauty, got me rent ready fer me, have you?' he asked as he licked his fat lips lecherously.

'Some of it, I'll make sure to have the rest ready for you the next time you call.' Nessie opened her hand and as he stared at the collection of ha'pennies and coppers he sneered, his nostrils widening repugnantly.

'That's no good to me, lass. The rent is three and sixpence per week, as you well know. There's just short of two bob there.'

'I'm quite aware of that,' Nessie answered coolly. Her face was outwardly calm but inside her stomach was churning. 'But Reuben sprained his ankle last week and had to have three days off work until he could put his weight on it again and it's made us short. We'll have the rest for you very soon.'

She had expected him to turn nasty, he was known for it hereabouts, but instead he surprised her when he leaned in and told her in a low voice, 'Well, just see as you have, pet... Otherwise we'll have to think of another way you can pay me, eh?' His putrid breath enveloped her as, reaching his hand forward, he suddenly tweaked her breast.

She sprang away from him as if she had been burned

as her cheeks flamed. He had left her in no doubt of what he wanted and Nessie felt sick to her stomach as she stared at the repulsive creature. Seth Grimshaw was forty if he was a day and even now he was at arm's length, the ripe smell of him assaulted her. He had a large moustache and the sight of the food caught in it made her want to gag. He was grossly overweight and his fat stomach strained against the buttons on his grubby, brightly coloured waistcoat. His hair was grey and plastered to his head with Macassar oil and Nessie found him totally repulsive.

'It will be here for you,' Nessie muttered primly as she thrust the money into his podgy fingers.

He grinned as he dropped the coins into the bag about his waist. 'See that it is,' he said, then he walked away without so much as another word.

Nessie hastily slammed the door before leaning heavily against it as she began to shake like a leaf in the wind. At that moment, Marcie's head popped around the back door and her eyes swiftly swept the room. 'Has he gone then?'

'Yes, he's gone.' Nessie sank on to the nearest chair, suddenly feeling weary. She was so tired of having to rob Peter to pay Paul and make ends meet, but what choice did she have? She had promised her mother, before she had been so cruelly taken away from them, that should anything ever happen to her she would keep the family together, and up to now she had, although she was well aware that she couldn't have managed it without the support of Reuben, her brother. He worked laying the train tracks that were springing up all over the country. Sometimes this meant that he had to work away from home but every Friday he turned up, as regular as clockwork, to tip his wages on to the table for her and Nessie wondered how they would ever manage without him. He was her rock and she depended on him.

Marcie, on the other hand, was a different matter altogether. Since leaving school, she'd worked in three different jobs but none of them had held her interest for long, much to Nessie's annoyance. Marcie wanted to be a lady and considered herself too good for manual work, so recently Nessie had suggested that they should change roles. She would go out to work to bring a little extra in while Marcie stayed at home to care for Joseph and keep the house running. But Marcie had been horrified at the idea. She was no fool and realised that staying at home would probably be harder than going out to work. 'No,' she had told Nessie, 'I'm going to wait until a rich man comes along and sweeps me off my feet, then I shall be waited on and spoiled.'

Nessie knew that the girl was living in cuckoo land. That sort of thing didn't happen to the likes of them. And yet, despite Marcie's selfishness, Nessie loved her and tried to turn a blind eye to her behaviour. Only the day before they'd had a terrible row after Nessie had sent Marcie to the market for some food. Admittedly, Marcie had shopped wisely and got everything on the list, but then finding she had a few precious pennies spare she had spent them on a length of red ribbon for her hair. Nessie had cried tears of rage and frustration. Marcie didn't seem to realise that those miserly few pence might mean the difference between them eating or not towards the end of the following week, and, worse still, she didn't seem to much care. But that was Marcie; she would always put herself first.

But all that faded into the background now as Nessie relived her confrontation with Seth Grimshaw in her mind. She shuddered. He'd made it more than obvious what he wanted from her and the thought of him laying his horrible hands on her made her tremble with fear. Somehow, she must find a way to pay him the rent next week, no matter what.

Traditional Welsh Cawl

This hearty, warming stew is one of Mrs Llewelyn's staples, and nothing like the watery version the postulants were fed!

You will need:

600-800g Bone-in lamb neck
1 Onion
2 large Maris Piper potatoes
1 Swede
2 Parsnips
2 Leeks
2 Carrots
2 Small turnips
1 Hard Conference pear
A small bunch of thyme
Salt and pepper
Welsh butter

The meat should make up about one third of the total weight of ingredients – you can use different quantities of any of the vegetables, as you prefer.

Method:

1. Using a large, heavy-bottom pan melt a small amount of butter. Season the lamb with salt and pepper then seal in the pan until brown on all sides.
2. Then add 2 litres of water, 2 teaspoons of salt and bring to a boil. Add the onion, whole. Leave to simmer for 15-20 minutes. Some fat from the meat will rise to the top of the pan; use a slotted spoon to skim this off.
3. After about 15 minutes the meat should be cooked through, remove it from the pan and allow to cool. Shred the meat, careful to remove all of the bones – discard these – and return the meat to the pan.
4. Add all of the vegetables, except for the leeks and pear, and bring back to the boil. Leave to simmer for at least an hour, or until the vegetables are soft.
5. Add the sliced leeks and pear, and simmer for another 10 minutes, with the lid on.
6. Taste and season, if needed, add some of the thyme.
7. Remove from the heat and chill in the fridge overnight, or for up to three days.
8. When you're ready to eat it, gently reheat in the pan until simmering. Serve in bowls, sprinkled with the remaining thyme, with crusty bread and a generous serving of Welsh butter or Caerphilly.
9. Enjoy!

Welsh Cakes or Pice
ar y maen

These traditional Welsh treats are a perfect afternoon snack to enjoy with a cup of tea

You will need:

225g Self-raising flour
110g Welsh salted butter, plus extra for greasing
1 free-range egg
50g Caster sugar, plus extra for dusting
A pinch of salt
65g Currants
A pinch of mixed spice, or nutmeg
A splash of milk, if needed

Method:

1. In a large bowl, mix the flour, spice and salt together.
2. Using your fingers rub in the butter, until you have a breadcrumb consistency.
3. Add in the sugar and currants and stir with a wooden spoon.
4. In a separate bowl, beat the egg with a fork.
5. Add the beaten egg to the dry ingredients and stir well, until you have a stiff dough that can be formed into a ball. If the mixture is too dry, add a splash of milk.

6. Roll the dough out until is it about 1/2cm thick. Cut into rounds using a biscuit cutter.

7. Grease a griddle or a heavy cast iron frying pan with some butter, wiping away the excess, then heat over a medium heat. Test that the griddle is hot enough by sprinkling a little water on it, if the water skips about and forms balls, it is ready.

8. Place the Welsh cakes on the griddle and bake for about 3 minutes on each side. They should be golden brown and have risen slightly.

9. Serve immediately, dusting with a little extra sugar.

10. Enjoy!